WHITE GARDENIA

By the same author

Wild Lavender

BELINDA ALEXANDRA

White Gardenia

HarperCollins*Publishers*

HarperCollins*Publishers*
77–85 Fulham Palace Road,
Hammersmith, London W6 8JB

www.harpercollins.co.uk

First published in Australia by
HarperCollins*Publishers* (Australia) 2002

This edition published by HarperCollins*Publishers* 2007

ISBN–13 978 0 00 720281 2
ISBN–10 0 00 720281 4

Typeset in Meridien by Palimpsest Book Production Limited,
Polmont, Stirlingshire

Printed and bound in Great Britain by
Clays Ltd, St Ives plc

Mixed Sources
Product group from well-managed
forests and other controlled sources
www.fsc.org Cert no. TT-COC-2139
© 1996 Forest Stewardship Council
FSC

For my family

Contents

PART ONE

ONE

Harbin, China

We Russians believe that if you knock a knife from the table to the floor, a male visitor will come, and if a bird flies into the room, the death of someone close to you is at hand. Both these events occurred in 1945, around my thirteenth birthday, but there had been no omens of dropped knives or stray birds to warn me.

The General appeared on the tenth day after my father's death. My mother and I were busy removing the black silk that had been draped over the mirrors and icons for the nine days of mourning. My memory of my mother on that day has never dimmed. Her ivory skin framed by wisps of dark hair, the pearl studs in her fleshy earlobes, and her fiery amber eyes piece together into a sharply focused photograph before me: my mother, a widow at thirty-three.

I recall her thin fingers folding the dark material with a languidness that was not usual. But then we were both shell-shocked by loss. When my father had set out on the morning of his doom, his eyes shining and his lips brushing my cheeks with parting kisses, I had no anticipation that my next view of him would be in a heavy oak coffin, his eyes closed and his waxen face remote in death. The lower part of the casket remained shut to hide the legs that had been mutilated in the twisted wreck of the car.

The night my father's body was laid out in the parlour, white candles on either side of the coffin, my mother bolted the garage doors shut and fastened them with a chain and padlock. I watched her from my bedroom window as she paced back and forth in front of the garage, her lips moving in a silent incantation. Every so often she would stop and push her hair back over her ears as if she were listening for something, but then she would shake her head and continue her pacing. The next morning I slipped out to look at the lock and chain. I understood what she had done. She had clasped shut the garage doors the way we would have clasped onto my father if we had known that to let him drive into the lashing rain would be to let him go forever.

In the days following the accident our grief was diverted by a constant rotation of visits from our Russian and Chinese friends. They arrived and left hourly, by foot or by rickshaw, leaving their neighbouring farms or city houses to fill our home with the aroma of roasted chicken and the murmur of condolences. Those from the land came laden with gifts of bread and cake or the field flowers that had survived Harbin's early frosts, while those from the city brought ivory and silk, a polite way of giving us money, for without my father, my mother and I faced hard times ahead.

Then there was the burial. The priest, craggy and knotted like an old tree, traced the sign of the cross in the chilly air before the casket was nailed shut. The thick-shouldered Russian men jabbed their spades into the dirt, dropping frozen clods of earth into the grave. They worked hard with set jaws and downcast eyes, sweat slipping from their faces, either out of respect for my father or to win the admiration of his beautiful widow. All the while our Chinese neighbours kept their respectful distance outside the cemetery gate, sympathetic but suspicious of our custom of burying our loved ones in the ground and abandoning them to the mercy of the elements.

4

Afterwards the funeral party returned to our home, a wooden house my father had built with his own hands after fleeing Russia and the Revolution. We sat down to a wake of semolina cakes and tea served from a samovar. The house had originally been a simple pitched-roof bungalow with stove pipes sticking out from the eaves, but when my father married my mother he built six more rooms and a second storey and filled them with lacquered cupboards, antique chairs and tapestries. He carved ornate window frames, erected a fat chimney and painted the walls the buttercup yellow of the dead Tsar's summer palace. Men like my father made Harbin what it was: a Chinese city full of displaced Russian nobility. People who attempted to recreate the world they had lost with ice sculptures and winter balls.

When our guests had said all that could be said, I followed behind my mother to see them off at the door. While they were putting on their coats and hats I spotted my ice skates hanging on a peg in the front entrance. The left blade was loose and I remembered that my father had intended to fix it before the winter. The numbness of the past few days gave way to a pain so sharp that it hurt my ribs and made my stomach churn. I squeezed my eyes shut against it. I saw a blue sky race towards me and a thin winter sun shining on ice. The memory of the year before came back to me. The solid Songhua River; the cheerful cries of the children struggling to stay upright on their skates; the young lovers gliding in pairs; the old people shuffling around in the centre, peering for fish through the sections where the ice was thin.

My father lifted me high on his shoulder, his blades scraping against the surface with the added weight. The sky became a blur of aqua and white. I was dizzy with laughter.

'Put me down, Papa,' I said, grinning into his blue eyes. 'I want to show you something.'

5

He set me down but didn't let me go until he was sure that I had my balance. I watched for a clearing and skated out into it, lifting one leg off the ice and spinning like a marionette.

'*Harashó! Harashó!*' My father clapped. He rubbed his gloved hand over his face and smiled so widely that his laugh lines seemed to come to life. My father was much older than my mother, having completed his university studies the year she was born. He had been one of the youngest colonels in the White Army and somehow, many years later, his gestures had remained a mix of youthful enthusiasm and military precision.

He held out his hands so I could skate to him, but I wanted to show off again. I pushed myself out further and started to turn, but my blade hit a bump and my foot twisted under me. I smacked against the ice on my hip and knocked the wind out of my lungs.

My father was at my side in an instant. He picked me up and skated with me in his arms to the riverbank. He set me down on a fallen tree trunk and ran his hands over my shoulders and ribs before slipping off the damaged boot.

'No broken bones,' he said, moving my foot between his palms. The air was freezing and he rubbed my skin to warm it. I stared at the white streaks that mingled with the ginger hair on his crown and bit my lip. The tears in my eyes were not from the pain but from the humiliation of having made a fool of myself. My father's thumb pressed against the swelling around my ankle and I flinched. Already the purple stain of a bruise was beginning to show.

'Anya, you are a white gardenia,' he smiled. 'Beautiful and pure. But we need to handle you with care because you bruise so easily.'

I rested my head on his shoulder, almost laughing but crying at the same time.

A tear splashed onto my wrist and dripped onto the tiles of the entranceway. I quickly wiped my face before my mother turned around. The guests were on their way out and we gave them one more wave and '*Da svidaniya*' before switching off the lights. My mother took one of the funeral candles from the parlour and we made our way up the stairs by its gentle glow. The flame trembled and I felt the quickness of my mother's breath on my skin. But I was afraid to look at her and see her suffering. I couldn't bear her grief any better than I could my own. I kissed her goodnight at her door and scurried up the stairs to my room in the loft, falling straight into bed and covering my face with a pillow so she wouldn't hear me sobbing. The man who had called me a white gardenia, who had lifted me on his shoulder and twirled me until I was dizzy with laughter, would not be there any more.

Once the official mourning period was over everyone seemed to dissolve back into their daily lives. My mother and I were abandoned, left to learn to live again.

After we had folded the cloths and stacked them in the linen press, my mother said that we should carry the flowers down to my father's favourite cherry tree. While she was helping me with the laces of my boots we heard our dogs, Sasha and Gogle, barking. I rushed to the window, anticipating another round of mourners, but instead I saw two Japanese soldiers waiting at the gate. One was middle-aged with a sabre in his belt and the long boots of a general. His square face was dignified and carved by deep wrinkles, but amusement twitched in the corners of his mouth when he eyed the two huskies leaping at the fence. The younger soldier stood motionless beside him, a clay doll illuminated only by the flicker of his narrow eyes. The colour leached completely from my mother's face when I told her the Japanese army was waiting at the gate.

From a crack in the front door I watched my mother speak with the men, first trying slow Russian and then Chinese. The younger soldier appeared to grasp the Chinese comfortably, while the General cast his gaze about the yard and house, and only paid attention when his aide translated my mother's answers for him. They were requesting something, bowing at the end of each sentence. This courtesy, not usually extended to the foreigners living in China, seemed to make my mother even uneasier. She was shaking her head, but giving her fear away in the flushed skin around her collar and in her trembling fingers which twisted and pulled at her sleeve cuffs.

In the past few months many Russians had received such visits. The Japanese high command and their assistants were moving into people's homes rather than living in army quarters. It was partly to protect them from Allied air raids but also to deter local resistance movements, either from White Russians turned Soviets or Chinese sympathisers. The only person we knew who had refused them was my father's friend, Professor Akimov, who owned an apartment in Modegow. He had disappeared one night and had never been heard from again. This, however, was the first time they had come this far from the city centre.

The General muttered something to his aide, and when I saw my mother calm the dogs and open the gate I scurried backwards into the house and hid under an armchair, pressing my face against the cold tiles of the entranceway. My mother entered the house first, holding the door for the General. He wiped his boots before coming inside and placed his hat down on the table next to me. I heard my mother take him into our sitting room. He seemed to be muttering his approval in Japanese, and although my mother continued to attempt basic conversation in Russian and Chinese, he gave no indication of understanding her. I wondered why he had left his aide at the gate. My mother and the General went upstairs and I could hear the creak of the floorboards in the spare room and the sound of cupboards being opened and shut. When they returned the General appeared pleased, but my mother's anxiety had travelled to her feet: she was changing her weight from one foot to the other and tapping her shoe. The General bowed and murmured, '*Doomo arigatoo gozaimashita.*' Thank you. When he picked up his hat he spotted me. His eyes were not like those of other Japanese soldiers I had seen. They were large and bulging, and when he opened them wide and smiled at me, the wrinkles on his forehead scrunched up towards his hairline and he seemed to transform into a large, friendly toad.

Every Sunday my mother, father and I had gathered at the home of our neighbours, Boris and Olga Pomerantsev, for a meal of borscht and rye bread. The elderly couple had been market farmers all their life, but they were gregarious and keen to improve their knowledge and often invited their Chinese acquaintances to join us. Until the Japanese invasion the gatherings had been lively affairs with music and readings from Pushkin, Tolstoy and Chinese poets, but as the occupation became more repressive the lunches became more subdued. All Chinese citizens were under constant surveillance, and those leaving the city had to show papers and get out of their cars or rickshaws to bow to the Japanese guards before they were allowed to move on their way. The only Chinese willing to do that for a social occasion other than a funeral or a wedding were Mr and Mrs Liu.

They had once been well-to-do industrialists, but their cotton factory had been taken over by the Japanese and they survived only because they had been prudent enough not to spend everything they had earned.

The Sunday after my father's mourning my mother waited until after the meal to tell our friends about the General. She spoke in broken whispers, running her hands over the lace tablecloth Olga brought out for special occasions, and cast glances at Mr Liu's sister, Ying-ying. The young woman was asleep in an armchair near the kitchen door, her breathing laboured and a sliver of saliva shining on her chin. It was unusual for Mr Liu to bring his sister to these occasions; he had always preferred to leave her in the care of his eldest daughters whenever he and his wife went out. But it seemed Ying-ying's depression was getting worse, swinging from days of listlessness to sudden outbursts of wailing and scratching the flesh of her arms until it bled. Mr Liu had sedated her with Chinese herbs and brought her with him, no longer confident that his children could cope.

My mother addressed us with careful words but her practised calmness only aggravated the sinking feeling in my stomach. She explained that the General would be renting the spare room in our house. She emphasised that his headquarters were in another village some distance away and that he would be spending most of his time there and so would not be such an imposition on us. She said that it had been agreed that no soldiers or other military attachés would be allowed to visit the house.

'Lina, no!' Olga cried. 'Such people!'

My mother's face blanched. 'How can I refuse him? If I do, I'll lose the house. Everything. I have to think of Anya.'

'Better no house than to live with such monsters,' said Olga. 'You and Anya can come and live here.'

Boris gripped my mother's shoulder with his farmer's hand, pink and rough with calluses. 'Olga, she will lose more than the house if she refuses.'

My mother lifted her apologetic eyes to the Lius and said, 'This will not look good in the eyes of my Chinese friends.'

Mrs Liu lowered her gaze but her husband turned his attention to his sister, who was stirring and mumbling names in her sleep. They were always the same names, whether Ying-ying was shouting them whilst Mrs Liu and her daughters held her down in the doctor's office, or whimpering them before sinking into one of her coma-like slumbers. She had come from Nanking with all the other bleeding and ruined refugees who had fled that city after the Japanese invasion. The names she called out were those of her three baby daughters, slit from throat to belly by the swords of Japanese soldiers. When the soldiers flung the girls' bodies onto a heap along with the bodies of the other children from their apartment block, one of the soldiers clamped Ying-ying's head between his fists so that she was forced to watch her daughters' tiny intestines spill to the ground and be fought over by guard dogs. Her husband and the other men were dragged into the street, marked and tied to stakes, and then the Japanese generals ordered the soldiers to plunge their bayonets through them for practice.

I slipped from the table unnoticed and ran outside to play with the cat who lived in the Pomerantsevs' garden. He was a stray with torn ears and a blind eye but he had grown fat and contented under Olga's attention. I pressed my face into his musky fur and wept. Stories like Ying-ying's were whispered all over Harbin and even I had seen enough of Japanese cruelty to hate them too.

The Japanese had annexed Manchuria in 1937, although it had been effectively invaded six years earlier. As the war became more intense, the Japanese issued an edict that all rice was to go to their army. The Chinese were reduced to acorn meal as a staple food, and this couldn't be digested by the very young or the sick. One day I was running along the twisted, leafy path by the river that flowed past our house. We had been let out from school early by our new Japanese principal, who had instructed us to go home and tell our parents of the recent Japanese victories in Manchuria. I was wearing my white convent uniform and enjoying the patterns the filtered sunlight made over me as I skipped along. I passed Doctor Chou, the local physician, on my way. Doctor Chou was trained in both Western and traditional medicine and was carrying a box of vials under his arm. He was famous for his sharp dress sense, and that day he was decked out in a well-cut Western suit and coat with a Panama hat. The mild weather seemed to please him too and we smiled at each other.

I passed him and reached the bend in the river where the forest was darkest and draped in vines. I was stunned by a loud shriek and stopped in my tracks when a Chinese farmer with a bruised and bleeding face lurched towards me. Japanese soldiers burst through the trees after him and surrounded us, waving their bayonets. The leader drew his sword and pressed it under the man's chin, making an indent in the flesh of his neck. He lifted the man's eyes to his, but I could see in their dimness and in the droop of his mouth that the light had already gone out of him. The farmer's jacket was streaming water and one of the soldiers took a knife and ripped open the left panel. Rice dropped in damp clumps to the ground.

The soldiers made the man kneel, taunting him and howling like wolves. The pack leader plunged his sword into the man's other jacket panel and blood and rice flowed out together. Vomit trickled from the man's lips. I heard glass smash and turned to see Doctor Chou standing behind me, his vials broken and leaking on the rocky path. Horror was etched in the grooves of his face. I stepped back, unnoticed by the soldiers, and into his outstretched arms.

The soldiers were grunting, excited by the smell of blood and fear. The leader pulled at the prisoner's collar, exposing his neck. In a single swoop he dropped his sword and sliced the man's head off at the shoulders. The bloody flesh rolled into the river, turning the water the colour of sorghum wine. The corpse remained upright, as if praying, and gushed blood in spurts. The soldiers stood back from it calmly and without guilt or disgust. Pools of blood and fluid collected around our feet and stained our shoes and the soldiers began to laugh. The killer lifted his sword to the sunlight and frowned at the muck that dripped from it. He looked around for something with which to clean it and laid eyes on my dress. He grabbed for me, but the outraged doctor pushed me further inside his coat, muttering curses at the soldiers. The leader grinned, mistaking Doctor Chou's curses for protests, and wiped his glistening sword across the doctor's shoulder. It must have disgusted Doctor Chou, who had just witnessed the murder of a fellow Chinese, but he remained silent in order to protect me.

My father was alive then, and that evening, after he had tucked me into bed and listened with restrained anger to my story, I heard him tell my mother on the landing: 'It's because their own leaders treat them so cruelly that they have lost all semblance of humanity. Their generals are to blame.'

At first the General brought little change to our lives and kept mainly to himself. He arrived with a futon, a gas cooker and a large trunk. We were only aware of his existence each morning, just after sunrise, when the black car would pull up outside our gate and the chickens in the yard would flutter as the General passed through them. And then in the evenings, when he would return late, weariness in his eyes, and give a nod to my mother and a smile to me before retiring to his room.

The General conducted himself with surprisingly good manners for a member of the occupying army. He paid rent and for anything he used, and after a while started bringing home rationed or banned items such as rice and sweet bean dumplings. He would place these luxuries, wrapped in cloth, on the dining table or kitchen bench before going to his room. My mother eyed the packages suspiciously and would not touch them, but she did not stop me from accepting the gifts. The General must have come to understand that my mother's goodwill could not be bought with items that had been taken from the Chinese, as the gifts were soon supplemented with secret acts of mending. One day we would find that a previously jammed window had been fixed, on another that a squeaky door had been oiled or a draughty corner sealed.

But it wasn't long before the General's presence became more invasive, like a potted vine that finds its way into the soil and takes over the garden.

On the fortieth day after my father's death, we visited the Pomerantsevs. The lunch was more light-hearted than usual, although it was only the four of us since the Lius would no longer come when we were invited.

Boris had managed to buy vodka, and even I was allowed some to 'warm' me. He amused us by suddenly whipping off his hat and revealing his closely cropped hair. My mother gingerly patted it and joked, 'Boris, who did this cruel thing to you? You look like a Siamese cat.'

Olga poured some more vodka, teasing me by pretending to pass over my glass several times, then scowled. 'He paid money for someone to do that to him! Some fancy new Chinese barber in the old quarter.'

Her husband grinned his yellow-toothed, happy grin and laughed. 'She's just upset because it looks better than when she does it.'

'When I saw you looking like such a fool, my weak old heart nearly gave out,' his wife retorted.

Boris took the vodka bottle and poured another round for everyone except his wife. When she frowned at him, he lifted his eyebrows and said: 'Mind your weak old heart now, Olga.'

My mother and I walked home, holding hands and kicking at the freshly fallen snow. She sang a song about gathering mushrooms. Every time she laughed little puffs of steam floated from her mouth. She looked beautiful, despite the grief that was etched behind her eyes. I wanted to be like her but I had inherited my father's strawberry blonde hair, blue eyes and freckles.

When we reached our gate, my mother's gaze narrowed at the sight of the Japanese lantern hanging over it. She rushed me inside, peeling off her coat and boots before helping me with mine. She jumped to the sitting room doorway, urging me to hurry so that I didn't catch cold from the tiled floor in the entranceway. When she turned to face the room she stiffened like a panicked cat. I stepped up behind her. Piled in one corner and covered with a red cloth was our furniture. Next to it a window alcove had been converted into a shrine complete with a scroll and ikebana flower arrangement. The rugs were gone and had been replaced by tatami mats.

My mother stormed through the house in search of the General, but he was not in his room or in the yard. We waited by the coal heater until nightfall, my mother rehearsing angry words for him. But the General did not come home that night and she lapsed into quiet despondency. We fell asleep, snuggled side by side near the dying fire.

The General did not return to the house until two days later, by which time exhaustion had drained the fight out of my mother. When he burst through the door with handfuls of tea, dress cloth and thread, he seemed to expect us to be grateful. In the delight and mischief in his eyes I saw my father again, the provider who found pleasure in securing treasures for his loved ones.

The General changed into a kimono of grey silk and set about cooking us vegetables and bean curd. My mother, whose elegant antique chairs had been packed away and who had no choice but to sit cross-legged on a cushion, stared out in front of her, purse-mouthed and indignant, while the house soaked in the aroma of sesame seed oil and soy sauce. I gaped at the lacquered plates the General set out on the low table, speechless but thankful for the small mercy that the General was cooking for us. I would have hated to see what would have happened had he

15

ordered my mother to cook for him. He was obviously not like the Japanese men I had seen in our village, whose women had to wait on them hand and foot, and who made their wives walk several paces behind them, burdened by the weight of whatever goods they had bought at the markets, while they strutted on ahead, empty-handed, heads held high. Olga once said that the Japanese race had no women, just donkeys.

The General placed the noodles in front of us and, with nothing more than a grunt of 'Itadakimasu', began eating. He seemed not to notice that my mother did not touch her plate, or that I sat staring at the juicy noodles, my mouth salivating. I was torn between my hunger pangs and my loyalty to my mother. As soon as the General finished eating, I rushed to clear the plates so that he wouldn't see that we had not eaten his meal. It was the best compromise I could make, for I did not want my mother's annoyance to bring any harm to her.

When I returned from the kitchen, the General was straightening out a roll of Japanese paper. It wasn't white and shiny like Western paper, nor was it completely matt. It was luminous. The General was on his hands and knees while my mother looked on, an exasperated expression on her face. The scene reminded me of a fable my father had once read to me about Marco Polo's first appearance before Kublai Khan, the ruler of China. In a gesture contrived to demonstrate European superiority, Polo's assistants un-ravelled a bolt of silk in front of the emperor and his courtiers. The material unfurled into a glistening stream that began with Polo and ended at the feet of Khan. After a moment's silence the emperor and his entourage burst into laughter. Polo soon discovered that it was hard to impress people who had been producing fine silk centuries before the Europeans stopped wearing animal skins.

The General beckoned for me to sit next to him and laid out an ink pot and calligraphy brush. He dipped the brush and set it to the paper, pouring out the feminine swirls of Japanese *hiragana*. I recognised the letters from the lessons we'd had when the Japanese had first taken over my school, before they decided it was better not to educate us at all and shut it down.

'Anya-chan,' the General said in his jumbled Russian, 'I teach you Japanese characters. Important for you to learn.'

I watched him deftly make the syllables come to life. *Ta, chi, tsu, te, to*. His fingers moved as if he were painting rather than writing and his hands mesmerised me. The skin was smooth and hairless, the nails as clean as bleached pebbles.

'You ought to be ashamed of yourself and your people,' cried my mother, snatching the paper from the General. She tried to tear it, but it was sinewy and pliant. So she scrunched it into a ball and threw it across the room. The paper dropped soundlessly to the floor.

I sucked in a breath. She glanced at me and stopped herself from saying anything more. She was trembling with anger but also with fear at what her outburst might cost us.

The General sat with his hands on his knees, not moving. The expression on his face was neutral. It was impossible to tell whether he was angry or just thinking. The tip of the brush dripped ink onto the tatami mat, where it spread out into a dark stain, like a wound. After a while the General reached into his kimono sleeve and took out a photograph and gave it to me. It was a picture of a woman in a black kimono and a young girl. The girl wore her hair in a topknot and had eyes as pretty as those of a deer. She looked almost the same age as me. The woman was glancing slightly out of the frame. Her hair was pulled away from her face. Her lips were powdered white and filled in with a narrow bow, but this couldn't hide the fullness of her mouth. The expression on her handsome face was formal, but something about the turn of her head suggested she was smiling at someone off camera.

'I have a little girl at home in Nagasaki with her mother and no father,' the General said. 'And you are a little girl without a father. I must take care of you.'

With that he stood up, bowed and left the room, leaving my mother and I standing with our mouths open, unable to think of anything to say.

Every second Tuesday the knife sharpener would come to our street. He was an old Russian with a lined face and mournful eyes. He had no hat and kept his head warm by wrapping it in rags. His sharpening wheel was strapped to a sled pulled by two Alsatians, and I would play with the dogs while my mother and our neighbours gathered to sharpen their knives and axes. One Tuesday Boris approached my mother and whispered that one of our neighbours, Nikolai Botkin, had disappeared. My mother's face froze for a moment before she whispered back, 'The Japanese or the Communists?'

Boris shrugged. 'I saw him only the day before yester-day at the barber in the old quarter. He talked too much. Boasted too much about how the Japs are losing the war and that they are just concealing it from us. The next day,' said Boris, clenching his hand and then springing it open to the air, 'he is gone. Like dust. That man's mouth was too big for his own good. You never know whose side the other customers are on. Some Russians want the Japs to win.'

At that moment there was a loud cry, 'Kazaaa!', and our garage doors flew open and a man ran out. He was naked, except for a knotted bandana pulled low on his brow. I didn't realise that it was the General until I saw him throw himself into the snow and leap up for joy. Boris tried to cover my eyes but through the gaps in his fingers I was startled to see the General's shrivelled appendage jiggling between his legs.

Olga slapped her knees and screeched with laughter,

while the other neighbours stared, open-mouthed, in amazement. But my mother saw the hot tub that had been constructed in her sacred garage and screamed. This last insult was too much for her to bear. Boris dropped his hands and I turned to see my mother as she had been before my father's death, her cheeks glowing and her eyes on fire. She raced into the yard, picking up a spade by the gate on her way. The General glanced from his hot tub to my mother, as if he were expecting her to marvel at his ingenuity.

'How dare you!' she screamed at him.

The smile died on his face but I could see that he couldn't comprehend her reaction.

'How dare you!' she screamed again, hitting him across the cheek with the spade handle.

Olga gasped but the General didn't seem worried about the neighbours witnessing my mother's insurrection. He didn't take his eyes from her face.

'It's one of the few things I have left to remember him by,' my mother said, losing her breath.

The General's face reddened. He stood up and retreated into the house without a word.

The following day the General dismantled the hot tub and offered us the wood for the fire. He took away the tatami mats and put back the Turkish carpets and sheepskin rugs for which my father had once traded his gold watch.

Later in the afternoon he asked if he could borrow my bicycle. My mother and I peered through the curtains to watch the General trundle down the road. My bike was too small for him. The pedals were short, so that with each rotation his knees passed his hips. But he handled the bicycle skilfully and in a few minutes disappeared through the trees.

By the time the General returned, my mother and I had adjusted the furniture and rugs back to almost the very inch where they had stood before.

The General glanced around the room. A shadow passed over his face. 'I wanted to make it beautiful for you but I did not succeed,' he said, using his foot to examine the magenta rug that had triumphed over his simple tatami. 'Perhaps we are too different.'

My mother almost smiled but stopped herself. I thought the General was about to leave, but he turned one more time to glance back at her, not at all like a regal military man but more like a shy boy who has been scolded by his mother. 'Maybe I have found something on whose beauty we can agree?' he said, reaching into his pocket and pulling out a glass box.

My mother hesitated before taking it from him, but in the end couldn't resist her own curiosity. I leaned forward, compelled to see what the General had brought. My mother opened the lid and a delicate scent wafted into the air. I knew it at once, although it was something I had never experienced before. The perfume became stronger, floating around the room and enveloping us in its spell. It was a blend of magic and romance, the exotic East and the decadent West. It made my heart ache and my skin tingle.

My mother's eyes were on me. They were glistening with tears. She held out the box and I stared at the creamy white flower inside. The sight of the perfect bloom set in a foliage of glossy green leaves conjured up a place where the light was dappled and birds sang day and night. I wanted to cry with the beauty of it, for instantly I knew the name of the flower, although until then I had only ever seen it in my imagination. The tree originated from China but was tropical and would not grow in Harbin where the frosts were brutal.

The white gardenia was a legend my father had spun for my mother and I many times. He had first seen the flower himself when he had accompanied his family to the Tsar's summer ball at the Grand Palace. He would describe to us the women in their flowing gowns with

20

jewels sparkling in their hair, the footmen and the carriages, and a supper of fresh caviar, smoked goose and *sterlet* soup served at round glass tables. Later there was a fireworks display choreographed to the music of Tchaikovsky's *Sleeping Beauty*. After meeting the Tsar and his family, my father walked into a room whose glass doors were thrown open to the garden. That was when he first saw them. The porcelain pots of gardenias had been imported from China for the occasion. In the summer air their delicate scent was intoxicating. The flowers seemed to nod and receive my father gracefully, as the Tsarina and her daughters had done just moments before. From that night on my father had been enamoured by the memory of northern white nights and a bewitching flower whose perfume conjured up paradise.

More than once my father had tried to purchase a bottle of the scent so that my mother and I could relive this memory too, but no one in Harbin had heard of the enchanting flower and his efforts were always in vain.

'Where did you get this?' my mother asked the General, running her fingertip over the dewy petals.

'From a Chinaman called Huang,' he answered. 'He has a hothouse outside of the city.'

But my mother barely heard his answer, her mind was a million miles away on a St Petersburg night. The General turned to go. I followed him to the foot of the stairs.

'Sir,' I whispered to him. 'How did you know?'

He raised his eyebrows and stared at me. His bruised cheek was the colour of a fresh plum.

'About the flower,' I said.

But the General only sighed, touched my shoulder and said, 'Goodnight.'

By the time spring came and the snow started melting there were rumours everywhere that the Japanese were losing the war. In the night I could hear planes and gunfire, which

Boris told us was the Soviets fighting the Japanese at the borders. 'God help us,' he said, 'if the Soviets get here before the Americans.'

I decided to find out whether the Japanese were really losing the war and hatched a plan to follow the General to his headquarters. My first two attempts to get up before him failed when I slept past my own usual waking time, but on the third day I was woken by a dream of my father. He was standing before me, smiling, and saying, 'Don't worry. You will seem all alone, but you won't be. I will send someone.' His image faded and I blinked at the early morning light making its way through my curtains. I leaped out of bed into the chilly air, and only had to pull on my coat and hat, having prepared myself by sleeping fully clothed and with my boots on. I sneaked out the kitchen door and to the side of the garage where I had hidden my bicycle. I crouched on the slushy ground and waited. A few minutes later the black car pulled up at our gate. The front door opened and the General strode out. When the car moved off, I jumped on my bicycle and pedalled furiously to keep even a discreet distance. The sky was cloudy and the road dark and muddy. When it reached the junction, the car stopped and I hid behind a tree. The driver reversed a short distance and changed direction, no longer heading along the road to the next village where the General had told us he went each day, but taking the main one to the city. I mounted my bicycle again but when I reached the junction I hit a rock and toppled over, slamming my shoulder into the ground. I winced in pain and looked at my bicycle. The front spokes had been bent by my boot. Tears leaked from my eyes and I limped back up the hill, walking the squealing bike next to me.

Just before I reached home I saw a Chinese man peek out from a grove of trees by the road. He looked as if he was waiting for me, so I crossed to the other side and began running with my wonky bicycle. But he soon caught up, greeting me in well-spoken Russian. There was something in his glassy-eyed gaze that made me afraid and I replied with silence. 'Why,' he asked, sighing as if he were talking to a naughty sister, 'do you let the Japanese stay with you?'

'We had nothing to do with it,' I answered, my eyes still averted. 'He just came and we couldn't say no.'

He took the handlebars of the bicycle, pretending to help me with it, and I noticed his gloves. They were padded and shaped as if he had apples in them instead of hands.

'They are very bad, the Japanese,' he continued. 'They have done terrible things. The Chinese people will not forget who helped us and who helped them.' His tone was kind and intimate but his words sent a chill through me and I forgot the ache in my shoulder. He stopped pushing the bicycle and laid it on its side. I wanted to run but I was frozen with fear. Slowly and deliberately he lifted his glove to my face and then pulled the material away with the grace of a magician. He held before me a mangled mess of badly healed flesh, twisted into a club with no fingers. I cried out at the horror of it but knew he was not doing it for effect alone; it was a warning. I left my bicycle and ran through the gate to my house. 'My name is Tang!' the man called out after me. 'Remember it!'

I turned when I reached the door but he was gone. I clambered up the stairs to my mother's bedroom, my heart beating like thunder in my chest. But when I pushed open the door I saw that she was still asleep, her dark hair spread over the pillow. I removed my coat, gently lifted the bedclothes and climbed in beside her. She sighed and brushed her hand against me before falling back into a sleep as still as death.

August was the month of my thirteenth birthday, and despite the war and my father's death, my mother was determined to keep our family tradition of taking me to the old quarter to celebrate. Boris and Olga drove us into the city that day; Olga wanted to buy some spices and Boris was going to get his hair cut again. Harbin was the place of my birth, and although many Chinese said that we Russians never belonged nor had any right to it, I felt that it somehow belonged to me. When we entered the city, I saw all that was familiar and home to me in the onion-domed churches, the pastel-coloured buildings and the elaborate colonnades. Like me, my mother was born in Harbin. She was the daughter of an engineer who had lost his job on the railways after the Revolution. It was my noble father who had somehow connected us to Russia and made us see ourselves in the architecture of the Tsars.

Boris and Olga dropped us off in the old quarter. It was unusually hot and humid that day, so my mother suggested we try the city's speciality, vanilla bean ice-cream. Our favourite café was bustling with people and much livelier than we had seen it in years. Everyone was talking about the rumours that the Japanese were about to surrender. My mother and I took a table near the window. A woman at the next table was telling her older companion that she had heard the Americans bombing the previous night, and that a Japanese official had been murdered in her district. Her companion nodded solemnly, running his hand through his grey beard and commenting, 'The Chinese would never dare do that if they didn't feel that they were winning.'

After my ice-cream, my mother and I took a walk around the quarter, noticing which shops were new and remembering the shops that had disappeared. A peddler of porcelain dolls tried to entice me with her wares, but my mother smiled at me and said, 'Don't worry, I have something for you at home.'

I spotted the red and white pole of a barber's shop with a sign in Chinese and Russian. 'Look, Mama!' I said. 'That must be Boris's barber.' I rushed to the window to peek inside. Boris was in the chair, his face covered in shaving foam. A few other customers were waiting, smoking and laughing like men with nothing much to do. Boris saw me in the mirror and turned and waved. The bald-headed barber, in an embroidered jacket, also looked up. He had a Confucian moustache and goatee and wore glasses with thick frames, the kind popular among Chinese men. But when he saw my face pressed against the window, he quickly turned his back to me.

'Come on, Anya,' my mother laughed, pulling my arm. 'Boris will get a bad haircut if you distract the barber. He might cut off his ear, and then Olga will be annoyed with you.'

I followed my mother obediently, but as we neared the corner I turned one more time towards the barber's shop. I couldn't see the barber through the shine on the glass, but I realised that I knew those eyes: they had been round and bulging and familiar to me.

When we returned home my mother sat me before her dressing table and reverently undid my girlish plaits and swept my hair into an elegant chignon like hers, with the hair parted at the side and bunched at the nape of the neck. She dabbed perfume behind my ears, then showed me a velvet box on her dresser. When she opened it I saw inside the gold and jade necklace my father had given her as a wedding present. She picked it up and kissed it, before placing it around my throat and fastening the clip.

'Mama!' I protested, knowing how much the necklace meant to her.

She pursed her lips. 'I want to give it to you now, Anya, because you are becoming a young woman. Your father would have been pleased to see you wear it on special occasions.'

I touched the necklace with trembling fingers. Although I missed seeing my father and talking with him, I felt that he was never far away. The jade seemed warm against my skin, not cold.

'He's with us, Mama,' I said. 'I know it.'

She nodded and sniffed back a tear. 'I have something else for you, Anya,' she said, opening the drawer near my knee and taking out a package wrapped in cloth. 'Something to remind you that you will always be my little girl.'

I took the package from her and untied the knot, excited to see what was inside. It was a matroshka doll with the smiling face of my late grandmother. I turned to my mother, knowing that she had painted it. She laughed and urged me to open it and find the next doll. I unscrewed the doll's torso and found that the second doll had dark hair and amber eyes. I smiled at my mother's joke, and knew that the following doll would have strawberry blonde hair and blue eyes, but when I saw it also had a smatter of freckles across its funny face, I burst into giggles. I opened that doll to find a smaller one and looked up again at my mother. 'Your daughter and my granddaughter,' she said. 'And with her smaller baby daughter inside her.'

I screwed all the dolls back together and lined them up on the dressing table, contemplating our matriarchal journey and wishing that my mother and I could always be just as we were at that moment.

Afterwards, in the kitchen, my mother placed an apple *pirog* before me. She was just about to cut the little pie when we heard the front door open. I glanced at the clock and knew it would be the General. He spent a long time in the entranceway before coming into the house. When he did finally enter the kitchen, he stumbled, his face a sickly colour. My mother asked if he was ill but he didn't answer her and collapsed into a chair, resting his head in his folded arms. My mother stood up, horrified, and asked me to fetch some warm tea and bread. When I offered these to the General, he looked up at me with red-rimmed eyes.

He glanced at my birthday pie and reached over to me, patting my head clumsily. I could smell the alcohol on his breath when he said, 'You are my daughter.' The General turned to my mother and with tears falling down his cheeks said to her, 'You are my wife.' Sitting back in the chair, he composed himself, wiping his face with the back of his hand. My mother offered him the tea and he took a sip and a slice of bread. His face was contorted with pain, but after a while it relaxed and he sighed as if he had reached a decision. He rose from the table and, turning to my mother, gave a charade performance of her hitting him with the spade handle after discovering his secret hot tub. He laughed then, and my mother looked at him, astonished for a moment, before laughing herself.

She asked him in slow Russian what he did before the war, had he always been a general. He looked confused for a moment, then pointed his finger to his nose and asked 'Me?' My mother nodded and repeated her question. He shook his head and closed the door behind him, muttering in Russian so well pronounced that he could have been one of us, 'Before all this madness? I was an actor. In the theatre.'

The next morning the General was gone. There was a note pinned to the kitchen door, written in precise Russian. My mother read it first, her frightened eyes scanning the words twice, then handed it to me. The General had instructed us to burn everything he had left in the garage and to burn the note after reading it. He said that he had placed our lives in great danger when his only wish had been to protect us. He told us that we must destroy every trace of him for our own sake.

My mother and I ran to the Pomerantsevs' house. Boris was chopping wood, but stopped when he saw us, wiping the sweat from his ruddy face and rushing us inside.

Olga was by the stove, twisting her knitting in her hands. She jumped out of her chair when she saw us. 'Have you heard?' she asked, white-faced and shaking. 'The Soviets are coming. The Japanese have surrendered.'

Her words seemed to shatter my mother. 'The Soviets or the Americans?' she asked, her voice rising in agitation.

I could feel myself inwardly willing that it was the Americans who were coming to liberate us with their wide smiles and bright flags. But Olga shook her head. 'The Soviets,' she cried. 'They are coming to help the Communists.'

My mother handed her the General's note. 'My God!' said Olga after reading it. She collapsed into her chair and passed the note to her husband.

'He spoke fluent Russian?' Boris asked. 'You didn't know?'

Boris began talking about an old friend in Shanghai, someone who would help us. The Americans were on their way there, he said, and my mother and I should go immediately. My mother asked if Boris and Olga would come too, but Boris shook his head and joked, 'Lina, what are they going to do to a couple of old reindeers like us? The daughter of a White Army colonel is a much better prize. You must get Anya out of here now.'

With the wood Boris had chopped for us we made a fire and burned the letter along with the General's bedding and eating utensils. I watched my mother's face as the flames rose and felt the same loneliness I saw written there. We were cremating a companion, someone we had never known or understood, but a companion just the same. My mother was relocking the garage when she noticed the trunk. It was jammed into a corner and hidden under some empty sacks. We lugged it out of its hiding place. The trunk was antique and beautifully carved with a picture of an old man with a long moustache holding a fan and gazing across a pond. My mother smashed the padlock with an axe and we lifted the lid together. The General's uniform was folded there. She picked it up and I saw an embroidered jacket in the bottom of the trunk. Underneath the jacket we found a false moustache and beard, some makeup, thick-rimmed glasses and a copy of the *New Pocket Atlas of China* folded in a sheet of old newspaper. My mother stared at me, puzzled. I said nothing. I hoped that if only I knew the General's secret we would be safe.

After we had burned everything, we turned over the soil and patted away the stain with the backs of our shovels.

My mother and I went to the district official's office to get a permit to go to Dairen where we hoped to board a ship to Shanghai. There were dozens of other Russians waiting in the corridors and on the staircase, and some other foreigners and Chinese too. They were all talking about the Soviets and how some of them were already in Harbin, rounding up the White Russians. An old lady beside us told my mother that the Japanese family next door to her had committed suicide, terrified of the vengeance of the Chinese. My mother asked her what had made Japan surrender, and she shrugged, but a young man answered that he had heard rumours of a new kind of bomb dropped on Japanese cities. The official's assistant came out and told us that no permits would be issued until all those seeking them had been interviewed by a member of the Communist party.

When we returned home our dogs were nowhere in sight and the door was unlocked and ajar. My mother paused before pushing it open, and just as her face on the day after my father's mourning remains in my memory, so is that moment imprinted on my mind, like a scene from a film played over and over again: my mother's hand on the door, the door swinging slowly open, the darkness and silence inside, and the incredible sense of knowing that someone was there, waiting for us.

My mother's hand dropped to her side and felt for mine. It wasn't trembling as it had since my father's death. It was warm and strong and decisive. We moved together, not taking off our shoes in the entranceway as we had always done, but continuing on into the sitting room. When I saw him there at the table, his mutilated hands resting before him, I wasn't surprised. It was as if I had been expecting him all along. My mother said nothing. She met his glassy eyes with a blank expression. He gave a bitter smile and motioned for us to sit down at the table with him. It was then that we noticed the other man, the one standing by the window. He was tall with piercing blue eyes and a moustache that hung from his lip like a winter fur.

Although it was summer, darkness fell quickly that evening. I remember the sensation of my mother's firm grip on my hand, the fading afternoon light retreating across the floor, and then the whistling sound of a storm beating against the unshuttered windows. Tang interviewed us first, his tight-lipped smile appearing whenever my mother answered his questions. He told us that the General had not been a general at all, but a spy who also masqueraded as a barber. He was fluent in Chinese and Russian, a master of disguise who used his skills to gather information on the Resistance. Because the Russians thought he was Chinese, they felt quite comfortable gathering at his shop and discussing their plans, and revealing those of their Chinese counterparts. I was glad then that I had not told my mother that I had understood who the General was as soon as I saw the costume in the trunk. Tang's face was fixed on my mother's and she looked so shocked that I felt sure he would believe she had no part in the General's work.

But even though it was obvious that my mother had not known who the General was, that we had not received any visitors while he lived with us, and that we were unaware that he could speak any language other than Japanese, it could not erase the hate Tang felt towards us. His whole person seemed to be inflamed with it. Such malice burned to only one goal: revenge.

'Madame Kozlova, have you heard of Unit 731?' he asked, restrained anger contorting his face. He seemed to be satisfied when my mother didn't answer. 'No, of course not. Nor would have your General Mizutani. Your cultured, well-spoken General Mizutani who bathed once a day and has never in his life killed a man with his own hands. But he seemed quite content to condemn people there, as you were to house a man whose countrymen have been slaughtering us. You and the General have as much blood on your hands as any army.'

Tang lifted his hand and waved the infected mess in front of my mother's face. 'You Russians, protected by your white skin and Western ways, don't know about the live experiments that took place in the district next to this one. I am the only survivor. One of the many they tied to stakes in the snow, so that their nice clean educated doctors could observe the effects of frostbite and gangrene in order to prevent it happening to their own soldiers. But perhaps we were the lucky ones. They always intended to shoot us in the end. Not like the others, whom they infected with plague then cut open without anaesthetic to observe the effects. I wonder if you could imagine the feeling of having your head sawn open while still alive? Or being raped by a doctor so that he could impregnate you then cut you open and look at the foetus.'

Horror pinched my mother's face but she never took her eyes off Tang. Seeing that he hadn't broken her, he flashed his cruel smile again, and using his clubbed hand and elbow removed a photograph from a folder on the table. It appeared to be of someone tied down on a table surrounded by doctors, but the overhead light was reflecting in the middle of it and I couldn't make it out clearly. He told my mother to pick it up; she looked at it and turned away.

31

'Perhaps I should show it to your daughter?' he said. 'They are about the same age.'

My mother's eyes flamed and she met his hate with her anger. 'My daughter is only a child. Hate me if you want, but what say has she had in anything?' She glanced at the photograph again and tears came to her eyes, but she blinked them away. Tang smiled, triumphant. He was about to say something when the other man coughed. I had almost forgotten the Russian, he had sat so quietly, gazing out the window, perhaps not listening at all.

When the Soviet officer questioned my mother, it was as if we had changed the script and were suddenly in a different play. He was unconcerned with Tang's thirst for revenge or details about the General. He acted as if the Japanese had never been in China; he had really come to grab my father's throat and, my father not being there, had settled on us. His questions to my mother were all about her family background and that of my father. He asked about the value of our house and my mother's assets, giving a little snort to each reply as if he were ticking off a form. 'Well,' he said, appraising me with his yellow-speckled eyes, 'you won't have such things in the Soviet Union.'

My mother asked him what he meant, and he replied with distaste, 'She is the daughter of a colonel of the Russian Imperialist Army. A supporter of the Tsar who turned his guns on his own people. She has his blood. And you,' he sneered at my mother, 'are of little interest to us but of great interest to the Chinese, it seems. They need examples of what is done to traitors. The Soviet Union just needs to call home its workers. Its *young*, able-bodied workers.'

My mother's face didn't change expression, but she gripped my hand tighter, squeezing the blood out of it and bruising the bones. But I didn't wince or cry out from the pain. I wanted her to hold me like that forever, to never let me go.

With the room spinning and me nearly passing out from

the pain of my mother's grip, Tang and the Soviet officer made their devil's bargain: my mother in exchange for me. The Russian got his able-bodied worker and the Chinese man got his revenge.

I stood on the tips of my toes, reaching upwards to the train window so that I could touch the fingertips of my mother's outstretched hand. She had pressed herself against the window frame so that she could be near to me. From the corner of my eye I could see Tang standing with the Soviet officer by the car. He was pacing like a hungry tiger, waiting to take me. There was much confusion on the station. An elderly couple were clinging to their son. A Soviet soldier shoved them away, forcing the young man onto a carriage, pushing him in the back as if he were a sack of potatoes not a person. In the cramped carriage he tried to turn to look at his mother one last time, but more men were pushed in behind him and he lost his chance.

My mother gripped the window bars and hoisted herself higher so I could see her face more clearly. She was very drawn with shadows under her eyes, but she was still beautiful. She told me my favourite stories over again and sang the song about the mushrooms to calm my tears. Other people were reaching their hands out of the train windows to say goodbye to their families and neighbours, but the soldiers beat them back. The guard near us was young, almost a boy, with porcelain skin and eyes like crystals. He must have taken pity on us for he turned his back to us and shielded our last moment from the view of others.

The train began to pull away. I held onto my mother's fingers as long as I could, side-stepping the people and boxes on the platform. I tried to keep up but the train gathered speed and I lost my grip. My mother was tugged away from me. She turned back, covering her mouth with her fist because she was no longer able to contain her own grief. My tears stung my eyes but I wouldn't blink. I watched the train until it disappeared from view. I fell against a lamppost, weakened by the hole that was opening up inside me. But an unseen hand held me upright. I heard my father say to me: 'You will seem all alone, but you won't be. I will send someone.'

TWO

The Paris of the East

After the train had gone there was a pause, like the interlude between a flash of lightning and the sound of thunder. I was afraid to turn and look at Tang. I imagined that he was creeping towards me, crawling as a spider does towards the moth it has caught in its web. There was no need to hurry, his prey was trapped. He could linger and savour the pleasure of his cleverness before devouring me. The Soviet officer would already be gone, my mother forgotten and his mind on other business. I was the daughter of a White Army colonel, but my mother would make a more useful labourer. Ideology was a catchcry to him. Practicality was more important. But Tang was not like that. He wanted his twisted justice done and would see this thing through until the end. I didn't know what he had planned for me, but I was sure it would be something lingering and unspeakable. He wouldn't just have me shot or thrown from a roof. He had said, 'I want you to live daily with the consequences of what you and your mother have done.' Perhaps my fate would be that of the Japanese girls in my district, the ones who had not been able to escape. The Communists shaved their heads then sold them to the Chinese brothels that served the lowest of the low: lepers without noses and men with such terrible venereal diseases that half their flesh was rotted away.

I swallowed. Another train was pulling in on the opposite platform. It would be easy . . . so much easier, I thought, staring at the heavy wheels, the metal tracks. My legs trembled, I inched a step forward, but my father's face flashed before me and I couldn't move any further. I caught sight of Tang out of the corner of my eye. He was indeed lurking towards me, taking his time. There was hunger, not relief, on his face now that my mother was gone. He was coming for more. It's over, I told myself. It's all over.

A firecracker exploded into the sky and I jumped back, startled by the sound. A crowd of people in Communist uniform swamped the station. I stared at them, not able to take in their sudden appearance. They were shouting 'Oora! Oora!' and waving bright flags and beating drums and cymbals. They had come to welcome the arrival of more Russian Communists. They marched directly between Tang and myself. I saw him trying to fight his way through them, but he became trapped in their parade. The people were circling him. He was screaming at them but they couldn't hear him above their cheers and music.

'Go!'

I looked up. It was the young Soviet soldier, the one with eyes like crystals. 'Go! Run!' he shouted, pushing me with the butt of his rifle. A hand grabbed mine and I was pulled through the crowd. I couldn't see who it was ahead of me. They dragged me through the wriggling onslaught. Everything was human sweat and the smell of gunpowder from the firecrackers. I glanced over my shoulder and saw that Tang was pushing through the crowd. He was gaining ground but the stumps of his hands hampered him. It was impossible for him to grab people to get them out of his way. He shouted orders to the young Soviet, who made as if to chase after me but purposely got himself tangled in the crowd. I was bumped and jostled, my shoulders and arms bashed and bruised. Up ahead through the sea of legs a car door opened up and I was thrust towards it. I recognised the hand then. I felt the calluses and knew the largeness of it. Boris.

I leaped into the car and Boris stepped on the pedal. Olga was in the passenger seat. 'Oh my darling Anya. My little Anya!' she cried. The road rolled away behind us. I looked through the back window. The crowd on the station was swelling, the disembarking Soviet soldiers adding to its number. I couldn't see Tang.

'Anya, get down under the blanket,' Boris said to me. I did as I was told, and I felt Olga piling things on top of me. 'Did you expect those people?' she asked her husband.

'No, I intended to grab Anya no matter what,' he said. 'But it seems that even the mad enthusiasm for the Communists can come in useful sometimes.'

A while later the car stopped and there were voices. The door opened and slammed. I heard Boris talking quietly outside. Olga was still in the front seat, wheezing under her breath. I felt sorry for her and her weak old heart. My own heart was beating wildly, and I clamped my mouth shut, as if that would somehow prevent anyone from hearing it.

Boris jumped back into the driver's seat and we moved on. 'A road block. I told them we have things to prepare for the Russians, and we are in a hurry,' he said.

Two or three hours passed before Boris said I could come out from under the blanket. Olga lifted the bags off me, which turned out to be sacks of grain and vegetables. We were driving along a dirt road surrounded by mountain ridges. There was no one in sight. The fields were deserted. Up ahead I could see a burned-out farmhouse. Boris drove into the storage shed. The whole place smelled of hay and smoke and I wondered who had lived there. I knew from the shrine-like shape of the gates that they had been Japanese.

'We will wait until dark before going to Dairen,' said Boris.

We got out of the car and he spread out a blanket on the floor and told me to sit on it. His wife opened a small basket and pulled out some dishes and cups. She scraped some *kasha* onto a plate for me, but I felt so sick I could hardly eat it.

'Take some, my darling,' she said. 'You need strength for the journey.'

I stared at Boris, who looked away.

'But we are staying together,' I said, feeling the fear constrict my throat. I knew that they were talking about sending me to Shanghai. 'You must come with me.'

Olga bit her lip and wiped her eyes with her sleeve. 'No, Anya. We must stay here or we will lead Tang straight to you. He is a vile creature who has not yet had his fill.'

Boris put his arm around my shoulders. I buried my face into his chest. I knew I would miss his smell, the smell of oats and wood. 'My friend, Sergei Nikolaievich, is a good man. He will take care of you,' he said, stroking my hair. 'Shanghai will be much safer for you.'

'And such fine things in Shanghai too,' said Olga, trying to make me smile. 'Sergei Nikolaievich is wealthy and will take you to shows and restaurants. It will bè much more fun than staying here with us.'

At nightfall, by back roads and across farms, the Pomerantsevs drove me to the port of Dairen where a ship was leaving for Shanghai at sunrise.

When we arrived at the dock, Olga cleaned my face with the sleeve of her dress and slipped the matroshka doll and jade necklace my mother had given me into my coat pocket. I wondered how she had saved them or understood their importance but I had no time to ask her before the ship's whistle sounded and the passengers were called on board.

'We have already sent word to Sergei Nikolaievich to expect you,' she said.

Boris helped me onto the gangway and handed me a small bag packed with a dress, a blanket and some food. 'Make your way in this world, little one,' he whispered to me, tears dripping down his face. 'Make your mother proud. All our dreams now rest with you.'

Later, on the Huangpu River approaching Shanghai, I remembered those words and wondered if I could live up to them.

How many days passed before the towering skyline of Shanghai loomed up in the distance, I do not remember. Perhaps two, perhaps more. I was not conscious of anything except a dark hole that seemed to have opened itself up in my heart, and the stench of opium smoke which choked the air day and night. The steamer was crammed with people fleeing the north, and several of the passengers lay about on their mats like emaciated cadavers, the stubs of their laced cigarettes clenched between their dirty fingers, their mouths like caverns in their faces. Before the war the foreigners had attempted to moderate the damage they had caused by imposing opium on China, but the Japanese invaders had used addiction to subdue the population. They had forced peasants in Manchuria to grow poppies and built factories in Harbin and Dairen to process it. The very poor injected it, the wealthy brewed it in pipes, and just about everyone else smoked it like tobacco. After eight years of occupation, it seemed that every Chinese male on the ship was addicted.

The afternoon we approached Shanghai, the steamer dipped and rose on the muddy river, sending bottles and children rolling. I gripped the railing, my gaze fastened on the makeshift houses that littered either side of the river-bank. They were windowless shacks propped one against the other like stacks of cards. Jammed next to them were rows of factories whose great furnaces exhaled gusts of smoke. The smoke wafted across the narrow, garbage-strewn streets and turned the air into one foul concoction of human waste and sulphur.

The other passengers displayed little interest in the metropolis we were approaching. They remained huddled in small groups, smoking or playing cards. The Russian man next to me was asleep on his blanket, an overturned bottle of vodka by his side and a stream of vomit running down his chest. A Chinese woman squatted next to him, cracking nuts with her teeth and feeding them to her two small children. I wondered how they could be so impassive when I felt that we were being slowly drawn into the world of the damned.

I saw that my knuckles were raw from the breeze and I shoved them into my pockets. My fingers nudged the matroshka doll and I began to cry.

Further on, the slums gave way to a stretch of ports and villages. Men and women lifted their straw hats and looked up at us from their fishing baskets and rice sacks. Dozens of sampans converged on the steamer like carp to a piece of bread. The occupants offered us chopsticks, incense, lumps of coal, and one even held up his daughter. The little girl's eyes were turned backwards with terror but she didn't struggle against him. The sight of her made the bruise on my hand twinge, the one my mother had pressed there on our last night in Harbin. It was still swollen and blue. The ache reminded me of the tightness with which she had held it, and the belief her grip had given me that we could never be separated, that she would never let me go.

It was only when we reached the Bund that I could grasp any sense of Shanghai's legendary wealth or beauty. The air was fresher there and the port full of cruise ships and a white ocean liner whose funnel was letting off steam in preparation for the journey ahead. Next to it a Japanese patrol boat with a gaping hole in the side and its bow half underwater listed against the dock. From the top deck of the steamer I could see the five-star hotel that had made the Bund famous: the Hotel Cathay with its arched windows and penthouse suites, and the line of rickshaws that curved around it like a long piece of string.

We disembarked into a waiting area at street level and were besieged by another wave of hawkers. But the wares the city peddlers offered us were much more exotic than those of the boat people: gold charms, ivory figurines, duck eggs. An old man pulled out a tiny crystal horse from a velvet bag and placed it in my palm. It had been diamond-cut and its planes sparkled in the sunlight. It made me think of the ice sculptures the Russians carved in Harbin, but I had no money in my pocket to spend and I had to hand it back to him.

Most of the passengers were greeted by relatives or whisked away in taxis or rickshaws. I stood alone in the subsiding babble of voices, nauseous with the panic that was rushing through my veins, my eyes flitting to every Western man, hoping that he would be Boris's friend. The Americans had rigged up open-air screens to play news-reels from around the world of the closure of the war. I watched the scenes of joyous people dancing in the streets, smiling soldiers returning home to their peaches-and-cream wives, the speeches by smug-looking presidents and prime ministers, all subtitled with Chinese characters. It was as if America was trying to convince us that everything would be all right again. The broadcast ended with an honour roll of those countries, organisations and individuals who had helped liberate China from the Japanese. There was one group conspicuously absent from it: the Communists.

A neatly dressed Chinese man appeared before me. He handed me a gold-edged card with my name written on it in a cramped, hurried hand. I nodded and he picked up my bag, gesturing for me to follow him. When he saw that I was hesitant, he said: 'It's okay. Mr Sergei sent me. He will meet you at his house.'

On the street, away from the river breeze, the sun produced a sweltering, semitropical heat. Hundreds of Chinese were crouched in the gutters cooking spicy broths or displaying trinkets on blankets. Between them, peddlers pushed wheelbarrows of rice and wood. The manservant helped me into a rickshaw and soon we were being pulled along a road filled with bicycles, rattling tramcars and shiny American Buicks and Packards. I turned my head to look up at the grand colonial buildings, never having seen a city like Shanghai in my life.

The streets off the Bund were a maze of narrow laneways with washing strung from window to window like flags. Baldheaded children with weepy eyes peered curiously from dark doorways. On every corner there seemed to be a food vendor frying something that smelled like rubber, and I was relieved when the rancid air gave way to the aroma of freshly baked bread. The rickshaw ran under an arch and came out into an oasis of cobblestoned streets, Art Deco lamps and shops displaying pastries and antiques in their windows. We turned into a street lined with maple trees and came to a stop outside a high concrete wall. The wall was lime-washed an elegant blue but my eyes fixed on the fragments of broken glass cemented to its top edge and the barbed wire wrapped around the branches of the trees that overhung it.

The manservant helped me down from the rickshaw and rang a bell next to the gate. A few seconds later the gate swung open and an elderly Chinese maid greeted us, her face colourless like a corpse against her black cheongsam. She didn't answer me when I introduced myself in Mandarin. She only lowered her eyes and guided me inside the compound.

The courtyard was dominated by a three-storey house with blue doors and lattice shutters. Another single-storey building was connected to the main house by a covered walkway and I assumed from the bedding slung over the windowsills that it was the servants' quarters. The man-servant handed my bag to the maid and disappeared into the smaller building. I followed the woman across the neat lawn and past flowerbeds bursting with roses the colour of blood.

The entrance hall was spacious with sea-green walls and

cream tiles. My footsteps echoed in the space while the maid's made no sound at all. The silence of the house stirred in me a queer sensation of transience, as if I had passed from life into something that was not life but not quite death either. At the end of the hall I could see another room decorated with red curtains and Persian carpets. Dozens of French and Chinese paintings hung on its pale walls. The maid was about to lead me there when I noticed the woman poised on the staircase. Her milky face was framed by blue-black hair styled in a sleek bob. She fingered the ostrich-feather collar of her dress and considered me for a moment with dark, severe eyes. 'A very pretty child indeed,' she said to the maid in English. 'But so serious-looking. What on earth will I do with that long face around me all day?'

Sergei Nikolaievich Kirillov was nothing like his American wife. When Amelia Kirillova led me into her husband's study, he immediately stood up from his cluttered desk and embraced me with kisses on both cheeks. His gait was heavy like a bear's and he was about twenty years older than his wife, who looked my mother's age. His eyes darted about keenly and, apart from his size, the only frightening thing about him was his thick eyebrows which made him look cross even when he was smiling.

There was another man sitting by the desk. 'This is Anya Kozlova,' Sergei Nikolaievich said to him. 'My friend's neighbour from Harbin. Her mother has been deported by the Soviets and we must take care of her. In return she is going to teach us the good manners of the old aristocrats.'

The other man grinned and stood up to shake my hand. His breath smelled of stale tobacco and his face had an unhealthy tinge to it. 'I am Alexei Igorevich Mikhailov,' he said, 'and God knows us Shanghailanders could do with some good manners.'

'I don't care what she teaches you as long as she speaks

English,' said Amelia, taking a cigarette from a case on the table and lighting it.

'Yes, madam, I do,' I said.

She gave me a look that wasn't quite a smile and pulled a tasselled cord by the door. 'Good then,' she said, 'you will have ample opportunity to show it off at dinner tonight. Sergei has invited someone he thinks will be very entertained by a young beauty who can speak Russian and English and teach him good manners.'

A child maid shuffled into the room, her head bowed. She couldn't have been more than six years old, with skin like caramel and her hair pulled into a topknot. 'This is Mei Lin,' Amelia said. 'When she actually manages to open her mouth she speaks only Chinese. But you probably do too. So she's all yours.'

The little girl was staring, as if mesmerised, at a point on the floor. Sergei Nikolaievich gave her a gentle push. She looked from the giant Russian to his willowy wife to me with wide, startled eyes.

'Rest for a while and come down when you are ready,' Sergei Nikolaievich said, squeezing my arm and leading me to the door. 'I feel for you and I hope tonight's dinner will put you in better spirits. Boris helped me when I lost everything in the Revolution. And I intend to repay that kindness to you.'

I let Mei Lin lead me to my room, although I would have preferred to have been left alone. My legs were trembling with fatigue and my head throbbed. Each stair was agony but Mei Lin's eyes were fixed on me with such innocent fondness that I couldn't help smiling at her. She returned the expression with her own brimming, baby-toothed grin.

My room was on the second floor, overlooking the garden. It had dark pine floors and gold-papered walls. An antique globe stood by the bay window and in the centre of the room was a four-poster bed. I walked to the bed and put my hand on the cashmere shawl covering it. As soon as my fingers touched the fabric I was filled with despair. It was a woman's room. The moment they had taken my mother away I had ceased to be a child. I covered my face with my hands and longed for my loft in Harbin. In my memory I could see each doll perched on the roof beam and hear each creak of the floorboards.

I turned from the bed and ran to the window, spinning the globe around until I located China. I traced an imaginary journey from Harbin to Moscow. 'God be with you, Mama,' I whispered, although in truth I had no idea where she was going. I took the matroshka doll from my pocket and assembled the four daughter dolls in a row on the dressing table. They were called nesting dolls because they represented a mother, a place where children could find rest. While Mei Lin ran a bath, I slipped the jade necklace into the top drawer.

There was a new dress hanging in the wardrobe. Mei Lin lifted herself on tiptoes to reach the hanger. She laid the blue velvet dress on the bed with the seriousness of an haute-couture saleswoman and then left me alone to bathe. She returned sometime later with a set of brushes and combed my hair with childish, awkward movements that scraped my neck and ears. But I bore it all patiently. It was as new to me as it was to her.

The dining room featured the same sea-green walls as the entrance but was even more elegant. The cornices and panels were painted gold and embellished with a maple leaf pattern. The motif was repeated on the frames of the red velvet chairs and the legs of the sideboard. I only had to look at the teak dining table and the chandelier that hung over it to know that Sergei Nikolaievich's suggestion that I teach him the ways of the old aristocrats had been in jest.

I could hear Sergei Nikolaievich and Amelia talking with their guests in the adjoining parlour but I hesitated before knocking on the door. I was exhausted, worn out by the events of the past week, and yet I felt obliged to put on a polite face and accept whatever hospitality they offered me. I didn't know anything about Sergei Nikolaievich except that he and Boris had once been friends and that he owned a nightclub. But before I could call out, the door opened and Sergei Nikolaievich appeared before me, grinning.

'Here she is,' he said, taking me by the arm and guiding me into the room. 'Gorgeous little thing, isn't she?'

Amelia was there, wearing a red evening dress, bare on one shoulder. Alexei Igorevich came towards me and introduced his plump wife, Lubov Vladimirovna Mikhailova. She threw her arms around me. 'Call me Luba, and for heaven's sake call my husband Alexei. We don't have such formalities here,' she said, kissing me with rouged lips. Behind her a young man of no more than seventeen waited with his arms clasped in front of him. When Luba stepped aside he introduced himself as Dmitri Yurievich Lubensky. 'But likewise, please just call me Dmitri,' he said, kissing my hand. His name and accent were Russian but he was not like any Russian man I had seen before. His sharply cut suit gave off a sheen in the lamplight and his hair was slicked back from his sculptured face, not brushed forward in the fashion of most Russian men. The blood rushed to the surface of my skin and I lowered my eyes.

Once we were seated the old Chinese maid served us shark's fin soup from a large tureen. I had heard of the famous dish, but I had never tried it. I swished the stringy soup around my bowl and took my first sweet mouthful. I looked up and saw that Dmitri was watching me, his fingers resting lightly on his chin. I couldn't tell if it was amusement or disapproval I saw on his face. But then he smiled kindly and said, 'I'm glad to see that we are introducing our northern princess to the delicacies of this city.'

Luba asked if he was excited that Sergei was going to make him the club's manager and Dmitri turned away to answer her. But I continued to study him. Next to me, he was the youngest person at the table and yet he seemed old for his age. In Harbin my schoolfriend's brother had been seventeen and he had still played with us. But I could not imagine Dmitri riding bicycles or running down the street in a rowdy game of tap and run.

Sergei Nikolaievich glanced over the rim of his champagne glass and winked. He raised his hand for a toast. 'Here's to the lovely Anna Victorovna Kozlova,' he said, using my full patronymic name. 'May she blossom as well as Dmitri has under my care.'

'Of course she will,' said Luba. 'Everyone blossoms under your generosity.'

The older woman was about to say something else when Amelia interrupted her by hitting a spoon against a wine glass. Her dress made her eyes look deeper and blacker, and if it were not for the drunk squint that twitched on her face, I would have thought her beautiful. 'If you don't all stop speaking in Russian,' she said through pursed lips, 'I'm going to ban these get-togethers. Speak in English, like I've told you to do.'

Sergei Nikolaievich let out a belly laugh and tried to rest his hand on his wife's clenched one. She pushed him away and turned her icy stare onto me. 'That's why you're here,' she spat. 'You're my little spy. When they speak Russian I can't trust any of them.' She threw the spoon down. It bounced off the table and clattered to the floor.

Sergei Nikolaievich's face turned pale. Alexei glanced awkwardly at his wife while Dmitri stared at his lap. The Old Maid scrambled for the spoon and retreated into the kitchen with it, as if by removing the spoon she could remove Amelia's source of anger.

Luba was the only one brave enough to retrieve the moment.

'We were just saying that Shanghai is full of opportunities,' she said. 'Something you've always claimed yourself.'

Amelia's eyes narrowed and she recoiled like a snake about to strike. But slowly a smile appeared on her face. Her shoulders relaxed and she slumped back into her chair, raising her glass with an unsteady hand.

'Yes,' she said, 'we *are* a room full of survivors. The Moscow-Shanghai survived the war and in another couple of months will be swinging again.'

The gathering raised their glasses, clinking them together. The maid returned with the second course and suddenly everyone's attention turned to the Peking duck, the excitement in their voices erasing the tension of the moment before. Only I seemed to be left with the awkward feeling of having witnessed something ominous.

After dinner we followed Sergei Nikolaievich and Amelia through their small ballroom to the library. I tried not to gape like a tourist at the fine tapestries and scrolls that lined the walls. 'This house is exquisite,' I confided in Luba. 'Sergei Nikolaievich's wife has very good taste.'

The older woman's face crinkled in amusement. 'My dear,' she whispered, 'his *first* wife had excellent taste. The house was built back in the days when Sergei was a tea merchant.'

The way she said 'first' chilled me. I was curious and afraid at the same time. I wondered what had happened to the woman who had created all the beauty and refinement I saw before me. How had Amelia come to replace her? But I was too shy to ask, and Luba seemed more interested in talking about other things.

'You know that Sergei was the most famous exporter of tea to the Russians? Well, the Revolution and the war have changed all that. Still, no one can say that he hasn't fought back. The Moscow-Shanghai is the most famous nightclub in the city.'

The library was a cosy room at the rear of the house.

Leather-bound volumes of Gogol, Pushkin and Tolstoy spilled from the wall-to-wall shelves, books I could never imagine Sergei Nikolaievich or Amelia reading. I ran my finger along the spines, trying to get a feeling for Sergei Nikolaievich's first wife. Her mysterious presence now seemed obvious in all the colours and textures I saw around me.

We sank into the leather couches while Sergei Nikolaievich laid out glasses and a new bottle of port. Dmitri handed me a glass and sat down next to me. 'So tell me what you think of this crazy, wonderful city,' he asked, 'this Paris of the East?'

'I haven't seen much of it. I only arrived today,' I told him.

'Of course, I'm sorry . . . I forgot,' he said, then smiled. 'Perhaps later on, when you settle in, I will show you Yuyuan Park.'

I shifted in my seat, aware that he sat so close to me that our faces were almost touching. He had arresting eyes, deep and mysterious like a forest. He was young but he exuded worldliness. Despite his smart clothes and polished skin, in his manner there was something of a swagger and a wariness. It was as if he wasn't comfortable in his surroundings.

Something dropped between us and Dmitri picked it up. A black, spike-heeled shoe. We looked up to see Amelia leaning against a bookcase, a bare white foot now matching her bare shoulder. 'What are you two whispering over there?' she hissed. 'Scoundrels! It's all Russian or whispers with you lot.'

Her husband and his companions paid no attention to her new outburst. Sergei Nikolaievich, Alexei and Luba were huddled by the open window, engrossed in their discussion of the horseraces. Only Dmitri stood up, laughing, and handed Amelia's shoe back to her. She cocked her head and looked at him with vixen eyes.

'I was just asking Anya about the Communists,' he lied. 'They are the reason she's here, you know.'

'She has nothing to fear from the Communists now,'

said Sergei Nikolaievich, turning away from his companions. 'The Europeans have made Shanghai into a massive money machine for China. They are not going to destroy it on some ideological whim. We survived the war and we will survive this.'

Later in the evening, when the guests had gone home and Amelia had passed out on the couch, I asked Sergei Nikolaievich if he had sent word to Boris and Olga Pomerantsev that I had arrived safely.

'Of course I have, my sweet child,' he said, covering his wife with a blanket and turning out the library lights. 'Boris and Olga adore you.'

The maid was waiting for us at the bottom of the stairs and began turning out the lights once we reached the first landing. 'And news of my mother?' I asked him hopefully. 'Did you ask them if they know anything?'

His eyes softened with pity. 'We will hope for the best, Anya,' he said, 'but it would be wiser for you to think of us as your family now.'

I woke up late the next morning, curled up in the fine linen sheets of my bed. I could hear the servants talking in the garden, the clatter of dishes being washed and the sound of a chair being dragged across the floor downstairs. The dappled sunlight on my curtains was pretty, but it couldn't cheer me. Each new day took me further away from my mother. And the thought of another day in the company of Amelia depressed me.

'Well, you slept well,' the American greeted me when I came down the stairs. She was dressed in a white dress with a belted waist. Apart from a slight puffiness under her eyes, she showed no sign of fatigue from the night before.

'Don't make a habit of tardiness, Anya,' she said. 'I don't like to be kept waiting and I'm only taking you shopping to please Sergei.' She handed me a purse, and when I

50

opened it I saw that it was full of hundred-dollar bills. 'Can you handle money, Anya? Are you good with numbers?' Her voice was high-pitched and she spoke in a hurry, as if she were on the verge of a fit.

'Yes, madam,' I answered. 'I can be trusted with money.'

She let out a shrill laugh. 'Well, let's see then.'

Amelia opened the front door and took off across the garden. I ran after her. The manservant was fixing a hinge on the gate and his eyes bulged with surprise when he saw us coming. 'Go call a rickshaw now!' she shouted at him. He looked from Amelia to me, as if trying to assess the emergency. Amelia grabbed him by the shoulder and pushed him out the gate. 'You know you must have one ready for me. Today is no exception. I'm already late.'

Once we were in the rickshaw Amelia calmed down. She almost laughed at her own impatience. 'You know,' she said, tugging at the ribbon that secured her hat to her head, 'all my husband could talk about this morning was you and how lovely you are. A real Russian beauty.' She put her hand on my knee. It was cold with no pulse, as if it belonged to something dead. 'Well, what do you think of that, Anya? You've only been in Shanghai a day and already you've made an impression on a man no one else can!'

Amelia frightened me. Something in her was snake-like and dark. And it was more apparent when we were alone than when we were with Sergei Nikolaievich. Her beady black eyes and lifeless skin warned of the venom beneath her smooth words. Tears prickled my eyes. I longed for my mother's warm strength, the courage and security I always felt when I was with her.

Amelia pulled her hand from my leg and snorted: 'Oh, don't be so serious, girl. If you are going to be so obnoxious, I'll have to give you away.'

The atmosphere on the streets of the French Concession was festive. The sun was out and women in colourful dresses, sandals and parasols were strolling along the wide pavements. Peddlers shouted out from stalls stacked with embroidered linen, silks and lace. Street entertainers were enticing people to spend a few idle moments to enjoy their acts. Amelia asked the rickshaw boy to stop so that we could watch a musician and his monkey. The creature, in a red-chequered vest and hat, was dancing to the sound of the man's accordion. He was pirouetting and leaping like a trained theatre performer rather than a wild animal, and in a few moments managed to attract a large crowd. When the music stopped, the monkey bowed and his audience was charmed. They clapped enthusiastically and the creature ran between their legs, holding up a hat for money. Almost everyone gave him something. Then suddenly he leaped onto the rickshaw, startling Amelia and making me scream. He perched himself between us and gazed at Amelia with adoring eyes. The audience was enthralled. Amelia batted her eyelids, knowing that everyone's attention was on her. She laughed and lifted her hand to her throat in a modest gesture I knew was fake. Then she pressed her fingers to her earlobes, taking out the pearl studs and tossing them into the monkey's hat. The audience screamed and hooted at Amelia's display of wealthy abandon. The monkey bounced back to its owner, but he had lost his audience to Amelia. Some of the men began calling out for her to tell them her name. But like a true performer Amelia knew to leave them wanting more. 'Come on,' she said, tapping the rickshaw boy's bony shoulders with her shoe, 'let's go.'

We turned off Bubbling Well Road into a narrow laneway known as the Street of a Thousand Nighties. It was crammed with tailor shops advertising their garments on mannequins propped up outside their doors or, as in one shop, with live models parading in the window. I followed Amelia to a street corner and a small store with such narrow steps I had to turn sideways to get up them. The shop was crowded with blouses and dresses hanging from ropes stretched wall to wall and smelled so strongly of fabric and bamboo that it made me sneeze. A Chinese woman jumped from behind a row of dresses and called out, 'Hello! Hello! You come for fit?'

But when she recognised Amelia the smile disappeared from her face. 'Good morning,' she said, looking at us with suspicious eyes. Amelia fingered a silk blouse and said to me, 'You choose a design you would like them to copy and they can make it up for you in a day.'

A small divan and a table had been set up by the shop's only window. The table was piled with catalogues and Amelia wandered over to it, picked up a catalogue and slowly turned the pages. She lit a cigarette and let the ash drop to the floor.

'How about this?' she said, holding up a picture of an emerald green cheongsam slashed to the thigh.

'She just girl. Too young for that dress,' the Chinese woman protested.

Amelia sniggered. 'Don't worry, Mrs Woo, Shanghai will soon make her old. You forget that I'm only twenty-five myself.' She laughed at her own joke and Mrs Woo pushed me with hard knuckles towards her bench at the back of the store. She pulled the tape measure from her collar and wrapped it around my waist. I stood straight and still for her, as my mother had taught me.

'Why you get involved with that woman?' Mrs Woo whispered to me. 'She no good. Her husband not as bad. But he stupid. His wife die of typhoid and he let that woman into his house because he lonely. No American want her . . .'

She stopped speaking when Amelia appeared with a handful of pictures she had torn from the catalogue. 'These, Mrs Woo,' she said, thrusting the ruined pages at the seamstress. 'We *are* a nightclub, you know,' she added, a catty smile on her face. 'And you are no Elsa Schiaparelli to tell us what or what not to wear.'

53

We left Mrs Woo with an order for three evening and four day dresses, which I assumed was the only reason the woman put up with Amelia's bad manners. From a department store on Nanking Road we bought underwear, shoes and gloves. On the pavement outside a beggar boy was scribbling the story of his plight with a piece of chalk. He was wearing a rough cotton loincloth, the skin on his shoulders and back burned painfully red by the sun.

'What does it say?' Amelia asked. I looked at the fine hand. My Chinese was not fluent but I could tell that the words had been written by someone educated and literate. The boy's story was that he had seen his mother and three sisters killed when the Japanese invaded Manchuria. One of his sisters had been tortured. He found her body by the roadside. Her nose, breasts and hands had been cut off by the soldiers. Only he and his father survived and they fled to Shanghai. They bought a rickshaw with all the money they had left. But one day the man's father was hit by a drunk foreigner driving too fast in his car. The father was still alive after the accident, with his legs broken and a large gash that exposed his skull on his forehead. He was bleeding profusely but the foreigner refused to take him to hospital in his car. Another rickshaw driver helped the boy cart his father to a doctor but it was too late. The man was dead. I read the last words out loud: 'I beg you, brothers and sisters, to hear my plight and help me. May the gods in heaven send you great riches for doing so.' The beggar boy looked up, amazed to see a Western girl reading Chinese. I slipped some coins into his hand.

'So that's how you will spend your money,' said Amelia, entwining her cold arm with mine. 'To help people who sit on pavements and do nothing to help themselves. I'd rather give it to the monkey. At least he strove to entertain me.'

For lunch we ate won-ton soup in a café filled with foreigners and rich Chinese. I had never seen such people, not even in Harbin before the worst of the war. The women were dressed in violet, sapphire or red silk dresses, their nails polished and their hair coiffured. The men were equally as stylish, in double-breasted suits and with pencil-thin moustaches. Afterwards Amelia took my purse to pay the bill at the counter and bought herself a packet of cigarettes and some chocolate for me. We strolled out onto the street, past the shops selling mah-jong sets, wicker furniture and love charms. I stopped to look at a store with dozens of canaries in bamboo cages hanging up outside it. The birds were all chirping and I was mesmerised by their pretty songs. I heard a cry and turned around to see two small boys looking at me. Their faces were creased and elfin and their eyes were full of menace. They seemed not quite human, holding up clawed hands. A pungent smell hit me and I realised their fingers were smeared with excreta. 'Give money or wipe on dress,' one of them said. At first I couldn't believe what was happening, but the boys crept closer and I felt in my pocket for my purse. Then I remembered I had given it to Amelia. I looked around for her but she was nowhere to be seen. 'I don't have money,' I pleaded with the boys. They responded by laughing and cursing me in Chinese. It was then that I noticed Amelia in the doorway of a hat shop across the road. My purse was in her hands.

'Please, help me. They want money,' I called out to her. She picked up a hat and studied it. At first I thought she hadn't heard me, but then she looked up, her mouth twisting into a smile. She shrugged and I realised that she had seen the whole thing. I stared at her hard face, her black eyes, but that only made her laugh more. One of the boys grabbed for my skirt, but before he could reach it the bird-keeper burst out from his store and swatted at the boy with a broom. The child ducked and scurried away with his companion through the rows of street stalls and between pedestrians, eventually disappearing from sight.

'Shanghai always like this,' the shopkeeper muttered, shaking his head. 'Now just get worse. Nothing but thieves and beggars. Cut off your fingers to get your rings.'

I glanced back to the doorway where Amelia had been standing a minute before. But it was empty.

Later I found Amelia in a pharmacy down the road. She was buying Dior perfume and an embroidered compact. 'Why wouldn't you help me?' I screamed at her, hot tears spilling down my face and dripping from my chin. 'Why do you treat me like you do?'

Amelia glared at me with disgust. She picked up her parcel and pushed me out the door. On the pavement she thrust her face into mine. Her eyes were bloodshot and furious.

'You're a foolish child,' she shouted at me, 'to rely on the kindness of others. Nothing is free in this city. Do you understand? Nothing! All kindness has a price! If you think people are going to help you for nothing, then you will end up like that beggar boy on the pavement!'

Amelia dug her fingers into my arm and dragged me to the kerb. She called out for a rickshaw. 'Now I'm going to the racing club to be with adults,' she said. 'You go home and find Sergei. He's always at home in the afternoon. Go and tell him what an evil woman I am. Go and cry to him about how badly I treat you.'

The rickshaw ride home was bumpy. The streets and the people became one blur of colour through my tears. I held my handkerchief to my mouth, terrified that I was going to be sick. I wanted to go home and I would tell Sergei Nikolaievich that I did not care about Tang, I wanted to be with the Pomerantsevs in Harbin again.

When I reached the gate I rang the bell until the Old Maid opened it. Despite my distress, she greeted me with the same expressionless face of the day before. I rushed past her and into the house. The hall was dark and silent, the windows and curtains had been closed to keep out the stifling afternoon heat. I stood in the parlour for a moment, unsure of what to do next. I passed the dining room and found Mei Lin asleep there, her tiny feet sticking out from under the table, the thumb of one hand in her mouth, the other clenching a cleaning cloth.

I hurried through the halls and corridors, terror rising in my blood. I ran up the stairs to the third floor and looked in every room until I came to the last one, the room at the end of the hall. The door was ajar and I knocked softly but there was no answer. I pushed it and it swung open. Inside, as with the rest of the house, the curtains were closed and the room was dark. The air was thick with the smell of human sweat. And something else: a cloying sweetness. When my eyes adjusted to the darkness I could see Sergei Nikolaievich slumped in his chair, his head on his chest. Behind him the shadowy figure of the manservant kept a ghoul-like watch.

'Sergei Nikolaievich,' I called out, my voice cracking. I was terrified that he was dead. But after a while Sergei Nikolaievich lifted his eyes. A blue haze rose up around him like a halo and with it came the reek of putrid air. He was sucking smoke from a long-stemmed pipe. I was startled by his face, sunken and grey, with eyes so hollow they looked like cavities in his skull. I edged away, not prepared for this new nightmare.

'I'm so sorry, my Anya,' he wheezed. 'So very, very sorry. But I'm lost, my little one. Lost.' He collapsed back into his seat, his head thrown back and his mouth open and gaping, struggling for breath like a dying man. The opium in the pipe gurgled and cooled into black ash.

I fled from the room, perspiration dripping from my face and neck. I made it to my bathroom just in time to throw up the soup I had eaten with Amelia. When I had finished I wiped my mouth with a towel and lay on the cool tiles, trying to steady my breathing. I heard Amelia's words in my head: *You're a foolish child to rely on the kindness of others. Nothing*

is free in this city. Do you understand? Nothing! All kindness has
a price!

In the mirror's reflection I could see the dresser with the matroshka dolls lined up on it. I closed my eyes and imagined a gold line stretching from Shanghai to Moscow. 'Mama, Mama,' I said to myself, 'keep safe. You survive, and I will survive, until we can find each other again.'

THREE

The Tango

The packages from Mrs Woo arrived a few days later, while Sergei Nikolaievich, Amelia and I were eating breakfast in the courtyard. I was drinking tea Russian-style, plain with a scoop of blackcurrant jam on the side for sweetness. Tea was all I ever had for breakfast, although every morning the table was laid with pancakes dripping with butter and honey, bananas, mandarins, pears, bowls of strawberries and grapes, scrambled eggs with melted cheese, sausages and triangles of toast. I was too nervous to have an appetite. My legs trembled under the glass tabletop. I spoke only when I was spoken to, and even then uttered not a syllable more than necessary. I was terrified of doing something that might bring on Amelia's ill humour. But neither Sergei Nikolaievich – who had given me permission to use his first name, Sergei – nor Amelia seemed to notice my timid behaviour. Sergei spoke cheerfully to me about the sparrows that visited the garden, and Amelia, for the most part, ignored me.

The bell on the gate rang and the maid brought up two brown-paper parcels with our address scribbled down the sides in English and Chinese. 'Open them,' Amelia said, clasping her talon-like fingers and smiling. She was pretending to be my ally for her husband, but I was not deceived. I turned to Sergei and held up the garments for him one by one. All the day dresses received his nods and 'ahs' of approval. 'Oh yes, that one is the prettiest,' he said, pointing to a cotton dress with a butterfly collar and a row of sunflowers embroidered on the neckline and belt. 'You should wear that tomorrow for our stroll in the park.' But when I opened the package of evening dresses and showed him the green cheongsam, Sergei's brow knotted and his eyes turned dark. He glared at Amelia and said to me, 'Anya, please go to your room.'

Sergei hadn't addressed me angrily, but being sent away from the table made me feel dejected. I shuffled through the hall and moped up the stairs, wondering what he was upset about and what he was going to say to Amelia. I hoped whatever it was wouldn't make her even more contemptuous of me.

'I told you that Anya is not coming with us to the club until she is older,' I heard him tell his wife. 'She has to go to school.'

I stopped on the landing, straining to listen. Amelia scoffed, 'Oh yes, we are going to hide the truth from her about who we are, aren't we? Make her spend some time with the nuns before we introduce her to the real world. I think she's already caught on to your habit. I can tell by the pitying way she looks at you.'

'She's not like girls from Shanghai. She is . . .' The rest of Sergei's sentence was drowned out by Mei Lin clumping up the stairs in wooden clogs, a pile of fresh linen stacked in her arms. I lifted my finger to my lips. 'Shhhh!' I said to her. Her birdlike face peered at me over the sheets. When she realised that I was eavesdropping, she put her finger over her own lips and burst into giggles. Sergei stood up and closed the front door, so I never got to hear the rest of the conversation that morning.

Later Sergei came to see me in my room. 'Next time I will get Luba to take you shopping,' he said, kissing the top of my head. 'Don't be disappointed, Anya. There is plenty of time for you to be the belle of the ball.'

* * *

60

My first month in Shanghai passed slowly and with no further news of my mother. I wrote two letters to the Pomerantsevs, describing Shanghai and my guardian in favourable terms so that they wouldn't worry. I signed my name Anya Kirillova, in case the letters were read by the Communists.

Sergei sent me to the Santa Sophia School for Girls in the French Concession. The school was run by Irish nuns and the students were a mix of Catholics, Orthodox Russians and some Chinese and Indian girls from wealthy families. The nuns were kind-hearted women from whose faces smiles shone more often than frowns. They were great believers in physical education and played baseball with the senior girls on Friday afternoons while the junior girls watched. The first time I saw my geography teacher, Sister Mary, sprinting from base to base with her habit hitched to her knees and being tagged by my history teacher, Sister Catherine, it took all my willpower not to laugh. The women were like giant cranes struggling for flight. But I didn't laugh. Nobody did. For while the sisters were usually sweet, they could also be exacting in their punishments. When Luba took me to enrol at the school, we witnessed the Mother Superior making her way along a line of girls propped up against the school wall. She was sniffing the girls' necks and hair. After each inhalation she twitched her nose and lifted her eyes to heaven as if she were tasting a cask of fine wine. Later I learned that she had been inspecting the girls for perfumed talc, scented hair tonics and other cosmetic enhancements that drew attention to themselves. The Mother Superior saw a direct connection between vanity and moral corruption. The one offending student she found that morning had been put on bathroom duty for a week.

Mathematics was taught by Sister Bernadette, a plump woman whose chin went straight to her neck. Her northern accent was as thick as butter, and it took me two days to work out that a certain word she kept repeating was 'parentheses'.

'Why are you frowning at me, Miss Anya?' she asked. 'Is there a problem regarding the *ahrentheses*?'

I shook my head and caught sight of two girls smiling at me from across the aisle. After the lesson they made their way over to my seat and introduced themselves as Kira and Regina. Regina was a petite dark-haired girl with violet eyes. Kira was as blonde as the sun.

'You're from Harbin, aren't you?' Kira said.

'Yes.'

'You can tell. We are from Harbin too but we came with our families to Shanghai before the war.'

'How can you tell I'm from Harbin?' I asked.

They laughed. Kira winked and whispered in my ear, 'You don't need Russian writing lessons.'

Kira's father was a doctor, Regina's a surgeon. We found out that we had elected almost the same classes for the coming term: French, English grammar, history, mathematics and geography. But while I took the afterhours art classes at the gymnasium, they rushed back to their homes at the posh end of Avenue Joffre for their piano and violin lessons.

Although we sat together in nearly every class, I sensed without asking that Regina's and Kira's parents would not have approved of their daughters coming to see me at Sergei's house nor would they have been comfortable with me in their own homes. So I never invited the girls and they never invited me. I was relieved in a way because I secretly feared that if I did invite them over, Amelia would have another drunken fit, and I would have been embarrassed to have such well brought up girls witness her behaviour. So while I often longed for their company, Regina, Kira and I had to make do with a friendship that began with prayers in the morning and ended with the school bell in the afternoon.

When I wasn't at school I was tiptoeing to Sergei's library and sneaking out to the garden with armfuls of books and my sketchpad. Two days after I had arrived at the house I discovered a gardenia tree in a sheltered part of the garden. It became my sacred spot and I spent almost every afternoon there, drowning myself in volumes of Proust and Gorky or sketching the blooms and plants around me. I would do anything I could to avoid crossing paths with Amelia.

Sometimes when Sergei returned home in the afternoon he would join me in the garden and we would talk for a while. I soon realised he was better read than I had assumed, and once he brought me the works of a Russian poet, Nikolai Gumilev. He read to me a poem about a giraffe in Africa which the poet had written to cheer his wife when she was depressed. Sergei's resonant voice made the words flow so eloquently that I could imagine the proud animal roaming the African plains. The picture carried me so far away from my sadness that I hoped the poem would never end. But always after an hour or so of talking, Sergei's fingers would start to tremble and his body begin to twitch, and I knew that I would lose his pleasant company to his habit. I would see then how much weariness lived in his eyes, and I understood that in his own way he too was avoiding Amelia.

One afternoon when I came home from school I was surprised to hear voices in the garden. I peered through the trees and saw Dmitri and Amelia sitting in wicker chairs near the lion-head fountain. There were two women with them. I caught glimpses of their bright dresses and hats through the tree ferns. The clinking of teacups and the sound of the women's laughter rippled through the garden like the whispers of ghosts. And for some reason Dmitri's voice, louder and deeper than the others, made my heart thump in my chest. He had offered to take me to Yuyuan and I was so bored and lonely I hoped that if he saw me he would remember his promise.

'Hello!' I said, bursting in on the little group.

Amelia raised her eyebrows and glanced scornfully over me. But I was so eager to see Dmitri I didn't care if she scolded me for intruding.

'Hello. How are you?' said Dmitri, standing up and dragging over an extra chair for me.

'It's a long time since I saw you,' I said.

Dmitri didn't answer me. He sank back into his own chair and lit a cigarette, humming a tune to himself. I cringed. It was not the enthusiastic welcome I'd imagined.

The two other women were about Dmitri's age and were dressed in mango and rose-coloured dresses with ruffles about the sleeves and necklines. The lines of their silk petticoats were visible beneath the sheer fabric. The girl closest to me smiled with lips rouged as dark as grapes. The severe line of kohl around her blue eyes made me think of an Egyptian goddess.

'I am Marie,' she said, stretching out a pale hand, the long nails sharpened to points. She nodded to the golden-haired beauty next to her. 'And this is my sister, Francine.'

'*Enchanté*,' Francine said, pushing her curls out of her eyes and leaning towards me. '*Comment allez-vous?* I heard you are studying French at school.'

'*Si vous parlez lentement je peux vous comprendre*,' I said, wondering who had been talking to her about me. Amelia wouldn't care if I spoke French or Swahili.

'*Vous parlez français très bien*,' exclaimed Francine. She wore a small diamond on her left hand. An engagement ring.

'*Merci beaucoup. J'ai plaisir à l'étudier.*'

Francine turned to Dmitri and whispered, 'She is charming. I want to adopt her. I think Philippe won't mind.'

Dmitri was staring at me. His gaze made me so self-conscious that I almost spilled the tea Francine handed to me.

'I can't believe you are the same girl I saw a few months ago,' he said. 'You look so different in your school uniform.'

A blush burned from my neck to my hair. Amelia sniggered and whispered something to Marie. I slumped back into my chair, barely able to breathe. I remembered how Dmitri had sat close to me that first night in Shanghai, his face near to mine as if we were confidants. Equals. Perhaps in the blue velvet dress he hadn't realised I was thirteen. What a contrast I must appear this afternoon: a child in a puffy blouse and pinafore, two tightly woven braids sticking out from under her straw hat. Not someone he would take to Yuyuan. Not when he could take Marie and Francine. I tucked my feet under the chair, suddenly ashamed of my school shoes and knee-high socks.

'You are very cute,' Francine said. 'I would like to take a photograph of you eating an ice-cream. And I've heard you are quite an artist too.'

'Yes, she copies the clothes from my fashion magazines,' sniggered Amelia.

I cringed in shame, too mortified to even look at Dmitri.

'What I hate about schoolgirls,' said Amelia, drumming her fingernails on her teacup and taking her time before plunging her dagger into me, 'is no matter how clean and tidy you send them off in the morning, they always return smelling like sweat and oranges.'

Marie roared with laughter, showing rows of little teeth like a piranha. 'How vulgar,' she said. 'I imagine it's all the running around and skipping rope they do.'

'And all the squashed fruit they sneak into their school bags,' Amelia added.

'Anya hardly smells like *that*,' said Dmitri. 'I was just taken aback by how young she is.'

'She's not that young, Dmitri,' said Amelia. 'She's just underdeveloped. When I was her age I already had breasts.'

'How mean they are being,' said Francine, brushing my braids off my shoulders. 'She has an elegance beyond her years. *Je l'aime bien. Anya, quelle est la date aujourd'hui?*'

But I did not want to practise French any more. Amelia

had hit her target and I was humiliated. I fumbled in my pocket for my handkerchief and pretended to sneeze. I did not want to add to my humiliation by letting them see the unhappiness in my eyes. It was as if they had held up a mirror for me and I had seen myself as never before. A scruffy schoolgirl with bruises on her knees.

'Come on then,' said Amelia, standing up. 'If you can't take a joke and are going to pull faces, then come inside with me. Let Dmitri enjoy the garden with his friends.'

I hoped Dmitri would protest and insist that I stay but he didn't, and I knew that I had sunk in his esteem and that he was no longer interested in me. I trailed after Amelia like an unwanted dog. I wished that I had never heard his voice in the garden that day. That I had gone straight into the house and to the library without saying a word to anyone. Once we were out of earshot, Amelia turned to me, her eyes flashing with pleasure at my pain. 'Well, you made a fool of yourself, didn't you? I thought you would have been taught better manners than to intrude where you have not been invited.' I didn't answer her. I hung my head and allowed myself to be corrected. Amelia strolled to the window and peered through the curtains. 'My friend Marie is such an attractive young woman,' she sighed. 'I do hope that she and Dmitri get on. He's at an age when a man looks for a companion.'

I spent the afternoon in my room, miserable. I kicked my French books under the bed and tried to drown myself in a volume on the history of Ancient Rome. From the garden I could hear laughter and the sound of music. I had never heard music like it before: carnal, enticing, creeping up to my window like the delicious scent of an exotic lily. I covered my ears against it and tried to concentrate on my book, but after a while the temptation to see what was going on became too much. I crept to the window and peeped out. Dmitri was dancing with Marie in the court-yard. Francine was bent over a record player, readjusting the needle each time the music stopped. One of Dmitri's hands rested between Marie's shoulderblades while the other clasped her fingers in his own. Cheeks pressed together, they were parading around in a kind of staccato walk. Marie was flushed, giggling stupidly with each step. Dmitri's expression was mock serious. 'Slow, slow, quick, quick, slow,' sang Francine, tapping out a rhythm for them with her hands. Marie was stiff and awkward, and tripped on the hem of her dress when Dmitri dipped her.

'I'm tired,' she complained. 'This is far too difficult. I would rather do the foxtrot.'

Francine swapped places with her sister. I wanted to shut my eyes, I was so sick with envy. She was by far the more graceful of the two sisters and in Dmitri's arms she brought elegance to the dance. Francine was like a ballet dancer, conveying everything from passion to anger and love in her eyes. Dmitri stopped pulling a face with her. He stood erect and appeared even more dashing. Together they looked like two Siamese cats locked in a mating ritual. I leaned further out the window, caught up by the dreamy tempo of the tango. I closed my eyes and imagined it was me down there in the courtyard, dancing with Dmitri.

A drop of water fell on my nose. I opened my eyes and saw that the sky had turned dark and an afternoon shower was splattering down. The dancers quickly gathered their things and rushed inside. I pulled shut my window and, as I did so, caught sight of myself in the dresser mirror.

'She's not young, she's just underdeveloped,' Amelia had said.

I glared at my reflection with loathing. I was slight for my age, having only grown an inch since my eleventh birthday. A few months before coming to Shanghai I had noticed the first sprouts of honey-coloured hair between my legs and under my arms. But I had remained painfully skinny with a flat chest and bottom. It had never bothered me until that afternoon; I had been indifferent to my physical growth.

67

But an impression had been made on me. I had come to see that Dmitri was a man, and suddenly I wanted to be a woman.

By the end of summer the tenuous truce between the Nationalist and Communist armies slid into civil war. There was no mail going in or out of Manchuria and I received no reply to my letters to the Pomerantsevs. I became driven by a desperate need to keep some sort of connection with my mother and began devouring every detail about Russia that I could find. I pored over the books in Sergei's library, searching out tales of steamers sailing on the Astrakhan, stories of the tundra and the taiga, the Ural and the Caucaus Mountains, the Arctic and the Black Sea. I pestered Sergei's friends for their memories of summer dachas, great cities of gold, grand statues reaching towards pale blue skies, and parades of soldiers. I tried to piece together a picture of Russia as my mother might see it, but instead found myself becoming lost in a landmass too big to imagine.

One day Amelia sent me on an errand to pick up mono-grammed table napkins for the club. Although I had been the one to drop off the material to the embroidery shop the week before, my mind was occupied by the news that the Soviets were battling for Berlin, and I shuffled along the avenues of the Concession without paying attention to where I was going. A man's shout snapped me out of my thoughts. Two people were bickering behind a fence. Their Chinese was too fast for me to understand, but when I glanced around at my surroundings I realised that I was lost. I was standing in a lane at the back of a row of derelict European-style houses. The shutters were barely holding on by their hinges and the peeling stucco walls were stained by rusty water-marks. Barbed wire curled over the fences and windowsills like ivy, and the yards were full of brackish puddles although it hadn't rained for weeks. I tried to retrace my steps but only became more confused in the maze of alleys that turned left and right with no logical pattern. The stench of urine was thick in the hot air and my path was blocked by scrawny chickens and geese. I clenched my fists in panic.

I turned a corner piled with rusty bed frames and an old icebox, and stumbled across a Russian café. White lace curtains were draped across the dirty windows. The Café Moskva was crammed between a grocer whose carrots and spinach stalks swooned limply in their buckets and a patisserie whose iced tea slices were speckled with dust. I was relieved to find something Russian and entered the café with the intention of asking directions. When I pushed open the screen door a bell rang. The smell of spiced sausage and vodka hit me as soon as I stepped into the dim interior. Chinese music was blaring from a radio balanced precariously on the counter, but it couldn't drown out the sound of flies circling the tin ceiling. An old woman, so shrivelled that she appeared to be on the verge of decay, squinted at me over the edge of her stained menu. She wore a crumpled velvet dress with lace at the throat and wrists, and in her grey hair a tiara with all the stones missing. Her lips moved and her eyes were dark and troubled. '*Dusha-dushi. Dusha-dushi,*' she muttered to me. *Speak soul to soul. Speak soul to soul.* At the table next to her an old man in a beret was scanning the menu, turning the yellowing pages frantically as if he were reading a detective novel. His companion had fierce blue eyes and black hair stretched back into a bun. She was biting her nails and scribbling words on a paper doily. The owner approached me with a menu, his cheeks rosy like borscht and his hairy stomach straining the buttons of his shirt. Two women in black dresses and shawls eyed my expensive shoes when I sat down.

'What can I bring you?' the owner asked.

'I want you to tell me about Russia,' I said on impulse.

The café owner rubbed his freckled hand over his cheeks and chin and sank into the chair opposite me like a man condemned. It was as if he had been waiting for me, for this day, this hour. He took a moment to gather his strength before describing to me the summer fields brimming with buttercups, birch trees, woods rich with the scent of pine needles and moss crushed underfoot. His eyes glistened when he recalled chasing squirrels, foxes and weasels as a child and the taste of his mother's dumplings served steaming on frozen winter nights.

The whole room stopped to pay attention, and when the owner was exhausted, the others joined in to fill in the spaces. The old woman howled like the lone wolf in the forest; the man in the beret sang out the tones of the massive church bells ringing on festive days; and the poet described peasant men and women harvesting fields bursting with wheat and barley. All the while the women in mourning kept wailing, punctuating every story with: 'And only in death will we return home.'

Hours passed like minutes, and it wasn't until the sun went down and the light in the windows changed from yellow to ash that I realised I had been in the café all afternoon. Sergei would probably be worried about where I was and Amelia would be angry when I told her that I hadn't picked up the napkins. Still I could not leave or interrupt these strange people. I sat listening until my legs and back ached from lack of movement, taking in every joyful shriek or downcast glance. I was captivated by the stories of a place that was opening up like a traveller's tale before me.

The following week, as the café owner had promised, a Soviet soldier was waiting for me. The man's face was sunken like a piece of pottery that had collapsed in the kiln. His nose and ears had been eaten away by frostbite and he'd wrapped gauze over the holes to keep the dust out. The air rattled in his throat, and I curled my toes to stop myself flinching from the reek of bile that blew across the table whenever he spoke.

70

'Don't be alarmed by my looks,' he told me. 'Mine is a lucky fate compared to the others. I made it to China.'

The soldier told me that he had been taken prisoner by the Germans. After the war, instead of welcoming them home, Stalin ordered all former prisoners of war to be transported to labour camps. The men were packed onto trains and ships riddled with rats and lice and sent to Siberia. It was punishment for having seen what Stalin was terrified they would tell others: that even when Germany was ravaged by war, its people lived better than the Russians. The soldier had escaped when his prison ship ran aground.

'When that happened,' he said, 'I felt the world open up before me and I fled across the ice. I could smell the fire and hear shouts behind me. The guards started shooting. Men fell dead around me, their mouths gaping and their eyes wide open. I expected to feel the hot metal rip of a bullet in my back too. But I kept running into the white nothingness. Soon all I could hear was the howling wind and I understood my fate was to survive.'

I did not turn away from the soldier or stop him talking when, for the price of hot tea and black bread, he described to me the burned villages, the famines and the crime, the rigged trials and mass deportations to Siberia where people dropped dead in the subzero air. His stories terrified me so much that my heart began to palpitate and I broke out in a sweat. But I continued to listen because I knew that he had come from the recent Russia. My mother's Russia.

'There are two possibilities,' he told me, softening the bread in the tea and gripping the edge of the table with the pain swallowing caused him. 'By the time your mother got to Russia they may not have cared that she was the widow of a White Army colonel and just stuck her in a factory as cheap labour and used her as an example of a reformed mind. Or they may have sent her to a gulag. If that was the case, unless she is a very strong woman, she is dead already.'

71

After the soldier had eaten, his eyes began to droop and he fell asleep, nestling his damaged head in his arms like a dying bird. I walked out into the midday light. Although it was still summer a sharp wind had risen and it stung my face and legs, making me shiver. I ran through the laneways, my eyes smarting and my teeth chattering. The soldier's words hung like chains on me. I saw my mother, gaunt and starving in a prison cell, or lying face down in the snow. I heard the sound of the train wheels and remembered her stricken face as she was carried far away from me. I could not fathom such a gruesome fate for the woman who was part of me, and yet I had no clue, not the slightest idea of what had happened to her. At least I had kissed my father's cold cheek and said goodbye. But with my mother there had been no final goodbye, no ending. Just a lonely longing from which there was no relief.

I wanted everything to stop, to have an end to the fears that prickled me, to find some peace. I tried to think of pleasant thoughts but I could only hear the soldier's words and see his brutalised face. *Unless she is a very strong woman, she is dead already.*

'Mama!' I cried out, covering my face with my hands.

Suddenly an old woman in a beaded scarf appeared next to me. I stumbled backwards, startled.

'Who are you looking for?' she asked, clutching my sleeve with her splintered nails.

I edged away but the woman shuffled towards me, peering at me with raven eyes. Her red lipstick was a slash of garish colour over her thin lips and the creases on her forehead were jammed with caked powder. 'You are searching for someone, aren't you?' she asked in a voice that sounded Russian, though I couldn't be quite sure. 'Bring me something of hers and I will tell you her fate.'

I tugged away from the woman and hurried down the street. Shanghai was full of cheats and tricksters preying on the desperation of others. But the words she shouted

72

after me stilled my breath. 'If she left something behind, she will come back for you.'

By the time I reached the house, my neck and arms were aching and a chill had set like ice in my bones. Zhun-ying, who everybody called the Old Maid, and Mei Lin were in the laundry near the servants' quarters. The laundry was a raised stone platform with a roof and temporary walls that were removed in summer. The Old Maid was wringing out towels and Mei Lin was helping her, water splashing in pools around their feet and dripping down the single step onto the grass. Mei Lin was singing something, and the normally grouchy Old Maid was laughing. The little girl's grin scrunched into a concerned frown when I lurched unsteadily up the step towards her and gripped onto the boiler handle for support. 'Please tell Sergei I won't be down for dinner tonight,' I told her. 'I've caught a cold and am going to bed.' Mei Lin nodded but the Old Maid scrutinised me with her inflamed gaze.

I collapsed onto my bed and the room's golden walls enveloped me like a shield. Outside, Mei Lin's laughter floated up into the summer air. Further in the distance I could hear the babble of traffic on the main road. I covered my eyes with the back of my arm, tormented by my alone-ness. I couldn't talk to Sergei about my mother. He skipped around the subject, cutting conversations short by suddenly remembering an urgent errand or paying attention to a distraction he normally would have ignored. His averted eyes and half-turned body always discouraged me from talking about her. I knew it was because of what grieving for his first wife had done to him. He once said that my pining might keep my mother alive in my imagination but in the end it would drive me mad.

I glanced at the matroshka dolls on my dresser and thought about the fortune teller. *If she left something behind, she will come back for you.* I slipped off the bed and opened the dresser drawer, lifting out the velvet box Sergei had given me for the jade necklace. I had not worn it since my thirteenth birthday. It was a sacred object which I laid out on the bed and wept over whenever I felt alone. The green stones reminded me of how much it meant to my mother to give it to me. I would close my eyes, trying to picture my father as a young man. I imagined how his heart must have been racing the day he walked with it hidden in his jacket on his way to give it to my mother. I opened the box and picked up the necklace. The stones seemed to vibrate with love. The matroshka dolls were mine, but somehow the necklace remained my mother's even though she had given it to me.

I had already dismissed the fortune teller as a fraud, a charlatan I would give a coin to so that she could tell me what I wanted to hear. *The regime in Russia will come to an end and your mother will come to Shanghai to find you.* Or perhaps, if she were an imaginative fraud, she would spin a fictitious story to comfort me. *Your mother will marry a kind hunter and live happily ever after in a house by a silver lake. She will always think fondly of you. And you will go on to marry a rich, handsome man and have many children.*

I wrapped the necklace in a scarf and hid it in my pocket. I decided that even if she turned out to be a liar it didn't matter. I just wanted to talk to someone about my mother, to hear something that would stop me thinking about the terrible tales the soldier had told me. But when I snuck out the front door and across the garden, I knew in my heart that I was yearning for more. I was hoping the fortune teller would be able to tell me my mother's real fate.

Before I reached the gate I heard the Old Maid cry out. I spun around to see her standing behind me, her face pale and angry. 'This is second time you disappear all afternoon. You make him worry,' she said, jabbing her finger into my breastbone.

I turned my back on her and hurried out the gate, slamming it behind me. But I was trembling as I did so. They were the first words the Old Maid had spoken to me since I had arrived in Shanghai.

Out on the street the icy breeze dissipated and the day turned into summer again. The sun was a flame in the blue sky and heat simmered up from the roadway, burning my feet through the soles of my shoes. Oily beads of sweat prickled my nose and my hair stuck to my neck. I clutched the necklace in my pocket. It was heavy but I felt calmer for having it there. I retraced the path back to the Café Moskva, searching in every old woman's face for the eyes of my fortune teller. But it was she who found me.

'I knew you would come back,' she said, stepping off the kerb in front of a bakery and falling into step with me. 'I will show you where we can talk. I will help you.'

The fortune teller linked her arm with mine. Her wrinkled flesh was soft and she smelled of talcum powder. Suddenly she didn't seem so garish, just aged and world-weary. She could have been my grandmother.

She led me to an apartment building a few streets away from the café, stopping every so often to catch her breath. A baby's crying echoed around the courtyard and I could hear two women trying to comfort it. The building's cement walls were cracked and weeds poked through the spaces. Water leaked out of a rusted drainpipe, creating pools of slime on the steps and pathway. A tabby cat was lapping up water from one. The scrawny animal blinked at us before clambering up a wooden fence and disappearing from view.

The building's entranceway was cold and piled with garbage. Hundreds of flies were buzzing over the food scraps that spewed from the overfilled cans. I squinted at the figure of a man at the end of the hall, backlit by the muted light of a single window. He was mopping the floor and I was surprised to see that the building had a cleaner. His eyes followed the old woman when we passed and I noticed there were crimson marks on his arms, one in the shape of a dragon. He rolled down his sleeve when he saw me looking at it.

We stopped in front of a metal door with a grille at the bottom. The old woman pulled out a key tied around her neck with a piece of string. The lock required some jiggling and, when she finally unhooked it, the door groaned open in protest. The woman rushed into the basement apartment but I stood on the threadbare doormat, peering inside. Pipes ran across the ceiling and the wallpaper was stained. Old newspapers covered the floor. The sheets were yellow and ripped, as if some animal lived there, sleeping, eating and urinating on the paper floor. The smell of dust and bad air made me queasy. When the woman realised that I hadn't followed her inside, she turned to me and shrugged. 'I can see from your clothes that you are used to better. But this is the best I can offer you.'

I blushed and stepped into the apartment, ashamed of my snobbery. In the centre of the room was a worn sofa, stuffing protruding from its seams. The woman brushed it with her hand and threw a musty-smelling rug over the cushions. 'Please. Sit,' she said. It was hotter in the apartment than it was outside. The mud-stained windows were shut, but I could hear footsteps and bicycle bells in the street beyond. The woman filled a kettle and lit the stove. The stove made the room even hotter and, when she wasn't looking, I lifted my handkerchief to my nose, trying to find relief in the fresh, laundered scent of the material. I glanced around the apartment, wondering if there was a bathroom. I couldn't understand how she could appear quite clean and yet live in such a filthy apartment.

'So many, many people in pain,' the old woman muttered. 'Everyone has lost someone: parents, husbands, sisters, brothers, children. I try to help, but there are so many of them.'

The kettle boiled and the woman poured the hot water into a chipped pot, setting it and two cups on the table in front of me.

'Did you bring me something of hers?' she asked, leaning forward and patting my knee.

I pulled the scarf from my pocket and unfolded it, placing the contents on the table. The old woman's eyes fixed on the necklace. She picked it up and dangled it in front of her face, captivated by the sight of it.

'It's jade,' she said.

'Yes. And gold.'

She cupped her other hand and dropped the necklace into it, weighing it in her palm. 'It's beautiful,' she said. 'And very old. You can't find jewellery like this now.'

'It is beautiful,' I agreed, and suddenly heard my father saying the same thing. A memory came to me. I was three years old and my parents and I were celebrating Christmas with some of their friends in the city. My father called out, 'Lina and Anya! Come quickly! Look at this magnificent tree!' My mother and I rushed into the room and found him standing by a giant evergreen, every limb decorated with apples, nuts and candies. I was lifted up in my mother's arms. My tiny fingers, sticky with ginger cake, played with the necklace around her swan-like throat.

'She likes that necklace, Lina,' said my father. 'It is beautiful on you.'

My mother, in a white lace dress with mistletoe in her hair, passed me to my father's shoulders so I could touch the glass snow queen at the top of the tree.

'When she is old enough, I shall give it to her,' my mother said. 'So she can remember us both.'

I turned to the old woman. 'Where is she?' I asked.

The woman clasped the necklace in her fist. It was a while before she answered. 'Your mother was taken away from you in the war. But she is safe. She knows how to survive.'

A spasm gripped my shoulders and arms. I lifted my hands to my face. Somehow I sensed it was true. My mother was still alive.

The woman sank deeper into her chair, pressing the necklace to her chest. Her eyeballs rolled under her lids like someone dreaming and her chest heaved. 'She is looking in Harbin for you but can't find you.'

I sat bolt upright. 'Harbin?'

Suddenly the woman's cheeks puffed out and her eyes bulged in a coughing spasm that rattled her small frame. She lifted her hand to her mouth and I saw bloodstained phlegm trickle down her wrist. I quickly poured some tea and passed it to her, but she waved it away. 'Water!' she gasped. 'Water!'

I rushed to the sink and turned on the tap. Brown mud exploded onto my dress and the floor. I turned the tap down and let the water run clear, glancing anxiously over my shoulder at the old woman. She was on the floor, clutching her chest and wheezing.

When I had enough clear water for half a glass I rushed back to her side. 'Shouldn't I boil it?' I asked, lifting the glass to her trembling lips. Her face was a terrible shade of grey, but after a few sips her convulsions settled and the blood came back to her cheeks.

'Have some tea,' she said, between gulps. 'I'm sorry. It's the dust. I keep the windows shut but it still gets in from the street.'

My hands were unsteady when I poured the tea. It was lukewarm and tasted of iron, but I took a couple of polite sips anyway. I wondered if she had tuberculosis, which was rife in this part of the city. Sergei would be furious if he found out I had been here. I took another mouthful of the foul-tasting tea and placed the cup back on the table.

'Please continue,' I said to her. 'Please tell me more about my mother.'

'I've had enough for one day,' she said. 'I'm sick.' But she no longer seemed ill. She was studying me. Waiting.

I reached into my dress, pulled out the notes I had hidden in my petticoat and laid them out on the table. 'Please!' I cried.

Her eyes drifted to my hands. I could feel my fingers

start to tremble. My arms were so heavy I couldn't lift them.

'Your mother,' said the old woman, 'has returned to Harbin to find you. But all the Russians there have fled and she doesn't know where you are now.'

I swallowed. My throat was tight and it was hard to breathe. I tried to stand up so that I could open the door for air, but my legs wouldn't move. 'But the Communists . . . they will kill her . . .' I began. My hands twitched, my throat contracted. 'How could she get out of Russia? The Soviets guard the border.' The woman's features were blurred in my vision. 'It's impossible,' I said.

'Not impossible,' said the old woman, standing. She loomed over me. 'Your mother is like you. Impulsive and determined.'

My stomach turned. My face burned with fever. I collapsed back into the chair, the ceiling spinning above me.

'How do you know these things about my mother?' I asked.

The woman laughed. It sent a chill through me. 'I watch, I listen to conversations, I guess,' she said. 'Besides, all redheads have strong wills.'

A sharp pain in my side jabbed me like a kick. I glanced at the teacup and understood. 'My mother isn't a redhead,' I said.

The woman held the necklace above me. I didn't attempt to grab at it. I knew it was lost. I heard the door open and a man's voice call out. Then nothing. Only blackness.

Men's voices brought me back to consciousness. They were arguing. My ears rang with their shouting. A light burned into my eyes and my chest ached. Something was lying across my stomach. I squinted at it and saw that it was my hand. The skin was scratched and bruised and the nails were broken and rimmed with dirt. My fingers were numb, and when I tried to move them I couldn't. Something hard was poking into my leg. I attempted to sit up but my head throbbed and I lay back down again.

'I don't know who she is,' one of the men was saying in broken English. 'She wandered into my café like that. I know she is from a good family because she is usually well dressed.'

'So you have seen her before?' the other man asked. The inflection was Indian.

'She has been to my café twice. Never said her name. Always asking about Russia.'

'She's very pretty. Perhaps you found her attractive?'

'No!'

After another attempt I managed to sit up and swing my feet to the floor. The blood rushed to my head and made me nauseous. When the blindness passed, the bars came into focus and I saw that I was in a prison cell. The door was open and I was sitting on a bench attached to the wall. A basin and a bucket were in one corner. The cement walls were covered with graffiti in every language imaginable. I glanced down at my bare feet. Like my hands, they were dirty and covered in scratches. A shiver passed through me and I realised that I was in my petticoat. I felt under the material, my underwear was missing too. I remembered the man in the hall. His vacant eyes, the scars on his hands. He must have been her accomplice. I started to cry, opening my knees and feeling between my legs for signs of injury. But there were none. Then I remembered the necklace and broke down weeping.

The policeman rushed into the cell. He was young, his skin as smooth and brown as honey. His uniform was neat with elaborate braids on his shoulders and he wore his hair in a turban. He straightened his jacket before kneeling down to talk to me. 'Do you have someone you can call?' he asked. 'I'm afraid that you have been robbed.'

Sergei and Dmitri arrived at the police station soon after. Sergei was so pale I could see the veins beneath his skin. Dmitri had to steady him with his arm.

Sergei handed me a dress and pair of shoes he had brought from the house. 'I hope these are all right, Anya,' he said, his voice tense with worry. 'Mei Lin fetched them for me.'

I washed myself in the basin with the rough cake of soap. 'Mother's necklace,' I wept, my airways choked with grief. I wanted to die. To climb into the sink and swirl away with the water. To never be seen again.

It was two in the morning when I led the policeman, Dmitri and Sergei back to the crumbling apartment building. It looked sinister in the moonlight, its cracked walls jutting into the night sky. Prostitutes and opium dealers were waiting in the courtyard but disappeared like cockroaches into shadows and crevices when they saw the policeman.

'Oh God! Forgive me, Anya,' Sergei said, putting his arm around my shoulders, 'for not letting you talk about your mother.'

I was disorientated in the dim hallway, hesitating in front of one door and then another, unsure which was the right one. I shut my eyes and tried to recall what the hall had looked like in the afternoon sunlight. I turned to a door behind me. It was the only one with a grille. The policeman and Sergei glanced at each other. 'This one?' the policeman asked.

We could hear someone moving about inside the apartment. I looked at Dmitri, but his eyes were turned away from me, his jaw set. A few months earlier I would have been excited to see him, but now I wondered why he had come.

The policeman knocked on the door. The rustling inside stopped but no one answered. He knocked again, then pounded the door with his fist. It was unlocked and swung open. Inside the apartment was dark and silent. Pale streaks of light leaked through the tiny windows from the street lamps outside.

'Who's there?' called the policeman. 'Come out!'

A shape scurried across the room. The policeman flicked on the light. We all jumped when we saw her. Her face was startled, like a wild animal. I recognised her mad eyes, the jewelless tiara perched lopsidedly on her head. The woman cried out as if in pain and sank into a corner, clutching her hands over her ears. *'Dusha-dushi,'* she said. *'Dusha-dushi.'*

The policeman sprang on her and dragged her up by the arm. The woman howled.

'No! Stop it!' I cried out. 'It's not her!'

The policeman let the woman go, she dropped to the floor. He wiped his hands on his trousers with disgust.

'I know her from the café,' I said. 'She's harmless.'

'Shh! Shh!' said the woman, holding her fingers to her lips and limping towards me. 'They've been here,' she said. 'They've come again.'

'Who?' I asked.

The woman grinned at me. Her teeth were yellow with decay. 'They come when I'm not home,' she said. 'They come and leave things here for me.'

Sergei stepped forward and helped the woman into a chair. 'Madame, please tell us who has been in your apartment,' he asked. 'There has been a crime.'

'The Tsar and Tsarina,' she said, picking up one of the teacups from the table and showing it to him. 'See.'

'I'm afraid we probably won't find your necklace,' said the policeman, opening the doors of the car for us. 'Those thieves have most likely already broken it up and sold the stones and chain separately. They spied on you and the old woman from the café. They won't return to this part of the city for some time.'

Sergei tucked a roll of bills into the policeman's pocket. 'Try,' he said, 'and there will be an even bigger reward waiting for you.'

The policeman nodded and patted his pocket. 'I will see what I can do.'

The next morning I opened my eyes and felt the sunlight dancing over me through the shifting curtains. There was a bowl of gardenias on the bedside table. I remembered putting them there a few days ago. I stared at the flowers and had a flash of optimism that I had been dreaming and that none of yesterday's events had really taken place. For a moment I believed that if I slipped out of bed and opened the top drawer of the dresser I would find the necklace again, safe in its box where it had been since I came to Shanghai. But then I caught sight of my leg poking out from under the ruffled sheets. Purple scratches crisscrossed over it like cracks on a porcelain vase. The sight of them brought reality bearing down on me. I pressed my fists to my eyes, trying to block out the images that came to torment me: the Soviet soldier, the derelict apartment stinking of faeces and dust, the necklace dangling from the gypsy's hand moments before I lost it.

Mei Lin came to open the curtains. I told her to leave them shut. I saw no point in getting up and facing the day. I could not imagine myself in school, the nuns looking at me with their bare, pale faces, asking why I hadn't been in my classes the day before.

Mei Lin put my breakfast tray on the side table. She lifted the cover before scuttling away like a thief. I had no appetite, just a pain in the pit of my stomach. Through the window the faint sound of Madame Butterfly's *'Un bel di'* drifted in on a ring of opium smoke. The realisation that Sergei was taking his fix early did nothing to lift my spirits. It was my fault. He had come to me late in the night. In the shadows, with his dark brow and worried eyes, he had looked like a tormented saint. 'You're too hot,' he had said, putting his hand on my forehead. 'I'm worried that the drug the old bag gave you is turning into poison.'

I was his nightmare relived again. He was terrified that

I might slip into death unnoticed. Sergei's first wife, Marina, contracted typhoid during the epidemic of 1914. He was by her bedside every day and night for the worst of her illness. Her skin felt like fire, her pulse beat erratically and her bright eyes turned dull and deathlike. He called in the finest physicians to save her with their forced-feedings, cold baths, fluid infusions and mysterious medicines. They managed to fight the primary infection but she died two weeks later from a massive internal haemorrhage. It was the only night Sergei had not been by Marina's side, and he had only left her then because the doctors and his staff had assured him that she was recovering and that he should sleep in a proper bed.

Sergei wanted to send for the doctor to examine me, but I clutched his trembling hand and held it against my cheek. He sank down to his knees and rested his chin on his elbows on the side of the bed. A giant bear of a man, kneeling like a child in prayer.

I must have fallen asleep soon after, for that was the last I remembered. Even in my misery I knew I was lucky to have Sergei. And that made me terrified that I would lose him too, without warning, as I had lost my mother and father.

Later, when Amelia was out at the races and Sergei was sleeping off his opium, Mei Lin brought me a note on a silver tray.

Come down. I want to talk to you and I won't be allowed up there.
    Dmitri.

I scrambled out of bed, smoothed my hair and grabbed a clean dress from the wardrobe. I took the stairs in twos and leaned over the balustrade when I reached the landing. Dmitri was waiting in the parlour, his hat and jacket beside him. His eyes were darting about the room and he was tapping his foot. He clutched something in his fist. I took a gulp of air and composed myself, trying to be as graceful as Francine and nothing at all like my girlish self.

When I stepped into the room he stood up and smiled. There were shadows under his eyes and his cheeks were puffy, as if he had slept badly.

'Anya,' he said, opening his hand and passing me a velvet pouch. 'This was all I could retrieve.'

I pulled the drawstrings open and poured the contents into my hand. Three green stones and part of a gold chain. I fingered the remains of my mother's necklace. The stones were scratched. They had been carelessly torn from the chain with no thought to their real worth. The sight of the jewels reminded me of the night my father's mangled body was brought into the house after the accident. My father was returned to us, but he was not the same. The men had brought him back in pieces.

'Thank you,' I said, trying to put on a brave smile. The policeman had said the necklace would be impossible to find. I was afraid to ask Dmitri how he had come across these pieces. What methods he had used. For I sensed that, like Sergei, he moved in a darker world sometimes. A place that had nothing to do with the handsome, well-spoken man who stood before me. A world that would never intrude on us.

'It was very kind of you,' I said. 'But I was stupid. I knew the old woman would lie to me. I just didn't expect her to rob me.'

Dmitri strolled to the window and stared at the garden. 'I don't suppose you've had much of an education for a place like Shanghai. The Russians you have grown up with have been . . . refined. I grew up among the lesser kind and I know what scum those people are.'

I studied him for a moment, the straightness of his back, his broad shoulders. I was overwhelmed by how handsome he was, yet his darkness was a mystery to me.

'You must think I'm very dull and spoilt,' I said.

He spun around, his eyes full of surprise. 'I think that you are very beautiful and very clever. I've never seen anyone like you . . . you're like someone from a book. A princess.'

I slipped the remains of my mother's necklace back into the pouch. 'That's not what you were thinking that afternoon I saw you in the garden. The day you were with Marie and Francine,' I said. 'You thought I was a stupid schoolgirl.'

'Never!' said Dmitri, looking genuinely alarmed. 'I thought Amelia was rude . . . and I was jealous.'

'Jealous? Of what?'

'I would have liked to have gone to a fine school. To have studied French and art.'

'Oh!' I said, staring at him in amazement. I had spent months thinking he looked down on me.

The parlour door opened and Mei Lin sprang into the room. When she saw Dmitri she froze and stepped back, shyly clinging to the arm of the sofa. She had lost her two front teeth the week before and lisped when she spoke. 'Mr Sergei asked if you would like tea now,' she said in polite Russian.

Dmitri laughed and slapped his knee. 'She must have learned that from you,' he said. 'She sounds like an aristocrat.'

'Would you like to stay for tea?' I asked him. 'Sergei would be pleased to see you.'

'Unfortunately I can't,' he replied, gathering up his hat and coat. 'I'm auditioning a new jazz band for the club.'

'And you would rather study French and art?'

Dmitri laughed again, and the sound of it ran over me like a warm wave. 'One day,' he said, 'Sergei will bend and bring you to the club.'

Outside, the air was fresh and the sun was blazing. I

had been depressed that morning, but Dmitri had lifted my spirits. The garden seemed alive with sounds, smells and colours. The doves were crooning and purple asters were blooming in the borders. I could smell the pungency of the moss that dappled the fountain and those parts of the wall that were in constant shade. I had an urge to link my arm with Dmitri's and skip with him to the gate, but I resisted it.

Dmitri glanced back at the house. 'Are you all right here, Anya?' he asked. 'It must be lonely.'

'I am used to it now,' I said. 'I have the library. And a few friends at school.'

He stopped and kicked at a piece of gravel on the path, frowning. 'I don't have much time because of the club,' he said, 'but perhaps I could visit you, if you like. What if I came for a couple of hours each Wednesday afternoon?'

'Yes,' I said, clapping my hands together. 'I would like that very much.'

The Old Maid opened the latch on the gate for us. I was afraid to look into her eyes. I wondered if she had heard what had happened to the necklace and despised me even more for it. But she was her usual grim-faced, silent self.

'What shall we do next Wednesday then?' Dmitri asked, whistling for a rickshaw. 'Do you want to play tennis?'

'No, I do enough of that at school,' I said. I imagined one of his smooth hands between my shoulderblades, the other clutching my fingers in his, our cheeks pressing. I bit my lip and studied Dmitri for some sign he felt the same way. But his face was a mask. I hesitated a moment before gushing: 'I want you to teach me the dance you did with Marie and Francine.' Dmitri stepped back, startled. I felt colour rush to my face but I wasn't going to back down. 'The tango,' I said.

He laughed, throwing his head back so I could see all his white teeth. 'That's a very forward dance, Anya. I think I would have to ask Sergei.'

'I've heard he was an excellent dancer himself once,' I replied, my voice turning wooden with nerves. Despite what Dmitri had said about thinking I was beautiful and clever, I could see that I was still a little girl in his eyes. 'Perhaps we can ask him to teach us.'

'Perhaps.' Dmitri laughed again. 'Although he is being very proper with you. I'm sure he will insist on the Viennese waltz.'

A rickshaw boy in torn shorts and a threadbare shirt pulled up to the gate. Dmitri gave him the address of the club. I watched him climb into the seat.

'Anya,' he called. I looked up and saw that he was leaning down towards me. I hoped he was going to kiss me, so I turned my cheek to him. But he cupped his hand to my ear and whispered: 'Anya, I want you to know that I understand. I lost my mother too when I was your age.'

The thump of my heart in my chest was so loud I barely heard him.

He signalled to the boy and the rickshaw moved off down the street. Just before it took the corner, Dmitri turned and waved. 'Next Wednesday then,' he shouted.

My skin was tingling. It felt so hot I thought it must be melting on my bones. I glanced over my shoulder and saw the Old Maid staring at me, her bone-thin hand holding the gate. I ran past her, back through the garden and into the house, my feelings a Chinese orchestra clashing and clanging within me.

FOUR

The Moscow-Shanghai

Winter in Shanghai was not as cold as in Harbin, but not as beautiful either. There was no whitewash of snow to blanket buildings and streets, no stalactites hanging from eaves like crystals, no retreat into peaceful silence. Instead there was an endless grey sky, a procession of pinch-faced bedraggled people in the dirty streets, and air so damp and full of sleet that one inhalation left me shuddering and melancholic.

The winter garden was monstrous. The flowerbeds were barren mud patches out of which only the hardiest of weeds would raise their heads. I surrounded the gardenia tree with mesh and a cover. The rest of the frost-nipped trees stood naked without leaves or snow. They cast forbidding shadows on my curtains at night, like skeletons standing up from their graves. The wind would howl through them, making the glass in the windowpanes shudder and the ceiling beams creak. I lay awake for hours many nights, crying for my mother and imagining that she was out there somewhere in the tempest, hungry and shivering.

But while the flowers and plants were lying dormant, my body was sprouting. First my legs grew longer, stretching towards the end of the bed so I could see I was going to be tall, like my parents. My waist thinned and my hips broadened, and my childish freckles began fading into ivory skin. Then, to my delight, buds of breasts began to swell out of my chest. I watched them with interest, expanding, pushing against my sweater like spring blooms. My hair remained strawberry blonde, but my eyebrows and lashes darkened, and my voice became more womanly. It seemed that the only feature apart from my hair that remained the same was my blue eyes. The changes were so rapid I couldn't help thinking that my growth the previous year must have been stunted, like a river blocked by a log, and that something had happened in Shanghai to dislodge the obstacle, sending forth a stream of startling changes.

I spent hours perched on the rim of the bathtub, peering in the mirror at the stranger I was becoming. I was both exhilarated and depressed about the changes in me. Each step towards womanhood was a step closer to Dmitri *and* a step away from the child I had been with my mother. I was no longer the young daughter to whom she had sung songs about mushrooms and whose stubby hand she had bruised because she held it so tightly, never wanting to let me go. I wondered if my mother would even recognise me.

Dmitri remained true to his promise and visited me every Wednesday. We moved the sofas and chairs to the sides of the ballroom and begged Sergei to teach us to dance. As Dmitri had predicted, Sergei insisted on the Viennese waltz. Under the stern eyes of the portraits hanging on the walls, Dmitri and I practised our turns and glides to perfection. Sergei was an exacting teacher, stopping us often to correct our footwork, our arms, the position of our heads. But I was happy beyond my expectations. What did it matter what style we danced or to what music, as long as I danced with Dmitri? When I was with him those few hours each week I could forget my sadness. At first I worried that Dmitri might only be coming because he felt sorry for me, or because Sergei had secretly urged him to do so. But I watched him like a cat eyeing a mouse, searching for signs of eagerness, and I found them. He was never late for our lessons, and seemed disappointed when our time was over, lingering in the hall longer than necessary to collect his coat and umbrella. Often, when he thought I wasn't looking, I would catch him staring at me. I would swiftly turn and he would glance away, pretending that his attention had been on something else.

By the time the daffodils were poking their heads through the soil and the birds were returning to the garden, my first period finally came. I asked Luba to tell Sergei that he had to let me go to the Moscow-Shanghai now. I was a woman. The reply was given to me on a silver card with a sprig of jasmine taped to it: *After your fifteenth birthday. You need more practice at being a woman.*

But Sergei did tell Dmitri that he would teach us the bolero. I was longing for the tango and, never having heard of the bolero, was disappointed.

'No, this dance is much more symbolic,' Dmitri reassured me. 'Sergei and Marina danced the bolero the day they got married. He would not be teaching it to us if he didn't think we were serious enough.'

The following week Sergei dimmed the lights in the ballroom. He positioned the needle on the record and set Dmitri and I so that we were opposite each other, me slightly to the right, and so close that the buttons of Dmitri's shirt pressed into me. I could feel Dmitri's pulse and the beat of his heart against my ribs. The amber light made Sergei's face look demonic and our shadows became grotesque shapes looming on the walls. The music was a relentless marching rhythm set to the beat of rolling drums. Then a flute, hypnotic as a snake charmer's pipe, began a melody. Trumpets full of bravado and horns full of passion joined in the frenzy. Sergei began dancing, teaching us the steps without words. Dmitri and I followed, keeping time with the clashing cymbals, dipping and rising, treading forwards then rocking slowly back, swaying our hips in the opposite direction to our feet. The music seized me and dragged me spiralling down into another world. For one moment I believed Dmitri and I were the king and queen of Spain presiding over our court, the next we were riding horseback across sweeping plains in the company of Don Quixote, and yet the next we were a Roman emperor and empress parading in a chariot before our subjects. The dance was a fantasy, the most erotic experience I had ever known. Sergei striding before us, his arms flowing softly over his head but his footwork masculine; Dmitri and I almost touching, lingering for a moment, then moving away. The music's melody repeated itself over and over again, plunging us in and out of each other, impelling us forward, seducing us, rising to a climax.

When Sergei came to a stop, Dmitri and I were breathless. We clung to each other, trembling. Sergei was a sorcerer who had taken us to the underworld and back again. I was burning with a fever but could not get my legs to move across the room to sit down.

The needle clicked off the record player and Sergei flicked on the lights. I was startled to see Amelia, a cigarette perched in the tips of her fingers and her black hair sleek like a mink's pelt against her pale face. The sight of her sent a shiver through me. She blew out a ring of cigarette smoke, considering me as if she were an army general gauging the size and nature of her enemy. I wished she would stop staring at me. She was grinding down the elation I felt after the bolero. She must have read my thoughts because she sniggered, turned on her heel and left.

I hadn't quite believed Sergei's promise to take me to the Moscow-Shanghai after my fifteenth birthday, but one day in August the following year he emerged from his study and announced that I would be going to the club that night. Amelia produced the emerald green dress Mrs Woo had sewn for me but I could barely get it over my head, I had grown so much. Sergei called a seamstress in for an urgent refitting. When she left, Mei Lin was sent to brush my hair. Amelia came after her, swinging a beauty case in her hand. She smudged rouge on my cheeks and lips and dabbed musky perfume on my wrists and behind my ears. When she had finished she leaned back and smiled, pleased with the result. 'I don't mind you so much now you're an adult,' she said. 'It's pouty children I can't stand.'

I knew she was lying. She still couldn't stand me.

I sat between her and Sergei in the car. Bubbling Well Road passed by like a silent movie. Young women of every nationality stood in the doorways of nightclubs, sparkling in their sequined dresses and feather boas. They waved to passers-by, soliciting customers with their smiles. Groups of revellers lurched along the crowded pavements, drunkenly bumping into other pedestrians and hawkers, while gamblers huddled together on the street corners, like bugs under the neon lights.

'Here we are!' announced Sergei. The door swung open and I was helped out of the car by a man in a Cossack's uniform. His hat was bear fur and I couldn't resist touching it, at the same time gaping at the magnificence that opened up before me. A red carpet ran up a set of wide stone steps, bordered on either side by gold-braid rope. A queue of men and women were waiting to get into the club, their gowns, furs, satins and jewels gleaming under the sepia-coloured lamps, the air electric with their chatter. At the top of the stairs was a portico with giant neoclassical columns and two marble lions guarding the entrance. Dmitri was waiting there. We exchanged smiles and he rushed down the stairs to meet us. 'Anya,' he said, his head close to mine. 'I will always have you to dance with from now on.'

Dmitri commanded respect as the nightclub's manager. When he directed us up the red carpet, the guests parted way in deference to him and more Cossacks bowed to us. Inside, the foyer was breathtaking. White artificial marble walls and gilded mirrors reflected the light of a giant chandelier hanging from a Byzantine ceiling. The false windows were painted in with a blue sky and white clouds and gave the impression of permanent twilight. The hall made me think of a photo-graph my father once showed me of the Tsar's palace and I remembered him telling me about the caged birds that would sing whenever anybody entered. But there were no singing birds at the Moscow-Shanghai, only a squad of young women in embroidered Russian dresses checking in the guests' coats and stoles.

The nightclub's interior had a different ambiance al-together. Wood-panelled walls and red Turkish rugs sur-rounded the dance floor which was crowded with people gyrating to the music spun out by the band. Among the glamorous couples, American, British and French officers were waltzing with pretty taxi dancers. Other patrons looked on from the mahogany chairs and velvet sofas, sipping cham-pagne or whisky and gesturing to waiters to bring them caviar and bread.

I breathed in the smoke-filled air. Just as had happened the afternoon Sergei taught us the bolero, I was being plunged into a new world. Only the Moscow-Shanghai was real.

Dmitri led us up a staircase to the restaurant which was on a mezzanine level overlooking the dance floor. Dozens of gas lamps decorated the tables, all of which were occu-pied. A waiter rushed by with flaming shashlik on a sword, filling the air with the aroma of tender lamb, onions and brandy. Everywhere I looked there were diamonds and furs, expensive wools and silks. Bankers and hotel managers sat down to discuss business with gangsters and taipans, while actors and actresses made eyes at diplomats and shipping officers.

Alexei and Luba were already seated at a table at the far end of the restaurant, a half-finished carafe of wine at Alexei's elbow. They were talking to two British shipping captains and their wives. The men stood up for us, while their tight-mouthed wives glanced from Amelia to myself with thinly disguised distaste. One of the women stared so hard at the splits in my dress that my skin began to tingle with embarrassment.

Waiters in tuxedos brought us food on silver platters, laying out a feast of oysters, *piroshki* filled with sweet pumpkin, *blini* with caviar, creamy asparagus soup and black bread. It was more food than we could possibly eat, but they kept the courses coming: fish in vodka sauce, chicken Kiev, compotes, and a dessert of cherries and chocolate cake.

One of the captains, Wilson, asked me how I liked Shanghai. I hadn't seen much of it, except Sergei's house, my school, the stores on the few routes I was allowed to walk on my own and a park in the French Concession, but I told him that I loved it. He nodded his approval and leaned closer to me to whisper: 'Most Russians in this city do not live like you, young lady. Look at those poor girls down there. Probably daughters of princes and nobles. Now they have to dance and entertain drunkards to earn a living.'

The other captain, whose name was Bingham, said he had heard that my mother had been taken to a labour camp. 'That Stalin madman won't be there forever,' he said, heaping my plate with vegetables and knocking over the pepper shaker in the process. 'There will be another revolution before the year's out, you'll see.'

'Who are these fools?' Sergei muttered to Dmitri.

'Investors,' Dmitri replied. 'So keep smiling.'

'No,' said Sergei. 'You will have to train Anya to do that now she is old enough. She's so much more charming than any of us.'

When the after-dinner port was served, I slipped away to the powder room and recognised the voices of the captains' wives speaking to each other across the stalls. One woman was saying to the other, 'That American woman should be ashamed of herself, not running around like the Queen of Sheba. She ruined a good man's happiness and now she's taken up with that Russian.'

'I know,' said the other woman. 'And who's that girl she's got with her?'

'I don't know,' answered the first. 'But you can bet before long she'll get a bad streak in her too.'

I pressed myself against the sink, dying to hear more, hoping my heels would not click on the tiled floor. Who was the good man whose life Amelia had ruined?

'Bill can spend his money how he likes,' said the first woman, 'but what good can come of associating with such riffraff? You know what those Russians are like.'

I let out a giggle and both women stopped talking. Their toilets flushed in unison and I dashed for the door.

At midnight the orchestra stopped and a Cuban band took over the stage. The rhythm of the stringed instruments was gentle at first, but as soon as the brass and percussion joined in the music changed tempo and I could feel the excitement rush through the crowd. Couples ran to the floor to dance the mambo and rumba, while those without partners joined in a conga line. I was entranced by the music, so savage and yet sophisticated. I found myself unconsciously tapping my foot and clicking my fingers along with the beat.

Luba let out a throaty laugh. She nudged Dmitri and pointed to me. 'Come on, Dmitri, take Anya out to dance and show us what Sergei has been teaching you.'

Dmitri smiled at me and offered his hand. I followed him to the dance floor, although I was terrified. To dance in the ballroom of Sergei's home was one thing, but on the dance floor at the Moscow-Shanghai was quite another. The mad rush of people rolling their hips and swinging their legs was like a wild frenzy. They danced as if their hearts would stop beating if they didn't. But Dmitri put one hand on my hip and clenched my fingers in his, and I felt safe. We moved together in short, syncopated steps, twisting our hips and rolling our shoulders. We were playful at first, and bumped knees and feet and into other people, laughing each time. But after a while we moved gracefully together and I found I had forgotten my self-consciousness.

'What is this music?' I asked Dmitri.

'They call it mango and merengue. Do you like it?'

'Yes, I like it very much,' I told him. 'Please don't let them stop.'

Dmitri threw his head back and laughed. 'I will tell them to play it every night for you, Anya! And tomorrow I will take you to Yuyuan.'

Dmitri and I danced every dance, sweat drenching our clothes and my hair falling loose over my shoulders. We only returned to the table when the last set was over. The captains and their wives had left but Sergei and the Michailovs stood up to applaud us. 'Bravo! Bravo!' Sergei shouted.

Amelia gave a weak smile and shoved napkins at us to wipe the perspiration from our faces and necks.

'Enough of making a fool of yourself, Anya.'

I ignored her nasty comment. 'Why don't you dance with Sergei?' I asked her. 'He's very good.'

My question was innocent, asked out of the high spirits dancing with Dmitri had given me. But Amelia arched like a cat. Her eyes glowered but she said nothing. The atmosphere between us, which had always been strained, became even tighter. I was aware of having made some terrible mistake, but I was not going to apologise for an imagined slight. We sat rigid in the car all the way home, opponents locked stubbornly in battle. Sergei made small talk about the traffic, I deliberately spoke only Russian, and Amelia stared directly ahead of her. But I knew even then that if it came to a strike, I could not win against her.

The following day I told Sergei that Dmitri had asked to meet with me. 'I'm glad you two have taken to each other,' he said, leaning close to me. 'It is the best that I could have wished for. Dmitri is like a son to me and you are like a daughter.'

Sergei had a business appointment, so immediately set about finding a substitute chaperone. Amelia refused outright, protesting that she had no intention of spending the day in the company of 'gooey-eyed teenagers'. Luba said she would have been delighted but was committed to a ladies' luncheon, and Alexei had come down with the flu. So it was the Old Maid who was sent out with me in the rickshaw. She sat in the seat, cold in her primness, and would neither answer my questions nor look at me whenever I tried to make conversation.

Dmitri and I met in the Yuyuan Gardens, in the old part of the city, at a traditional tea-house overlooking a lake and out to the mountains. He was waiting under the shade of a willow tree, wearing a cream linen suit that brought out the green in his eyes. The tea-house's ochre walls and upturned roof reminded me of a tea-chest we had in the house in Harbin. The day was hot and Dmitri suggested we sit on the top floor to catch the breeze. He invited the maid to sit at our table, but she took her place at the table next to us, staring stoically out to the pretty vista of winding walkways and pavilions, although I suspected she was listening with keen ears to everything we said.

A waitress brought us jasmine tea in ceramic cups. 'It's the oldest park in the city,' Dmitri told me. 'And much nicer than the ones in the French Concession. You know they used to have signs that read: "No Dogs or Chinese".'

'It's awful to be poor,' I told him. 'I thought I had seen enough of it when the Japanese invaded Harbin. But I have never seen anything like the poverty in Shanghai.'

'There are many Russians poorer than Chinese here,' Dmitri said, taking a metal case from his pocket and pulling out a cigarette. 'My father had to work as a chauffeur for a rich Chinese family when he came to Shanghai. I think it gave them pleasure to see a white man in desperate circumstances.'

A lazy breeze drifted across the table, lifting the napkins

and cooling the tea. The Old Maid had fallen asleep, her eyes closed and her head resting on the windowpane. Dmitri and I grinned at each other.

'I saw those Russian girls last night,' I confided in him. 'The ones who are paid to dance with customers.'

Dmitri studied me for a moment, his face serious and his eyes narrowed. 'You're kidding me, Anya? Those girls make good money and are not required to compromise themselves to do it. Maybe a few promises here, a flirtatious comment there, show a little flesh and charm the customers into drinking and spending a bit more than they otherwise would. But nothing more than that. There are women in much worse circumstances.'

He turned away then and the silence was awkward between us. I pinched my arm, feeling stupid and condescending when all I had wanted was for Dmitri to admire me.

'Do you think about your mother much?' he asked me.

'All the time,' I told him. 'She's on my mind all the time.'

'I know,' he said, signalling to the waitress to bring us more tea.

'Do you think it's true,' I asked him, 'that there will be another revolution in Russia?'

'I wouldn't wait for it, Anya.'

Dmitri's flippant tone stabbed me and I cringed. When he saw my reaction his face softened. He glanced over his shoulder to check the maid was still asleep before taking my fingers in his warm hand. 'My father and his friends waited every day for years for the aristocracy to be restored in Russia, wasting their lives away hoping for something that never happened,' he said. 'With all my heart I pray that your mother will be released, Anya. All I'm saying is that you mustn't wait around for it. You have to help yourself now.'

'Amelia would say something like that,' I told him.

He laughed. 'Oh? Well, I can understand that. We are

sort of similar. We've both had to fight our way in this world, starting with nothing. At least she knows what she wants and how to get it.'

'She frightens me.'

Dmitri cocked his head, surprised. 'She does? Well, you shouldn't let her. She's all spit and no bite. She's a jealous person, and envious people are always insecure.'

Dmitri accompanied us back to the house where the maids were polishing the furniture and cleaning the carpets. Amelia was nowhere in sight. Sergei had just arrived home himself and waited for us by the front door.

'I hope you had a nice time at Yuyuan together,' he said.

'Wonderful,' I replied, stepping up to kiss him. His face was clammy and his eyes glazed over, a sign he was going to take his fix.

'Stay with us a while,' Dmitri said to him.

'No, I must get on with things,' said Sergei. He stepped back from us and reached for the doorknob but his fingers were trembling and he couldn't grasp it.

'I'll help you with it . . .' Dmitri said, leaning across. Sergei looked at him with tormented eyes, but as soon as the door opened he hurried away, almost knocking a maid over in his rush. I looked into Dmitri's face and saw the anguish on it.

'You know, don't you?' I said.

Dmitri covered his eyes with his hand. 'We're going to lose him, Anya. Just like I lost my father.'

My second night at the Moscow-Shanghai was a disappointment, and my excitement fell flat as soon as I entered the club. Instead of the ritzy clientele of the previous night, the club was full of razor-shaved marines and sailors. On stage an all-white swing band was blasting out dance numbers, and the bright nylon dresses of the Russian girls turned the dance floor into a cheap carnival. There were too many men and not enough women. Those men without partners waited in groups at the bar or in the restaurant which had become a de facto drinking area. The men's voices were loud with testosterone and rowdy. When they laughed or shouted their orders to the harried bartenders, the sound of their revelry was often louder than the music.

'We don't like them in the club,' Sergei confided in me, 'and usually our prices keep them out. But since the war, discriminating against them is considered bad form. So on Thursday nights it's half-price drinks and dances.'

The maître d'hôtel guided us to a table at the far corner of the room. Amelia excused herself to go to the powder room and I glanced about for Dmitri, wondering why he hadn't joined us. I spotted him at the edge of the dance floor, near the steps that led to the bar. His arms were folded across his chest and he was hunching his shoulders backwards and forwards nervously.

'Poor kid,' Sergei said to me. 'He guards this place with his life. I'm fond of it, but if it went up in flames I wouldn't care so much.'

'Dmitri is concerned about you,' I told him.

Sergei winced and picked up a napkin, dabbing his lips and chin. 'He lost his own father when he was a boy. His mother had to take in men just to get enough to eat.'

'Oh,' I said, remembering Dmitri's reaction to my ignorance about the Russian dancers. I burned with shame. 'When was this?'

'At the start of the war. Dmitri's used to surviving on his own.'

'He told me that he lost his mother when he was young. But I have never asked him how she died and he has never told me.'

Sergei stared at me, as if he was weighing up how much he should say to me. 'She took the wrong man in one day. A sailor,' he said, lowering his voice. 'He killed her.'

'Oh!' I cried, digging my fingers into Sergei's arm. 'Our poor Dmitri!'

Sergei shrugged. 'He found her, Anya. Imagine what that did to the kid. The navy tried the monster and hung him. But what good is that to a boy who has lost his mother?'

I stared at the whirling dancers, too sad to cry and too overwhelmed to think of any response.

Sergei nudged me with his elbow. 'Go tell Dmitri not to worry,' he said. 'Other clubs have had trouble, but never this one. It's a favourite with their officers. They wouldn't dare.'

I was grateful to Sergei for giving me an excuse to approach Dmitri. The dance floor was an orgy of heat and writhing limbs. I could barely see my way through the flailing arms and flushed faces. The dancers were growing wilder like the music, the beat of the percussion instruments rising to a climax. A Russian girl was dancing so vigorously that one of her large breasts began to protrude over the low-cut neckline of her dress. At first only her crimson nipple slipped above the fabric, but the harder she danced, the more of her flesh became exposed. After one energetic leap her whole breast tumbled out into full view. She made no attempt to fix herself and no one else seemed to notice.

Someone tapped my back. 'Hey, looker! Here's my ticket.' I could feel the shadow of the man behind me and smell the alcohol sweating out of his skin. There was lust in his slurred voice. 'You, sweetheart. I'm talking to you.' From somewhere in the crowd a female voice shouted: 'Leave her alone. She's the boss's kid.'

Dmitri's eyes widened when he saw me heading towards him. He lunged into the crowd and pulled me to the side of the dance floor.

'I told them not to bring you here tonight,' he said, lifting me up onto the step behind him. 'Sometimes I wonder if either of them has any sense left.'

'Sergei said to tell you he doesn't think there will be trouble,' I told him.

'It's a hot and drunken night. And I'm not taking any chances.' Dmitri gestured to one of the waiters and whispered in his ear. The waiter hurried away and returned a few moments later with a glass of champagne.

'Here,' said Dmitri. 'You can have some of this and then I'm sending you home.'

I took the glass from him and drank a single sip. 'Hmmm, nice champagne,' I teased. 'French, I believe?'

He grinned. 'Anya, I want you to be here, to work with me. But not on these nights. It doesn't become you. You're too good for this crowd.'

A marine bumped into me, almost knocking me down the steps. He straightened himself and grabbed drunkenly for my waist. His arms were a web of badly cut tattoos. I shuffled back from him, frightened by the aggression in his bloodshot eyes. His hand swiped at me, landing like a rope around my wrist. He yanked me onto the dance floor. My shoulder cracked and I dropped the champagne glass. It smashed on the floor and was crushed under somebody's foot.

'You're a little skinny,' the marine said, clutching at my hips. 'But I like slim women.'

Dmitri was between us in a second. 'Excuse me, sir,' he said, 'but you're mistaken. She's not a dancer.'

'If she's got two legs and a hole, she is,' the marine grinned, wiping the slaver from his lips with his fingertips.

I didn't see Dmitri hit the marine, so quickly did it happen. I only saw the man fall backwards, blood spurting from his mouth, surprise in his eyes. His head smacked the floor and he lay there for a moment, dazed. Then he tried to lift himself onto his elbow, but before he could get up Dmitri dropped his knee into the man's neck and started pounding into his face with his fist. Everything became slow motion then. The dancers moved away into a wide circle. The band stopped playing. Dmitri's hands were covered in blood and saliva. The marine's face was turning into pulp before my eyes.

Sergei burst through the crowd and tried to pull Dmitri away. 'Have you gone mad?' he shouted. But his words were lost. Dmitri was kicking the marine in the ribs. Bones cracked under the force. The man rolled over in pain and Dmitri stomped on his groin.

Three marines, thick-necked and square-fisted, came to their shipmate's rescue. One of them lifted the bleeding man by his shirtsleeves and dragged him off the floor. The other two grabbed Dmitri and knocked him to the ground. Panic hit the crowd then. Everyone was convinced they were about to witness a murder. The British, French and Italian sailors started shouting abuse at the marines. The marines shouted back. Some of them tried calling their fellows to order, telling them not to disgrace their country, while others fuelled the violence. Fist fights broke out like spot fires. Patrons started gathering their belongings and rushing for the exits, clawing against each other to get out. The Russian dancers fled to the safety of the powder room while the chefs and waiters ran about moving precious vases and statues. The word must have got out on the street because, although some guests were fleeing, the room was also filling up with reinforcements. American soldiers were hitting marines, the marines were striking the French, and the French were fighting the British sailors.

The marines had Dmitri in a headlock. His mouth twisted in agony. An Italian sailor and another marine came to his assistance, but they were no match for the burly men. Sergei picked up a chair and smashed it across the back of one of the marines, knocking him unconscious. Encouraged by his success the Italian wrestled the other marine to the floor. But the last marine, the biggest of the three, retained his grip on Dmitri, pushing his head against the floor and trying to break his neck. I screamed and looked around the room for help. I spotted Amelia in the restaurant, she had a knife in her hand and was trying to make it down the steps through the crowd. Dmitri was choking, spittle dribbling from his mouth. Sergei thumped the marine with his bear-like fists, but it had no effect. Dmitri's hand was twisted behind him. His fingers grabbed for my shoe and squeezed the toes. I couldn't take any more, I threw myself against the marine and bit his ear with all my might. Blood and salt burst into my mouth. The marine yelped and let go of Dmitri. He pushed me off him and I spat out the bloody pink flesh. The marine's face turned ashen when he saw that I had half his ear in my lap. He clasped his hand to his head and fled.

'*Benissimo!*' the Italian sailor said to me. 'Now go wash your mouth out.'

When I returned from the bathroom I could hear the sirens and whistles of the military police outside. The police stormed into the building, clubbing indiscriminately and adding to the casualty count. I ran outside to see ambulances carting off the wounded. It looked like wartime all over again.

I searched through the mayhem for Dmitri and Sergei and found them on the steps with Amelia, seeing off the injured as if they were seeing off VIP guests on any normal night. Dmitri's eye was black and his lips so swollen that he barely looked human. Still, he managed to smile boyishly when he saw me.

'It's the end of us,' I wailed. 'They'll close us down now, won't they?'

Dmitri's brow lifted in surprise. Sergei laughed. 'Dmitri,' he said, 'I do believe that after only two nights Anya cares.' Even Amelia, the sleeve of her dress torn and her hair dishevelled, smiled at me.

'It's like that, isn't it, Anya?' said Dmitri. 'It's like the music. The place gets into your blood. You're really one of us now. A Shanghailander.'

The limousine pulled up and Amelia climbed in, gesturing for me to follow her. 'The boys made the mess and the boys can clean up,' she said.

The marine's sticky blood was still on the front of my dress. It clung to my skin. I looked at it and began to sob.

'For God's sake,' said Amelia, grabbing my arm and pulling me into the car. 'This is Shanghai not Harbin. Tomorrow it will be business as usual and tonight will be forgotten. We will still be the hottest nightclub in town.'

FIVE

Roses

The next morning while I was braiding my hair for school, Mei Lin tapped on the door and told me that Sergei was on the telephone. I clumped down the stairs, stifling a yawn. My skin was dry and my throat hurt. The stink of stale cigarette smoke lingered in my hair. I wasn't looking forward to Sister Mary's boring geography lesson before lunch. I pictured myself falling asleep somewhere between the Canary Islands and Greece and being made to write out a hundred times on the blackboard the reason for my fatigue. I imagined the surprise on Sister Mary's face when I picked up the piece of chalk and began writing on the board: *I was at the Moscow-Shanghai last night and didn't get enough sleep.*

I enjoyed my French and art lessons, but now I had danced the bolero and seen the Moscow-Shanghai, I was too grown up for school. My sanctuary of textbooks and paints didn't match the excitement and glamour of the world that had opened up to me.

I put my hairbrush on the stand in the hall and picked up the telephone receiver.

'Anya!' Sergei's voice bellowed down the line. 'Now you are an employee of the club I need you down here at eleven o'clock!'

'But what about school?'

'Do you think you've had enough of school? Or do you still want to go?'

My hand flew to my mouth. I bumped the table and sent the hairbrush clattering to the floor. 'I've had enough!' I cried. 'I was only thinking that just this minute! I can always continue to read and learn on my own.'

Sergei laughed and whispered to someone else in the room with him. The other person, a man, laughed too. 'Well, get ready and come to the club then,' he said. 'And wear your prettiest dress. You must always look fashionable from now on.'

I slammed down the receiver and hurried up the stairs, ripping off my school uniform as I went. The tiredness I had been feeling only a few moments before vanished.

'Mei Lin! Mei Lin!' I called out. 'Help me get dressed!'

The girl stepped out on the landing, her eyes wide.

'Come on.' I grabbed her little arm and dragged her into my room. 'From now on you are the maid to an employee of the Moscow-Shanghai!'

The Moscow-Shanghai was buzzing with activity. A team of Chinese workmen were scrubbing the stairs with brooms and buckets of soapy water. One of the windows had been broken in the previous night's riot and a repairman was fixing the glass. In the dance hall maids were mopping down the floor and wiping the tables. Chefs' assistants rushed in and out through the kitchen swing doors, collecting the boxes of celery, onions and beetroots passed to them by a delivery man through the side entrance. I pushed back my hair from my face and smoothed my dress. My outfit had been chosen with Luba one day after school. We had seen it in a catalogue from America. It was a pink shift dress with a layer of tulle over the top. There were rosettes around the neckline and hem. It was low cut, but the material was gathered at the bust, so it didn't appear too immodest. I hoped Sergei would approve of it and not embarrass me by sending me home to change. I asked one of the kitchen hands where

I could find Sergei and he pointed to a corridor and a door marked 'Office'.

But it was Dmitri's voice that answered my knock. 'Come in,' he called.

He was standing near a stone fireplace, smoking a cigarette. His face was bruised and swollen and his arm was in a sling. But at least I could tell it was Dmitri this morning and, despite his wounds, I thought him as handsome as ever. He eyed my dress and I could tell by his smile that he was pleased with what he saw too.

'How are you this morning?' He pushed open the louvred shutters and let more light into the room. On the window sill was a model of the Venus de Milo. It and the blue and white porcelain vase on the mantelpiece were the only decorative pieces in the office. Everything else was starkly modern. A teak desk and red leather chairs dominated the room, which was fastidiously neat, not a paper or open book in sight.

The window looked out onto an alleyway which, unlike most Shanghai backstreets, was clean. A beauty salon, café and sweet shop stood side by side there. The shops' green awnings were open and blooms of red geraniums burst from the window boxes.

'Sergei told me to come,' I said.

Dmitri stubbed out his cigarette on the grate. 'He's gone somewhere with Alexei. They won't be back today.'

'I don't understand. Sergei said—'

'Anya, it was me who wanted to speak to you.'

I wasn't sure whether to be delighted or afraid. I sat down in the chair by the window. Dmitri seated himself opposite me. The expression on his face was so grave I was worried that something serious had taken place, that there was a problem with the club because of what had happened the previous night.

He pointed out the window. 'If you look out there over to the west you will see some dilapidated rooftops. That's where you lost your mother's necklace.'

His comment baffled me. Why was he bringing up such an unhappy memory? Had he somehow found the rest of the necklace?

'That's where I come from,' he said. 'That is where I was born.'

I was surprised to see his hand tremble. He fumbled with a cigarette, dropping it into his lap. I had an urge to take his shaking hand and kiss it, to comfort him somehow. But I had no idea what was wrong. I picked up his cigarette and held the lighter steady for him. A strange expression crept into his eyes, as if he were remembering something painful. I couldn't stand the sight of his hurt. It jabbed like a knife straight into my own heart.

'Dmitri, you don't have to tell me this,' I said. 'You know I don't care where you came from.'

'Anya, there is something important I have to tell you. You'll need to know it in order to make a decision.'

His words were ominous. I swallowed. A vein in my neck started to throb.

'My parents came from St Petersburg. When they left their home it was in the dead of night. They took nothing with them because there was no time. My father's tea was left steaming on the table, my mother's embroidery lay on her seat by the fire. They had received word of the revolt too late and escaped Russia with only their lives. When they reached Shanghai my father found work as a labourer and then, after I was born, as a chauffeur. But he never recovered from the loss of the life he had known. He had bad nerves, on account of the war. He drank and smoked away most of the meagre money he earned. It was my mother who put aside her pride to scrub the floors of rich Chinese women to keep a roof over our heads. Then he overdosed on opium one day and left her with debts her cleaning work couldn't pay. My mother was forced into . . . another means to earn money to keep food on our table.'

'Sergei told me about your mother,' I said, desperate to

spare him the pain. 'My mother also had to make a decision that seemed morally wrong in order to keep me safe.
A mother will do anything to save her child.'

'Anya, I know Sergei told you about my mother. And I
know you have such a kind heart that you can understand.
But listen to me, please. Because these are the forces that
shaped me.'

I sat back in my chair, chastised. 'I promise not to
interrupt any more.'

He nodded. 'For as long as I can remember I wanted to
be rich. I didn't want to live in a wretched, grotty shack
that stank of the sewers and was so damp that the coldness of it stayed in my bones, even in summer. The boys
around me were all begging or thieving or working in factories that would keep them poor forever. But I swore I would
never become the coward my father had been. I would not
give in, regardless of what I had to sacrifice. I would find
a way to make money, and I would make life good for
myself and my mother.

'At first I tried honest jobs. Although I had never been
to school I was smart and my mother had taught me to
read. But all I could make was money enough for a little
more food, and I wanted more than that. It's fine to be
fussy about what you do if you are rich. But street rats?
Scum like me? We have to be more cunning. So you know
what I did? I hung outside the bars and clubs where rich
people went. And when they came out I would ask them
for work. I don't mean rich people like Sergei or Alexei . . .
I mean . . . opium lords. They don't care who you are or
where you've come from or how old you are. In fact, the
less suspect you are, the better.'

He stopped, searching my face for signs of the effect his
words were having on me. I didn't like what I was hearing, but I was determined to keep silent until he had
finished.

'The opium lords were amused that such a young boy

knew who they were and wanted to work for them,' he continued, standing up and gripping the back of his chair with his good hand. 'I used to run messages for them from one end of town to the other. Once I delivered a severed hand. It was a warning. I never spent a cent I earned on myself. I hid it in my mattress. I was saving up for a better place, nicer things for my mother. But before that could ever happen she was murdered . . .'

He let go of the chair and moved to the fireplace, clenching his fingers. He composed himself, then began again. 'After my mother's death I became even more determined to be rich. If we had been rich, my mother wouldn't have been murdered. That was what I figured anyway. I still think that. I would rather be dead than poor again, because if you are poor you are as good as dead anyway.

'I'm not proud of everything I have done. But I don't regret anything either. I'm glad I'm alive. By the time I was fifteen I had a broad back and strong chest. And I was good-looking too. The opium lords would joke that I was their handsome bodyguard. It was prestigious to have a White Russian in their entourage. They would buy me silk suits and take me with them into the best clubs in town.

'Then one night I delivered a package to the French Concession. When I was taking something direct from one of the lords, you could be sure that it was heading for a classy joint. Not the dens the middlemen serve: dim, stinking and filled with desperate customers like my father. Not the hovels the rickshaw boys go to so they can stick their arms through a hole in a wall and get a hit from a needle. The one that night turned out to be the best in the Concession. It looked more like a five-star hotel than a brothel: black lacquer furniture, silk screens, French and Chinese porcelain, an Italian fountain in the lobby. It was teeming with Eurasian and white girls.

'I took my deal to the madame of the house. She laughed when she read the note from the lord, gave me a kiss on the cheek and a pair of gold cufflinks for my trouble. On my way out I passed a room with the door partly open. I could hear the whispers of women coming from inside. Out of curiosity, I peered through the crack and saw a man lying on the bed. Two girls were going through his pockets, which even in the ritzy joints is the standard practice whenever someone passes out. They searched his clothes and found something around his neck. It looked to me like a ring on a chain. They tried to undo the clasp but couldn't get their little hands around the back of his thick neck. One of them started biting the chain, as if she was going to break it with her teeth. I could have just shut the door and left. But the man looked vulnerable. Maybe he reminded me of my father. Without really thinking, I burst in on the girls and told them they had better leave the man alone as he was a good friend of the Red Dragon. They backed off, scared. I thought that was funny so I yelled at them to call the house doormen to help me get the man into a rickshaw. It took four of us to do it. "The Moscow-Shanghai," one of the doormen whispered to me when we were ready to leave. "He's the owner of the Moscow-Shanghai."'

I blushed. I didn't want Dmitri to continue with the story. This was not the Sergei I knew.

Dmitri glanced at me and laughed. 'I guess I don't have to tell you who that man was, Anya. I was surprised. The Moscow-Shanghai was the top nightclub in the city. Even someone like the Red Dragon wouldn't have been good enough to go there. Anyway, in the rickshaw Sergei started to wake up. The first thing he did was to grab for the chain around his neck. "It's safe," I told him. "But they cleaned out your pockets."

'By the time we got to the club, it was closed. A couple of waiters were smoking out the back and I called them to help me get Sergei inside. We lifted him onto a couch in the office. He was in pretty bad shape. "How old are you,

113

kid?" he asked me. When I told him, he laughed. "I've heard of you," he said.

'The next day I found Sergei standing on my doorstep. He was out of place in the slums with his finely cut coat and the gold watch on his wrist. He was lucky he was left alone. I think it was his size and that fierce expression of his which protected him. Any other man would have been a sitting duck. "Those lords you are working for are just making fun of you," he said. "You're their amusement and they'll throw you away like an old whore when the novelty wears off. I want you to come and work for me. I'll train you to manage my club."

'So Sergei paid the lords off and took me back to his home, the house you are living in now. My God! Do you think I'd ever seen a place like that in my life? When I stepped into the hallway I thought my eyes would burn with the beauty of it. You didn't think that, did you, Anya, when you first saw it? It's because you're accustomed to luxurious things. But I was like an adventurer in a foreign territory. Sergei thought it was amusing, me gawking at the paintings, fingering every vase, staring at the plates on the table like I'd never eaten off a dish before. I had never seen anything so elegant. The opium lords had mansions, but they were full of gaudy statues, red walls and gongs. Symbols of power. Not of wealth. Sergei's house had something else. An essence. I knew then that if I had a house like that I would have real wealth. Not the kind someone can take away from you. Not the kind that makes you feel as though you are living with a knife at your back. A house like that would transform me from scum to a gentleman. I wanted to be more than just rich then. What Sergei had, I wanted too.

'Sergei introduced me to Amelia. But I only had to talk to her for a minute to know she wasn't responsible for the way the house looked. She was like me, a stranger to luxury. Although she's a sly one too. Even if she wasn't born to it, she can smell it out like a weasel. But she only knows how to make herself appealing so she can get some of it for herself. She doesn't know how to create it.'

He laughed then, to himself. And I realised for the first time that he had affection for Amelia. The way he spoke so casually about her revealed it. My spine prickled. But I knew I had to accept it. They had known each other for a long time before I had come along. And Dmitri had told me before that they were two of a kind.

'But she's nervous,' he said, turning to look at me. 'Have you noticed that, Anya? Jumpy. When you've fought for it, you have to protect it. You can never quite relax. People who are born into wealth don't know that. Even when they have lost everything, they still act as if money is nothing.

'Later, I found out about Marina. She had decorated the house. Sergei just threw the money at her. He didn't know what she was buying half the time. He loved her so much he gave her all he had. Then one day he opened his eyes and found himself living in a palace. He told me it was because he was just a merchant with money but Marina was an aristocrat and aristocrats had good taste. I asked him what "aristocrat" meant and he said. "Someone of good birth and breeding."'

Dmitri paused for a moment, resting his head on the mantelpiece. My mind wandered to my father. He had filled our house with beautiful and unique things, but he had lost his wealth when he left Russia. Perhaps it was true what Dmitri said. My father wouldn't have known how to be poor if he had tried. I remembered him always saying that it was better to go without than to settle for something of crude quality.

'Anyway,' Dmitri said, 'Sergei hired me to help with his club and rewarded me well for my efforts. He told me that I was like a son to him and that, as he had no children of his own, Amelia and I would get the nightclub when he dies. The day I walked into the club and the clients greeted me as if I was as good as any of them, I knew I had achieved my goal. I was rich. I live in fine rooms in Lafayette. My suits are all handmade in England. I have a maid and a butler. There is nothing I lack. Except the essential thing. I tried to emulate what I saw in Sergei's house and couldn't do it. My ottoman, my mahogany chairs, my Turkish rugs do not sit together in casual elegance as they do in Sergei's library. No matter how I arrange things, my apartment looks like a flashy department store. Amelia tried to help me. "All men are clumsy," she said. But she's only good with stuff that's new and showy. That's not what I wanted. When I tried to explain, she stared at me and said: "Why would you want your furniture to look old?"

'Then one day you appeared, Anya. I watched you sip your first taste of shark's fin soup, taking it all in your stride. In an instant I saw that you had exactly the essence . . . the element . . . that all of us, even Sergei, lack. You wouldn't see it of course, to you it's as natural as breathing. When you sit to eat, you eat calmly. Not like an animal expecting its food to be snatched away. Have you ever noticed that, Anya? How delicately you eat? And the rest of us, always shovelling our food down like we're running off to war. This is the girl who is going to lift me out of the mud, I told myself. This is the girl who can turn me from scum into a king.

'The day you first arrived in Shanghai, right after you lost your mother, you talked to me about a painting in Sergei's library. Do you remember? It was French Impressionist and you told me how the frame made all the difference to the painting. I couldn't see it until you formed a box with your hands and told me to look through your fingers. Later, the day after you lost your mother's necklace, you walked with me to the gate and pointed out that the asters were just starting to bloom in the garden. Anya, even when your heart is heavy, you talk about small details as if they were the most significant things in the world. Big things like money you rarely talk about. Or when you do, you talk about them as though they were unimportant.'

Dmitri started to pace the room, the colour heightened in his cheeks as he thought of more and more ways I had impressed him. I still had no idea where he was leading with his story. Did he want me to decorate his home? I asked him that and he clapped his hands, laughing until he had tears running down his face.

He rubbed his eyes, then calmed down and said, 'One day you got yourself lost in the world of my scum, and when Sergei came running half mad to tell me that, I went half mad too. Then we found you. Those pieces of shit had torn your clothes and scratched your skin with their filthy claws. But they didn't manage to lower you to their level. Even sitting there in the prison cell, wearing nothing but rags, you managed to be dignified.

'That night Sergei came to see me, crying so fiercely I thought that you had died. He loves you. Do you know that, Anya? You've opened a part of his heart that has been closed for a long time. If he'd had you, he never would have turned to opium. But it's too late now. He knows he's not going to live forever. And who's going to take care of you then?

'I wanted him to ask me to take care of you. But he was so protective of you, I was afraid he thought I wasn't good enough for you. That no matter how wealthy I became, no matter how much he said he loved me, I couldn't have you. That it made no difference what I wore or what I ate or to whom I talked, I would always be scum.

'I searched the backstreets of the Concession trying to find pieces of your mother's necklace. I was trying to be a man worthy of you. But the next day, as if by magic, you said you wanted to have dancing lessons with me. *With me*. My God, you caught me off guard with that request! And then I saw something that I had never considered before.

Right there in your cornflower blue eyes. *You* were in love with *me*.

'Sergei himself took one look at us dancing together and he knew it too. He saw himself and Marina, thirty years earlier. I understood that when he taught us the bolero, he was giving you to me. Even he couldn't stop what was happening naturally. History repeating.'

Dmitri hesitated there for I had risen out of my seat and was leaning against the window.

'Anya, please don't cry,' he said, rushing to my side. 'It wasn't my intention to upset you.'

I tried to speak but I couldn't. All I could do was make gagging sounds, like a child. My head was swimming. I had woken up expecting another normal day at school and suddenly Dmitri was telling me things I couldn't grasp.

'Isn't it what you want too?' he asked, touching my shoulder and turning me around to face him. 'Sergei said we can get married as soon as you turn sixteen.'

The room seemed hazy to me. I was in love with Dmitri, but his sudden proposal of marriage and the way he had gone about it left me bewildered and uncertain. He had prepared for it, but his words had hit me like an explosion. The clock on the mantelpiece struck twelve and startled me. I was suddenly aware of other sounds: the maids sweeping the hallways, a cook sharpening a knife, someone singing 'La Vie En Rose'. I stared up at Dmitri. He smiled at me through his bruised lips and my confusion gave way to a rush of love. Could it really be true that Dmitri and I were going to be married? He must have seen the change in my expression for he dropped to his knees.

'Anna Victorovna Kozlova, will you marry me?' he asked, kissing my hands.

'Yes,' I told him, half laughing, half crying. 'Yes, Dmitri Yurievich Lubensky, I will.'

*   *   *

In the afternoon Dmitri announced our engagement, and Sergei came out to see me in my spot near the gardenia tree. He took my hands in his own, tears in the corners of his eyes. 'What shall we do for a wedding?' he asked. 'If my beloved Marina was here . . . and your mother . . . what a time we would have!'

Sergei sat down next to me and together we looked up at the sunlight sparkling through the leaves of the trees. He pulled out a crumpled piece of paper from his pocket and smoothed it out on his knee. 'I've been carrying around this poem by Anna Akhmatova because it touched me,' he said. 'And now I want to read it to you.

> 'It was dawn when they took you. I followed,
> As a widow walks after the bier.
> By the icons – a candle, burnt hollow;
> In the bed-room – the children, in tears.
> Your lips – cool from the kiss of the icon,
> Still to think – the cold sweat of your brow . . .
> Like the wives of Streltsy, now I come
> To wail under the Kremlin's gaunt towers.'

When Sergei read those words my chest tightened and I began to cry, an eruption of the tears I had held in for years, crying so sharp and painful that I thought my heart and ribs would burst with it. Sergei wept too, his bear-like chest heaving with his own secret grief. He put his arms around me and we pressed our wet cheeks together. When our sobs subsided, we began to laugh.

'I'm going to make you the most beautiful wedding,' he said, wiping the back of his hand across his reddened mouth.

'I feel her in me,' I told him. 'And one day I know that I will find her.'

That night Amelia, Luba and I draped ourselves in long satin gowns. The men put on their best tuxedos. We all squeezed into the limousine and headed for the Moscow-Shanghai. Because of the fight the night before we had closed the club. Everything had been repaired but closing for one night was good for publicity. It was the only night we had the whole place to ourselves. Sergei flicked on a switch, sending a waterfall of light onto the dance floor. Dmitri disappeared into the office and returned a few moments later with a wireless. We all waltzed around the dance floor to 'J'ai Deux Amours', balancing our champagne glasses in our free hands and trying to sing like Josephine Baker. 'Paris . . . Paris,' crooned Sergei, his face pressed to Amelia's cheek. The light reflecting off his shoulders and circling his head made him look like an angel.

By midnight my eyes were beginning to droop. I slumped against Dmitri.

'I'll take you home,' he whispered. 'I think you've been worn out by too much excitement.'

On the doorstep Dmitri pulled me close and kissed me on the lips. The lushness of his mouth surprised me. The warmth of him sent tingles down my spine. He parted his lips, aroused, and probed my mouth with his tongue. I drank in the taste of him, sipping his kisses like champagne. Then the door opened behind us and the Old Maid yelled out. Dmitri stood back and laughed.

'We are getting married, you know,' he said to her. But she flashed her eyes at him and pointed with her sharp chin to the gate.

After Dmitri left, the Old Maid turned the lock and I made my way up the stairs, dabbing at the moisture Dmitri's kiss had left on my lips.

The air in my room was oppressive. The windows were open but the maids had drawn the curtains when they turned down the bed in order to keep the mosquitoes out. The heat trapped inside reminded me of a greenhouse. Thick and humid. A drop of sweat trailed down my throat. I turned off the light and opened the drapes. Dmitri was standing in the garden, looking up at me. I smiled and he waved. 'Goodnight, Anya,' he said, and turned back to the path and disappeared out of the gate like a thief. Happiness bubbled through me. Our kiss had felt like a good luck charm, sealing our union together. I stripped off my dress and flung it over a chair, enjoying the relief of air on my skin. I padded over to the bed and collapsed into it.

The night air remained sticky and motionless. Instead of kicking my sheets off I managed to twist myself up in them, spinning a tight cocoon around me. I woke in the early hours of the morning, hot and irritated. Amelia and Sergei were arguing downstairs, every word as clear as two glasses clinking, so still was the air.

'What are you doing, you old fool?' Amelia was saying, her voice slurred by alcohol. 'Why are you going to so much trouble for them? Look at all this stuff. Where have you been keeping it?'

I could hear the sound of cups against plates and cutlery being thrown on the table. Sergei answered, 'They are like our . . . like my children. This is my happiest moment in years.'

Amelia let out one of her high-pitched laughs. 'You know they are only getting married because they can't wait to *fuck* each other! If they really loved each other they would wait until she was eighteen.'

'Go to bed. I'm ashamed of you,' Sergei said, his voice raised but calm. 'Marina and I were the same age as Dmitri and Anya when we got married.'

'Oh yes. Marina,' said Amelia.

The house fell silent. A few minutes later there were footsteps in the hall and my door opened. Amelia appeared, a blur of black hair and a white nightdress. She stood watching me, unaware that I was awake. I shivered as if her gaze were a long, sharp fingernail tracing down my spine.

'When are you all going to stop living in the past?' she said in a low voice.

I tried not to twitch under her stare. I feigned a sleepy sigh and she retreated, leaving the door open behind her.

I waited until I heard the click of Amelia's bedroom lock before slipping out of bed and going downstairs. The floorboards were cool against my burning feet and my damp fingers stuck to the balustrade. The air smelled of lemon oil and dust. The first floor was dark and empty. I wondered if Sergei had gone to bed too, until I saw the flickering line of light coming from under the dining room door. I tiptoed across the hall and pressed my ear to the carved wood. Beautiful strains of music floated from the other side. A lilting melody, so intense and intriguing it seemed to enter my blood and sting my skin from underneath. I hesitated a moment before turning the door handle.

The windows had all been flung open and an old gramophone was perched on the sideboard. In the dim light I could see that the table was covered with boxes. Some of them had been opened, spilling out paper stuffing so yellow and cracked that it crumpled in my hands. Towers of plates and dishes were stacked according to pattern. I picked up one. It was edged in gold and stamped with a family crest. There was a moan. I looked up to see the outline of Sergei slumped in a chair by the fireplace. I grimaced, expecting to see the noisome blue flame rise around him. But Sergei wasn't smoking opium, and from that night on he never would again. His hand was hanging limply by his side and I thought he might be asleep. His foot was resting on the side of an open suitcase, out of which billowed something that looked like a puffy white cloud.

'Dvorak's Requiem,' he said, turning to look at me. His face was shadowed, but I could see the haggardness around his eyes and the mottled blue of his lips. 'She loved this part. Listen.'

I moved towards him and sat on the armrest of the chair, cradling his head in my arms. The music swelled around us. The violins and drums rose into a storm I longed would pass. Sergei's hand clenched mine. I pressed his fingers to my lips.

'We never stop missing them, do we, Anya?' he said. 'Life doesn't go on like they tell you it does. It stops. Only the days go on.'

I leaned over and ran my hand over the white object in the suitcase. It was silky to touch. Sergei tugged the lamp cord and in the brighter light I could see that I was clutching folds of fabric.

'Take it out,' he said.

I lifted the material up and saw that it was a wedding gown. The silk was old but well preserved.

Together Sergei and I laid the heavy dress out on the table. I admired the beading, and the swirls on the embroidered bodice reminded me of the spiralling suns of Van Gogh. I was sure I could smell the fragrance of violets lingering in the fabric. Sergei opened another suitcase and removed something wrapped in tissue paper. He laid the gold crown and veil at the head of the dress while I smoothed out the skirt. The train was trimmed with blue, red and gold satin bands. The colours of a noble Russian.

Sergei gazed at the dress, a memory of a happier past in his eyes. I knew what he was going to ask me even before he said it.

Dmitri and I were married shortly after my sixteenth birthday, amidst the heady fragrance of a thousand flowers. Sergei had spent the previous day searching out the city's finest florists and private gardens. He and the manservant had returned with a car loaded with exotic florals and cuts on their hands. They had transformed the entrance hall of the Moscow-Shanghai into an aromatic garden. Duchess de Brabant roses with their double-cupped blooms filled the air with a sweet raspberry scent. Clusters of canary-yellow Perle des Jardins, with a fragrance like freshly ground tea, burst out from their glossy dark green foliage.

In amongst the voluptuous roses, Sergei set elegant white calla lilies and lady's-slipper orchids. To this intoxicating mix he added pewter bowls piled with cherries, spiced apples and grapes, so that the overall effect was one of complete sensual abandon.

Sergei led me into the hall and Dmitri turned to look at me. When he saw me in Marina's wedding dress, a bouquet of violets in my hand, his eyes filled with tears. He rushed to me and pressed his clean-shaven face to my cheek. 'Anya, we are here at last,' he said. 'You are a princess and you have made me a prince.'

We were a stateless people. Our marriage meant little in the eyes of the endorsed church, or the foreign and Chinese governments. But through his connections. Sergei had been able to find a French official willing to act as a celebrant. Unfortunately, the poor man's hay fever was so bad he had to stop every few sentences to blow his inflamed nose. Later, Luba told me that the official had arrived early and upon seeing the beautiful roses had rushed towards them, inhaling their perfume like a thirsty man drinking water, although he knew the flowers would make him sick. 'It's the power of beauty,' she said, smoothing my veil. 'Use it while you can.'

While Dmitri and I exchanged vows, Sergei stood beside me, with Alexei and Luba a step behind. Amelia sat aloof by one of the false windows, looking like a carnation among the roses in her frilly red dress and hat. She sipped champagne from a fluted glass, her face turned towards the painted blue sky as if we were all on a picnic and she was admiring some other view. But I was so happy that day that even her peevish rudeness amused me. Amelia couldn't stand not being the centre of attention. But no one rebuked her or made comment. After all, she had dressed up and come. And for the little affection we could expect from Amelia, that seemed enough.

After we had taken our vows, Dmitri and I kissed. Luba

marched around us three times carrying an icon of Saint Peter, while her husband and Sergei cracked whips and shouted to keep evil spirits away. The official concluded the ceremony with a sneeze so strong that one of the vases toppled over. It smashed onto the floor, sending a scented river of petals floating towards our feet. 'I'm so sorry,' he apologised.

'No!' we all cheered. 'It's good luck! You have frightened the devil!'

Sergei prepared the wedding feast himself. He had arrived at the club's kitchen at five o'clock that morning, with armloads of fresh vegetables and meats from the market. His hair and fingers were tinged with the aromas of the exotic herbs he had ground to present before us a banquet of eggplant caviar, *solyanka*, steamed salmon and *dviena sterlet* in champagne sauce.

'My God,' said the official, his eyes ogling the food. 'I was always grateful to be born French and now I find myself wishing I were a Russian!'

'In Russia the mothers always feed the bride and groom at the wedding, like two baby birds,' Sergei said, carving slices of meat and placing them before Dmitri and myself. 'I am both of your mothers now.'

Sergei's eyes brimmed with happiness, but he looked tired. He was pallid and his lips were chapped. 'You've worked too hard,' I told him. 'Please rest. Let Dmitri and me take care of you.'

But Sergei shook his head. It was a gesture I had seen many times in the months leading up to our wedding. Sergei had abandoned his lost opium afternoons as easily as one might discard a hobby, and instead threw himself into preparing for the day. He worked from the first light of morning, always thinking of better and greater plans than those he had made the day before. He bought Dmitri and I an apartment not far from the house and refused to let either of us see it. 'Not until it's finished. Not until your wedding night,' he said. He claimed to have hired carpenters, but I suspected from the way he returned each day smelling of resin and sawdust that he was decorating it himself. Despite my urges to rest, he would not. 'Don't worry about me,' he said, brushing my cheek with his blistered hands. 'You can't imagine how happy I am. I feel life inside me, rushing in my veins, singing in my ears. It's as if she is here by my side again.'

We ate and drank until the small hours of the morning, singing traditional Russian songs and smashing our glasses on the floor to display defiance of anything that might try to harm our new marriage. When Dmitri and I were ready to leave, Luba brought me an armful of roses. 'Bathe in them,' she said, 'then give him the water to drink and he will love you forever.' Afterwards, Sergei dropped Dmitri and myself at the doorstep of our new apartment building and slipped the keys into Dmitri's hand. He kissed us and said, 'I have loved you both as if you were my own.'

After Sergei's car had disappeared down the street, Dmitri unlocked the frosted glass doors and we rushed through the foyer and up the staircase to the second floor. The building was two storeys and our apartment was one of three on the upper level. A gold nameplate was attached to the door: 'Lubensky'. I ran my fingertips over the cursive writing. That was my name now. Lubenskya. I felt excited and sad at the same time.

Dmitri showed me the key. It was a beautiful design. Wrought iron with a Parisian bow. 'For eternity,' he said. We clasped each other's fingers and turned the lock together.

The apartment's drawing room was large with high ceilings and tall windows facing onto the street. The windows were bare, but carved pelmets for drapes had already been set in place. On the outside of the glass I could see flower-boxes brimming with violets hanging from each sill. I smiled, pleased that Sergei had planted Marina's favourite flower. There was a fireplace and opposite it a comfortable-looking

126

French sofa. Everything smelled like polish and new fabric. My eyes rested on a glass display cabinet in the corner of the room and I walked across the *Savonierre* carpet to see what was in it. I peered through the glass and saw my matroshka dolls smiling back at me. I lifted my hand to my mouth and tried not to cry. I had wept many times over in the days leading up to our wedding, knowing that my mother would not be here to share the most important day of my life. 'He thinks of everything,' I said. 'Everything here has been done with love.'

I looked up, still clutching the roses to my bosom. Dmitri was standing in an arched doorway. Behind him I could see a hallway leading to a bathroom. The ceiling was low, like a doll's house, and both it and the walls were covered with floral paper. It reminded me of the garden Sergei had created for our wedding. I walked towards Dmitri and together we approached the bath. He took the roses from me and dropped them in the basin. For a long time we didn't say anything. We stood, looking into each other's eyes, listening to the rhythm of each other's breathing. Then Dmitri reached for my shoulders and slowly began undoing the clasps on my dress. My skin tingled with his touch. Although we had been promised to each other for a year, we had never been intimate. Sergei would not have allowed it. Dmitri tugged the dress forward over my shoulders and let it slip down my legs to the floor.

I filled the bath while Dmitri tore off his shirt and pants. I was mesmerised by the beauty of his skin, his broad chest with the spray of dark hair down the sternum. He stood behind me and lifted my petticoat above my waist, then over my breasts and head. I felt his penis push against my thigh. He took the flowers from the basin and together we sprinkled the petals over the surface of the water. The bath was cool on my skin but did nothing to dampen my desire. Dmitri slipped in beside me and took scoops of water in his hands and swallowed it.

In the bedroom there were two bay windows facing an inner courtyard. Like the windows in the drawing room they had pelmets but no curtains. A jungle of ferns in pots on the ledges provided privacy. Dmitri and I embraced. A puddle of water gathered on the floorboards around our feet. My flesh pressed against his burning skin made me think of two candles melting together.

'Do you think this is the kind of bed the nobility spent their wedding nights in?' he asked, his hands slipping into mine. The corners of his eyes crinkled with his smile. He tugged me towards the bronze bed and pushed me down onto the red coverlet. 'You smell like flowers,' I said, kissing a droplet from one of his eyebrows.

Dmitri slipped his arm around my shoulders and traced over my breasts with his fingertips. A ripple of pleasure ran from my neck to my toes. I felt Dmitri's tongue flick against my skin. I pushed my hands against his shoulders and tried to wriggle away, but his arms encircled me tighter. I thought of myself and my mother lying in a summer field, the smell of grass on our clothes and in our hair. She liked to pull off my shoes and tickle my feet. I would laugh and struggle against her, both ecstatic and uncomfortable with the pleasure of her touch. That was how I felt when Dmitri touched me.

Dmitri's hands moved down to my hips. His hair tickled my stomach when he slid himself between my legs. He pushed my knees open and I felt the blood rush to my face. In shyness I tried to close them, but he pressed my legs further apart and kissed the skin between my thighs. The scent of roses floated up around us and I opened up to him like a bloom.

A sound jolted us. The telephone was ringing. We sat up. Dmitri glanced over his shoulder, his eyes pensive. 'It's a wrong number,' he said. 'No one would call us now.'

We listened to the telephone ring out. When it didn't ring again, Dmitri lifted himself and pressed his face into my neck. I stroked his hair. It smelled like vanilla.

128

'Don't think about it,' he said, pulling me further up on the bed. 'It was a wrong number.' He paused above me, eyes half closed, and I drew him down. Our lips met. I could feel him pushing into me. I gripped the skin of his back. Something in my stomach fluttered, as if a bird was trapped there. The warmth of him burst into me, making lights dance before my eyes. I wrapped my legs around him and bit into his shoulder.

But long after Dmitri and I collapsed back into the rumpled bedsheets, and he fell asleep with his arm draped over my chest, the ring of the telephone echoed on in my mind. And I was filled with dread.

SIX

Requiem

The flutter of wings woke me the next morning. Through sleepy eyes I glimpsed the dove perched on the windowsill. Dmitri must have opened the window during the night because the bird was on the inside ledge, coaxing me from my dreams with her rhythmic cooing. I pulled the bed-covers aside and slipped into the chilly morning air. Dmitri's eyes flickered open and his hand fell to my hip. 'Roses,' he murmured. He lapsed back into deep sleep and I tucked his hand under the sheet again.

'Shoo!' I whispered to the bird, waving her away, but she skimmed through my fingers and landed on the dresser. She was the colour of a magnolia flower and tame. I stretched out my arm and made kissing sounds with my lips, trying to entice her to fly to me. But she darted through the dressing room and into the corridor. I snatched my robe from the hook on the door and dashed after her.

In the grey light the furniture that had looked so homely the night before suddenly seemed austere and formal. I studied the exposed stone walls, the furnishings, the polished wood, and wondered what had changed. The bird landed on a lampshade, almost losing her balance when it toppled from its stand. I closed the door to the corridor and opened one of the windows. The street outside was cobble-stoned and picturesque. Set between two stone cottages was a bakery. A bicycle was propped against the flyscreen

130

door and the light was on inside. After a few minutes a boy stepped through the door, his arms laden with bags of bread. He tossed them into a basket tied to the bicycle's handlebars and pedalled away. A woman in a floral dress and cardigan peered out the door after him, her breath making rings of steam in the frosty air. The dove swept over my shoulder and flew out the window of her own accord. I watched her tumble and swoop through the air, flying higher and higher above the rooftops until she disappeared into the cloudy sky.

The telephone rang and startled me. I picked up the receiver. It was Amelia.

'Get Dmitri!'

It was one of her orders. But instead of feeling annoyed at her intrusion, I was puzzled. She sounded even more highly strung than usual and out of breath.

Dmitri was already striding across the carpet, pulling on his pyjama shirt. His face was wrinkled with a sleepy frown.

I passed him the receiver. 'What is it?' he asked, his voice hoarse.

Amelia's muffled conversation through the receiver was incessant. I imagined she had arranged brunch at the Hotel Cathay or some other interruption, anything to prevent Dmitri and I enjoying our first morning as a married couple alone. I looked around for matches to light the fire and found a box on the bookshelf. I was about to light one when I caught sight of Dmitri out of the corner of my eye. His skin had turned alabaster.

'Calm down,' he was saying. 'You stay there in case he calls.'

Dmitri put down the receiver and stared at me. 'Sergei went out driving by himself last night and didn't come home.'

Pins and needles jabbed into my palms and the soles of my feet. At any other time I wouldn't have been so concerned. I would have assumed that Sergei was at the club sleeping off the previous day's festivities. But things had changed. Shanghai was more dangerous than ever. The civil war had sent Communist spies everywhere, and in the last week there had been eight assassinations of Chinese and foreign businessmen. The thought of Sergei in the hands of the Communists was too horrible to bear.

Dmitri and I searched the trunks the maids had packed for us. All we could find were summer clothes and light coats. We put them on, but as soon as we were outside a wind like a demon bit into our exposed fingers and faces and my bare legs. I shivered from the cold and Dmitri put his arm around me.

'Sergei never liked to drive,' he said, 'I don't understand why he didn't wake the servant to take him where he wanted to go. If he was stupid enough to drive out of the French Concession . . .'

I clenched Dmitri's waist, not wanting to imagine that Sergei had come to harm.

'Who was it that called last night?' I asked. 'Amelia?'

Dmitri winced. 'No, it wasn't her.'

I could feel the tremble under his skin. Dread fell over us like a dark cloud and we marched grimly onwards. Tears burned in my eyes. The first day of my marriage was supposed to be my happiest. Instead it was full of gloom.

'Come on, Anya,' said Dmitri, quickening his pace. 'He's probably asleep in the club and all this drama is for nothing.'

The doors to the entrance hall were locked, but when we tried the side door we found that it was open. Dmitri ran his palm down the jamb, looking for signs of a break-in, but there were none and we smiled at each other. 'I knew he would be here,' Dmitri said. Amelia had told him that she'd been ringing the club since the early morning, but if Sergei was sleeping off alcohol, or opium, he may not have heard the telephone.

The scent of roses in the foyer was overpowering. I

pressed my face to the dewy petals, drinking in their perfume. They were a pleasant memory.

'Sergei!' Dmitri called out. There was no response. I ran into the hall and followed him across the dance floor, my footsteps echoing in the vacant space. I was filled with sadness and couldn't understand why. The office was empty. Nothing had been disturbed except for the telephone. It was sprawled out on the floor. The base was cracked and the receiver cord was twisted around the leg of a chair.

We searched the restaurant, looking under the tables and behind the reception desk. We ran through the kitchen and the bathrooms, and even climbed the narrow staircase to the rooftop, but there was no sign of Sergei anywhere in the club.

'What now?' I asked Dmitri. 'At least we know it was Sergei who telephoned us.'

Dmitri rubbed his hand over his jaw. 'I want you to go home and wait for me there,' he said.

I watched Dmitri scramble down the stone steps and hail a rickshaw. I knew where he was going. He was heading for the slums and backstreets of the Concession, where I had once been robbed of my mother's necklace. And if he couldn't find Sergei there, he would head to West Chessboard Street where the stench of opium would still be trapped in the narrow alleys. The false shopfronts would be going up and the dealers would be packing away their wares for the day.

On my way back to the apartment I passed teashops, incense merchants and butchers opening up their businesses. When I reached the cobblestoned street at the rear of the building I found it deserted. There was no sign of the boy on his bicycle or his mother. I searched in my purse for the door key but something sweet made my nose itch and stopped me in my tracks. The scent of violets. I looked up at the window boxes but knew that the smell could not be coming from there.

133

I spotted the grille and bonnet of Sergei's limousine. It was poking out of a laneway between the bakery and a house. I wondered how Dmitri and I had missed it before. I ran across the street towards the car and saw Sergei sitting in the front seat, watching me. He was smiling, one hand resting on the wheel. I cried out with relief.

'We've been worried about you!' I said, throwing myself on the shiny bonnet. 'Have you been there all night?' From the angle of the bonnet the glary sky reflected in the windscreen and hid Sergei's face from me. I squinted at him, wondering why he didn't answer me. 'I've been thinking of nothing but Communists and assassinations all morning, and here you are!' I said.

There was no sound from the car. I slipped off the bonnet and squeezed between the wall and the passenger side. I wrenched the door open. A putrid smell hit me. The blood drained from my face. Sergei's lap was stained with vomit. He was sitting unnaturally still.

I reached for his face but it was cold and stretched like leather. His eyes were congealed. His top lip was curled back, baring his teeth. He hadn't been smiling at all.

'No!' I cried. 'No!' I clutched his arms, unable to comprehend the sight before me. I shook him. When he didn't respond, I grabbed him harder. It was as if I couldn't believe what I was seeing was real and if I just shook the corpse long enough it would turn into Sergei again. One of his hands clenched his knee, something shiny glinting in the curve of his fist. I prised open his fingers and managed to grasp the object. A wedding ring. I wiped at the tears in my eyes, trying to see the pattern that was engraved on it. A circle of doves flying on a band of white gold. I ignored the stench and rested my head on Sergei's shoulder, weeping. When I did so, I was sure I heard him speak to me. 'Bury me with it,' he said. 'I want to go to her.'

*   *   *

134

Two days later we gathered in the club's foyer for the funeral. The wedding roses were already turning brown at their tips, like the leaves outside. They drooped their heads as if in mourning. The lilies shrivelled and wrinkled like maidens fading into old women before their time. The servants added cloves and cinnamon to the floral display, so that the air became at once spicy and gloomy, reminding us that the darker months were on their way. They also burned vanilla beans, hoping the loam-like aroma would hide the smell that seeped from the carved oak coffin.

After discovering Sergei, I had called the manservant to help me take him back to the house. Dmitri met us there. Amelia called a doctor. He examined the body and pronounced death from a heart attack. Dmitri and I washed Sergei as lovingly as parents bathe a newborn and laid him to rest on a table in the front parlour, intending to call the undertaker the following day. But in the evening Amelia called us back to the house. 'The whole place smells of him. There is nowhere to escape.'

When we arrived, the house was engulfed in a fetid odour. We examined the body and saw red welts on the face and neck and that the hands were covered with purple spots. Sergei was putrefying in front of us, decaying much faster than normal. It was as though his body was willing itself to dissolve from this world as rapidly as possible, to return to dust without delay.

Autumn fell like a guillotine the day of the funeral, cutting us off from the last of the blue summer skies and cloaking us in hues of steely grey. A drizzly rain dampened our faces, and a wind that gathered strength from north and south blew in gusts and froze us to the bone. We buried Sergei in the Russian Cemetery, under the shadow of the orthodox crosses and amid the smell of rotting leaves and damp earth. I teetered at the edge of the grave, staring at the coffin that cradled Sergei like a womb. If Amelia had disliked me before Sergei's death, she hated me with a fierceness after it. She pressed herself against my side, nudging me with her shoulder as if she hoped I would fall into the grave too. 'You killed him, you selfish girl,' she whispered in a raspy voice. 'You worked him to his death. He was as strong as an ox until your wedding.'

Afterwards at the wake Dmitri and I gorged ourselves on ginger biscuits, longing to taste sweetness again in our numb mouths. Amelia had managed to distract herself in between funeral arrangements with trips to the races and shopping expeditions, while Dmitri and I had wandered like ghosts in the apartment, devoid of our senses of taste and smell. Every day we discovered on a bookshelf or in a cupboard some new object, a photograph in a frame, a trinket, an ornament, which Sergei had lovingly chosen for us. His intention had been to bring us joy each time we found one, but in the shadow of his death those objects pierced us like arrows. In bed we clung to each other, not as newlyweds but as drowning people, staring into each other's ashen faces and searching for answers.

'Don't blame yourselves,' Luba tried to comfort us. 'I don't believe he was afraid to disturb you on your wedding night. I think he knew he was going to die and wanted to be near you. You reminded him so much of himself and Marina.'

We never told Amelia that we buried Sergei with his wedding ring on his finger and that the grave next to his, with the Russian inscription and the two engraved doves, one living, one dead, was Marina's.

The day after the funeral, Alexei called us to his office for the reading of the will. It should have been a straightforward affair. Dmitri owned the apartment, Amelia would get the house, and the Moscow-Shanghai would be divided between them. But the way Luba hovered nervously, twisting the tie of her scarf and trembling when she served the tea, made me think something was wrong. Dmitri and I huddled together on the sofa while Amelia sank into a leather armchair by the window, her sharp features bathed in the frosty morning light. Her eyes were narrowed and once again she reminded me of a coiled snake about to strike. I understood the ferocity of her hate for me. It stemmed from her sense of self-preservation. Sergei had been much closer to me than anyone else for the past year.

Alexei kept us in suspense, shuffling papers around on his desk and taking his time to light his pipe. His movements were clumsy and slow, weighted down by the grief he felt for the man who had been his friend for over thirty years.

'I'm not going to draw this out,' he said at last. 'Sergei's final will, revoking all other previous wills and made the twenty-first day of August, 1947, is simple and plain.' He rubbed his eyes and put on his glasses before addressing Dmitri and Amelia. 'Although he loved you all equally and dearly, and you may be perplexed by his choice, his wishes are clear and exact: "I Sergei Nikolaievich Kirillov bequeath all my wordly belongings, including my house and all its possessions, and my business, the Moscow-Shanghai, to Anna Victorovna Kozlova."'

Alexei's words were met with stunned silence. Nobody moved. I think we were waiting for him to say something more, to make some qualifications. Instead he removed his glasses and said, 'That's it.' My mouth turned so dry I couldn't close it. Dmitri stood up and walked to the window. Amelia sank down into her chair. What had just taken place seemed unreal to me. How could Sergei, whom I loved and trusted, do such a thing to me? He had betrayed Dmitri for all his years of loyalty and made me his accomplice. My mind raced to think of a reason, but it made no sense.

'He made this will when Anya and I got engaged?' Dmitri asked.

'The date would indicate so,' said Alexei.

'The date would indicate so,' repeated Amelia, her face full of scorn. 'Are you not his lawyer? Did you not advise him on his will?'

'As you know, Amelia, Sergei has not been well for some time. I witnessed his will but I did not advise it,' Alexei replied.

'Do lawyers take wills from people they suspect to be not of sound mind and body? I think not!' Amelia spat, leaning across his desk. Her fangs were drawn and she was ready to strike.

Alexei shrugged. It gave the impression he was enjoying the sight of Amelia being undone.

'I believe Anya to be a young woman of impeccable character,' he said. 'As a wife she will share everything she has with Dmitri, and, as you have been so charitable to her, I'm sure she will show the same kindness towards you.'

Amelia sprang from her chair. 'She came here as a pauper,' she said, not looking at me. 'She was never meant to stay. We gave her charity. Do you understand? Charity. And he turns his back on Dmitri and me and gives her everything!'

Dmitri crossed the room and stood above me. He took my chin in his hand and looked into my eyes. 'Did you know anything about this?' he asked. I paled at the question. 'No!' I cried. He grasped my hand to help me off the sofa. It was the gesture of a loving husband, but as soon as our skin touched I felt his blood turn cold.

I did not miss the hate in Amelia's eyes as she watched us leave. Her expression was a knife in my back.

Dmitri did not utter one word to me on the way home. Nor did he say anything once we were in the privacy of our apartment. He spent the afternoon slouched on the window ledge, smoking and gazing at the street below. The burden of conversation fell to me and I was too weary to carry it. I cried, and my tears dripped into the carrot soup I prepared for supper. I cut myself when I sliced the bread and I let the blood drip into the dough. I thought that maybe if Dmitri tasted my grief he would believe in my innocence.

In the evening Dmitri sat rigid-backed, staring into the fire. He turned away from me, while I faced him full on, vulnerable and longing to be forgiven for something that wasn't my fault.

It wasn't until I rose to go to bed that he finally spoke to me. 'He didn't trust me in the end, did he?' he said. 'After all that talk about me being like a son, he still saw me as scum underneath. Not good enough to be trusted.'

The muscles in my back tensed. My mind was moving in two different directions at once. I was both relieved and terrified that Dmitri was finally talking to me. 'Don't think that way,' I said. 'Sergei adored you. It's as Alexei said: he wasn't of a right mind.'

Dmitri rubbed his hands over his haggard face. It hurt me to see the bitterness in his eyes. I longed to hold him, to make love with him again. I would have given anything to see desire instead of misery on his face. We had had only one night of real love and happiness. Since then everything had been a descent into decay and rot. Bitterness made our home reek the way Sergei's perishing corpse had pervaded the house with its smell.

'And what's mine is yours anyway,' I continued. 'You haven't lost the club.'

'Then why not have the decency to give it to the husband in the first place?'

We lapsed into hostile silence again, Dmitri moving back to the window and me retreating to the kitchen door. I wanted to shout out at the injustice of my situation. Sergei had lovingly prepared the apartment for us and then, with one sweep of his will, had turned it into a battlefield.

'I never understood his relationship with Amelia,' I said.

'Sometimes it seemed like they hated each other. Perhaps he was afraid of her influence on you?'

Dmitri turned to me with such spite in his eyes that it sent a chill through me. His hands clenched into fists. 'The worst of it is not what he has done to me, but what he has done to Amelia,' he said. 'She built that club up while he was busy soaking his brain with opium, lost in illusions of his glorious past. Without her he'd be just another rotting Russian lying in the gutter. It's easy to pick on her because she was born in the street, because she doesn't have fine aristocratic manners. But what do those manners really mean? Tell me who is more honest?'

'Dmitri,' I cried. 'What are you talking about? Who do you mean?'

Dmitri slid off the window ledge and strode to the door. I followed him. He had taken his coat from the closet, and was slipping it on.

'Dmitri, don't go!' I begged, and realised what I meant was: *'Don't go to her.'*

He fastened the buttons of the coat and tied the belt, oblivious to me.

'What has been done can be undone,' I said. 'We can divide the Moscow-Shanghai between the two of you. I'll legally give it to you and you can decide what you want to give to Amelia. Then both of you can run it as you always have, independent of me.'

Dmitri stopped buttoning his coat and glanced at me. The tautness in his face softened and my heart leaped with hope.

'That would be the decent thing to do,' he said. 'And to let her stay in the house, even if it is yours now.'

'Of course, I had no intention of doing otherwise.'

Dmitri stretched out his arms. I ran into them, burying my face into the folds of his coat. I felt him press his lips to my hair and I inhaled his familiar scent. It will be all right between us, I told myself. This will pass and he will love me again.

But the coldness was still there in his body. It was impenetrable, like armour between us.

The following week I was shopping on Nanking Road. There had been a reprieve in the weather after the bitter cold of the previous week and the street was packed with people enjoying the fragile rays of the midday sun. Businessmen poured out of their offices and banks for lunch; women with shopping carts greeted each other on street corners, and everywhere I turned there were street vendors. The smell of the vendors' spicy meats and roasting walnuts made me hungry. I was reading the menu in the window of an Italian café, deciding between *zuppa di cozze* and *spaghetti marinara* when suddenly there was a scream so shrill and dreadful it made my heart stop. People began to scurry in all directions, terror on their faces. I was jostled along with them. But the crowd was hedged in by two army trucks at each end of the block and I found myself jammed against a shop window, a heavy-set man pressing so hard against me that I thought my ribs would break. I slipped past him and into the writhing crowd. Everyone was struggling against each other, trying to stay away from whatever was happening on the street.

I was propelled to the front of the crowd and I found myself face to face with a group of Nationalist army soldiers. The soldiers were pointing their rifles at a line of young Chinese men and women kneeling in the gutter with their hands linked behind their heads. The students didn't seem frightened, only disorientated. One of the girls was squinting at the crowd and I noticed her glasses were caught in the collar of her jacket. They were cracked, as if they had been knocked from her face. Two army captains were standing off to the side, arguing with each other in hushed tones. Suddenly one broke away from the other. He strode up behind the first boy in the line, pulled a pistol from his belt and fired at the boy's head. The boy's face contorted with the impact of the bullet. A spurt of blood like a fountain shot up from the wound. He collapsed on the pavement, blood oozing around him. I was struck dumb with horror, but others in the crowd screamed or cried out in protest.

The captain moved rapidly along the line, executing each of the students as casually as a gardener picking off dead blooms. They dropped one by one, their faces twisting and twitching in death. When the captain reached the near-sighted girl, I ran forward without thinking, as if to protect her. He glared at me with savage eyes, and an English woman grabbed my arm and pulled me back into the crowd. She tucked my head against her shoulder. 'Don't look!' she said. The pistol fired and I wrenched away from the woman. The girl didn't die instantly like the others. It hadn't been a clean shot. Half the side of her head was blown away. A loose flap of skin was dangling by her ear. She fell forwards and dragged herself along the pavement. The soldiers followed alongside, kicking her and poking at her with their rifles. She whim-pered, 'Mama, Mama,' before becoming still. I stared at her lifeless form, the gaping wound on her head, and imagined a mother somewhere, waiting for a daughter who would never come home.

A Sikh policeman pushed through the crowd. He yelled at the soldiers and pointed to the bodies strewn on the pavement. 'You have no right to be here!' he shouted. 'This is not your territory.'

The soldiers ignored him and climbed back into their trucks. The captain who had done the killing turned to the crowd and said, 'Those who have sympathy for the Communists will die with the Communists. This is my warning: what I did to them, they will surely do to you if you let them into Shanghai.'

I hurried along Nanking Road, barely aware of where I was going. My mind was a jumble of images and sounds. I bumped into people and shopping carts, bruising my arms and hips and not noticing. I thought mostly of Tang. His twisted smile, his mangled hands, his need for revenge. I hadn't seen the ugliness of his hate in the eyes of those fresh-faced students.

I found myself in front of the Moscow-Shanghai and rushed inside. Dmitri and Amelia were in the office, examining the account books with their new lawyer, an American called Bridges. The air was heavy with their collective cigarette smoke and they were frowning in concentration. Although the tension between Dmitri and myself had faded, and even Amelia had been civil after she had realised I wasn't going to oust her from the house, it was only because of my desperation that I interrupted them so boldly.

'What is it?' asked Dmitri, getting out of his chair. His eyes were full of concern and I wondered what I looked like.

He helped me to sit down and brushed my hair away from my face. I was touched by his tenderness and blurted out what I had seen, stopping every so often to swallow the tears that choked me. They listened to my story intently and when I had finished were silent for a long time. Amelia tapped her long red nails on the desk, and Dmitri wandered to the window, jacking it open for air.

'These are not good times,' said Bridges, rubbing his sideburns.

'I believe Sergei,' said Dmitri. 'We survived the war and we will survive this.'

'The only wise words he had to offer,' Amelia scoffed, taking a fresh cigarette and lighting it.

'What about the rumours?' asked Bridges. 'We are hearing them more and more. And one day there is no bread, another day there is no rice.'

'What rumours?' I asked.

Bridges glanced at me, the hairy fist of one hand pressed against the palm of the other. 'They say that the Communist army has regrouped and is approaching the Yangtze, that all over the country Nationalist generals are deserting and joining forces with the Communists. That they plan to take Shanghai.'

I drew in a breath. A tremble travelled from my legs to my arms. I thought I was going to be sick.

'What are you frightening Anya for?' said Dmitri. 'Is this the time to be telling her such things? After what she has just seen?'

'It's nonsense,' said Amelia. 'The club is doing better than ever. It is full of British, French and Italians. It's only the lily-livered Americans who are getting nervous. So what if the Communists come? They want the Chinese, not us.'

'What about the curfew?' said Bridges.

'What curfew?' I asked.

Dmitri frowned at Bridges. 'It's only for the winter. To preserve fuel and other supplies. Nothing to worry about.'

'What curfew?' I repeated, looking from Bridges to Dmitri.

'We can only open four nights a week. And only until eleven-thirty,' said Bridges.

'A mere rationing precaution,' said Dmitri. 'It was more severe during the war.'

'Another American lily-livered act,' added Amelia.

'It's only for the winter,' said Dmitri. 'Nothing to worry about at all.'

The next day Luba came to see me. She was dressed in a cobalt blue suit with a corsage of posies pinned to the lapel. At first I felt awkward because Dmitri and Amelia had fired her husband as the club's lawyer, but Luba did not behave any differently towards me. 'Anya, look how pale and skinny you've become,' she said. 'We shall get you a proper meal. At my club.'

I invited her in and she brushed past me, glancing around the apartment as if she were looking for someone. She rushed over to the display cabinet and examined the dolls, then picked up a jade Buddha on the bookshelf and studied it, and ran her hands over the exposed stone walls.

Then I understood what she was looking for in the things she touched.

'I miss him like I miss my own father,' I said.

Her face twitched. 'I miss him too.'

Her eyes met mine and she turned away to look at a painting of the Chinese Gardens. The mid-morning sun was shining through the curtainless windows. It bounced off Luba's wavy hair, turning it into a halo. It reminded me of the way the light had flooded over Sergei's shoulders when he danced at the Moscow-Shanghai the night of our engagement party. Although Luba was part of our clique, I had never got to know her very well. She was one of those women who took so well to the role of being someone's wife that it was impossible to think of her as any more than an extension of her husband. She had always appeared a robust, fleshy doll on her husband's arm, smiling through gleaming gold teeth but never revealing her thoughts. Suddenly, in a moment, we had become allies, both of us daring to remember Sergei with affection.

'I'll get dressed,' I said. Then on impulse I asked her, 'Were you in love with him?'

She laughed. 'No, but I did love him,' she said. 'He was my cousin.'

Luba's club was off the Bubbling Well Road. It was stylish in a shabby kind of way. The curtains were elegant but faded and the oriental carpets were grand but worn. The floor-to-ceiling windows looked out over a rockery garden with a fountain and magnolia trees. The club attracted the well-to-do wives who couldn't get into the British clubs. It was full of German, Dutch and French women mostly about Luba's age. The dining hall was noisy with the babble of their conversations and the clanking of plates and glasses being whisked around on silver trolleys by Chinese waiters.

Luba and I shared a bottle of champagne and ordered chicken Kiev and Vienna schnitzel, with white chocolate cheesecake for dessert. I felt as if I were seeing her for the first time. Looking at her was like looking at Sergei. I couldn't believe that I hadn't noticed the similarities before. The same bear-like roundness. Her plump hands on her knife and fork were age-spotted but perfectly manicured; her shoulders were hunched but she held her chin high. Her skin looked pliant and well fed. She opened a compact and powdered her nose. There was a little splatter of pockmarks on her left cheek but her face was so neatly madeup that they were hardly noticeable. Although she wasn't anything like my real mother, there was something maternal about Luba that made me feel warmly towards her. Or perhaps it was because I saw Sergei living on in her.

'How come neither of you mentioned being cousins?' I asked after the main-course dishes had been cleared away.

Luba shook her head. 'Because of Amelia. Sergei wouldn't listen to us when we told him not to marry her. He was lonely and she was looking for an easy ride to luxury. As you know, the law in Shanghai is complicated for Russians. All the other foreigners are subject to the laws of their own countries but we are subject to Chinese laws on most things. We had to take whatever steps we could to protect my assets.'

Luba scanned the room for the waiter but he was busy taking orders at a large table of women. Not wanting to wait for service, she grabbed the neck of the champagne bottle and refilled our glasses.

'Anya, I have to warn you,' she said.

'Warn me about what?'

She smoothed the tablecloth with her hand. 'Alexei advised Sergei to make that new will, and to cut Dmitri out of it.'

My mouth dropped open. 'So Sergei wasn't in an irresponsible state of mind?'

'No.'

'That will nearly broke up my marriage,' I said, my voice

tightening. 'Why would your husband advise Sergei to do such a thing?'

Luba slammed her glass down, sending up a splash of champagne. 'Because Dmitri never listened to Sergei when he tried to warn him about Amelia. When they married, Sergei gave Amelia jewels and money. But he never promised her the Moscow-Shanghai. That wasn't meant for anybody until Dmitri came along. And yet somehow Amelia managed to convince Dmitri that they were going to share it after Sergei's death.'

I shook my head. I wasn't ready to tell Luba that I had signed over the club to Dmitri for that specific purpose. 'I still don't understand any of this,' I said.

Luba studied me for a moment. I sensed there was more to the story than she had revealed, but she wanted to make sure I was strong enough to hear it before continuing. I hoped she would decide that I wasn't. I couldn't bear to listen to any more.

The waiter arrived with the dessert trolley and placed between us the cheesecake we had ordered to share. When he left, Luba picked up a fork and cut into the creamy cake. 'Do you know what Amelia really wants?' she asked me.

I shrugged. 'We all know Amelia. She wants her own way.'

Luba shook her head. Leaning forward, she whispered, 'Not her own way. Not really. She wants people's souls.'

It sounded so melodramatic that I almost laughed, but something in Luba's eyes stopped me. I could feel my pulse in my throat.

'She devours them, Anya,' she continued. 'She had Sergei's soul before you came along and freed him. And now you're taking Dmitri away from her too. Do you think she's going to be pleased with that? Sergei's given you a chance to cut her out of your life like a cancer. Dmitri's not strong enough to do it. That's why Sergei left the club to you.'

I let out a little snort and took a bite of the cheesecake, trying to hide the terror that was starting to creep through my veins. 'Luba, you can't really believe that she wants Dmitri's soul. I know she's awful but she's not the devil.'

Luba dropped her fork onto her plate. 'Do you know what kind of woman she is, Anya? I mean, really know? Amelia came to China with an opium trader. When he was assassinated by a Chinese gang, she started pursuing a young American banker whose wife and two children were still in New York. He tried to break away from her, so she wrote a letter full of lies to his wife. The young woman filled a bath with hot water and slit her wrists.'

The cake's tangy sweetness turned bitter in my mouth. I remembered my first night at the Moscow-Shanghai and how one of the captain's wives had said that Amelia had ruined a good man's life.

'Luba, you're frightening me,' I said. 'Please just tell me what it is that you are trying to warn me about.'

A shadow seemed to pass over the room. My back stiffened. Luba shivered as if she had sensed the blackness too. 'She's capable of anything. I don't believe Sergei had a heart attack. I believe she poisoned him.'

I dropped my napkin onto the table and stood up, looking in the direction of the ladies' room. 'Excuse me,' I said, fighting the black specks that were swimming before my eyes.

Luba grabbed my wrist and pushed me back down into my seat. 'Anya, you are not a little girl any more. Sergei isn't here to take care of you now, you must face reality. You must rid yourself of that woman. She is a snake in waiting. Waiting to swallow you whole.'

SEVEN

The Fall

Dmitri's prediction that we would be untouched by the civil war was proved wrong by the end of November. Refugees from the countryside were pouring into Shanghai, struggling across frozen paddy fields and muddy roads, carrying all they could in rickshaws and wheelbarrows. There were too many of them to beg. They starved before our eyes, dropping dead in the streets like shrunken bundles of clothing. The slums swelled and every vacant building was invaded by squatters. In the streets they hovered over feeble fires and suffocated their children when they couldn't bear to see them suffer any longer. The stench of death mingled with the chilly air. People walked the streets with handkerchiefs over their noses; restaurants and hotels sprayed their interiors with perfumes and installed airlocks to keep the odours out. Every morning garbage trucks motored around the city, picking up the dead.

The Nationalist government continued to censor the newspapers, and all we read about were Paris fashions and cricket matches in England. Although inflation was crippling the economy, the trams and shopping strips were plastered with advertisements for new household appliances. The commercial moguls of Shanghai were trying to convince us that everything was normal. But they couldn't stop the whispers in cafés, theatres, libraries and drawing rooms. The Communist army was camped on the banks of the Yangtze, studying us. They were waiting out the winter, gathering their strength before they marched into Shanghai.

One morning Dmitri returned later than usual from the club. I hadn't accompanied him the night before because I was suffering from a bad cold. I was still feverish when I met him at the door. His face was haggard and forlorn. His eyes were bloodshot.

'What's the matter?' I asked, helping him with his coat.

'I don't want you to come to the club any more,' he said.

I wiped my nose with a handkerchief. I was nauseous so I sat on the sofa. 'What's happened?'

'Our clientele are too scared to come out at night. It's getting harder to cover our costs. The head chef has fled to Hong Kong and I have just had to pay someone half as good twice as much money to join us from the Imperial.'

Dmitri took a bottle of whisky and a glass from the cabinet and poured himself a drink. 'I'm going to have to lower our prices in order to attract more people . . . just until we get through this thing.' He turned to me. He stooped, like a man who has taken a blow. 'I don't want you to see it. I don't want my wife entertaining sailors and factory foremen.'

'Is it as bad as that?'

Dmitri slumped next to me. He laid his head in my lap and closed his eyes. I stroked his hair. He was only twenty, but the stress of the past few months had brought up a ripple of wrinkles on his forehead. I ran my finger over the bumps, smoothing them away. I loved the feel of his skin, strong and velvety, like good suede.

We both fell asleep and for the first time in a long time I dreamed of Harbin. I wandered towards the house and heard familiar laughter. Boris and Olga were standing by the fire with their cat. My father was pruning roses to go in a vase, a cigarette perched on the rim of his lip, his hands taking deft snips at the thorns and stems. He smiled when I passed by. Out of the window the green fields of my childhood spread out before me and I saw my mother standing by the river. I ran outside, the wet grass whipping at my feet. I was out of breath and crying by the time I touched the hem of her dress. She lifted her fingers to her lips, and then pressed them to mine. She faded and I blinked into the morning.

Dmitri was still asleep next to me on the sofa, his face squashed against the cushion. His breathing was deep and peaceful. Even when I gently kissed his eyelids, he didn't stir. I rubbed my cheek against his shoulder and then clasped my arms around him like a drowning person clinging to a log.

By the evening my cold had turned into a fever and my cough was so violent that I was spitting blood. Dmitri called a doctor who arrived just before midnight. The doctor's hair was a white cloud above his ruddy face and his nose resembled a mushroom. I thought he looked like a fairytale goblin when he warmed his stethoscope in his papery hands and listened to the rasp in my chest.

'You were foolish not to have called me sooner,' he said, dipping a thermometer into my mouth. 'Your chest is infected, and unless you promise to stay in bed until you are completely well, I will put you in hospital.'

The thermometer tasted of menthol. I sank back into the pillows, folding my arms across my aching rib cage. Dmitri crouched beside me, massaging my neck and shoulders to ease the pain. 'Anya, please get better,' he whispered.

For the first week of my illness Dmitri attempted to nurse me and take care of the club as well. But my cough cut into the few hours of sleep he tried to snatch in the late mornings and afternoons. The circles under his eyes and his pallid complexion alarmed me. We couldn't afford for him to get sick too. I hadn't got around to hiring a maid or a cook, so I asked Dmitri to send Mei Lin to look after me and suggested that he should try to get some rest at the house.

I was bedridden most of December. Each night brought fevers and bad dreams. I saw Tang and the Communists marching towards me. The farmer I had seen executed by the Japanese appeared nightly in my dreams, pleading with me with his mournful eyes. He'd reach out his hand and I would take it, but I couldn't feel his pulse and I knew that he was already condemned. Once, when I thought I was awake, I saw a young Chinese girl lying beside me, her broken glasses caught on her collar and her mangled head bleeding onto the sheets. 'Mama! Mama!' she wailed.

Sometimes I dreamed of Sergei and would wake up crying. I tried to test myself, to see if I could really believe that Amelia had poisoned him, but despite Luba's conviction, I simply couldn't. If anything, since Dmitri had made Amelia his partner at the club, she had been more cordial to me than ever. And when she had heard I was ill, she had sent her manservant over with a beautiful bunch of lilies.

By mid December Dmitri was spending most of his time at the club trying to keep it afloat. He had moved his things back to the house because it was easier for him to stay there. I was lonely and bored. I tried to concentrate on the books Luba brought me but my eyes tired quickly and I ended up spending hours staring up at the ceiling, too weak to even sit in a chair by the window. After three weeks, even though the fever had subsided and my cough had eased, I still couldn't make it from the bedroom to the sofa on my own.

Dmitri came to see me early on the Western Christmas Eve. Mei Lin, whose cooking skills were improving all the time, prepared deep-fried spiced fish and spinach.

'It's good to see you eating real food again,' Dmitri said. 'You'll be better before you know it.'

'When I'm better, I'm going to put on my best dress and knock them dead at the club. I'm going to help you like a wife should.'

152

Dmitri's face twitched, as though something had irritated his eyes. I looked at him and he turned away. 'That would be nice,' he said.

At first I was puzzled by his reaction. But then I remembered that he was ashamed of the new clientele. I don't care, I thought, I love you, Dmitri. I'm your wife and I want to be by your side, no matter what.

Later in the evening, after Dmitri had left, Alexei and Luba brought me a gift. I opened the box and found a cashmere shawl inside. The shawl was a delicate damson colour and I draped it over my shoulders to show it off for them. 'It's very becoming on you,' Alexei said. 'It's pretty against your hair.'

The Michailovs left and I watched them from the window walking down the street. Just before they turned the corner, Alexei hooked his arm around his wife's waist. The movement was easy and relaxed, the touch of confident affection that comes from having been intimate for years. I wondered if Dmitri and I would be like that one day, but the thought made me despondent. We had been married for just three months and already we were spending the festive season apart.

Things seemed much better the next day when Dmitri came to see me. He was grinning from ear to ear and patted me playfully on the hip. 'You should have seen it last night!' he said. 'It was almost like the old days. Everyone seems sick of this stupid war. The Thorns, the Rodens, the Fairbanks, they were all there. Madame Degas turned up with her poodle and asked after you. Everyone had a good time and agreed to come back on New Year's Eve.'

'I'm better now,' I told Dmitri. 'I've stopped coughing. When will you come back to the apartment?'

'I see that,' said Dmitri, kissing my cheek. 'After New Year's Eve. I have a lot to do until then.'

Dmitri tore off his clothes and ran a bath, ordering Mei Lin to bring him a whisky. I caught sight of my pale complexion in the hall mirror. There were black splotches under my eyes and the skin around my nostrils and lips was flaking. 'You look terrible,' I told my reflection. 'But whatever it takes, you must go to that party too.'

'*Give me a good field and I'll bring you golden wheat*,' I heard Dmitri sing in the bath. It was an old song about bringing in the harvest. His singing made me smile. Give me one more week's rest and a day at the beauty parlour, and I'll go to your party, I thought. Then I had an even better idea. I'd keep my intention a surprise until the last moment. My appearance would be a late Christmas gift to him.

The steps of the Moscow-Shanghai were deserted when I arrived there on New Year's Eve. It was a blustery night and there was no red carpet or gold-braid rope set out for a glittering crowd. The two marble lions seemed to stare down at me when I stepped out of the taxi and onto the icy steps. A damp wind ruffled my hair. It irritated my windpipe and I started to wheeze, but nothing was going to stop me from seeing my surprise through. I clutched the collar of my coat and ran up the steps.

I was relieved to see hordes of people in the foyer, filling the white space with colour. Their laughter echoed off the chandelier and gilded mirrors. I lapped up the sight of them. I could only imagine the down-market patrons Dmitri had said he had entertained to keep the club going, because the people I saw tugging off layers of fine wools and silks and handing them to the cloak-girls were the old crowd. You could taste their scent in the air: oriental perfume, fur, good tobacco and money.

I checked in my coat and noticed a young man watching me. He was leaning on the counter, a glass of gin balanced in his fingers. The man's eyes flitted over my dress and he gave me a smile that was more like a wink. I was wearing the emerald green cheongsam, the dress I had worn the first time I had visited the club. I wore it as a good luck charm, for the Moscow-Shanghai and for myself. I slipped past my admirer and searched for Dmitri.

I was almost crushed in the crowd heading for the ballroom. On stage, a black band in aubergine suits were playing hard jazz. The musicians were sharp-looking. Their straight teeth and ebony skin glistened under the lights. The floor was packed with people shaking to the squeals of the trumpet and saxophone. I caught sight of Dmitri by the stage door, talking to a waiter. He had cut his hair. It was short above the ears and across his forehead. The style made him appear younger. It amused me to think that we had both gone back in time, me in my dress and Dmitri with his short hair. The waiter left and Dmitri glanced in my direction but didn't recognise me until I moved closer. When he did, he frowned. I was taken aback by his displeasure. Amelia rushed up to him and said something. But when he didn't react she followed his gaze to where I was standing. A look of suspicion passed over her face. But what did she have to be suspicious of in me?

Dmitri pushed his way towards me. 'Anya, you should be at home,' he said, clutching my shoulders as if I were on the verge of collapse.

'Don't worry,' I said. 'I'll only stay until midnight. I wanted to support you.'

Dmitri still didn't smile. He only shrugged and said, 'Come on then. Let's get a drink in the restaurant.'

I followed him up the stairs. The maître d'hôtel seated us at a table overlooking the floor. I noticed Dmitri glance at my dress.

'Do you remember it?' I asked.

'Yes,' he said, his eyes glistening. I thought for a moment that he had tears in them, but it was just a trick of the light.

The waiter brought us a bottle of wine and filled our glasses. We ate two small *blinis* with caviar and sour cream. Dmitri leaned over and touched my hair. 'You're a beautiful girl,' he said.

A ripple of pleasure ran through me. I moved closer to him, aching with hope for the happiness that had escaped us since Sergei's will. We are going to be all right, I told myself. Everything is going to be better from now on.

He looked away from me and studied his hands. 'I don't want there to be lies between us, Anya.'

'There are no lies,' I said.

'Amelia and I are lovers.'

My breath caught in my throat. 'What?'

'It wasn't intentional. I loved you when I married you,' Dmitri said.

I edged away from him. Goosebumps sprang up on my chest and arms. 'What?' My insides twisted. My senses started deserting me one by one. The music slowed down, my vision became blurry, I gripped my wine glass but I couldn't feel it.

'She's a woman,' he said. 'Right now that's what I need. A woman.'

I stood up from the table, knocking over my glass. Red wine splashed across the white cloth. Dmitri didn't notice. The space between us became distorted. Instead of being at the same table we seemed to be on separate sides of the room. Dmitri was smiling to himself. The stranger who had once been my husband wasn't looking at me. He was miles away. A man in love with somebody else.

'There's always been something there,' he said, 'but it took Sergei's death to open the door.'

The twisting sensation inside me turned into a crushing pain. If I walk away, none of it will be true, I told myself. I turned my back on Dmitri and edged my way through the tables. People looked up from their meals or stopped mid-sentence to stare at me. I tried to hold my head high, to look like the perfect hostess, but tears mixed with face powder ran down my cheeks. 'Are you all right?' a man asked me. 'Yes, yes,' I said, but my knees buckled under me. I clutched at the passing drinks waiter. We toppled over together, a champagne glass splintering beneath me.

Some time later I came to and found myself in the apartment with Mei Lin tweezing pieces of glass out of my shoulder. She had numbed the area with ice, but my entire shoulder had swollen into a plum-coloured lump. The cheongsam hung over a chair by the cupboard; the bloodstained hole on the sleeve looked like a gunshot wound. Dmitri watched us from beside the fireplace.

'If it's clean,' he told Mei Lin, 'bind it up and we'll call the doctor tomorrow.'

The girl stared at him, sensing that something was wrong. She pressed a wad of cotton gauze to the wound and secured it with a bandage. When she'd finished she gave Dmitri one final glare before scuttling away.

'She's becoming insolent, that little one. You shouldn't spoil her so much,' he said, pulling on his coat.

I stood up and swayed like a drunk woman. 'Dmitri! I'm your wife!'

'I've explained the situation to you,' he said. 'I have to get back to the club.'

I leaned against the door, unable to comprehend what was happening. How could Dmitri be doing this? How could Dmitri say he was in love with *her*? *With Amelia?* My face pinched and I started to cry. The tears were so savage against my inflamed ribs that I gasped for breath.

'Come on,' said Dmitri, trying to move past me. I blinked through my tears at him. There was a hardness in his face that I had not seen before. I knew then that all the tears in the world would not change anything.

One illness gave way to another. Mei Lin tried to make me eat breakfast the next morning, but I couldn't keep down even a mouthful of scrambled eggs. A broken heart was much worse than a fever. Every part of me ached with pain. I could barely breathe. Dmitri had betrayed me and left me alone. I had no one. No father, no mother, no guardian, no husband.

Luba was at the door less than an hour after I called her. Her hair was usually impeccably groomed, but this morning strands were sticking up at the back. One side of her dress collar was tucked into her neckline. I felt a strange sense of comfort when I saw my confusion reflected in her appearance.

She took one look at me and rushed to the bathroom, returning with a damp washcloth and wiping my face.

'The worst thing about this is that you tried to warn me,' I said.

'When you've had a rest and something to eat,' she said, 'you will see things are not as bad as they seem.'

I closed my eyes and clenched my fists. How could things be worse? Wasn't it Luba who had told me that Amelia had driven a woman to suicide and that she had some sort of dark influence over Dmitri's soul?

'You won't believe me,' she said, 'but now that it's happened, I can see there are a lot of things in your favour. Things I didn't consider before.'

'I did everything Sergei tried to protect me from,' I said, sinking down onto the sofa. 'I gave them the club.'

Luba sat down next to me. 'I know, but the club's the club, and with the war on who knows what will happen to it. The important thing is that you still own the house and everything in it.'

'I don't care about the house or the money,' I said, beating my sore chest with my fist. 'When you warned me, I thought you meant Amelia was after my money, not my husband.' I took a painful breath. 'Dmitri doesn't love me any more. I'm all alone.'

'Oh, I think Dmitri will come to his senses,' said Luba. 'He won't want an immoral American for a wife. He's more vain than Sergei ever was. He'll come to his senses sooner or later. Besides, she's almost ten years older than him.'

'What good will that do me?'

'Well, he can't marry her unless he divorces you. And I can't see him doing that. Even if he tried to, you could fight it.'

'He loves her,' I said. 'He doesn't want me. That's what he told me.'

'Anya! Do you think that she really wants him? He's a boy. She's manipulating him to get back at you. And he's all muddled with stress and grief.'

'I don't want him. Not after he's been with her.'

Luba put her arm around me. 'Cry, but not too much. It would be hard to be a married woman and not under-stand the nature of men. They find something to amuse themselves with in the most unlikely of women, then suddenly one day it's all over and they're back on your doorstep as if nothing ever happened. Alexei gave me so much grief when we were young.'

I cringed at her detached practicality, but I knew that she was trying to comfort me and that she was the only ally I had left.

'I'll make a lunch booking for us at the ladies' club,' she said, patting my back. 'A meal and a drink will make you feel better. Everything will work out, Anya, if you behave calmly.'

Going out was the last thing I felt like doing, but I obeyed Luba when she insisted that I bathe and get dressed. I knew what she was trying to do. If I stayed in the apartment I would be finished. Anything that stopped in Shanghai was doomed. Sick beggars who fainted in the street perished in Shanghai, along with deserted babies and exhausted rick-shaw boys. Shanghai was only for the strong. And the secret of survival was to keep moving.

I made it through the weeks after the demise of my marriage by shutting down. I did not allow myself the indulgence of thinking. If I thought about what had happened, I stopped.

As soon as I stopped I could feel myself dying inside, just as a soldier who has stopped moving feels himself freezing in the snow. I tried to believe what Luba had said about Dmitri and Amelia's affair being a temporary liaison, that they didn't truly love each other. That illusion vanished the day I saw them together.

I was on the Bund, looking for a rickshaw to take me home after lunch with Luba. My head was light with the champagne I had been drinking to ease my loneliness. The weather was cold and I was wearing my full-length fur coat with the hood on, my scarf pulled up around my face. My heart almost stopped when I saw the familiar limousine pull up to the kerb just a metre away from me. Dmitri stepped out. He was so close to me and didn't know it. I could have brushed my finger down his cheek if I wanted to. The sound of the traffic faded and he and I seemed alone, trapped in time. Then he reached inside the car. I flinched when I recognised the gloveless, sharp-nailed fingers that clasped his hand. Amelia slipped out, wearing a red cape with a sable wrap around her throat. She looked like a beautiful demon. I died inside when I saw the admiration on Dmitri's face. He hooked his arm around her waist with the same intimate touch I had seen Alexei give Luba on Christmas Eve. Dmitri and Amelia disappeared into the city crowd, and I disappeared some-where inside myself. Something told me that the Dmitri I knew was dead and I was a sixteen-year-old widow.

I slipped into a pattern of sleeping late into the morn-ing. Around one o'clock I would take a rickshaw to Luba's club and linger over my food, letting lunch spill into high tea. In the afternoons there was jazz or Mozart in the main foyer, and I would listen to it until the sun went down and the waiters began dressing the tables for dinner. I would have stayed for that meal too, if I hadn't been so self-conscious. I was the youngest woman by at least five years. I'd even had to lie about my age on the membership form so that I could go to the club without Luba accompanying me.

One day, I was sitting at my usual table and glancing through the *North China Daily News*. There was nothing about the progress of the civil war in the paper, except to say that the Nationalists and Mao Zedong were attempting a truce. A truce between such opposing forces was unlikely. I could never be sure what was true and what was propaganda in those days. I looked up from the paper and glanced out the window at the winter-bare rockery. I saw someone watching me in the reflection. I turned to see a tall woman in a floral dress, a matching scarf knotted around her throat.

'I am Anouck,' the woman said. 'You are here every day. You speak English?' Her own English was heavy, weighed down by a Dutch accent. She glanced at the chair opposite me.

'Yes, a little,' I said, gesturing for her to sit down.

There were wisps of gold in Anouck's brown hair and her skin seemed naturally tanned. Her mouth was the only thing that marred her prettiness. When she smiled her top lip disappeared. It made her look severe. Nature was cruel. It created loveliness and then spoiled it.

'No, you speak it well,' she said. 'I've heard you. A Russian with a slight American accent. My husband . . . he was American.'

I picked up the 'was' in her sentence and studied her more closely. She couldn't have been more than twenty-three. When I didn't react, she said, 'My husband . . . he is dead.'

'I'm sorry,' I said. 'Was it the war?'

'I sometimes think so. And your husband?' she asked, pointing to my wedding ring.

I blushed. She had seen me at the club more often than was seemly for a young woman with a husband. I glanced down at the intertwined gold bands and cursed myself for not having taken the ring off. Then I saw her mouth twitch and I caught on. We were both smiling but it was impossible to miss that we shared the same afflicted look in our eyes.

'My husband . . . he is . . . dead too,' I said.

'I see,' she said, smiling.

Anouck proved to be a lively distraction. My appearance at the club became less frequent after she introduced me to other young 'widows'. Together we filled our days with shopping and our nights with dinners at the Palace Hotel or the Imperial. The other women spent their cheating husbands' money by the handful. Anouck called it 'the womanly art of revenge'. The money I had was mine, and I had no desire for revenge. But like the other women I wanted to escape the pain and humiliation my husband had caused me.

Anouck convinced me to join the 'language and culture afternoons' at the American consulate. Once a week, the consul-general invited foreigners to mingle with staff in the elegant drawing room of his house. For the first hour we would speak in English, discussing various artistic movements and literature. Never politics. Afterwards we would pair off with whichever staff member wished to learn our native language. Some of the participants were very serious about the lessons, but for most of us it was an excuse to meet people and gorge ourselves on the pecan pies that were served at each meeting. The only American who signed up to learn Russian was a tall, gangly young man named Dan Richards. I liked him the moment I set eyes on him. He had ginger hair, curly and closely cropped. His skin was freckled and his pale eyes were ringed by fine lines, which became deeper when he smiled.

'*Dobryy den*, Mrs Lubensky,' he said, shaking my hand. '*Minya zavut* Daniel.' His pronunciation was terrible, but his earnestness was so charming that I found myself smiling sincerely for the first time in a long time.

'Do you want to be a spy?' I teased him.

His eyes flashed with surprise. 'No, I've hardly got the nature for it,' he said. 'My grandfather was a diplomat in Moscow before the Revolution. He spoke highly of the Russians and I have always been intrigued by them. So when Anouck announced that she was bringing her lovely Russian friend, I decided to ditch the old gargoyle who has been trying to teach me French grammar and take up Russian instead!'

The language and culture afternoons became something to live for through the dreary, drizzly onset of spring. Dan Richards was funny and charming, and I regretted that we were both married for I could have easily fallen in love with him. His jokes and his gentlemanly demeanour helped me to forget Dmitri a little. He spoke of his pregnant wife with such fondness and respect that he made me want to trust someone. Listening to him, I could believe in the possibility of love again. I started to feel like the person I had been before my mother was taken away, someone who believed that people were good.

Then one afternoon Dan was late for his lesson. I watched the other groups engaged in their conversations and tried to occupy myself by memorising the names and dates of the presidents whose dour-faced portraits hung on the walls. When Dan arrived he was out of breath. There were beads of rain in his hair and on his eyelashes and his shoes were scuffed. He rubbed his hands nervously over his knees and forgot words a minute after I pronounced them for him.

'What's the matter?' I asked him.

'It's Polly. I've just sent her back to the States.'

'Why?'

He rubbed his lips together as if his mouth were dry. 'The political situation here has become too uncertain,' he said. 'When the Japanese invaded they stuck plenty of American women and children in camps. I'm not taking

163

any chances. If you were my wife I would send you away too,' he said.

I was touched by his concern. 'We Russians have nowhere to go,' I told him. 'China is our home.'

He glanced about the room before bringing his face close to mine. 'Anya,' he said, 'this is confidential information but Chiang Kai-shek is about to abandon the city. The American government has told us that they will not be giving the Nationalist government any more help. Our weapons have been falling into the hands of the Communists each time one of the Nationalist generals decides to cross over to the other side. The British have instructed their citizens to stand by their businesses. But we've outdone our stay in China. It's time for us to go.'

Later, during the cakes and refreshments, Dan slipped a note into my hand and pressed it there. 'Think about it, Anya,' he said. 'A Cossack named Grigori Bologov has been negotiating with the International Refugee Organisation to get your people out of Shanghai. There is a ship leaving soon for the Philippines. If you stay, the Chinese Communists will send you to the Soviet Union. The last group of Shanghai Russians who returned there after the war were executed as spies.'

I ran home in the rain, clutching Bologov's address in my hand. I was depressed and frightened. Leave China? Where would I go? Leaving China would be abandoning my mother. How would she ever know where to find me? I thought of the happy and pregnant Mrs Richards, safely on her way back to America and soon to be joined by a kind-hearted, faithful husband who loved her. How random a thing was fate. Why had I been destined to meet Dmitri? I placed my hands on my flat stomach. I no longer had a husband, but perhaps I could be happy again with a child. I imagined a little girl, dark-haired and with amber eyes like my mother.

The apartment was gloomy. Mei Lin wasn't there and I

assumed she must have gone shopping or be taking a nap in the maid's room. I closed the door behind me and started taking off my coat. A chill prickled my neck. The spicy smell of tobacco stung my nose. I squinted at the shadow on the sofa until it took form. Dmitri. The red tip of his cigarette glowed like a coal in the blackness. I stared at his faint outline, trying to decide if he was real or an apparition. I switched on the light. He glanced at me but said nothing, drawing in and out on the cigarette as if he couldn't breathe without it. I walked into the kitchen and put the kettle on the stove. The steam hissed from the spout and I made myself a cup of tea without offering him anything.

'I put the rest of your things in a trunk in the hall closet,' I told him. 'In case you were wondering why you couldn't find them. Lock the door when you go.'

I shut the bedroom door behind me. I was too tired for words and in no mood to be hurt any more by Dmitri. I kicked off my shoes and tugged my dress over my head. The room was cold. I slipped under the bedcovers and listened to the rain. My heart was thumping in my chest. But I wasn't sure if it was Dmitri or Dan who had caused that. I stared at the clock on the bedside table, the gold miniature that the Michailovs had given us on our engagement. An hour passed and I assumed Dmitri must have left. But just as my eyes began to droop, I heard the bedroom door open and Dmitri's step on the floorboards. I rolled on my side, feigning sleep. I held my breath when I felt the weight of his body sink into the mattress. His skin was like frost. He rested his hand on my hip and I turned to stone.

'Go away,' I said.

His hand gripped tighter.

'You can't do what you did and then come back.'

Dmitri didn't say anything. His breathing was the sound of a man spent. I pinched my arm until the skin bled.

165

'I don't love you any more,' I said.

His hand moved across my back. The skin was no longer soft like suede. It was sandpaper. I slapped him away but he clasped my cheeks in his hands, forcing me to face him. Even in the darkness I could see his gauntness. She had taken him whole and returned him empty.

'I don't love you any more,' I said.

Hot tears dripped onto my face. They burned into my skin like sulphur.

'Whatever you want, I'll give it to you,' he sobbed.

I pushed him away from me and struggled out of the bed. 'I don't want you,' I said. 'I don't want you any more.'

Dmitri and I ate breakfast the next morning at the Brazilian café on Avenue Joffre. He sat with his legs stretched out in the streak of sunshine gleaming through the window. His eyes were closed and his mind seemed far away. I picked out the mushrooms from my omelette with a fork, saving them for last. *Mushrooms in the woods lie hidden like secret treasures, waiting for eager hands to pluck them.* I remembered my mother singing to me. The café was empty except for the moustached waiter who hovered at the counter, pretending to clean it. The air smelled of wood, oil and onions. Even now, whenever I come across that combination of aromas, I remember the morning after Dmitri came back to me.

I wanted to know if he had come back to me because he loved me or because things had gone wrong with Amelia. But I couldn't bring myself to ask him. The words lay on my tongue like a foul taste. The uncertainty was a barrier between us. To talk of her was to conjure her up, and I was too afraid to do that.

After a while he sat up and rolled his shoulders. 'You have to move back to the house,' he said.

The thought of even seeing the house made my stomach

166

turn. I didn't want to live in the place where Dmitri had been with Amelia. I did not want to see betrayal in every piece of furniture. I baulked at the idea of sleeping in my old bed after it had been defiled.

'No, I don't want to,' I said, pushing my plate aside.

'It's safer at the house. And for now that's what we have to think about.'

'I don't want to go to the house. I don't even want to see it.'

Dmitri rubbed his face. 'If the Communists storm the city, they will come to the Concession via your street first. The apartment has no protection. At least the house has the wall.'

He was right, but I still didn't want to go. 'What do you think they will do if they come?' I asked. 'Will they send us to the Soviet Union like they did to my mother?'

Dmitri shrugged. 'No. Who will make money for them? They will take over the government and seize Chinese businesses. It's the looting and rioting I'm concerned about.'

Dmitri stood up to go. When he saw that I was hesitant he reached out his hand. 'Anya, I want you to be with me,' he said.

My heart dropped when I saw the house. The garden was muddy from the rain. No one had bothered to prune the rosebushes. They had turned into menacing vines snaking up the walls, digging their tentacles into the window frames and leaving brown scars on the paint. The gardenia tree had lost all its leaves and was nothing more than a stick poking up through the ground. Even the soil in the beds looked clumped and dejected: no one had planted bulbs for spring. I heard Mei Lin singing in the laundry and realised that Dmitri must have moved her to the house yesterday.

The Old Maid opened the door and smiled when she saw me. The expression transformed her sunken eyes. For a moment she looked radiant. In all the years I had known her she had not smiled at me once. Suddenly, as we were balanced on the brink of disaster, she had decided to like me. Dmitri helped her drag my suitcases into the entrance and I wondered when the other servants had left.

The walls of the drawing room were bare, all the paintings were gone. There were holes where the light fittings had been removed.

'I stored them away. To be safe,' Dmitri said.

The Old Maid opened the trunks and started carrying my clothes up the stairs. I waited until she was out of earshot before I turned to Dmitri and said, 'Don't lie to me. Don't lie any more.'

He flinched as if I had struck him.

'You sold them to keep the club. I'm not stupid. I'm not a little girl, despite what you think. I'm old, Dmitri. Look at me. I'm old.'

Dmitri slipped his hand over my mouth and held me against his chest. He was exhausted. Old too. I could feel it through his skin. His heart was barely beating. He clutched me, pressing his cheek against mine. 'She took them when she left.'

The words stung like a slap. My heart bore down on my rib cage. I thought it might burst into the pit of my stomach. So *she* had left *him*. He hadn't chosen me over her at all. I pulled away from him and sank back against the sideboard. 'Is she gone?' I asked.

'Yes,' he said, watching me.

I sucked in a breath, teetering between two worlds. One where I took my suitcases and headed back to the apartment, and the other where I stayed with Dmitri. I pressed my palms against my forehead. 'Then we will put her behind us,' I said. 'She is out of our lives.'

Dmitri fell against me and wept into my neck.

'"She", "Her", "Gone". That's how we will talk of her now,' I said.

*   *   *

168

The Nationalist army tanks roared through the city day and night and the street-corner execution of Communist supporters became a daily occurrence. Once, on my way to the markets, I passed four severed heads spiked on street signs and didn't even notice until a girl and her mother behind me screamed. In those last days the streets always smelled of blood.

The new curfew limited us to opening the club only three nights a week, which was a blessing in a way because we were short-staffed. All our top chefs had left for Taiwan or Hong Kong and it was hard to find any musicians who were not Russian. But on the nights we did open, the old patrons were there in their finery.

'I'm not going to let a bunch of disgruntled peasants spoil my fun,' Madame Degas told me one evening, taking a long drag through her cigarette holder. 'They'll spoil everything if we let them.' Her poodle had been run over by a car, but she had stoically replaced it with a parrot named Phi-Phi.

Her sentiment was reflected in the faces of the other patrons who stayed on in Shanghai. The British and American businessmen, the Dutch shipping merchants, the nervous Chinese entrepreneurs. An obsessive kind of joie de vivre kept us going.

Despite the mayhem in the streets outside, we drank cheap wine as if it were vintage stock and nibbled at cubes of ham the way we once ate caviar. When there were blackouts, we lit candles. Dmitri and I waltzed on the dance floor every night like newlyweds. The war, Sergei's death and Amelia had all come to seem a strange dream.

On the evenings the club was closed, Dmitri and I stayed at home. We read to each other or listened to records. In the midst of the disintegration of the city we had become a normal married couple. Amelia was nothing more than a ghost in the house. Sometimes I caught a whiff of her scent on a cushion or found a sleek dark hair on a brush or tile.

169

But I never saw her or heard from her, until one evening, several weeks after I had moved back into the house, when the telephone rang and the Old Maid answered it. In the absence of the manservant the old woman had taken to speaking English and answering the telephone like a butler. I could tell who the caller was by the way the Old Maid shuffled into the room, nervously avoiding my glance. She whispered something to Dmitri. 'Tell her I am not at home,' he said. The Old Maid returned to the hall and was about to deliver the message when Dmitri called out loud enough so that Amelia would have heard him: 'Tell her not to call here again.'

The next day Luba sent me an urgent message to meet her at the club. We hadn't seen each other for a month and when I found her sitting in the foyer in a smart hat but with a face as drawn as a dead woman's, I almost cried with the shock of it.

'Are you all right?' I asked her.

'We are leaving the house,' she said. 'We depart for Hong Kong tonight. This is the last day for exit visas. Anya, you must come with us.'

'I can't,' I told her.

'It will be impossible for you to get an exit visa otherwise. Alexei has a brother in Hong Kong. You can pose as our daughter.'

I had never seen Luba in such an overwrought state. She had been my voice of calm through my marriage crisis. But when I looked at the other women in the room, the few regulars who were left, all of them had the same panic-stricken eyes.

'Dmitri came back to me,' I said. 'I know he won't leave the club and I must stay with my husband.' I bit my lip and stared at my hands. Another person was slipping away from me. If Luba left Shanghai, we weren't likely to meet again.

She opened her handbag and pulled out a handkerchief.

'I told you he would come back,' she said, dabbing at her eyes. 'I'd help you both to get out, but you're right about Dmitri. He won't leave the club. I wish he was still friends with my husband. Alexei might have been able to convince him to leave.'

The maître d'hôtel called us to say our usual table was ready. After he seated us, Luba ordered a bottle of the best champagne, and the cheesecake for dessert.

When the champagne arrived, she almost gulped down her first glass. 'I'll send you our address in Hong Kong,' she said. 'If you need our help in any way, you let me know. Though I would be a lot happier if I knew you were intending to leave.'

'There's still quite a crowd going to the club,' I told her. 'But if they start leaving, I promise I will talk to Dmitri about going too.'

Luba nodded. 'I have news about what happened to Amelia,' she said.

I dug my nails into the seat of my chair. I wasn't sure I wanted to know.

'I heard she started chasing after a Texan with money. But that man was smarter than her usual prey. He took what he wanted and then left her. She's been outdone this time.'

I told her what had happened the previous night and how Dmitri had told Amelia never to call again.

The champagne seemed to have helped Luba's nerves. A smile came to her face. 'So the bitch had to have one more try,' she said. 'Don't worry, Anya. He's out from under her spell now. Forgive him, and love him with all your heart.'

'I will,' I said. But I wished we hadn't spoken about Amelia. She was a virus that lay dormant in the system until you mentioned her.

Luba took another swig of champagne. 'The woman's a fool,' she said. 'She's been telling people about some rich connections she has in Los Angeles. She's talking about her own nightclub, the Moscow-LA. What a joke.'

It was raining when we came out of the club. I kissed Luba goodbye and was grateful for the numbing properties of champagne. I watched her push her way through the crowds to get to a rickshaw. What has happened to us all? I wondered. Those of us who had once waltzed on the dance floor of the Moscow-Shanghai and tried to sing like Josephine Baker.

The night was full of the wail of sirens and in the distance there was gunfire. The next morning I found Dmitri standing ankle-deep in the muddy garden.

'They closed the club,' he said.

His face was ashen. In his despairing eyes I saw the young Dmitri. A boy who had lost his mother.

He shook his head in disbelief. 'We are ruined,' he said.

'It's only until everything settles down,' I told him. 'I'm prepared. We have enough of everything to last us a few months.'

'Didn't you hear the news?' he said. 'The Communists have taken over. They want all foreigners out. All of us. The American consulate and the International Refugee Organisation have arranged a ship.'

'Then let's get out,' I said. 'We'll start again.'

Dmitri sank to his knees in the mud. 'Did you hear what I said, Anya? *Refugees*. We can't take anything with us.'

'Let's just go, Dmitri. We are lucky somebody wants to help us.'

He brought his muddy hands to his face and covered his eyes. 'We're going to be poor.'

The word 'poor' seemed to break him but I felt strangely relieved. We weren't going to be poor. We were going to be free. I hadn't wanted to leave China because it had seemed the only connection to my mother. But the China we had known didn't exist any more. It had slipped through

172

our hands in a second. None of us should have tried taking it in the first place. Even my mother would have seen the open door before me, a chance for Dmitri and I to start again.

The Old Maid's face dropped when I told her that she and Mei Lin should leave because it wasn't safe to be in our house. I packed whatever food I could for them into trunks, and sewed a pouch full of money and told the Old Maid to hide it in her dress. Mei Lin clung to me. Dmitri had to help me lift her into the rickshaw. 'You must go with your old friend,' I told her. She was still crying when the rickshaw moved off, and for a moment I thought of keeping her with me. But I knew they would never let her out.

Dmitri and I made love to the sound of bomber planes and the thunder of distant explosions. 'Can you forgive me, Anya? Can you really forgive me?' he asked afterwards. I told him that I already had.

In the morning a torrential rain was falling. It beat like gunfire against the roof. I slid out of Dmitri's embrace and moved to the window. The rain was washing down the street in great floods. I turned to Dmitri's naked form on the bed and wished that the rain could wash away the past too. He stirred and blinked at me.

'Never mind the rain,' he mumbled. 'I will go by foot to the consulate. You pack our suitcases. I will come back and get you tonight.'

'It's going to be all right,' I told him, helping him with his shirt and coat. 'They aren't going to kill us. They are just telling us to get out.'

He touched my cheek. 'Do you really think we can start again?'

Together we walked through the house, knowing that by the end of the day we would never again recline on its elegant furniture or gaze out its grand windows. I wondered what would become of it, to what use the Communists would put it. I was grateful Sergei wouldn't have to witness the destruction of Marina's beloved home. I kissed Dmitri and watched him run up the garden path, hunched against the rain. I felt the urge to go with him, but there was little time and I had to prepare for our journey.

I spent the day breaking up my jewellery and sewing the stones and pearls into the toes of our socks and the seams of our underwear. I hid the remaining pieces of my mother's jade necklace in the base of my matroshka doll. I had no practical clothes that I could pack, so I stuffed my most expensive dresses into my suitcase in the hope that at least I would be able to sell them. I was terrified and excited at the same time. We couldn't be sure that the Communists would let us out. Not if they were like Tang. They might execute us in their thirst for revenge. But I sang as I worked. I was happy and in love again. When darkness fell I shut all the curtains and cooked by candle-light, using every ingredient in the kitchen to prepare a feast. I spread out a white tablecloth on the floor and set it with our wedding dishes and glasses, the last time we would use them.

When Dmitri did not return in the evening I convinced myself not to think the worst. I speculated that the rain would keep the Communists at bay for at least another day and that Dmitri was streetwise enough to stay out of trouble. 'The worst is over,' I muttered to myself like a mantra and curled up on the floor. 'The worst is over.'

When Dmitri hadn't returned by morning, I tried to call the consulate but the lines were down. I waited an-other two hours, nervous sweat pooling under my arms and slipping down my back. The rain eased and I threw on my coat and boots and ran to the consulate. The halls and waiting areas were crammed with people. I was given a ticket and told to wait my turn. I scanned the crowds desperately for Dmitri.

I spotted Dan Richards coming out of his office and called out to him. He recognised me and waved me over.

'Awful business, Anya,' he said, taking my coat and shutting the door to his office behind us. 'Can I get you some tea?'

'I'm looking for my husband,' I told him, trying to quell the panic that was churning inside me. 'He came here yesterday to get us passage on the refugee ship. But he hasn't returned.'

Concern washed over Dan's kind face. He helped me into a seat and patted my arm. 'Please don't worry,' he said. 'Everything has been chaotic here. I'll find out what has happened.'

He disappeared down the hall. I sat, numb like a stone, eyeing the Chinese antiques and books that were half packed into boxes.

Dan returned an hour later, his face gaunt. I rose out of the chair, terrified that Dmitri was dead. Dan had a paper in his hands and lifted it up to me. I saw the photograph of Dmitri. The eyes that I loved so much.

'Anya, is this your husband? Dmitri Lubensky?'

I nodded, fear screaming in my ears.

'Good God, Anya!' he cried, sinking into his chair and running his hand through his unkempt hair. 'Dmitri Lubensky married Amelia Millman last night and left for America this morning.'

I stood in front of the Moscow-Shanghai, staring at its boarded-up doors and windows. The rain had stopped. Guns were sounding nearby. My eyes drank in the portico, the stone steps, the white lions that guarded the entrance. Was I trying to remember or forget it all? Sergei, Dmitri and I dancing to the Cuban band, the wedding, the funeral, the last days. A family scurried by on the street behind me. The mother shooed her crying children like a hen. The father was bent over, pulling a cart of trunks and suitcases which I knew would be seized before they even got to the dock.

Dan had given me one hour to return to the consulate. From there he had secured for me passage on a United Nations ship headed for the Philippines. I was going to be a refugee, but I was going to be one alone. The pearls and stones in my stocking toes jabbed me. All my other jewellery would be looted when the hordes broke into the house. All of it except my wedding ring. I lifted my hand and stared at its bands in the glary light. I climbed the steps towards the growling marble lion closest to the door and placed the ring on its tongue. My offering to Mao Zedong.

PART TWO

EIGHT

The Island

The ship that took us from Shanghai groaned and listed to one side. It lurched forward at full speed, smoke billowing from its funnels. I watched the city slip further and further into the distance, waves splashing over my feet. The buildings of the Bund were devoid of light and activity, like grieving relatives at a funeral. The streets were quiet, waiting for what would come next. Once we reached the mouth of the river the refugees on board wept and laughed. One held up the white, blue and red royal flag. We had been saved. Other rescue ships had been shot at or sunk before they reached that point. The passengers sprang from railing to railing, hugging each other, buoyant with relief. Only I seemed to be sinking, weighed down by a loss wrapped around me like an anchor. I was being dragged down into the river, the murky water rushing over my head.

Dmitri's second betrayal had unleashed a longing for my mother stronger than I had experienced in all the years we had been separated. I called her up from the past. I saw her face in the overcast sky and in the white wake that spread like a sheet between me and the country where I had been born. Her image was the only thing that could bring comfort. Only she could help name the wretchedness that tormented me.

I was in exile and without love for the second time.

I didn't recognise the other people on the ship, though

179

many of them seemed to know each other. All the Russians I knew had escaped China by other means. But there were quite a few wealthy people mixed in with the middle-class families, the shopkeepers, the opera singers, the pick-pockets, poets and prostitutes. We privileged ones were the most ridiculous. The first night in the mess hall we arrived for dinner in our furs and evening attire. We dipped bent spoons into chipped soup bowls and failed to notice the metal cups and frayed napkins that were our tableware. We were so lost in our illusions of who we had once been that we could have been dining at the Imperial for all we knew. After the meal we were handed the cleaning roster for the next twenty days at sea. The woman next to me accepted it in her diamond-ringed fingers as if it were a dessert menu and then squinted at the piece of paper in puzzlement. 'I don't understand,' she said, looking around for whoever was responsible. 'Surely they can't mean me?'

The next day one of the ship's orderlies handed me a plain blue dress from a pile of clothes he was pushing around on a trolley. It was a size too big and was worn around the waistband and the sleeves. The cream lining was stained and it smelled musty. I slipped it on under the garish bathroom light and stared in the mirror. *Is this what you were afraid of, Dmitri? That we would be wearing other people's clothes?*

I gripped the sides of the sink. The room seemed to spin around me. Did Dmitri want a club called the Moscow-LA so badly that he had been prepared to sacrifice me? I had not seen treachery in his eyes the morning he left for the consulate. When I helped him to button his coat, I had no reason to believe that he would not return for me. So what had happened after that? How had Amelia intercepted him? I closed my eyes and imagined her red mouth whispering spells of persuasion: 'It will be so easy for you to start again . . . the Nationalist government destroyed thousands of documents before they fled. There's probably nothing formal to say you're married. Nothing the United States would know about anyway.' I heard Dmitri affirming 'I do' at their hurried wedding. Did he flinch, I asked myself, at the moment he murdered me?

It was the thought of how much I loved him and how little he loved me that was driving me to madness. Dmitri's love was like Shanghai. It had only existed on the surface of things. Underneath it was corrupt and rotten. His love was not like my mother's love, although both had left their mark on me.

Most of the refugees on the ship were cheerful. The women gathered at the railings to talk and stare at the sea, the men sang as they mopped decks, the children skipped rope together and shared toys. But every night they would gaze out of their cabin windows to search for the moon and stars and check the ship's position. They had learned not to trust anyone. It was only when they saw the celestial markers that they could sleep, reassured that they were still en route to the Philippines and were not being transported to the Soviet Union.

If they had sent me to a labour camp, I wouldn't have cared. I was dead already.

They on the other hand, behaved as though they were grateful. They scrubbed the decks and peeled potatoes with little complaint and talked of the countries that might accept them after the Philippines. France, Australia, the United States, Argentina, Chile, Paraguay. The places rolled off their tongues like poetry. I had no plan, no idea what the future held. The pain in my heart was so deep that I thought I was going to die of it before we ever reached shore. I scrubbed the decks along with the other refugees, but while they took breaks, I went on rubbing fittings and railings until my hands were bleeding from windburn and blisters. I only stopped whenever the supervisor tapped me on the shoulder. 'Anya, your energy is remarkable but you must go get something to eat.' I was in purgatory, trying to buy my way out. As long as I felt pain, I would live. As long as there was punishment, there was hope of redemption.

Six days into the journey I awoke with a burning pain on my left cheek. The skin had turned red and raw and was full of hard cysts that looked like insect bites. The ship's doctor examined it and shook his head. 'It's caused by anxiety. It will go when you get some rest.'

But the disfiguration didn't go. It stayed with me the whole journey, marking me out like a leper.

On the fifteenth day the steamy heat of the tropics passed over us like a cloud. The steel blue water transformed into an azure ocean and the smell of tropical pines perfumed the air. We passed islands with steep cliffs and sandbanks of white coral. Each sunset was a fiery rainbow sizzling on the horizon. Tropical birds fluttered on and off the decks, some so tame that they would jump onto our hands and shoulders without fear. But such natural beauty made some of the Shanghai Russians uneasy. Rumours of voodoo and sacrifices spread throughout the ship. Someone asked the captain if it was true that Tubabao Island was a leper colony and he assured us that the island had been sprayed with DDT and any lepers moved long ago.

'Don't forget you're the last ship,' he told us. 'Your fellow countrymen and women are already there, ready to welcome you.'

On the twenty-second day there was a shout from one of the crew and we rushed out onto the decks for our first view of the island. I shielded my eyes from the sun and squinted into the distance. Tubabao protruded from the sea, mute, mysterious and shrouded in a fragile mist. Two giant mountains, covered in jungle, mimicked the curves of a woman resting on her side. Snuggled in the arch of her stomach and thighs was a cove of alabaster sand and coconut palms. The only sign of civilisation was a jetty reaching out from the tip of the beach.

We anchored and our luggage was unloaded. Later in the afternoon we were sorted into groups and taken to the beach in a creaky barge that reeked of oil and seaweed. The barge moved slowly and the Filipino captain pointed to the clear sea beneath us. Schools of rainbow-coloured fish skittered under the boat and something that looked like a stingray lifted itself from the sandy bottom. I was sitting next to a middle-aged woman in high heels and a hat with a silk flower in the brim. Her hands were neatly tucked into her lap and she was perched on the splintery wooden bench as though she were on her way to a health spa for the day, when in reality none of us knew what even the next hour would bring. It struck me then how absurd our situation had become. Those of us who had known the bustle and stink, the noise and frenzy of one of the world's most cosmopolitan cities were about to make our home on a remote island in the Pacific.

Four buses waited for us at the end of the jetty. They were rundown, the glass was missing from the windows and the panels were warped with rust. An American navy man with hair like steel wool and a sunburned forehead stepped out of one and told us to get onboard. There weren't enough seats so most of us had to stand. A young boy offered me his seat and I sunk gratefully into it. My thighs stuck to the burning leather and, when I was sure no one was looking, I slipped my stockings down to my ankles and hid them in my pocket. The air on my stinging legs and feet was a relief.

The bus bumped and rattled over the furrows in the dirt road. The air steamed with the aroma of the banana trees that lined our path. Every so often we passed a nipa hut and a Filipino hawker would hold up a pineapple or soda drink for us to see. The American shouted above the roaring motor that he was Captain Richard Connor, one of the IRO officials based on the island.

The camp itself was only a short distance from the beach, but the primitiveness of the road made the journey seem longer. The buses parked next to an open-air café, empty of patrons. The bar was made of thatched palm leaves. Card tables and fold-up chairs were half buried in the sandy soil. I looked at the chalkboard menu: cuttlefish in coconut milk, sugar pancakes and lemonade. Connor led us by foot down a paved path between rows of army tents. Some of the flaps were rolled up to let in the afternoon breeze. The insides were crammed with camp beds and overturned crates that served as tables and chairs. Many had a single light bulb strapped to the centre pole and a primus stove near the entrance. In one tent the crates had been covered with matching cloths and set with a dinner service made from coconut shells. I was amazed at what some people had managed to get out of China. I saw sewing machines, rocking chairs and even a statue. Those belonged to the people who had left first, those who had not waited for the Communists to land on their doorsteps before evacuating.

'Where is everyone?' the woman with the flower in her hat asked Connor.

He grinned. 'Down at the beach, I suspect. When you're off duty, that's where you will want to be too.'

We passed a large tent with open sides. Inside four stout women were bent over a vat of boiling water. They turned their sweaty faces towards us and shouted, '*Oora!*' Their smiles were genuine but their welcome filled me with homesickness. Where was I?

Captain Connor led us to a square in the middle of the city of tents. He stood on a wooden stage, while we sat in the scorching sun and listened to his instructions. He told us that the camp was divided into districts, each with its own supervisor, communal kitchen and shower block. Our area backed onto a jungle ravine, a 'disadvantageous position in terms of wildlife and safety'. Therefore our first task

184

would be to clear it. I could barely hear the captain through the pulse in my head when he talked about the deadly 'one minute snakes' and about the pirates who crept out of the jungle at night armed with bolo knives and who had mugged three people already.

Single women were usually put two to a tent, but due to our proximity to the uncleared jungle all the women in our district were put in tents of four or six. I was assigned a tent with three young women from the countryside around Tsingtao who had come to the island earlier on the *Cristobal*. Their names were Nina, Galina and Ludmila. They were not like Shanghai girls. They were robust with rosy looks and hearty laughs. They helped me collect my trunk and showed me where the bedding was issued.

'You're very young to be here on your own. How old are you?' Ludmila asked.

'Twenty-one,' I lied.

They were surprised but not suspicious. I made up my mind in that moment that I would never talk of my past. It hurt too much. I could speak about my mother because I was not ashamed of her. But I would never mention Dmitri again. I thought of how Dan Richards had signed my papers to get me out of Shanghai. He had struck out 'Lubenskya' and written my maiden name, 'Kozlova'. 'Trust me,' he said. 'There will be a day when you'll be glad that man's name doesn't belong to you.'

Already I was longing to be free of it.

'What did you do in Shanghai?' Nina asked.

I hesitated a moment. 'I was a governess,' I said. 'To the children of an American diplomat.'

'You have nice clothes for a governess,' said Galina, sitting cross-legged on the baked-mud floor and watching me unpack. She swept her fingers over the green cheongsam poking out of the corner of my trunk. I tucked the corners of the sheets under my mattress. 'I was expected to help entertain,' I said. But when I looked up I saw that her expression was innocent. There had been nothing behind her remark. And the two other girls seemed more fascinated than sceptical.

I reached into the suitcase and pulled out the dress. I flinched when I saw that Mei Lin had repaired the shoulder. 'Have it,' I said to Galina. 'I'm too tall for it these days anyway.'

Galina jumped up, pressing the dress against her chest and laughing. I cringed at the side splits. It was too sexy for any governess, even those exceptional ones who 'entertained'.

'No, I'm too fat,' she said, handing it back to me. 'But thank you for your kindness.'

I held the dress out for the other girls but they giggled. 'It's too fancy for us,' said Nina.

Later, on our way to the dining tent, Ludmila squeezed my arm. 'Don't look so sad,' she said. 'It all seems a bit much at first, but when you see the beach and the boys you'll forget your troubles.'

Her kindness made me despise myself more. She thought I was one of them. A young, carefree woman. How could I tell them I had lost my youth long ago? That Shanghai had ravished it?

The district dining tent was illuminated by three twenty-five-watt bulbs. In the dim light I could make out about a dozen long tables. We were served boiled macaroni and meat hash on tin plates. The people from my ship picked at their food while the seasoned Tubabao hands wiped their plates clean with slices of bread. An old man spat plum pits straight onto the sand floor.

When she saw that I wasn't eating, Galina pressed a can of sardines into my hand. 'Add them to the macaroni,' she said. 'For a bit of taste.'

Ludmila nudged Nina. 'Anya looks terrified.'

'Anya,' Nina said, pulling at her hair, 'soon you'll look like us. Suntan and frizzy hair. You'll be a Tubabao native.'

*   *   *

186

I woke up late the next morning. The air in the tent was hot and stank of burned canvas. Galina, Ludmila and Nina were gone. Their unmade beds still held the impressions of their bodies. I blinked at the crumpled army-issue sheets, wondering where they had gone. But I was glad of the peace. I did not want to answer any more questions. The girls were kind, but I was a million miles away from them. They had their families on the island, I was alone. Nina had seven brothers and sisters, and I had none. They were maidens waiting for their first kiss. I was a seventeen year old who had been abandoned by her husband.

A lizard wriggled along the inside of the tent. It was teasing a bird on the outside. The lizard blinked its boggle eyes and strutted past the bird several times. I could see the bird's shadow flapping its wings and pecking at the canvas in predatory frustration. I flung my blanket aside and sat up.

A crate propped against the centre pole served as a communal dressing table. Among the beads and brushes covering it was a hand mirror with a Chinese dragon on the back. I picked it up and examined my cheek. In the bright light the rash looked even more inflamed. I stared at it for a while, trying to get used to my new face. I was scarred. Ugly. My eyes looked small and cruel.

I kicked open my trunk. The only sundress I had brought was too elegant for the beach. Italian silk with a glass bead trim. It would have to do.

The tents I passed on my way to the district supervisor's office were full of people. Some were sleeping off the night watch or San Miguel, the local drink. Others were washing dishes and clearing breakfast plates. Some sat in deckchairs outside their tents, reading or talking like people on holiday. Young men with sun-browned faces and clear eyes watched me walk by. I lifted my chin to show them my damaged cheek, warning them that I was unavailable, without and within.

The district supervisor worked from a Nissen hut with a

concrete floor and sun-faded pictures of the Tsar and Tsarina posted above the doorway. I knocked on the flyscreen door and waited.

'Come in,' a voice called out.

I crept into the dark space. My eyes squinted to adjust to the dimness inside the hut. I could just make out a camp bed by the door and a window at the far end of the room. The air reeked of mosquito repellent and motor grease.

'Careful,' the voice said. I blinked and turned in its direction. The hut was hot but cooler than my tent. The district supervisor gradually came into view, sitting at his desk. A small lamp gave off a ring of light but didn't shine on his face. From his silhouette I could see he was a muscular man with square shoulders. He was stooped over something, concentrating on it. I moved towards him, stepping over bits of wire, screws, rope and a rubber tyre. He was holding a screwdriver and working on a transformer. His nails were ragged and dirty, but his skin was brown and smooth.

'You're late, Anna Victorovna,' he said. 'The day has already started.'

'I know. I'm sorry.'

'This is not Shanghai any more,' he said, motioning for me to sit down on a stool opposite him.

'I know.' I tried to catch a glimpse of his face, but all I could see was his strong jaw and tightly clenched lips.

He took some papers from a pile next to him. 'You have friends in high places,' he said. 'You've only just arrived but you will be working in the IRO administration office. The others from your ship are going to have to clear the jungle.'

'I'm lucky then.'

The district supervisor rubbed his hands together and laughed. He sat back in his chair and folded his arms behind his head. The lips relaxed. They were full and smiling. 'What do you think of our tent city? Is it glamorous enough for you?'

I didn't know how to answer him. There was no sarcasm in his tone. He wasn't trying to belittle me, rather he spoke as if he saw the irony of our situation and was trying to make light of it.

He picked up a photograph from his desk and handed it to me. The picture was of a group of men standing by a pile of army tents. I studied their unshaven faces. The young man in front was crouching, holding a stake. He had big shoulders and a broad back. I recognised the full lips and the jaw. But there was something wrong with the eyes. I tried to hold the picture closer to the light, but the district supervisor took the photograph back from me.

'We were the first people sent to Tubabao,' he said. 'You should have seen it then. The IRO dropped us here without tools. We had to dig the toilets and the trenches with whatever we could find. One of the men was an engineer and he went around collecting bits of machinery the Americans had left from when they used this island as a war base. Within a week he had created his own electricity generator. That's the kind of resourcefulness that wins my respect.'

'I'm grateful for everything Dan Richards has done for me. I hope I will contribute to the island in some way.'

The district supervisor was quiet for a moment. I couldn't help thinking that he was studying me. The mysterious lips curved into a grin full of mischief. It was a warm smile that lit up the hut in a flash. It made me like him, despite his harsh manner. There was something of a bear in the man. He reminded me of Sergei.

'I'm Ivan Mikhailovich Nakhimovsky. But under the circumstances let's just call each other Anya and Ivan,' he said, reaching out his hand. 'I hope my joking didn't upset you.'

'Not at all,' I said, clasping his fingers. 'I am sure you are used to dealing with a lot of haughty Shanghailanders.'

'Yes. But you're not a true Shanghailander,' he said. 'You

were born in Harbin and I heard you worked hard on the ship.'

After I had completed the registration and employment forms, Ivan walked me to the door. 'If you need anything,' he said, shaking my hand again, 'please come and see me.'

I stepped into the sunshine and he tugged me back by the arm, pointing with his rough finger to my cheek. 'You have tropical worm there. Go to the hospital immediately. They should have treated you for it on the ship.'

But it was Ivan's own face that caught me by surprise. He was young, perhaps twenty-five or twenty-six. He had classic Russian features. A wide jaw, strong cheekbones, deep-set blue eyes. But running from his forehead down the corner of his right eye to his nose was a scar like a scorch mark. Where the injury had clipped his eye the flesh had healed badly and the lid was partly closed.

He caught sight of my expression and stepped back into the shadow, turning away from me. I was sorry for my reaction because I liked him.

'Go. Hurry,' he said, 'before the doctor goes to the beach for the day.'

The hospital was near the market and the main road. It was a long wooden building with an overhanging roof and no glass in the windows. A young Filipino girl led me through the ward to a doctor. The beds were all empty except for a woman resting with a small baby asleep on her chest. The doctor was a Russian and, as I later learned, a volunteer from among the refugees. He and the other volunteer medical staff had built the hospital from scratch, begging the IRO and Filipino government for medicine or buying it on the black market. I sat on a rough bench while the doctor examined my cheek, stretching the skin with his fingers. 'Just as well you came to me now,' he said, rinsing his hands in a bowl of water held up by the girl. 'Parasites like that can live on for ages, destroying the tissue.'

190

The doctor gave me two injections, one into my jaw and another stinging one near my eye. My face prickled as if someone had slapped it. He handed me a tube of cream that read 'Sample only' on the label. I slipped off the bench and almost fainted. 'Sit for a while before you go,' the doctor told me. I did as he said, but as soon as I was out of the hospital I became nauseous again. There was a courtyard beside the hospital with palm trees and canvas chairs. It had been set up for day patients. I stumbled over to one of the chairs and collapsed into it, the blood singing in my ears.

'Is that girl all right? Go check,' I heard an old woman's voice say.

The sun was hot through the leaves of the trees. I could hear the ocean rumble in the background. There was a rustle of material and then a woman's voice. 'Can I get you some water?' she asked. 'It's very hot.'

I blinked my watering eyes, trying to focus on the shadowed figure against the cloudless sky.

'I'm okay,' I said. 'I just had some injections and they've made me weak.'

The woman crouched next to me. Her curly brown hair was tied high on her head with a scarf. 'She's fine, Grandmother,' she called out to the other woman.

'I'm Irina,' the young woman said, her smile full of white teeth. Her mouth was out of proportion to her face, but she emanated light. It shone on her lips, in her eyes, through her olive skin. When she smiled she was beautiful.

I introduced myself to her and her grandmother. The old lady was stretched out on a banana chair under a tree, her feet barely reaching the end. The grandmother told me her name was Ruselina Leonidovna Levitskya.

'Grandmother hasn't been well,' said Irina. 'The heat doesn't agree with her.'

'What's wrong with you?' Ruselina asked me. Her hair was white but she had the same brown eyes as her granddaughter.

I pushed back my hair and showed them my cheek.

'You poor thing,' said Irina. 'I had something like that on my leg. But it's all gone now.' She lifted her skirt to show me her dimpled but stainless knee.

'Have you seen the beach?' Ruselina asked.

'No, I only arrived yesterday.'

She clasped her hands to her face. 'It's beautiful. Can you swim?'

'Yes,' I said. 'But I've only ever swum in a pool. Not the ocean.'

'Then come,' Irina said, stretching out her hand. 'And be anointed.'

On the way to the beach we stopped by Irina and Ruselina's tent. Two rows of conch shells marked the path to the door. Inside, a crimson sheet draped from corner to corner across the ceiling gave everything a warm pink hue. I was amazed at how many clothes the women had managed to pack inside a plywood wardrobe. There were feather boas, hats and a skirt made from bits of chipped mirror. Irina flung me a white swimming costume.

'It's Grandmother's,' she said. 'She's stylish and slim like you.'

My sundress was sticky against my hot skin. It felt good to peel it off. The air rushed over my body and my skin tingled with relief. The costume fitted around my hips but was tight over my bust. It made the flesh of my breasts swell upwards, like a French corset. At first I was embarrassed by it, but then I shrugged and decided not to care. I hadn't worn so little in the open since I was a child. It made me feel free again. Irina slipped on a suit that was magenta and silver-green. She looked like an exotic parrot.

'What did you do in Shanghai?' she asked me.

I told her my governess story and asked her what she did. 'I was a cabaret singer. My grandmother played the piano.'

She saw my surprise and blushed a little. 'Nothing fancy,' she said. 'Not the Moscow-Shanghai or anything as classy as that. Smaller places. Grandmother and I made dresses between jobs to support ourselves. She made all my costumes.'

Irina didn't notice me flinch at the mention of the Moscow-Shanghai. The recollection of it was a shock. Had I really believed that I would never have to think of it again? There must be hundreds of people on the island who had heard of it. It had been a Shanghai icon. I just hoped none of them would recognise me. Sergei, Dmitri, the Michailovs and I had not been typical Russians. Not the way my father, mother and I had been when we lived in Harbin. It felt strange to be amongst my people again.

The path to the beach passed a steep ravine. A jeep was parked on the side of the road and four Filipino military policemen crouched around it, smoking and sharing jokes. They straightened up as we walked by.

'They keep watch for pirates,' Irina said. 'You'd better be careful on your side of the camp.'

I wrapped my towel over my thighs and used the ends to cover my breasts. But Irina strode by the men with her towel over her shoulder, aware but unashamed of the electric effect her voluptuous body and swinging hips had on them.

The beach was a dreamscape. The sand was as white as foam and dotted with coconuts and millions of tiny shells. It was deserted except for a couple of brown retrievers sleeping under a palm tree. The dogs lifted their heads as we passed. The water was flat and clear under the midday sun. I had never swum in the ocean before but I ran towards it without fear or hesitation. Goosebumps of pleasure pinched my skin when I broke the surface. Schools of silver fish flickered past. I threw my head back and floated on the crystal mirror of the ocean's skin. Irina dived and resurfaced, blinking away drops of water from her lashes. *Anointed*. That was the word she had used. It was how I felt. I could feel the worm on my cheek shrinking, the sun and the salt acting like antiseptic on the wound. Shanghai was washing off me. I was basking in nature, a girl from Harbin again.

'Do you know anyone from Harbin here?' I asked Irina.

'Yes,' she said. 'My grandmother was born there. Why?'

'I want to find someone who knew my mother,' I said.

Irina and I lay on our towels under a palm tree, sleepy like the two dogs.

'My parents were killed in the bombing of Shanghai, when I was eight,' she said. 'My grandmother came to take care of me then. It's possible she knew your mother in Harbin. Although she lived in a different district.'

A motor rumbled behind us, disturbing our peace. I thought of the Filipino police and jumped up. But it was Ivan, waving at us from the driver's seat of a jeep. At first I thought the jeep had been painted in camouflage, but when I looked at it more closely I saw that it was moss and corrosion that gave the panels their mottled appearance.

'Do you want to see the top of the island?' he asked. 'I'm not supposed to take anyone there. But I've heard it's haunted and I think I might need two virgins to protect me.'

'You're full of stories, Ivan,' Irina laughed, standing up and brushing the sand off her legs. She wrapped her towel around her waist and, before I could say anything, hoisted herself into the jeep. 'Come on, Anya,' she said. 'Join the tour. It's free.'

'Did you go to the doctor?' Ivan asked me when I clambered on.

I was careful this time not to stare too closely at his face. 'Yes,' I said, 'but I'm surprised it was tropical worm. I got it just out of Shanghai.'

'The ship you came on has done more than one journey. A lot of us have had the same thing. But you're the first I've seen with it on the face. That's the most dangerous place to have it. Too close to your eyes.'

The sandy beach track stretched for a mile, after which the coconut and nipa palms gave way to monstrous trees that crouched over us like demons. Their twisted trunks were draped in vines and parasitic plants. We passed a waterfall with an old wooden sign nailed to the rock: 'Beware of snakes near the water supply'.

A few minutes after the waterfall, Ivan brought the jeep to a stop. A mountain of blackened rocks blocked our path. Once the motor was off the unnatural quiet made me uneasy. There was no sound of birds singing, or the ocean or the wind. Something caught my attention, a pair of eyes on the rocks. I studied the mountain more closely and gradually came to see the relief of saints and papaya trees etched into it. A shiver pinched my spine. I had seen something like it before in Shanghai, but this Spanish church was ancient. A scatter of broken tiles was all that was left of the collapsed steeple, but the rest of the building was intact. Tiny ferns had taken root in every crack and I imagined the lepers, who had been on the island before the Americans arrived, milling around it and wondering if God had forsaken them the same way their fellow human beings had when they brought them here to die.

'Stay in the jeep. Don't get out for any reason,' Ivan said, looking directly at me. 'There are snakes every-where . . . and old weapons. Doesn't matter if I get blown to bits, but not pretty girls like you two.'

I understood why he had asked us to come then, why he had come looking for us on the beach. It was bravado. He had noticed my reaction to his face and he wanted to show me that he was not afraid for me to see it. I was glad that he had done it. It made me admire him because I was not like that. The mark on my cheek was not as bad as the scar on his face and yet it made me want to hide.

195

He threw aside a blanket and the hunter's knife underneath it gleamed in the sunlight. He tucked the knife into his belt and threw a coil of rope over his shoulder. I watched him disappear into the jungle.

'He's looking for more materials. They are going to build a movie screen,' Irina explained.

'He's risking his life for a movie screen?' I asked.

'This island's like Ivan's home,' said Irina. 'A reason to go on living.'

'I see,' I said, and we lapsed into silence.

We waited over an hour, sucking in the still air and staring into the jungle for any sign of movement. The sea had dried on my skin and I could taste the salt on my lips.

Irina turned to me. 'I heard that he was a baker in Tsingtao,' she said. 'During the war the Japanese discovered some Russians sending radio messages to a US ship. They took random revenge on the Russian population. They tied his wife and two baby daughters up in their shop and set it alight. He got that scar trying to save them.'

I sat down in the back of the jeep and rested my head on my knees. 'How awful,' I said. There was nothing more profound I could say. None of us had escaped the war unscarred. The agony I woke up to every morning was the same agony other people were experiencing too. The Tubabao sun bore down on my neck. I had only been there a day and already it was having an effect on me. It had magical powers. Powers to heal and to terrify, to drive you to madness or to relieve your pain. For the past month I had thought that I was alone. I was glad to have met Irina and Ivan. If they could find reasons to go on living, perhaps I would too.

A week later I was at my job in the IRO office, typing a letter on a manual machine with a missing Y key. I had learned to compensate for the typewriter's shortcoming by substituting Y words for ones without the missing letter.

'Yearly' became 'annual', 'young' became 'adolescent' and 'Yours truly' changed to 'With deepest regards'. My English vocabulary improved rapidly. However, I did strike a problem with Russian names, many of which contained Ys. For those I would type a V and painstakingly pencil in a stem.

The office was a Nissen hut with one open side, two desks and a filing cabinet. My chair scraped noisily on the cement floor every time I moved, and I had to peg the top of my papers so that they wouldn't fly away in the sea breeze. I worked five hours a day and was paid one American dollar and a can of fruit a week. I was one of the few people paid for their work, most of the other refugees were expected to work for free.

On that afternoon Captain Connor was being annoyed by a persistent fly. He swatted at it, but the insect eluded him for over an hour. It landed on the report I had just typed and in exasperation Captain Connor squashed it with his fist, then looked guiltily at me.

'Shall I type that page again?' I asked.

Such accidents were common in our office but to retype a full page perfectly, when I had never used a typewriter before coming to the island, was a laborious task.

'No, no,' said Captain Connor, lifting the paper and flicking the fly's remains off it with his fingers. 'It's almost the end of your day and the thing landed right at the end of a paragraph. It looks like an exclamation mark.'

I fitted the cloth cover over the keys and locked the typewriter away in its special box. I was picking up my bag to leave when Irina turned up.

'Anya, guess what?' she said. 'I'm going to sing cabaret on the main stage this weekend. Will you come?'

'Of course!' I cried. 'How exciting!'

'Grandmother is excited too. She's not well enough to play the piano, so I wondered if you could take her and keep her company?'

'I will,' I said. 'And I will wear my best evening dress to mark the occasion.'

Irina's eyes flashed. 'Grandmother loves getting dressed up! She's been racking her brains about your mother all week. I think she has found someone on the island who can help you.'

I had to bite my lip to stop it trembling. It was four years since I had seen my mother. I was a little girl when we were parted. After all that had happened to me, she had started to seem like a dream. If I could talk to someone about her, I knew she would become real again.

On the evening of Irina's concert, Ruselina and I trampled through the ferns to the main square. We clutched our evening dresses at the hems, mindful that they shouldn't get snagged on the thick grass. I was wearing a ruby evening gown and the damson shawl the Michailovs had given me for Christmas. Ruselina's white hair was piled up on her crown. The style went well with her empire dress. She looked like a member of the Tsar's court. Although she was frail and clung tightly to my arm, her cheeks were rosy and her eyes sparkled.

'I've been talking to people from Harbin about your mother,' she said. 'One of my old friends from the city thinks she knew an Alina Pavlovna Kozlova. She's very old and her memory comes and goes, but I can take you to see her.'

We passed a tree full of flying foxes hanging like fruit from its branches. The foxes took flight when they heard us, transforming into black angels winging across the sapphire sky. We stopped to watch their silent journey.

I was thrilled with Ruselina's news. Although I understood that the woman from Harbin probably couldn't shed any more light on my mother's fate, to find someone who knew her, to whom I could talk of her, was as close as I could get to her then.

Ivan met us outside his hut. When he saw our outfits

he rushed back inside and returned with a stool in one hand, a wooden crate in the other, and a cushion pressed under each armpit. 'I can't have elegant women like you sitting on the grass,' he said.

We reached the main square and found ushers with wetted-down hair and sun-bleached jackets directing people to seating areas. The whole camp seemed to have turned out for the concert. Ruselina, Ivan and I were sent to the VIP section near the stage. I saw doctors and nurses carrying people on stretchers. There had been a dengue fever outbreak a few weeks before I arrived on the island and the medical volunteers were carrying the patients from the convalescing tents to a special section marked 'hospital'.

The show opened with a variety of acts including poetry readings, some comedy skits, a mini ballet and even an acrobat. When the evening light faded into darkness and the lights came on, Irina appeared on the stage in a red flamenco dress. The audience stood up and cheered. A young girl with braids and a short skirt lifted herself up to the piano stool to accompany her. The girl waited for the audience to be still before placing her hands over the keys. She couldn't have been more than nine but her fingers were magic. She conjured up a sad melody that pierced the night. Irina's voice melded with it. The audience was mesmerised. Even the children were well behaved and quiet. It seemed we were all holding our breath, afraid to miss a single note. Irina sang about a woman who had lost her lover in the war, but who could be happy when she remembered him. The words brought tears to my eyes. *'They told me you would never return, but I didn't believe them. Train after train returned without you, but in the end I was right. As long as I can see you in my heart, you are with me always.'*

I remembered my mother's friend in Harbin, an opera singer I knew only as Katya. Her voice could make you feel that your heart was going to break. She said it was because when she sang a sad piece she thought about the fiancé she had lost in the Revolution. I looked at Irina standing on the stage, her dress glimmering against her gold skin. What was she thinking about? A mother and father who would never hold her again? She was an orphan. So was I. An orphan of sorts.

Afterwards, Irina sang cabaret songs in French as well as Russian, and the audience clapped along. But it was the first one that moved me most.

'What a tremendous thing it is,' I said, half to myself, 'to give other people hope.'

'You'll find her,' Ruselina said.

I turned to her, unsure of the meaning of her words.

'You'll find your mother, Anya,' she said, pressing her fingers into my arm. 'You'll see, you'll find her.'

NINE

Typhoon

A week later Ruselina and I were walking along the sandy path to her friend's tent in the Ninth District. After Irina's concert Ruselina's health had deteriorated and we proceeded slowly. She clung to my arm for support and helped herself along with a cane she had bought from a beach vendor for a dollar. Too much exertion shortened her breath and left her doubled over and wheezing. Yet, despite her feebleness, I felt it was me who was leaning against her that afternoon.

'Tell me something about your friend,' I asked her. 'How did she know my mother?'

Ruselina stopped and used the back of her sleeve to dab the sweat from her forehead. 'Her name is Raisa Eduardovna,' she said. 'She is ninety-five years old, lived in Harbin most of her married life, and was brought to Tubabao by her son and his wife. I think she met your mother only once, but the occasion seems to have left an impression on her.'

'When did she leave Harbin?'

'After the war. The same time you did.'

My heart prickled with yearning. Sergei's imposed silence on my mother had wounded me, although he had meant well. I had read that some tribes in Africa dealt with their grief by never speaking of someone again if they left the tribe or died. I wondered how they could do that. To love someone was to always be thinking about them, whether they were with you or not. Not being able to speak freely about my mother in that period when I had first been separated from her had made her seem mythical and remote. At least a few times a day I tried to recall the texture of her skin, the timbre of her voice, our exact difference in height the last time I saw her. I was terrified that if I forgot any of those details, I would start to forget her.

We turned down a track choked with banana trees and headed towards a ten-man tent. When we reached the thatched fence that encircled it and opened the gate, I felt my mother's presence. It was as though she were pulling me towards her. She wanted to be remembered.

Ruselina had visited her friend many times but this was the first time I had been inside the enclosure. The tent was the 'mansion' of Tubabao Island. The spacious marquee had been further enlarged by an annexe of woven palm leaves which served as a kitchen and dining room. A trimmed lawn of bull grass ran all the way up to the edges of the porch, which was bordered by a row of hibiscus trees. In the far corner of the yard a vegetable patch of tropical greens was thriving, while in front of it four chickens were pecking at a mound of food scraps. I helped Ruselina onto the porch and we smiled at each other when we saw the row of shoes on it, neatly arranged in descending order of size. The largest was a pair of men's hiking boots, the smallest a pair of baby shoes. Someone was banging something inside the tent. Ruselina called out and the chickens beat their wings and squabbled with surprise. Two of them took flight, landing on the roof of the annexe. I had heard that the chickens people bought from the Filipinos could fly quite high. I'd also heard that the eggs they laid tasted like fish.

The tent flap lifted and three small children tumbled out. They were all golden-haired girls. The youngest was a baby still in nappies and just learning to walk. The eldest was about four. When she smiled her dimples reminded me of Cupid. 'Pink hair,' she giggled, pointing at me. Her inquisitiveness made me laugh too.

Inside the tent, Raisa's daughter-in-law and granddaughter were bent over planks of wood. They each held a hammer in their fist and gripped a line of nails between their teeth.

'Hello,' said Ruselina.

The women looked up, their faces red with exertion. They had tucked their skirts into their underwear, turning them into shorts. The older woman spat the nails out of her mouth and laughed.

'Hello,' she said, standing up to greet us. 'You must excuse us. We're building a floor.' She was plump with an upturned nose and chestnut hair that fell in waves to her shoulders. She must have been fifty years old but her face was as smooth as a girl of nineteen's. I held up the cans of salmon Ruselina and I had brought as a gift. 'My goodness!' she said, taking them from me. 'I'll have to make a salmon pie, and you'll have to return to eat it.'

The woman introduced herself as Mariya and her fair-haired daughter as Natasha. 'My husband and son-in-law are out fishing for our dinner,' she said. 'Mother has been taking a rest. She'll be pleased to see you.'

A voice called out from behind a curtain. Mariya pulled the screen aside and I saw an old woman lying on a bed. 'Just as well you're almost deaf, Mother,' Mariya said, bending to kiss the woman's head. 'Otherwise how could you have slept through our racket?'

Mariya helped her mother-in-law to sit up and then arranged two chairs for Ruselina and myself on either side of the bed. 'Come on,' she said. 'Sit down. She's awake now and ready to talk.' I took my place by Raisa's side. She was older than Ruselina and her veins protruded through her parched skin like worms. Her legs were wasted and the toes so bent with arthritis they were curled over. I leaned over to kiss her cheek and she gripped my hand with a strength that belied her withered frame. I didn't feel sorry for her the way I sometimes felt sorry for Ruselina. Raisa was infirm and not long for the world, but I envied her. An old woman surrounded by her happy, productive family. She could have little to regret in life.

'Who is this beautiful girl?' she asked, still clutching my hand and turning to Mariya. Her daughter-in-law leaned over and spoke into her ear. 'She is a friend of Ruselina's.'

Raisa peered at our faces, searching for Ruselina. She recognised her friend and grinned through toothless gums. 'Ah, Ruselina. I've heard you've not been well.'

'I'm good enough now, my dear friend,' Ruselina replied. 'This is Anna Victorovna Kozlova.'

'Kozlova?' Raisa glanced at me.

'Yes, the daughter of Alina Pavlovna. The woman you think you met,' said Ruselina.

Raisa fell silent, distracted by her thoughts. The air in the tent was hot, even though Mariya had rolled up the flaps on the rear and side windows. I edged forward on my chair so that my legs wouldn't stick to the wood. A trickle of saliva gathered on Raisa's chin. Natasha gently wiped it away with the corner of her apron. I thought the old woman had fallen asleep when she jolted upright and stared at me. 'I met your mother once,' she said. 'I remember her well because she was so striking. Everyone was taken with her that day. She was slim with lovely eyes.'

My legs went weak. I thought I was going to swoon with the mention of my long-kept secret, my mother. I clutched the side of the bed, no longer aware of the others in the room. They disappeared from my mind as soon as Raisa spoke. I could only see the old woman lying in front of me and wait for each slurred word.

'It was a long time ago,' Raisa sighed. 'It was at a summer party in the city. It must have been 1929. She arrived with her parents and was wearing an elegant lilac dress.

I thought her very poised and liked her because she was interested in everything other people said. She was a very good listener.'

'That was before she married my father,' I said. 'You've done well to remember that far back.'

Raisa smiled. 'I thought I was already old back then. But I'm much older now. All I have to think about now is my past.'

'Was that the only time you saw her?'

'Yes. I didn't see her after that. There were quite a few of us in Harbin and we didn't all move in the same circles. But I did hear that she married a cultured man and that they lived in a nice house on the outskirts of the city.'

Raisa's chin dropped to her chest and she sank deeper into the bed, lying there like a deflated balloon. Her recollection seemed to have drained her. Mariya scooped water from a bowl and lifted the glass to her mother-in-law's lips. Natasha excused herself to watch her children. I listened to the cries of the girls playing in the yard. I could hear the chickens cluck when Natasha passed by them. Suddenly Raisa's face contorted. The water dribbled out of her mouth then gushed out like a fountain. She began to cry.

'We were fools to have stayed for the war,' she said. 'The smart ones left for Shanghai long before the Soviets came.' Her voice was raspy, constricted with pain.

Ruselina tried to make her more comfortable but she tugged away from her.

'I heard the Soviets took your mother,' Raisa said, lifting her age-spotted hand to her forehead. 'But where she went, I don't know. It may have been for the best. They did such terrible things to those who stayed behind.'

'Take a rest, Mama,' said Mariya, lifting the glass of water again to the old woman's lips, but Raisa pushed her hand away. She was shivering despite the heat, and I wrapped her shawl around her shoulders. Her arms were so thin I was afraid they would splinter in my hands.

'She's tired, Anya,' Ruselina said. 'Maybe she can tell us more another day.'

She stood up to leave. My heart was torn with guilt. I didn't want to make Raisa suffer, but I also didn't want to leave until she had told me everything she knew about my mother.

'I'm sorry,' said Mariya. 'Some days she's clearer than others. I'll tell you if she says anything more.'

I picked up Ruselina's cane and was offering her my arm when Raisa called out. She struggled up on her elbows. Her eyes were red-rimmed and wild. 'Your mother had neighbours, Boris and Olga Pomerantsev, didn't she?' she asked. 'They chose to stay in Harbin even when the Soviets came.'

'Yes,' I said.

Raisa sank back into the cushions and covered her face with her hands. A low wail rose in her throat. 'The Soviets took all the young ones, the ones they could make work,' she said, half to me, half to herself. 'I heard they took Pomerantsev because he was still strong, even for an old man. But they shot his wife. She had a bad heart. Did you know that?'

I don't remember walking back to Ruselina's tent. Mariya and Natasha must have helped us at least some of the way, because I don't see how Ruselina could have supported me on her own. I was in shock and my mind was blank except for one image: Tang. Boris and Olga's fate reeked of him. I remember sinking onto Irina's bed and pressing my face into the pillow. I yearned for sleep, for unconsciousness, for a respite from the agonising pain that gripped my insides. But it wouldn't come. My swollen eyelids sprang open when I tried to close them. My heart pumped like a piston in my chest.

Ruselina sat beside me and rubbed my back. 'It's not what I expected,' she said. 'I wanted to make you happy.'

I looked up at her haggard face. There were hollows

206

under her eyes and her lips were blue. I hated the distress I was causing her. But the more I tried to be calm the worse the pain became.

'I was stupid to believe nothing bad would happen to them,' I said, remembering Olga's frightened eyes and the tears on her husband's cheeks. 'They knew they were going to die for helping me.'

Ruselina sighed. 'Anya, you were thirteen years old. Old people know they have choices to make. If it had been you or Irina, I would have done the same thing.'

I rested my head on her shoulder and was surprised to find that it was steadier than I had expected. My need seemed to give Ruselina strength. She stroked my hair and embraced me as if I were her own child.

'In my life I have lost my parents and a brother, a baby, my son and my daughter-in-law. It's one thing to die old, quite another to be cut down when you are young. Your friends wanted you to live,' she said.

I hugged her tighter. I wanted to tell Ruselina that I loved her, but the words got lost somewhere in my throat.

'Their sacrifice was their gift to you,' she said, kissing my forehead. 'Honour it by living with courage. They couldn't ask for more than that.'

'I want to thank them,' I said.

'Yes, you do that,' said Ruselina. 'I'll be all right until Irina gets back. Go and do something to respect your friends.'

I stumbled down the path to the beach, almost blind with tears. But the trills of the crickets and the chirps of the birds in the bushes comforted me. In their music I heard Olga's cheerful voice. She was telling me not to grieve, that she didn't feel pain and wasn't afraid any more. The day's merciless sun had softened and, filtered through the trees, it caressed me with a gentle touch. I longed to press my face into Olga's dough-sprinkled bosom and tell her how much she had meant to me.

When I reached the beach the sea was grey and sombre. A circle of seagulls screamed overhead. The last of the sun's rays burned into a shimmering line down the ocean's centre and a mist floated in the air. I dropped to my knees in the sand and built a mound as high as my chest. When I had finished, I pressed a garland of shells around its point. My teeth clenched each time I imagined Olga dragged from her hearth and shot. Did she scream? I couldn't think of her without thinking about Boris. They were swans. Mated for life. He wouldn't have lasted a day without her. Did they make him watch? My tears dented the sand like raindrops. I built another mound and formed a bridge of sand between the two. I guarded my memorial, listening to the pounding and hissing of the waves, until the sun disappeared into the ocean. When the orange mirage faded and the sky dimmed, I said Boris and Olga's names three times to the wind so that they would know I remembered them.

I found Ivan waiting for me under a light on the path back to my tent. He was holding a basket covered with a checked cloth. When I approached him, he lifted the cloth and uncovered a batch of fresh *pryaniki*. The honey and ginger smell of the cakes mingled with the sea air and the scent of the palm leaves. Such a cold climate tradition seemed out of place on the island. I had no idea how he had managed to get the ingredients, let alone bake them.

'My very best, for you,' he said, holding the basket towards me.

I tried to smile but I couldn't. 'I'm not good company now, Ivan,' I said.

'I know. I took my *pryaniki* to Ruselina and she told me what happened.'

I bit my lip. I had cried so much on the beach that I didn't think I could cry any more. Still a heavy droplet slipped down my face and onto my wrist.

'There's a rock ledge just above the lagoon,' he said. 'I

go there when I'm sad and it makes me feel better. I'll take you there.'

I drew a line in the sand with my foot. He was being kind and I was touched by his compassion. But I wasn't sure if I wanted to be with someone or be alone.

'As long as we don't talk,' I said. 'I'm not in the mood for talking.'

'We won't talk,' he said. 'We'll just sit.'

I followed Ivan along a sandy track to an outcrop of rocks. The stars had come out and their reflections shone like blurry flowers on the water. The ocean was a deep mauve. We sat down on a ledge protected on two sides by large boulders. The rock surface was still warm from the sun and I leaned my back against it, listening to the waves swirl and drip in the crevices beneath us. Ivan offered me the basket of cakes. I took one although I wasn't hungry. The sweet dough crumbled in my mouth and brought back memories of Christmas in Harbin: my mother's advent calendar on the mantelpiece, the coldness of the pane against my cheek when I peered through the window and watched my father collect wood, staring down at my feet and seeing snowflakes in the creases of my boots. I couldn't believe that I had travelled so far from the cocooned world of my childhood.

True to his promise, Ivan didn't try to speak. At first it felt strange to sit with someone I didn't know very well and not say anything. Normal people can ask each other simple intro-ductory questions to get better acquainted, but as I thought of things I could ask Ivan, I realised there was little we could say to each other that wouldn't inflict some sort of pain. I couldn't ask him about his baking, he couldn't ask me about Shanghai. Neither of us could ask each other if we were married. Even an innocent comment on the ocean was poten-tially awkward. Galina had told me how much more beauti-ful the beaches of Tsingtao were compared to Tubabao. But how could I mention Tsingtao to Ivan without reminding him of what he had lost there? I breathed in the briny scent of the waves and pressed my palms under my chin. It was easier for people like Ivan and myself, people living in the aftermath, to ask nothing rather than risk trespassing on each other's fragile memories.

I scratched my cheek. The worm on my face had died, leaving a flat, mottled patch of skin. There were few mirrors on Tubabao and little time for vanity, but whenever I caught a glimpse of the mark in the reflection of a tin can or a pail of water, I was shocked by my appearance. I was no longer myself. The scar was like the mark of Dmitri, a crack in a vase that reminds the owner time and time again of how it toppled from its base before she could save it. Whenever I saw it, the memory of Dmitri's betrayal stung me like a whip. I tried not to think about him and Amelia in America, their easy life of cars, big houses and running water.

I searched the sky and found the small but beautiful constellation Ruselina had pointed out to me a few nights before. I offered a silent prayer up to it, and imagined that Boris and Olga were there. Then, thinking about them, I felt the tears sting my eyes again.

Ivan was sitting with his back curved and his arms on his knees, lost in his own thoughts.

'There's the Southern Cross,' I said. 'The sailors in the southern hemisphere use it to guide them.'

Ivan turned to me. 'You're talking,' he said.

I blushed although I had no idea why I should feel embarrassed. 'Can't I talk?'

'Yes, but you said you didn't want to.'

'That was an hour ago.'

'I was enjoying the silence,' he said. 'I thought I was getting to know you better.'

Although it was dark he must have seen me smile. I felt him smile too. I turned back to the stars. What was it about this curious man that made me feel brave? I never would have thought it could be so comfortable to sit with anyone for so long and not say anything. Ivan had presence. Being with him was like leaning against a rock you knew would never falter. He must have been in pain too, but his loss seemed to have made him stronger. I, on the other hand, thought that if I suffered any more loss, I would go crazy with it.

'I was only joking,' he said, passing me the basket of cakes. 'What did you want to tell me?'

'Oh no,' I said. 'You are right. It feels good to be quiet and still.'

We were silent again and it was just as comfortable as before. The waves settled down, and one by one the camp lights started to go out. I glanced at Ivan. He was leaning against the rock with his face turned towards the sky. I wondered what he was thinking.

Ruselina had said that the best way to honour the Pomerantsevs was to live with courage. I had waited for my mother but she had not returned to me nor had there been any news about her. But I was not a little girl any more, restrained by the whims of others. I was old enough to search for her on my own. And yet, despite my longing for her, I dreaded the idea that I might discover that she too had been tortured and executed. I squeezed my eyes shut and made my wish on the Southern Cross, asking Boris and Olga to help me. I would use my courage to find her.

'I'm ready to go back,' I told Ivan.

He nodded and stood up, holding out his hand to help me to my feet. I took his fingers and he gripped me with such strength that it was as if he had read my mind and was supporting me.

'How would I go about finding someone in a Soviet labour camp?' I asked Captain Connor when I arrived for work at the IRO office the next day. He was sitting at his desk eating a poached egg and bacon. The egg was bleeding across his plate and he soaked it up with a slice of bread before answering me.

'It's very difficult,' he said. 'We are at a stalemate with the Russians. Stalin is a madman.' He glanced up at me. He was a man of good manners and didn't ask any questions. 'My best advice,' he continued, 'would be for you to get in touch with the Red Cross in your country of settlement. They've been doing marvellous work in helping people trace their relatives after the Holocaust.'

The countries of settlement was the question occupying everyone's mind. After Tubabao, where would we go? The IRO and the community leaders had petitioned many countries, begging them to let us in, but they had not received replies. Tubabao was lush and fruitful and we should have been enjoying the respite, but our future was uncertain. Even on a tropical island we were always in the shadow of gloom. There had been one suicide and two attempted ones already. How much longer could we be expected to wait?

It was only after the United Nations forced the issue that the countries started to respond. Captain Connor and the other officials met at the office. They arranged their chairs in a circle, donned their eyeglasses and lit cigarettes before discussing the options. The United States government would only accept those people who had sponsors already living in America; Australia was interested in young people on the condition they sign a contract to work in any job required by the government for the first two years; France offered hospital beds to the elderly or the sick either to live out their days or to recover until they were fit to be moved elsewhere; and Argentina, Chile and Santo Domingo opened their doors without restrictions.

I sat at my typewriter, staring at the blank paper, paralysed. I had no idea where I would go or what would become of me. I could not imagine myself anywhere but

China. I realised that ever since I arrived in Tubabao I had kept a secret hope that we would eventually be taken home.

I waited for the officials to leave before asking Captain Connor if he thought it might be possible for us to return to China one day.

He looked at me as if I had asked him if I thought it was possible that one day we would all grow wings and turn into birds. 'Anya, there is no China for you people any more.'

A few days later I received a letter from Dan Richards urging me to come to America under his guarantee. 'Don't go to Australia,' he wrote. 'They are putting intellectuals to work on railways. South America is out of the question. And you can't trust the Europeans. Don't forget how they betrayed the Lienz Cossacks.'

Irina and Ruselina were despondent. They wanted to go to the United States but didn't have the money or sponsorship requirements. I ached for them each time I saw how they would listen with keen ears and longing eyes whenever anyone mentioned the lively nightclubs and cabarets of New York. I replied to Dan that I would take up his offer, and asked if he could do something to help my friends.

One evening Ruselina, Irina and I were playing Chinese checkers in their tent. The sky had been overcast all day and the humidity so oppressive that we'd had to call a nurse to the tent to massage Ruselina's lungs to help her breathe. It was the dry season, which on Tubabao meant it only rained once a day. We had been dreading the wet. Even when it rained lightly, all sorts of jungle creatures took refuge in the tents. Twice a rat had jumped out of Galina's suitcase, and our tent was riddled with spiders. The transparent lizards were famous for laying their eggs in people's underwear and shoes. A woman from the Second District woke up one morning to find a brown snake coiled on her lap. It had curled there for warmth and she had to lie still for hours until it slithered away of its own accord.

It wasn't the season for tropical storms yet but that day there had been something menacing in the sky. Ruselina, Irina and I watched it, seeing evil shapes form in the clouds. First a goblin-like creature with burning eyes where the sun shone through; then a round-faced man with a malicious mouth and peaked eyebrows, and finally a shape that moved across the sky like a dragon. Later in the afternoon a strong wind picked up, knocking over plates and bringing down washing lines. 'I don't like this,' Ruselina said. 'Something bad is coming.'

Then the rain started. We waited for it to stop, which it usually did after half an hour or so. But the rain didn't cease, it became heavier each hour. We watched it overflow the trenches, washing mud and anything else that stood in its way down the road. When it started to flood the tent, Irina and I ran outside and, with our neighbours' help, dug deeper trenches and furrows leading away from the tents. The rain whipped against our skin like sand, turning it red. Tents without good centre poles collapsed in the downpour, and the occupants had to struggle against the wind to re-erect them. By nightfall the power was down.

'Don't go home,' Irina said. 'Stay here tonight.'

I accepted her invitation without hesitation. The track to my tent was lined with coconut trees and, whenever the wind picked up, dozens of the rock-like fruits would crash to the ground. I was afraid that one would fall on my head and always ran through the grove with my hands raised above me as a shield. The girls in my tent laughed at my paranoid behaviour, until one day a coconut fell on Ludmila's foot and she was in a cast for a month.

We lit a gas lamp and continued with checkers, but by nine o'clock even games couldn't relieve the hunger pangs pinching our stomachs. 'I've got something,' said Irina, shuffling around in a basket on top of the wardrobe. She took out a packet of biscuits and laid a plate on the table. She tipped the packet and a fat lizard fell out among the crumbs, followed by dozens of her wriggling babies. 'Pffumpt!' Irina screamed, dropping the packet to the floor. The lizards scurried in all directions and Ruselina laughed so much she began to wheeze.

The camp siren blasted and we froze. It sounded again. One blast signalled twelve noon and 18:00 hours. Two was to call the district leaders to a meeting. The siren repeated its shrill cry. Three was for everyone to meet in the square. We looked at each other. Surely they couldn't expect us to meet in such weather? The siren blasted again. Four was for fire. Irina crouched beside her bed, frantically searching underneath it for her sandals. I grabbed the spare blanket from the wardrobe. Ruselina sat stoically in her chair, waiting for us. The fifth blast sent a chill down my back. Irina and I turned to one another, mirroring each other's disbelief. The final blast was long and sinister. The fifth call had never been used before. It meant typhoon.

We could feel the rush of panic in the tents around us. Voices cried out in the storm. A few minutes later the district official appeared at our tent. His clothes were saturated and clung to him like a second skin. The dread in his face ignited our own. He tossed us some pieces of rope.

'What do you want us to do with these?' Irina asked.

'I've given you four to tie down the things in your tent. The others are for you to bring to the square in five minutes. You are going to have to strap yourselves to trees.'

'You must be joking,' said Ruselina.

The district official shivered, his eyes bulging with terror. 'I don't know how many of us are going to make it. The army base received the warning too late. They think the sea is going to cover the island.'

We joined the rush of people crashing through the jungle to the main square. The wind was so strong we had to dig our feet into the sandy soil to struggle against it. A woman collapsed to her knees nearby, crying out with fear. I ran to her, leaving Irina to look after Ruselina. 'Come on,' I said, pulling the woman up by her arm. Her coat flapped open and I saw the baby in a sling on her chest. It was tiny, with closed eyes, no more than a few hours old. My heart stung at the sight of its helplessness. 'It will be all right,' I told the woman. 'I will help you.' But terror had got the better of her. She clung to me, weighing me down and holding me back. We were drowning together in the angry air. 'Take my baby,' she pleaded. 'Leave me.'

It will be all right, I had said. I thought of all the times I had thought things would be all right, and loathed myself. I thought I would have been reunited with my mother by now, I had been convinced my marriage would be a happy one, I had trusted Dmitri, I had run to Raisa expecting wonderful stories about my mother. I had never been in a typhoon before. What right did I have to tell anyone that things would be all right?

In the square volunteers perched on tree stumps held up spotlights so that people wouldn't trip on the ropes and bags of emergency supplies. Captain Connor was standing on a rock, shouting directions into a megaphone. The district officials and the police were sorting people into groups. Small children were taken from their parents and herded into the walk-in refrigerator in the main kitchen. A Polish nurse was put in charge of them. 'Please take them too,' I said to the nurse, leading the woman and baby to her. 'She's just given birth.'

'Take her to the hospital,' the nurse said. 'That's where they are going to keep the sick and the mothers with young babies.'

Ruselina took the child from the woman's arms and Irina and I helped her towards the hospital. 'Where's the father?' asked Irina. 'Gone,' replied the woman, her eyes distant. 'He left me for another woman two months ago.'

216

'And he didn't even come back to help his child?' Ruselina shook her head and whispered to me, 'Men are no good.'

I thought of Dmitri. Perhaps it was true.

The hospital was already crowded when we arrived. Doctors and nurses were pushing the beds together to make room for more stretchers. I recognised Mariya and Natasha, busy nailing planks across the windows. Ivan was dragging a cupboard in front of a door. A harried-looking nurse took the child from Ruselina and led the woman to a bench where another young mother was nursing a child.

'Can my grandmother stay here too?' Irina asked the nurse. The nurse threw up her arms and I could see that she was about to say no when Irina flashed her dazzling smile. The nurse's refusal never left her mouth. Her lips twisted, as if she were resisting the smile that was breaking out across her own face. She nodded towards the rooms at the back of the hospital. 'I can't give her a bed,' the nurse said. 'But I can put her in a chair in a consulting room.'

'But I don't want to be here alone,' protested Ruselina when we helped her into a chair. 'I'm well enough to come with you.'

'Don't be foolish, Grandmother! This building is the best on the island.' Irina rapped her knuckles against the wall. 'Look! It's made of solid wood.'

'Where are you going to go?' asked Ruselina. The frailty in her voice pricked my heart.

'The young people have to run to the top of the island,' Irina said, trying to be cheerful. 'So you will have to imagine Anya and myself doing that.'

Ruselina reached out and grabbed Irina's hand, pressing it into mine. 'Don't let go of each other. You're all I've got.'

Irina and I kissed Ruselina and hurried back out into the rain to join the line of people picking up the ropes and torches and scrambling up the mountain track. Ivan struggled through the crowd to meet us. 'Actually, I've saved a special spot for you two,' he said. We put down the ropes but kept one torch and followed him to a small Nissen hut in a clearing behind the hospital.

The hut had three barred windows and was dark inside. Ivan shuffled in his pocket and produced a key. He tugged my palm towards him and dropped the key into it.

'No, we can't,' I said. 'It's a solid building. You should give it to the sick or the children.'

Ivan raised his eyebrows and laughed. 'Oh, so you think I'm giving you some special privilege, do you, Anya?' he said. 'I'm sure you two get a lot of favours on account of your good looks, but I'm putting you to work.'

Ivan gestured for me to unlock the hut. I pushed the key into the lock and opened the door but I couldn't see anything but darkness inside. 'I have no spare volunteers left to look after them,' he said. 'All the nurses are occupied elsewhere. But don't worry. They are harmless.'

'Who are "they"?' asked Irina.

'Ah, my Irina,' Ivan said. 'Your voice has won my heart. But you need to win my respect too if you want me to truly admire you.'

Ivan laughed again and bounded off into the rain, leaping over fallen branches and debris with the nimbleness of a stag. I watched him disappear into a grove and out of sight. There was a 'crack!' in the sky and a palm tree crashed to the ground, splattering mud over our dresses and missing us by no more than a foot. Irina and I clambered into the hut and struggled to close the door behind us.

The air inside reeked of sun-parched linen and disinfectant. I stepped forward and bumped into something hard. I ran my hand around the edges of it. A table.

'I think it's a storeroom,' I said, rubbing the bruise on my thigh.

Something scuttled by us. Fur brushed across my feet. 'Rats!' I cried. Irina flicked on the torch and we found ourselves face to face with a startled kitten. She was white with pink eyes. 'Hello, cat,' said Irina, crouching down and stretching out her hand. The kitten scampered to Irina and rubbed her chin against her knees. The cat's fur was shiny, not dusty like most animals on the island. I jumped back when Irina did, both of us staring at the same thing: a pair of human feet illuminated by the circle of torchlight. They were lying toes up on a sheet. My first thought was that we were in the mortuary but I realised it was too hot for that. Irina traced the beam up the striped pyjama pants to the face of a young man. He was asleep, his eyes tightly closed and a sliver of drool glistening on his chin. I edged closer and touched his shoulder. The man didn't stir but his flesh was warm.

I whispered to Irina, 'He must be sedated because I don't see how else he could be sleeping through the commotion outside.'

She curled her fingers around my wrist, crunching the bones, and flicked the torch over the rest of the room. There was a wooden table with a pile of paperback novels neatly stacked on it and a metal cupboard near the door. We searched behind us and both jumped when we saw an old woman squinting at us from a bed in the far corner. Irina redirected the torchlight out of the woman's eyes.

'I'm sorry,' Irina said. 'We didn't realise there was anybody else here.'

But in the instant the beam had illuminated the woman's face, I had recognised her. She was better fed and cleaner than the last time we had met, but there was no mistaking her. All that was missing was her tiara and her worried expression.

'*Dusha-dushi*,' the old woman said.

Another voice, a man's, called out from a shadowy corner. 'I'm Joe,' he said. 'Joe like Poe like Poe like Poe like Poe. Although my mother called me Igor. It's Joe like Poe.'

Irina gripped my wrist, making it ache. 'What is it?' she asked.

But I was too occupied trying to believe what Ivan had done to answer her. He'd put us in charge of the mental patients.

By the time the head of the storm hit the island, the hut was rattling and shaking like a motorcar on a bumpy road. A stone struck one of the windows and a crack began to zigzag across the glass. I searched the cupboard for tape to seal it. I managed to paste some down before the fracture reached the frame. We couldn't hear anything outside above the howl of the wind. Only once did the young man wake up, looking at us through glazed eyes. 'Whaat's thaat?' he asked. But before we could answer him, he turned over on his stomach and lapsed back into a deep slumber. The kitten sprang onto his bed and, after some deliberation over the most comfortable spot to settle, curled herself into a ball in the crook of his knees.

'They must both be deaf,' said Irina.

The old woman slipped out of bed and twirled around the hut in a silent ballet. We wanted to preserve the torchlight so Irina switched it off, but as soon as she did the woman began hissing like a snake and shaking the latch on the door. Irina switched the torch back on and held the beam on the woman, who danced in the spotlight like a girl of sixteen. 'Joe' stopped his monotonous self-introduction to applaud her performance and then announced that he wanted to go to the toilet. Irina searched under the beds for a pan, and when she found one, handed it to him. But he shook his head and insisted that he be let outside. I made him stand with one foot in the door and clutched his pyjama shirt while he urinated against the side of the hut. I was terrified that he was going to run off or get blown away by the storm. After he had relieved himself, he stared up at the sky and refused to come back inside. Irina had to keep

220

the torch on the old lady while helping me drag Joe back into the hut. His pyjamas were soaked and we had nothing to change him into. We struggled to pull off his wet clothes and wrapped him in a sheet. But once he was warm again, he flung the sheet off and insisted on remaining nude. 'I'm Joe like Poe like Poe like Poe,' he muttered, parading up and down the length of the hut on his skinny legs, bare as the day he was born.

'You and I are never going to make good nurses,' Irina said.

'They're sedated too. That makes us extra hopeless,' I replied.

Irina and I laughed. It was the only spot of joy we would know all night.

The howling outside rose to a frenzy. In one gust, an airborne tree was propelled into the hut. It rammed into the wall, denting the metal inwards. The cupboard doors flung open and trays and cups crashed to the floor. The old lady stopped dancing, startled like a child caught playing past her bedtime. She clambered into her bed, pulling the blankets over her head.

The wind was battering the tree against the wall of the hut. Small tears sprung up everywhere and leaves poked through the gaps. Irina and I knocked the books from the table and turned it on its side, jamming the top against the wall as a brace.

'I don't like this,' said Irina, turning off the torchlight. 'I can hear the waves coming.'

'You can't,' I said. 'It's something else.'

'No,' said Irina. 'It's the ocean. Listen.'

'It's Joe like Poe, you know,' Joe shouted out.

'Shhh!' I scolded him.

Joe sniffed and climbed under his bed, continuing to mutter under his breath.

Raindrops struck the sides of the hut and rang like bullets. The screws holding the walls to the cement floor groaned under the pressure of the wind. Irina grabbed my hand. I squeezed it back, remembering what Ruselina had said about not letting go of each other. The old lady threw her arms around me and clung on so tightly that I couldn't move. The young man and his cat slept on peacefully. Joe retreated somewhere deeper into the shadows. I couldn't hear him.

Suddenly the door stopped rattling and was silent. The walls slid back into position. The flapping of canvas and trees ceased. I thought I had gone deaf. It took a few moments to register that the wind outside had calmed. Irina lifted her head and turned on the torch. Joe crawled out from under his bed. I could hear voices in the hills, moans and cheers. People were calling out to each other from their positions in the jungle. A man was shouting out to his wife, 'Valentina, I love you! After all these years I still love you!'

But nobody moved. Even the calm had something evil in it.

'I'm going to check on Grandmother,' Irina said.

'Don't go out!' All the feeling had gone from my legs. I couldn't have stood up if I had tried. 'It's not over. It's just the eye.'

Irina frowned at me. She snatched her hand away from the door latch, her mouth open in horror. The handle was vibrating. We stared at it. In the distance the ocean let out a roar. The voices in the jungle rose in panic. The wind lifted again, moaning through the stripped trees. Before long it changed form and was screeching like a demon, moving in reverse and picking up all the debris lifted by the head of the storm. Branches crashed against the hut. Irina shook the young man awake and dragged him under the bed. She fixed the cat in the crook of his arm. Together we set the table upright and pushed Joe and the old woman under it with us.

'I'm Joe like Poe. Like Poe. Like Poe,' he whimpered in my ear.

Irina and I pressed our faces together. There was a fetid odour. Joe had emptied his bowels.

Something crashed onto the roof. Shreds of metal fell around us. Rain began to drip inside. A few drops at first, then a waterfall. The wind thudded against the walls. I cried out when I saw the side of the hut lift, held to the ground only by the screws on the other side. The metal screeched and the hut opened up like a bread box. We gaped at the furious sky. The books fluttered around us before being flung to all corners of the room. We clung onto the table legs but the table began to inch along the floor. Joe struggled from my grasp and stood up, reaching towards the sky.

'Get down!' Irina screamed. But it was too late. A flying branch struck him on the back of the head. The shock knocked him to the ground. He was blown across the cement floor like a leaf. Irina managed to catch him, scissor-like, between her feet before he was forced between the jaws of metal and the floor. If the wall came down again, he would be sliced in two. But Joe was wet and slipped from her grip. I tried to reach for his hand but the old lady was holding me and I couldn't reach far enough. I grabbed him by the hair. He cried out because it started to tear in my fingers. 'Let him go!' Irina shouted. 'He'll pull you with him.' I managed to slip one hand under Joe's arm and grip him by the shoulder, but in that position my head was out in the open. Leaves and sticks stabbed into me, stinging my flesh like marauding insects. I closed my eyes, wondering what object would strike me. What piece of flying debris would end my life.

'I'm Joeee,' Joe cried out. He slipped from my grasp and was blown against the cupboard. It toppled over but fell onto the bed under which the young man was hiding. The cupboard missed Joe's head by an inch. He was trapped, but as long as the bed didn't shift, he was safe.

'Don't move!' I cried out. My voice was drowned by an

223

ear-splitting shriek. I watched as the wall was ripped off its last hinges and flung into the air. It seemed to spin for ages, an ominous shadow floating in the sky. I wondered where it would land. Who it would kill.

'God help us!' Irina screamed.

Then, with no warning, the wind stopped. The wall dropped from the sky and spliced through a nearby tree, becoming stuck in the branches. The tree had given its life for ours. I could hear the ocean toss and roar, summoning the storm back into it.

Something warm dripped onto my arm. I rubbed it. It was sticky. Blood. I thought it must have been from Irina because I didn't feel anything. I turned on the torch and searched her head with my fingertips but couldn't find a wound. Still the blood continued to drip. I turned to the old woman. My stomach heaved. She had put her teeth straight through her bottom lip. I tore my petticoat and folded the material into a wad, holding it against her mouth to stop the bleeding.

Irina pressed her face into her knees, trying not to cry. I blinked the water from my eyes and surveyed the damage. Joe was sprawled on the floor like a fish stranded on the beach. There were grazes on his forehead and elbows but otherwise he seemed unhurt. The young man was awake but quiet. His kitten stood, drenched, back arched, hissing in the corner.

'I'm Joe like Poe, like Poe,' Joe muttered to the cement.

Nobody else said anything for a good half-hour.

TEN

Countries of Settlement

The storm had transformed the island into a stagnating swamp. At first light we emerged from the wreckage and gathered in the square. We looked small among the fractured and tottering trees. Muddy roots protruded from deep, gaping holes in the earth. People were staggering down the path from the mountain, their clothes ripped and wet and their hair caked with sand. I searched for Ivan, holding my breath until I saw him towards the rear, coils of rope slung over his shoulders like limp snakes.

The hospital was still standing and a crowd milled around it. Ruselina was stationed in the doorway, directing people into groups with her walking stick. There were hundreds of them, dishevelled, hobbling, bleeding. The doctors and nurses, themselves bedraggled and weary, administered whatever they could from their meagre supplies. A young doctor sat on a crate opposite the *dusha-dushi* woman, stitching her lip. The procedure must have been excruciatingly painful without strong anaesthetic, but the woman sat quietly, her agony given away only by the trembling hands she clutched to her chin.

Irina and I embraced Ruselina and then ran ahead of the others to the camp. The sight of it struck us with mute heartbreak. Torn flies and strips of canvas flapped in the morning breeze like rotting clothes on a skeleton. The roads were deep gullies, their surfaces stamped with the

225

pulverised remains of bed linen and broken crockery. Many of the things people had struggled so hard to salvage from China had been devoured. The endless piles of broken chairs and tables, upturned beds and scattered toys was too much to bear. An old woman brushed past us, holding up the torn, water-damaged photograph of a child. 'It was all I had left of him. And even it is gone,' she cried, looking at me. Her sunken mouth quivered as if she expected an answer. But I had no words to say.

Irina returned to the hospital to help Ruselina. I walked through the camp towards the Eighth District, loose stones rattling under my feet. I had nothing to fear from the coconuts any more. The trees were bare of fruit and the shells lay cracked and scattered on the ground. There was an unpleasant scent in the air. I traced it to the body of a puppy on the path, a snapped tent pole speared into its swollen stomach. Ants and flies were busy at work on the wound. I shuddered when I imagined a child searching for her pet. I picked up a strip of palm bark and dug a shallow grave. When I had finished, I tugged the pole from the dog's belly and dragged her by the paws into the hole. I hesitated a moment before covering it with sand, unsure if I was doing the right thing. But I remembered my own childhood and I knew that there were things a child should never see.

The dense jungle surrounding the Eighth District had saved it. The tents had collapsed and drifted limply to the ground, but they weren't shredded beyond repair like those in the Third and Fourth Districts. Beds were strewn across the area but few of them were broken, and at one site, although the tent itself had been flung into the trees, the furniture was upright and neatly arranged, as if the owners had only stepped away a minute before.

I bit my cracked lips until they bled when I saw my trunk. It had been lashed against a tree with a skilfully knotted rope and was still intact. I was filled with gratitude to whichever girl had taken the trouble with it in my absence. The lock was jammed and I couldn't prise it open. I grabbed a nearby rock and smashed the clasp with it. The evening clothes inside were damp and gritty with sand but I didn't care about them. I fumbled underneath the fabrics, praying that my hand would find what I searched for. When I touched wood, I screamed with relief and pulled out the matroshka doll. It was unscathed and I kissed it over and over again, like a mother who has found her lost child.

The sea was the colour of milky tea. Bits of vegetation and flotage bobbed on its surface. The morning light glinting on the waves made it seem harmless, nothing like the enraged monster that had threatened to swallow us last night. Nearby, on the small strip of sand that remained, a priest was leading a group of people in a prayer of thanks. I didn't believe in God, but I bowed my head in respect anyway. We had a lot to be grateful for. By some miracle, not one human life had been lost. I closed my eyes and gave in to the balm of numbness.

Later I found Captain Connor standing in front of the IRO office. The metal walls were full of pits and some of the filing cabinets were overturned. He looked surreal in the midst of the catastrophe, with his neatly pressed uniform and the part in his hair so straight that the red of his sunburned scalp shone through. The only sign of the storm on him was a splash of mud on his boots.

He smiled at me as if this was just another day and I was arriving for work as usual. He pointed to the cluster of Nissen huts that were used for storage. Some were in worse condition than our office, their walls bent so badly out of shape that they probably could no longer be used. 'If one good thing comes of this disaster,' he said, 'it will be that they realise they have to get us off this island sooner rather than later.'

By the time I returned to the hospital, the Filipino and

American soldiers from Guam had arrived to help. Ivan and the other officials were lifting jerry cans of fuel and drinking water from the back of an army truck, while the soldiers busied themselves erecting tents for the patients who couldn't fit into the hospital. Volunteers were boiling water to sterilise the hospital instruments and bandages, or preparing food under a makeshift canopy.

The beaten, soggy grass was crowded with people sleeping on rugs. Ruselina was one of them. Irina sat next to her, stroking her grandmother's white hair. Ruselina had said that she would sacrifice herself for Irina or me, and that we were all she had in the world. I watched the two women from behind a tree, clutching the matroshka doll to my chest. They were all I had too.

I saw Ivan drag a sack of rice to the cooking tent. I wanted to assist too, but all the courage had drained out of me. Ivan straightened up, rubbing his back, and his eye caught mine. He strode towards me, a grin on his face and his hands on his hips. But his expression changed when he saw my face.

'I can't move,' I said.

He reached out his arms. 'It's all right, Anya,' he said, clutching me to his chest. 'It's not as bad as it seems. No one is seriously hurt and things can always be repaired or replaced.'

I pressed my face against him, listening to his steady heartbeat and letting his warmth flow into me. For a moment I was home again. A treasured child in Harbin. I could smell freshly made bread, hear the fire crackling in the parlour, feel the softness of bear fur under my feet. And for the first time in a long while I heard her voice: *I'm here, my little girl, so close you could touch me.* A truck engine started up and the spell was broken. I stepped back from Ivan, opening my mouth to speak but unable to utter a word.

He took my hand in his rough fingers, but gently, as if

he were afraid of breaking it. 'Come on, Anya,' he said. 'Let's find somewhere for you to rest.'

The weeks following the storm were full of hopes and heartaches. The American navy based in Manila arrived in ships laden with supplies. We watched the sailors march up the beach, sacks slung over their broad shoulders, and in a matter of two days re-erect Tent City. The new city was much more orderly than the old one, which had been laid out in a hurry, with no forward planning and insufficient tools. The roads were rebuilt with deeper gutters and paving and the jungle was cleared from around our bathroom blocks and kitchens. But the neat construction filled us with unease rather than pleasure. There was something uncomfortably permanent in the way the new camp was built and, despite Captain Connor's hopes, there was still no word from our 'countries of settlement'.

The Russian Society in America heard about the disaster and sent us an urgent message: 'Tell us not just what you need to survive, but what you need to be happy.' The society gathered material from its members, many of whom had become wealthy in the United States, but also from companies who were prepared to donate spoiled stock. Captain Connor and I spent a night working on a wish list that included one small present for each person. We requested records, tennis rackets, playing cards, pencil sets and books for our library and lending store, but also asked for scented soap, chocolate, writing journals, sketchpads, hair combs, handkerchiefs and a small toy for each child under twelve. We received a reply within a fortnight: 'All items requested have been obtained. We are also sending you Bibles, two guitars, a violin, thirteen bolts of dress material, six samovars, twenty-five raincoats and one hundred copies of Chekov's play *The Cherry Orchard* with the cover missing.'

The barge was due to arrive a month later and Captain

Connor and I waited for it, excited as two mischievous children. We watched for the ship for six weeks but it never arrived. Captain Connor made investigations through the IRO office in Manila. All the goods had been intercepted by corrupt officials and sold on the black market.

Ivan came to see me at the IRO office one afternoon. I squinted at his figure in the doorway, not recognising him at first. His shirt was pressed and his hair was clean, not sprinkled with sawdust and leaves as usual. He was leaning idly against the doorpost, but his fingers were thrumming on his hip and I knew he was up to something.

'You've been spying on me,' I said.

He shrugged and glanced about the room. 'No, I haven't,' he said. 'I just came to see how you are.'

'Yes, you have,' I said. 'Captain Connor left just a minute ago on an errand. And then you appeared. You must have watched him go.'

Ivan's eyes fell on a frayed wicker chair we saved for guests. His face was turned away from me but I could see him smile. 'I have a plan to boost everyone's morale,' he said, 'and I didn't know if Connor would approve.'

Ivan dragged the chair in front of my desk and then perched on it like a giant on a thimble. 'I've built the projector and the screen. All I need is a movie.' His hand moved to his eye. I didn't like the way it hovered there, as if he were trying to mask it. Was he still conscious of his disfigurement in front of me? He needn't have been. The scar was prominent but you only had to know Ivan for a day before you stopped noticing it. His personality was the thing about him that stayed in your mind. My own cheek twinged. I didn't like to see weakness in Ivan, or vulnerability. He was my rock. I needed him to be strong.

'We've got plenty of movies.' I pointed to the crate of film reels that Captain Connor had resorted to using as a footrest. 'We've just never had a projector.'

'Come on, Anya,' said Ivan, leaning forward with his hands on his knees. The nails were scrubbed, another change. 'Those are old. The kind our parents would have watched. We need a good movie.'

His good eye was clear like water. It was dark blue and bottomless. I imagined if I looked closely enough into that eye I would see Ivan's past etched there. His dead children, his wife, his bakery, floating just below the surface. If I peered deeper perhaps I would see right into his boyhood and know who he was before his face had been disfigured. His eye belied the youthfulness of his voice, his boyish vigour, just as his scarred face belied the gracefulness of his body.

'I need you to persuade him,' Ivan said.

It required no effort at all to convince Captain Connor of the value of Ivan's plan. The captain was infuriated that we were still on the island with the typhoon season approaching and was determined to milk the guilty conscience of the IRO. I requested a recent movie; Captain Connor demanded no less than a Hollywood prerelease. He must have been convincing. We did not have to wait in disappointment this time for a barge that never arrived. The film was airlifted to us within a fortnight, under guard, along with medical supplies.

The premiere of *On the Town* was announced in the *Tubabao Gazette* and everyone on the island talked of little else until the opening night. Ivan built seats for Ruselina, Irina and myself out of palm logs and we sat in style next to his projection box. Ivan was in high spirits. 'We've done it, Anya!' he said, pointing at all the people. 'Look at this happy crowd!'

It was like the old days, before the storm. Families set out blankets and cushions and spread before themselves miniature feasts of tinned fish and bread. Young boys dangled their legs from tree branches, couples reclined arm in arm under the stars, and the more ingenious gawked from their self-created 'box' seats, complete with bedsheet canopies in case of rain. Frogs croaked and mosquitoes nipped incessantly at our exposed flesh, but no one cared. When the movie began we all jumped up to cheer. Irina threw back her head and laughed. 'You funny girl,' she said to me. 'You know most of us won't understand this. It's all in English.'

Ivan glanced up from the projector and wiped his brow. He smiled at me. 'It's a love story. What's there to understand?'

'It's a musical,' I said, pinching Irina's arm. 'And it's set in New York. So you'll get to see the city you've been dreaming about.'

'Good for you, Anya!' Ruselina said, patting my back. 'Good for you!'

It was true that when Captain Connor had shown me the list of possible movies, I had chosen *On The Town* with Irina and Ruselina in mind. But when Gene Kelly, Frank Sinatra and Jules Munshin sprang from their naval ship and began to dance and sing their way through New York, it was me who was watching them with amazed eyes. New York was a place such as I had never seen before, more dazzling than Shanghai. Its monuments loomed up like pillars to the gods: the Empire State Building, the Statue of Liberty, Times Square. Everyone moved with energy and zest, the traffic buzzed and tooted, and even the office girls were dressed in haute couture. I drank in every movement, every note, every colour.

When the leading men returned to the ship and their pretty girls waved them farewell, I had tears in my eyes. All the way back to my tent I sang numbers from the musical.

The film ran for a week and I was there every night. The editor of the *Tubabao Gazette* asked me to write an article about the film for the paper. I wrote an enthusiastic piece about New York and went overboard by including sketches of all the outfits the female characters had worn.

'You express yourself well,' the editor said when I gave

232

him my copy. 'We should get you to write a fashion column for the newsletter.'

The idea of fashion on Tubabao made us both laugh out loud.

I was dizzy with a feeling I had not experienced for a long time. Deep-running optimism. Suddenly I had all sorts of hopes. Dreams that had been lost in the drudgery of my daily life. I believed that I could be beautiful again, that I would fall in love with a man as handsome as Gene Kelly, that I was capable of living my life with verve and in a world of modern appliances.

A week later I received a letter from Dan Richards saying that he would help Ruselina and Irina to get to America too, and Captain Connor received notice that immigration officers from the countries of settlement would be arriving the next month to process our visas and arrange transport off the island. Suddenly it seemed as if everyone's wishes were coming true.

'When we go to America,' I told Ruselina and Irina, 'I'm going to study and be an anthropologist like Ann Miller. And you, Irina, should learn to dance like Vera-Ellen.'

'Why would you study boring anthropology when you write such good articles?' Irina said. 'You should be a journalist.'

'And what will I do while you two career women are gallivanting about with young men?' asked Ruselina, fanning herself and feigning indignation.

Irina threw her arms around Ruselina's shoulders. 'Grandmother, I guess you will just have to drive cabs like Betty Garrett.'

Ruselina and Irina laughed until Ruselina had a coughing fit. But I was serious.

No matter how sophisticated we had been in our past lives, every man, woman and child waited on the beach to watch the representatives from our countries of settlement disembark from the United Nations' ship. We stared, open-mouthed, with the awe of people who had lived too long in isolation and had forgotten how dark the sun had made their skin. The serious-looking men and women who stepped onto the barge wore pristine suits and dresses, while our clothes and hair were stiff with salt. A joke started among us: 'If you are in New York or San Francisco and you see a man walking by with a package under his arm, don't ask him, "What are they issuing today?"'

We laughed at ourselves, but secretly I think we all wondered if we could ever adjust to normal life again.

The first night the IRO officials treated the guests to pig cooked on a spit. Filipino chefs were brought in and a white marquee was erected. While the representatives dined at tables with linen cloths and crystal glasses, we looked on and trembled, our future in their hands.

Later I met Ivan on the way to my tent. It was dark but there was a full moon and his shoulders were silhouetted against the sky.

'I'm going to Australia,' he said. 'I've been trying to find you to tell you.'

I hardly knew anything about that country but I imagined it was wild and hard. Such a young country would welcome an industrious, hardworking man like Ivan. But I was frightened for him too. America was largely tame. Australia was supposed to be writhing with beastly things: dangerous snakes and spiders, crocodiles and sharks.

'I see,' I said.

'I'm going to a city called Melbourne,' he said. 'They say you can make a fortune there if you work hard.'

'When do you leave?'

Ivan didn't answer me. He stood with his hands in his pockets. I lowered my eyes. It felt awkward between us. Saying goodbye to friends hadn't got any easier for me.

'You will succeed at anything you put your mind to, Ivan. Everyone says that,' I told him.

He nodded. I wondered what he was thinking, why he was being so strange and why he wasn't making his usual witty remarks. I was about to make some excuse to go back to my tent when he suddenly said, 'Anya, I want you to come with me!'

'What?' I said, stepping back.

'As my wife. I want to work hard for you and make you happy.'

The situation seemed unreal. Ivan was proposing to me? How had our friendship suddenly come to this? 'Ivan . . .' I stumbled, but I had no idea how to begin or end. I cared about him but I didn't love him. It wasn't his scar, it was that I was sure I would never feel anything more than friendship for him. I hated Dmitri but I still loved him too.

'I can't, Ivan . . .'

He moved closer to me. I could feel the heat from his body. I was tall for a girl but he stood a foot above me and his shoulders were twice as wide. 'Anya, who is going to take care of you after this? After the island?'

'I'm not looking for someone to take care of me,' I said.

Ivan was silent for a moment, then he said, 'I know why you're afraid. But I will never betray you. I will never desert you.'

The skin around my hairline prickled. There was something behind his words. Did he know about Dmitri?

I tried to protect my threatened heart by being angry. 'I won't marry you, Ivan. But if you have something more to say then you should say it.'

He hesitated, rubbing the back of his neck and looking towards the sky.

'Go on,' I said.

'You never talk about it. I respect you for that . . . but I know what happened with your husband. The American consulate had to give a reason to the IRO for sending a seventeen-year-old girl to Tubabao on her own.'

I saw spots before my eyes. There was a lump in my

throat. I tried to swallow it but it remained there, choking me. 'Who else have you told?' I asked. My voice quivered. I was still trying to sound angry, but it wasn't convincing.

'People from Shanghai know about the Moscow-Shanghai, Anya. You were in the social pages. Those from other cities probably don't know.'

He took another step forward, but I slipped back further into the darkness.

'Why hasn't someone confronted me then?' I asked. 'Seeing that I'm such a liar.'

'You're not a liar, Anya. You're just scared. Those who do know like you too much to force you to talk about things you'd rather forget.'

I thought I was going to be sick. I wished that Ivan had not proposed to me. I wanted to go on pretending that I had been a governess so I would never have to think of the Moscow-Shanghai again. I would have liked to have kept the memory of Ivan as the kind man who sat with me on the rock ledge the night I found out about the Pomerantsevs. But what had been said was of such magnitude that it couldn't be undone. In a few moments our relationship had changed forever.

'Ivan, I won't marry you,' I said. 'Find someone else. Someone who isn't already married!'

I made to run past him but he blocked me, grabbing my shoulders and holding me against his chest. I stayed there for a moment before I began to struggle against him. He let me go, his arms falling to his sides. I ran through the dark back to my tent, groping my way like a frightened animal. I wasn't sure what had scared me most: Ivan's proposal or the idea of losing him.

The foreign consulates set up tents to facilitate immigration interviews and the issuing of visas. We were allocated numbers and waited our turn outside in the hot sun. Ruselina, Irina and I were only required to fill in official forms and take a medical examination. We were not grilled about Communist affiliations or family history as the other immigrants were. When I heard that many of the applicants wishing to go to the United States had been rejected, I could only close my eyes and silently thank Dan Richards.

'It's finally happening,' said Irina. 'I can't believe it.' She clutched the forms in front of her as though they were fistfuls of money. For the weeks following she practised her scales while I sat on the beach, staring out to sea, pondering then dismissing the thought that Dmitri might try to find me. My life on Tubabao was so far removed from the one I had lived in Shanghai, I thought I had forgotten him. But Ivan's proposal had dredged up the pain. I listened to the sea swell in its lazy rhythm and wondered if Dmitri and Amelia were happy together. That would have been the ultimate betrayal.

A short time later the naval transport vessel, the *Captain Greely*, arrived to take the last of the immigrants who were going to Australia. The rest had left earlier on other transport ships. Those going to the United States travelled by sea to Manila, and from there by army transport plane or boat to Los Angeles, San Francisco or New York. Those of us left behind watched the camp shrink. It was the end of October and we were still in danger of typhoons, so Captain Connor moved the camp to the sheltered side of the island.

Ruselina was unwell the day the *Captain Greely* left and Irina and I took her to the hospital before rushing to Ivan's hut to help him pack. I hadn't told Irina and Ruselina about Ivan's proposal, hoping to avoid any further embarrassment for the both of us. I was also ashamed that I had lied to them about being a governess in Shanghai, although I wasn't sure if they had learned the truth or not. Since the night of the proposal Ivan and I had avoided each other but I couldn't not wish him farewell.

We found him standing outside his hut, looking over it like a man about to put down his favourite horse. My heart stung for him. He had done so much to be proud of here, it must have been hard for him to leave.

'Australia will be just like one big Tubabao!' I blurted out.

Ivan turned to me with an unfamiliar expression, a distance in his eyes. I flinched but didn't let it wound me. All my life precious people had come and gone and I was learning not to cling to anyone any more. I told myself that Ivan was just one more goodbye and that I ought to get used to them.

'I can't believe you've packed everything already,' said Irina.

Ivan's stony face broke into his usual smile and he held up a box for us to see. 'I've packed everything I need in here,' he grinned. 'I challenge you to do the same.'

'You can always find what you want,' I said, recalling the scavenger hunts. 'You'll have no problem in your new home.'

It was sunny but a choppy wind was whipping the ocean into bumps of white froth. The breeze absorbed all other sound. Only in the distance could we hear the cries of the sailors calling out instructions as they prepared to load the ship. By the time we reached the jetty, it was already crowded with people and baggage. Everyone was animated. They spoke in high voices and, although they nodded enthusiastically to one another, no one was really listening to what anybody else was saying. Everyone's attention was fixed in one way or another on the ship dipping on the ocean in the distance, the vessel that was going to take them away to a new country and life.

'How will we write to you?' Irina asked Ivan. 'You've been such a good friend, you must never be a stranger.'

'I know!' I said, grabbing the pencil Ivan had perched behind his ear. I wrote Dan Richards's address on Ivan's box. When I stood up and handed back the pencil I saw tears in Ivan's eyes and quickly turned away.

I loathed myself. Ivan was a good man and I had hurt

him. I wished he had fallen in love with Irina. She had a purer heart. Shadows from the past didn't haunt her the way they did me.

It took the sailors over three hours to load the people and luggage onto the ship. Ivan waited for the last barge. When he stepped onto it, he turned to wave to us. I stepped forward, wanting to say something but not knowing what. Perhaps if I had been able to swallow the stone-like obstruction in my throat, I would have told Ivan that nothing was his fault, that I was in so much pain I wasn't much good to anyone. At the very least I would have liked to thank him, for I would never see him again. But all I could do was smile stupidly and wave back.

'We'll miss him,' Irina said, putting her arm around me.

'I am always thinking of America,' I said. 'How different our lives will be. It scares me to think that we could be so happy.'

Ruselina was waiting for us on the hospital steps.

'What are you doing out here?' Irina asked. 'It's too hot. You should be inside.'

Ruselina's face was ghastly. There were black shadows beneath her skin. The expression in her eyes stopped us short. A nurse hovered behind her in the darkness of the doorway.

'What is it?' asked Irina, her voice cracking with agitation.

Ruselina swallowed, then with a raspy breath said, 'My X-rays came back. I don't understand. I was clear when I left China.'

I gripped the balustrade and looked down at the sand. The sun made it glisten like diamonds. I knew she was about to tell us something terrible, something that would change everything. I stared at the shiny grains of sand and imagined them opening up and swallowing all my hope.

Irina looked desperately from her grandmother to the nurse. 'What's the matter?' she asked.

The nurse moved into the sunshine where her freckles stood out more boldly. Her eyes darted about like a frightened horse. *'Teebeeshnik.* TB,' she said. 'Very sick. Might die. Can't go to America no more.'

For two weeks Irina and I waited anxiously for the final word from the United States Immigration Department. Although Captain Connor was usually aloof and professional, I could see how thoughtfully he spoke to Irina and I was grateful. The problem was that the United States would not accept people with tuberculosis and, although there had been exceptions made on humanitarian grounds, such cases were rare.

The message came in early one morning and Captain Connor called us to his office to deliver it.

'They won't take her in America,' he said, biting his pencil, a habit he detested in other people. 'We'll be moving her to France in the next few days.'

I thought of Ruselina in the hospital, doped up on streptomycin, and wondered if she could survive such a long journey. I tore the skin from around one of my nails and didn't even notice until the blood began to run down my hand.

'I don't care where I have to go,' said Irina. 'As long as she gets better.'

Captain Connor cringed and stood up. 'That's the problem,' he said, rubbing his brow. 'France won't take you. Only the sick. You and Anya can still go to America but I can't guarantee that they will take your grandmother, even if she gets better.'

I asked Captain Connor to telegram Dan Richards, but Dan could only give us the same answer.

For the next few days I suffered with Irina the awful choice that lay before her. I watched her twist her hair and cry herself to sleep. We walked around the island together for hours. I even took her to Ivan's rock ledge but we couldn't find any peace there either.

'Captain Connor said America *may* take Grandmother if she gets an all-clear. But it's not a guarantee. The Australian consulate, on the other hand, has agreed to take her when she's better on the condition that I work there for two years,' she said.

We held on to each other. Was I going to lose Irina and Ruselina too?

One night, while Irina tossed and turned in her bed, I took a walk on the beach. I couldn't bear to think of Ruselina and Irina separated. If the French were humanitarian enough to take the sick and the old, I didn't doubt that Ruselina would get the best care. But I couldn't help seeing what was happening to them as something similar to what happened to my mother and me. Irina had lost her parents when she was eight years old, and now she was about to be cast off on her own again. I couldn't help Ruselina being sick, but perhaps I could put her mind at rest. I sat down in the warm sand and looked up at the stars. The Southern Cross was shining brightly. Boris and Olga had given their lives for mine and Ruselina had said the best way to honour that was to live with courage. I pressed my face into my hands and hoped that I was a person worthy of their sacrifice. 'Mother,' I whispered, thinking about dazzling New York and the life I hoped to build there, 'Mother, I hope I'm a person who can make a sacrifice for somebody else.'

The following afternoon I was hanging out the washing when Irina came to me. Her face had colour in it again and she seemed peaceful. She had resigned herself to something and I was anxious to find out what she had decided. I pursed my lips and steeled myself for her answer.

'I will go to Australia,' she said bravely. 'I'm not taking any chances. As long as Grandmother gets better and we can be together, I don't care. There are more important things than singing in ritzy nightclubs and visiting the Statue of Liberty.'

I nodded and returned to hanging out the washing, although I had barely enough strength to lift a slip.

Irina perched herself on an upturned bucket and watched me. 'You must tell me all about America, Anya. You must write and not forget me or Grandmother,' she said, entwining her fingers on her knee and swinging her foot. She was trying to hold back her tears but a single droplet fell from her eye and caught on the curl of her lip.

The blood rushed to my head and air surged into my lungs. I felt like a swimmer drawing a breath before launching herself from the diving board. I pegged a skirt to the line and strode up to Irina, grabbing her hand and pressing it into mine. Irina looked up at me. The tear slid from her lip onto my wrist. I had trouble saying the words at first, I couldn't get them out in one sentence. 'Ruselina said that we're all she's got.'

Irina didn't take her eyes from my face. She opened her mouth to say something but stopped herself. She squeezed my hand tightly.

'Irina, I . . . will not forget you . . . nor Ruselina,' I said, 'because I am coming with you.'

ELEVEN

Australia

I had been uprooted twice in my life but nothing could have prepared me for the shock of Australia. A few days after Ruselina was taken to France, Irina and I were flown from Manila to Sydney by army plane, so exhausted neither of us could remember much of the journey except for the furnace that blew over us when we changed planes in Darwin. We arrived at Sydney airport early in the morning. An immigration official by the name of Mr Kolros greeted us and helped us through customs. He had emigrated from Czechoslovakia a year earlier and spoke some Russian and English. Mr Kolros answered our questions about rents, food and employment politely, but when I asked him if he liked Sydney he ground his teeth and replied, 'Sydney is good. It's the Australians who take some getting used to.'

Irina clutched my arm, trembling with the influenza she had caught en route. We struggled to keep up with Mr Kolros, who strode through the arrivals area as if he had something more important to do at half past four in the morning than wait for us. There was a taxi waiting outside and he tossed our suitcases into the boot and paid the driver the fare to take us to the wharf, where we were to join a group of migrants from Europe.

Mr Kolros helped us into the taxi and wished us well before shutting the door. I couldn't stop thinking about what he had said about the Australians.

'Welcome to Sydney, girls,' the driver greeted us, leaning over the front seat and speaking from the corner of his mouth. His English sounded unusual, it crackled like a log fire. 'I'll do the scenic route. It won't take us much longer this time of the morning.'

Irina and I squinted through the windows, trying to catch a glimpse of our new city. But Sydney was cloaked in darkness. The sun hadn't risen yet and there was a curfew on electricity usage because of the shortages after the war. All I could see were rows of terrace houses and grocers with their shutters rolled down. On one of the streets a dog with a black patch around his eye cocked his leg against a fence. A stray or a pet? I couldn't tell. But he looked better fed than we did.

'This is the city proper,' the driver said, turning into a street lined with shops. Irina and I eyed the mannequins in the department store windows. While Shanghai would still have been bustling with life at this time of the morning, Sydney was quiet and empty. There wasn't a cleaner, a policeman or a prostitute in sight. Not even a stray drunk staggering home. The Town Hall and its clock tower could have been shipped directly from Second Empire Paris, and the square between the hall and the church next to it created spaciousness that didn't exist in Chinese cities. Shanghai wouldn't have been Shanghai without its congestion and chaos.

The lower end of the street was bordered by Classical and Victorian style buildings, and one that looked like an Italianate palace, stamped with the initials 'GPO'. Further along, the harbour loomed up ahead of us. I strained my neck to see the massive steel bridge that stretched across the black expanse of water. It seemed to be the tallest structure in the city. The headlights of the dozen or so cars passing over it winked at us like stars.

'Is that the Harbour Bridge?' I asked the driver.

'Sure is,' he said. 'The one and only. My father worked as a painter on it.'

We passed under the bridge and soon found ourselves on a strip lined by warehouses. The driver stopped in front of a sign that read 'Pier 2'. Although Mr Kolros had paid the driver already, I thought perhaps he would want a tip. When he took our suitcases from the boot, I searched my purse for the only American dollar I had left. I tried to pass it to the driver but he shook his head. 'You might need it,' he said.

Australians, I thought. So far so good.

Irina and I hesitated at the boom gate. A cold wind blew from the water, bringing with it the smell of brine and tar. The breeze bit through our cotton dresses. It was November and we had been expecting Australia to be warm. The IRO ship from Marseille was docked in the port. Hundreds of German, Czechoslovakian, Polish, Yugoslavian and Hungarian migrants were pouring down the gangways. The scene made me think of Noah and his ark, such was the variety of their accents and appearances. Men hobbled beneath the weight of wooden trunks. Women scuttled after them, bundles of bedding and cooking pots tucked under their arms. Children ran between their legs, calling out in their mother tongues, eager to see their new country.

We asked the guard where we should wait and he pointed to a train on the dock. Irina and I entered one of the carriages and found it empty. We struggled along the aisle, pinching our noses against the reek of fresh paint, and sat down in the first compartment we could find. The seats were hard leather and the air was thick with dust.

'I think it's a goods train,' Irina said.

'I think you are right.' I opened my suitcase, pulled out one of the blankets I had brought from Tubabao and wrapped it around Irina's shoulders.

Through the grime on the window we watched the wharfies unload the ship's cargo with a crane. Seagulls swooped overhead, squawking and screeching. The birds were the only things I had seen in the city that were familiar to me.

The ship's passengers had to scramble over the piles of luggage to get their suitcases and trunks. A little girl in a pink coat and white stockings stood near the gangway, crying. She had lost her parents in the chaos. I saw a wharfie crouch down to talk to her, but she only shook her curly head and cried more. He glared around the crowd, then picked the girl up and put her on his shoulders, parading her around in the hope of finding her parents.

Once they had their luggage the passengers were directed to a building with the words 'The Commonwealth of Australia Department of Immigration' painted above the door. I realised then how lucky Irina and I had been to travel to Australia by plane. Although the trip had been rough between Manila and Darwin, our journey had been quick and we were the only two passengers. The people from the ship looked haggard and ill. Over an hour later they began to emerge from the building and make their way towards the train.

'Are they all going to fit?' Irina asked.

'Surely not,' I said. 'Mr Kolros said that it will be a long trip to the camp.'

To our horror we watched the stationmaster round the passengers up like cattle and direct them to the doors. Elbows, arms and suitcases blocked our view as people pushed against each other to get inside. Unlike us, the Europeans were overdressed for the weather. They all seemed to be wearing two coats and several dresses or shirts each, as if they had saved on packing space by wearing everything they owned. A man in a pinstriped suit appeared at the compartment door. His face was smooth and young but his hair was white.

'*Czy jest wolne miejsce?*' he asked. '*Czy pani rozumie po polsku?*'

I knew a few basic phrases in Polish, which has some similarities to Russian, but I had to guess that he wanted a seat. I nodded my head and indicated for him to come inside. He was followed by a woman, and an old lady with two scarves tied over her head.

'*Przepraszam,*' the old lady said when she sat next to me. But I had exhausted all my Polish. She glanced at me. We didn't speak the same language but we both had the same anxious look in our eyes.

Three Czechoslovakian men left their luggage in the aisle and took standing positions in the compartment. On one of the men's sleeve was a dark patch in the shape of a star. I had heard what had happened to the Jews in Europe, and the tales were one of the few things that stopped me feeling sorry for my own situation.

With so many people in the compartment, the air quickly became stuffy, and Irina cracked the window open for air. Our fellow passengers' clothes reeked of stale cigarette smoke, sweat and dust. Their faces were gaunt and pale, souvenirs of their long journey. My dress, and Irina's too, smelled of scorched cotton, sea salt and airplane fuel. Our hair was streaked with blonde from the sun and greasy at the roots. We hadn't been able to wash for three days.

Once the last group of passengers boarded we could see out the window again. The morning light was breaking across the sky, revealing the sandstone and granite details of the buildings we had not been able to see when it was dark. The modern and Art Deco buildings of downtown Sydney weren't as tall as those in Shanghai but the sky above them was pristine blue. Past the helm of the ship the sun was sending golden rays shimmering across the water and I could see some red-roofed houses dotted along the foreshore. I pressed my palms together and brought my hands to my lips. Those beams of sunlight on the water were beautiful. There was no reference for the harbour in anything in my past. Its colour was the mythical hue of a mermaid's eyes.

The stationmaster waved his flag and blew his whistle.

The train shunted forward. The smell of coal was more oppressive than the air in the compartment and Irina shut the window. All of us crowded to the window to see the city when the train left the port. Through my square of the glass I saw prewar-style cars motoring along the streets in an orderly fashion; there were no traffic jams, tooting horns or rickshaws as in Shanghai. The train passed an apartment building. The lobby door opened and a woman in a white dress, hat and gloves stepped out. She looked like a model in a perfume advertisement. The image of the woman blended with the image of the harbour, and I felt excited about Australia for the first time.

But a few minutes later we were passing rows of fibro-cement houses with tin roofs and untidy gardens, and my excitement turned to despair. I hoped what was true of other cities was also true of Sydney, that only the very poor lived near rail lines. The view from the window was a reminder that we were not in America. Gene Kelly and Frank Sinatra would not dance merrily through this place. Even in the city there had been no great pillars to the gods. No Empire State Building. No Statue of Liberty. No Times Square. Only a street of elegant buildings and a bridge.

The younger Polish woman reached into her handbag and pulled out a package wrapped in cloth. The smell of bread and boiled eggs mixed in with the human scent in the air. She offered Irina and me a square of egg sandwich each. I accepted my piece gratefully. I was hungry because I hadn't eaten breakfast. Even Irina, who had no appetite because of the influenza, accepted her piece with a smile.

'*Smacznego!*' Irina said. '*Bon appétit.*'

'How many languages do you speak?' I asked her.

'None except Russian,' she said, grinning. 'But I can sing in German and French.'

I turned back to the window and saw that the view had

changed again. We were passing market farms with lettuce, carrots and tomato vines planted in rows. Birds skittered through the fields. The houses seemed as solitary as the outhouses that stood in their yards. We passed through train stations that I would have thought deserted if not for their well-tended rosebushes and neatly painted signs.

'Perhaps Ivan will be at the camp,' Irina said.

'Melbourne is south,' I told her. 'A long way from here.'

'Then we must write to him soon. He will be surprised that we are in Australia.'

Irina's mention of Ivan brought back the unhappy memory of those last weeks in Tubabao and I squirmed in my seat. I told her that I would write to Ivan, but I didn't sound convincing, even to myself. Irina regarded me curiously for a moment, but said nothing more. She wrapped the blanket tighter around her shoulders and rested her head against the side of the seat. 'What is this place we are going to?' she yawned. 'I want to stay in the city.' A moment later she was asleep.

I played with the clasp of my handbag. It seemed strange that the elegant accessory in my lap had accompanied me all the way from Shanghai and was on its way with me to a refugee camp somewhere in the Australian countryside. The first time I had used the suede bag was to go to lunch with Luba at her ladies' club. The lunch had been before Dmitri was unfaithful to me, and before I ever thought I would live anywhere else but China. The skin had faded in the Tubabao sun and there was a tear along the side. I fingered the scar on my face and wondered if the handbag and I were sharing a common destiny. I opened it and pressed my fingers against the matroshka doll inside. I thought about the day my mother was taken away and wondered what she had seen on her way to Russia. Had it been as alien to her as the scenery outside was to me?

I bit my lip and steeled myself, remembering my vow to be courageous. As soon as I could, I would contact the

Red Cross. I told myself not to be worried about what kind of work I would be given or where I had to live; the only thing that mattered was finding my mother.

A while later the train started to climb, winding its way through a forest of white-barked trees so tall they almost blotted out the sun. They were unlike any trees I had seen before, ghostly and elegant, broad leaves quivering in the breeze. Later I would learn their names: blue gum, peppermint gum, stringy-bark, mottled gum, scribbly gum. But on that morning, they were yet another mystery to me.

The train jolted and came to a stop, sending passengers and luggage flying. I lifted my hand just in time to stop a box falling on Irina's head.

'Meal stop!' the conductor called out.

The Polish family looked to me to interpret the instruction. I gestured to them that we were getting off the train.

We stepped outside onto a little station surrounded by gullies of gum trees and sheer sandstone cliffs. The air was as fresh and sharp as menthol. Where the rock had been cut for the track there were crevices in the face of the stone. Water seeped through the cracks and mosses, liverworts and lichens clung there with tenacity. From all directions the atmosphere was alive with sounds: water trickling over rocks, the rustle of animals moving through the leaf litter, and birds. Never before had I heard such a chorus of birdsong.

A group of women were waiting for us on the platform, positioned like a small army behind trestle tables and soup urns. Their weather-beaten faces sized us up.

I turned around to find Irina and was shocked to see that she was bending over the side of the platform, holding a handkerchief to her mouth. I rushed towards her as a trickle of vomit fell from her lips and dripped onto the tracks.

'It's just the flu and the motion of the train. It's nothing,' she said.

'Can you eat something?' I rubbed my palm over her feverish forehead. It was not a good time to be sick.

'Maybe some soup.'

'Sit down,' I told her. 'I'll bring you something.'

I stood in line with the others, glancing over my shoulder every so often to check on Irina. She was sitting on the edge of the platform, her blanket wrapped over her head so that she looked like a woman from the Middle East. I felt a tug on my sleeve and turned around to see a gnome-faced woman with a bowl of onion-smelling soup in her hands.

'Is she very sick?' the woman asked, handing me the bowl. 'I brought it to you to save you standing in line.' Like the taxi driver her voice was dry and crackled. The timbre of it warmed me.

'It's the change in weather and the journey,' I said. 'We expected Australia to be warm.'

The woman laughed and folded her arms across her ample chest. 'My word, the weather can change, love. But I suspect it will be hot where you are going. Dry as a bone in the Central West this month, I hear.'

'We came from an island where it was always hot,' I said.

'Well, you're on a big island now,' she smiled, rocking back and forth on the balls of her feet. 'Not that you will believe it once you're inland.'

I thanked her for the soup and carried it to Irina. She tried a mouthful and shook her head. 'My nose is blocked but I can still smell the fat. What is it?'

'Sheep meat, I think.'

Irina pushed the bowl towards me. 'You'd better eat it, if you can. It tastes like lanolin to me.'

After eating, we were instructed to board the train again. I offered the Czechoslovakian men my seat, if they wanted to take turns to sit down, but they declined. The one with

251

the faded star on his coat could speak a little English and said, 'No. You take care of your friend. We will sit on our suitcases when we get tired.'

The sun lowered and we entered a world of raw granite and grassland. White-barked trees stood like ghostly sentries in the endless fields staked out with barbed-wire fences. Flocks of sheep dotted the hills. Every so often a farmhouse with smoke rising from the chimney came into view. Each one had a corrugated water tank perched on stilts next to it. The old Polish lady and Irina were asleep, lulled by the motion of the train and the length of the journey. But the rest of us couldn't take our eyes off the strange world outside.

The woman opposite me began to cry and her husband scolded her. But I could see in the nervous twitch of his mouth that he was trying to quell his own fear. My stomach churned. I felt calmer if I looked above the land, to the sun spinning gold and violet threads across the sky.

Just before dusk the train slowed and came to a stop. Irina and the old woman woke up and glanced about them. There were voices, then the sounds of the doors rattling open. Fresh air rolled over us. Men and women in brown army uniforms and broad-rimmed hats hurried by the windows. I could see a convoy of buses and a couple of trucks parked in the copper-coloured dirt. The buses weren't like the ones we had on Tubabao. They were pristine and new. An ambulance pulled up alongside them and waited with its motor running.

There was no station and the soldiers were dragging ramps up to the doors so that people could get out. We started to collect our things but when the old woman looked out the window she screamed. The Polish man and woman tried to calm her, but the old woman squatted and wedged herself behind her seat, panting like a frightened animal.

252

A soldier, a boy with a sunburned neck and freckles on his cheeks, rushed to the compartment.

'What's the problem?' he asked.

The young Polish woman took one look at his uniform and backed into the corner with her mother, throwing her arms protectively around her. It was then I noticed the tattooed number on her arm poking through her sleeve.

'What's the matter?' the soldier asked, looking around at us. He was shuffling his hands in his pockets, searching for something, and trembling as if he himself were on the verge of a fit. 'Does anyone speak their language?'

'They are Jews,' said the Czechoslovakian who could speak English. 'Think what this must look like to them.'

The soldier frowned, puzzled. But receiving some sort of explanation for the hysterical behaviour, even if he didn't understand it, seemed to calm him. He straightened his spine and puffed out his chest, and began taking control of the situation. 'Do you speak English?' he asked me. I nodded and he told me and Irina to make our way to the buses, explaining that perhaps if the women saw us go willingly they would be more confident about following us. I helped Irina out of her seat, but she almost swooned and we stumbled over a suitcase. 'Is she sick?' the soldier asked. The veins in his forehead were starting to show and his chin was tucked into his neck, but he still managed to sound compassionate. 'You can take her to the ambulance. They'll take her to the hospital if she needs it.'

I considered translating what he said for Irina, but decided against it. She might be better off at the hospital, but she would not agree to being separated from me.

Outside the train we were told by the soldiers to take our luggage to the trucks and then to board the buses. A flock of pink and grey parrots had settled on a bare patch of dirt and seemed to be watching us. They were pretty birds and looked out of place in this environment. They seemed more suited to a tropical island than the grassy hills that surrounded us. I turned back to the train door to see what was happening with the Polish family. The soldier and the Czechoslovakian were helping the women down the ramp. The Polish man was following with their suitcases. The young woman seemed calmer and even smiled at me, but the old woman's eyes were darting about like a madwoman's and she was almost doubled over with her fear. I squeezed my hands into fists, digging the nails into my skin and trying to stop myself from crying. What hope did that woman have? The situation was hard enough for myself and Irina. I glanced down at my sandals. My toes were covered in dust.

It was dark when the convoy of buses came to a stop outside a barricade. The camp guard stepped out of his box and lifted the post for us to go through. Our bus jerked forward, followed by the others, into the campsite. I pressed my face against the glass and saw the Australian flag flapping from a pole in the centre of the driveway. Radiating out from this point were rows of army barracks, most of them wooden but some made from corrugated iron. The ground between the huts was hardened dirt with tufts of grass and weeds poking through the cracks. Rabbits scampered around the campsite as freely as chickens in a farmyard.

The driver told us to disembark and make our way to the dining hall directly ahead of us. Irina and I followed the others to something that looked like a small aircraft hangar with windows. Inside we found rows of tables covered with brown paper and spread with sandwiches, sponge cakes and cups for tea and coffee. The agitated voices of the passengers echoed off the unlined walls and the bare light bulbs gave their tired complexions an even more sickly tinge. Irina sank down onto one of the seats and rested her face in her palms. A man with woolly black hair noticed her as he passed. He was carrying a clipboard and wore some sort of badge on his coat. 'Red Cross. Top of the hill,' he said, tapping her shoulder. 'Go there or we'll all be ill.'

I was excited to hear that there was a Red Cross office in the camp and slid into the seat next to Irina. I told her what the man had said, only I phrased it more politely. 'We'll go tomorrow,' she said, pressing her hand into mine. 'I'm not up to it tonight.'

The man with the clipboard stepped onto a podium and announced in heavily accented English that shortly we would be sorted into groups for accommodation. Men and women would be accommodated separately. Children would be accommodated with either parent according to their age and sex. The news was quickly translated around the hall and voices began to cry out in protest.

'You can't separate us!' one man said, standing up. He pointed to the woman and two small children with him. 'This is my family. We were separated all through the war.'

I told Irina what was happening. 'How can they do such a thing?' she said, still speaking into her palms. 'People need their families at times like these.'

A tear dripped down her face and onto the brown paper. I put my arm around her and rested my head against her shoulder. We *were* each other's family. Our roles had become reversed. Irina was older and of a more sanguine disposition than I was and it was usually she who gave me encouragement. But Ruselina was ill and far away, and Irina was in a new country whose people spoke a language she didn't understand. On top of all that, she was sick. I realised that it was up to me to be strong, and I was terrified. It was taking all my strength to keep my own spirits up. How would I ever be able to lift Irina's as well?

Our block supervisor was a Hungarian woman named Aimka Berczi. She had a bland face but long, delicate hands. She issued us with cards on which were printed our names, countries of birth, vessels of arrival and room numbers. She told us to go to our barracks and get some sleep. The camp director, Colonel Brighton, would address us in the morning.

My eyes were watering with exhaustion and Irina could barely stand, but as soon as I opened the door to our wooden shack I wished I had been more forceful about making her go to the hospital. The first thing I saw was a bare light bulb dangling from the ceiling and a bug flittering around it. There were twenty camp beds crammed side by side on the wooden floor. Washing was strung over fold-up chairs and suitcases and the air was dank and musty. Most of the beds were already occupied by sleeping women, so Irina and I headed for the two spare ones at the end of the room. One of the women, an old lady with bobby pins in her hair, looked up when we passed her bed. She propped herself on her elbow and whispered, '*Sind Sie Deutsche?*'

I shook my head because I couldn't understand her.

'No, not German,' she said in English. 'Russian. I can tell by your cheekbones.' The woman had grooves like scars around her mouth. She was probably only sixty years old, but the lines made her look eighty.

'Yes, Russian,' I said.

The woman seemed disappointed but smiled just the same. 'Tell me when you are ready and I will turn out the light.'

'I am Anya Kozlova and my friend is Irina Levitskya,' I told her. I helped Irina down onto one of the rickety cots and put our suitcases at the foot of the beds, where I noticed everyone else kept theirs. 'We are Russians from China.'

The woman relaxed a little. 'I'm pleased to meet you,' she said. 'My name is Elsa Lehmann. And tomorrow you will learn that everyone in this room hates me.'

'Why?' I asked.

The woman shook her head. 'Because they are Poles and Hungarians and I am German.'

I didn't know how to continue the conversation after she said that, so I turned my attention to making our beds. We had been issued with four army blankets and a pillow each. The breeze outside had been cool, but there was no air circulation in the hut and it was hard to breathe. Irina asked what the woman had said, so I explained Elsa's situation to her.

'Is she here alone?' Irina asked.

I translated the question for Elsa who said, 'I came with my husband, a doctor, and the one son who survived the war. They sent them to Queensland to cut cane.'

'I'm sorry to hear that,' I said. I wondered what the Australian government had in mind when it encouraged families from around the world to come to its shores and then separated them.

I helped Irina tuck in her sheets and one blanket then fixed my own. I was self-conscious about the fusty odour that rose from our feet and underwear when we changed into our nightclothes, but Elsa was already asleep. I tiptoed over to her bed and pulled the light switch.

'I guess we will find out tomorrow if they like or hate Russians,' Irina said, closing her eyes and drifting off to sleep.

I climbed into the bed and pulled the sheets over me. It was too hot for blankets. I turned from my back to my side and onto my back again, exhausted but unable to sleep. I opened my eyes and stared at the ceiling, listening to Irina's breathing. If the Australians could separate Elsa from her husband and son, how much more likely were they to separate us? And if they could send a doctor to cut cane, what kind of work would they give us? I squeezed my palms against the side of my head and pushed the thoughts from my mind. I focused instead on the idea of finding my mother. Whatever lay ahead, I must be strong.

I pulled the sheet up to my throat and tried to catch a glimpse of the world through the gap in the wall, but all I could see were the silhouettes of the hills in the distance and a few stars. Finally my fatigue got the better of my fear and I fell asleep.

* * *

The morning light flickered over the flaking paint on the floorboards. A rooster greeted the day with a cry. From somewhere nearby a horse snorted and sheep were bleating. I rubbed my eyes and sat up. Irina's eyes were squeezed shut, as if she was resisting the idea of waking up. Everyone else was fast asleep too and the air in the hut was stale and hot. There was a gap between two of the planks in the wall next to my bed and I could see golden light sparkling off the tin roofs and fences. A truck was parked outside and a dusty sheepdog crouched under it. The dog pricked up his ears when he spotted me spying on him. He wagged his tail and yelped. I quickly lay down, not wanting his bark to wake the others.

As the light increased, the other women began to stir, kicking their bedsheets aside like caterpillars emerging from cocoons. I said good morning to Elsa but she averted her eyes, gathered a brunch coat and towel and scurried out the door. The other women, who looked to be in their twenties and thirties, blinked at me, wondering when Irina and I had appeared. I said hello and tried to introduce myself. A few of them smiled back and one girl, whose English was not as fluent as mine, commented that it was awkward that we didn't have a common language between us.

Irina pushed herself up onto her pillow and combed her hair with her fingers. She had flakes of sleep in her eyelashes and her lips looked dry.

'How are you?' I asked her.

'Not good,' she said, swallowing hard. 'I'll stay in bed.'

'I'll bring you some food. You must eat something.'

Irina shook her head. 'Just water, please. Don't bring back any of that soup.'

'How about beef stroganoff with vodka, then?'

Irina grinned and lay back down, covering her eyes with her arm. 'Go and discover Australia, Anya Kozlova,' she said. 'And tell me all about it when you get back.'

I didn't have a robe or brunch coat. Not even a towel.

But I couldn't stand the musky smell of my hair and skin any longer. I took the cleanest-looking blanket from the ones we had been issued and a bar of soap I had brought from Tubabao. I held them up to the girl who could speak some English, hoping she would understand what I wanted. She pointed to a map on the back of the door. The ablutions block was marked with a red X. I thanked her and picked out the last fresh dress from my suitcase before heading out into the sunshine.

The barracks in our area were almost identical. Here and there people had taken time to put curtains up or create flowerbeds with pieces of rock, but there was none of the pride and solidarity of Tubabao. But then we had all been Russians. I had only been in Australia a day and already I had seen racial tensions. I wondered why they didn't organise all the migrants and refugees into our national groups, it would have been easier for us to communicate and for them to administer, but then I recalled the phrase they used on our identity cards – 'New Australians' – and I remembered that they wanted us to assimilate. I thought about the term 'New Australian' and decided I liked it. I wanted to be new again.

My jovial mood left me when I stepped into the toilet block. I would have put my foot straight into an overflowing pan if the stench hadn't stopped me first. I clasped the blanket to my nose and looked around the hut in horror. There were no doors on the cubicles, just leaking pans set low on the ground with blowflies buzzing around them. The seats were caked with excreta and dirty paper was clumped on the wet floor. There had been two chain toilets in the dining hall but that would not be sufficient for the whole camp. 'Do they think we are animals?' I screamed, hurrying back out into the air.

I had never seen conditions so foul for white people, not even in Shanghai. After seeing Sydney I thought that Australia was going to be an advanced country. Surely the camp organisers knew about disease? We had eaten at the army base in Darwin, and I began to wonder if Irina had something worse than influenza, perhaps hepatitis or even cholera.

I heard voices from the shower block and glanced inside. It was clean but the shower stalls were nothing more than rusty tin sheets with gaps. Two women were showering with their children. I was so upset that I forgot all about privacy and tore off my nightdress, huddled under the pathetic dribble of the shower rose and cried.

At breakfast my fears grew worse. We were served sausages, ham and eggs. Some people discovered maggots in their meat and one woman rushed out of the hall to be sick. I didn't eat the meat, I only drank the acidic-tasting tea with three teaspoons of sugar and a piece of bread. A Polish group near me complained about the bread. They told one of the Australian kitchen hands that it was too doughy. He shrugged and told them that was how it was delivered. The Chinese bread I ate in Harbin was steamed and much more sticky, so I was used to it. I was more concerned about how clean the kitchen was and whether the cooks understood anything about hygiene. My hair hung in limp strands around my ears and my skin smelled like wool from the blanket. I couldn't believe how far I had fallen. A year ago I had been a new bride with an elegant apartment, married to the manager of the most famous nightclub in Shanghai. Now I was a refugee. I felt the degradation of it more keenly than I had on Tubabao.

Irina had been asleep when I returned from my shower, and I was relieved that I didn't have to face her until I had a chance to compose myself. I had promised myself that I would never complain to her about Australia. She would blame herself for making me come, although it had been my choice. I thought of Dmitri in America and my spine prickled. But to my surprise I didn't focus too long on him before my thoughts started shifting to Ivan. What would he have made of all this?

A man in army uniform entered the hall and made his way past the tables to the podium. He climbed up the step and waited for us to fall silent, clasping a swatch of cardboard sheets to his side and coughing once into his fist. It was only when he had the attention of every person in the room that he began to speak.

'Good morning, ladies and gentlemen. Welcome to Australia,' he said. 'My name is Colonel Brighton. I am the camp director.' He put the sheets of cardboard down on the podium and picked up the first sign, holding it up so that everyone could see. It had his name written on it in large letters so neatly printed that they could have been typed.

'I hope that those of you who can speak English will translate what I have to say for your friends,' he continued. 'Unfortunately, my translators are busy with something else this morning.' He smiled at us from beneath his dark moustache. His uniform was too tight and made him look like a little boy who had been tucked firmly into his bed.

Until the Colonel addressed us, my arrival in Australia had seemed like a dream. But when he started talking about our work contracts with the Commonwealth Employment Service and how we must be prepared to do any sort of work, even if we considered it beneath us, to pay back our passages to Australia, the magnitude of what Irina and I had done hit me. I glanced around at the sea of anxious faces and wondered whether the announcement was worse for those who couldn't understand English or whether it was affording them the luxury of a few more minutes' reprieve from reality?

I dug my fingers into my palms and tried to follow the Colonel's lecture on the Australian currency, the state and federal political systems, and the relationship to the British

monarchy. For each new subject he held up a card to illus-
trate the main points and ended his talk with, 'And I
implore you all, both young and old, to learn as much
English as you possibly can while you are here. Your success
in Australia will depend on it.'

There wasn't a sound in the room when Colonel
Brighton finished speaking, but he simply grinned at us
like Father Christmas. 'Oh, by the way, there is someone
I need to see,' he said, glancing at his notebook. 'Can Anya
Kozlova please come forward?'

I was startled by the mention of my name. Why was I
being singled out from three hundred new arrivals? I made
my way through the tables to the Colonel, tucking my hair
behind my ears and wondering if something had happened
to Irina. A crowd of people had gathered around him to
ask questions. 'But we don't want to live in countryside.
In city,' a man with a patch on his eye was insisting.

No, I told myself, Irina is safe. I wondered if maybe Ivan
had heard we were in Australia and was trying to contact
us. I dismissed that thought too. Ivan's ship was bound for
Sydney, but he had told us he intended to go straight to
Melbourne by train. He had enough funds to stay out of
a camp.

'Ah, you're Anya?' said the Colonel, when he saw me
waiting. 'Come with me, please.'

Colonel Brighton marched at a sprightly pace towards
the administrative area and I had to almost skip to keep
up with him. We passed more rows of barracks, kitchens
and laundries and a post office, and I began to appreciate
the size of the camp. The Colonel told me that the camp
used to belong to the army and that a lot of ex-army
barracks were being turned into migrant accommodation
all over the country. Although I was anxious to know why
he wanted to see me, his small talk assured me that it
wasn't anything too serious.

'So you're Russian, Anya. Where from?'

'I was born in Harbin in China. I've never been to Russia. But I spent a lot of time in Shanghai.'

He tucked his cardboard signs further under his arm and frowned at a broken window in one of the huts. 'Report that to the maintenance office,' he told a man sitting on the steps, before turning back to me. 'My wife is English. Rose has read a lot of books about Russia. She reads a lot of books in general. So where were you born? Moscow?'

I didn't take the Colonel's lack of concentration to heart. He was shorter than me with deep-set eyes and a receding hairline. The lines on his forehead and his button nose made his face seem comical, although his upright posture and his manner of speaking were serious. There was something likeable about him, he was efficient without being cold. The Colonel had mentioned that there were over three thousand people in the camp. How could he remember us all?

Colonel Brighton's office was a wooden hut not far from the cinema hall. He pushed open the door and ushered me inside. A woman with red hair and horn-rimmed glasses glanced up from her desk, her fingers perched over a typewriter.

'This is my secretary, Dorothy,' the Colonel said.

The woman smoothed the folds of her floral dress and pinched her lips into a smile.

'I am pleased to meet you,' I said. 'I am Anya Kozlova.'

Dorothy glanced over me before deciding to fix her gaze on my straggly hair. I blushed and looked away. Behind her were two unoccupied desks, and another desk from which a bald man in a fawn-coloured shirt and tie smiled at us. 'And this is the welfare officer,' the Colonel said, indicating the man. 'Ernie Howard.'

'Pleased to meet you,' Ernie said, getting up from his seat and shaking my hand.

'Anya's from Russia. She arrived last night,' the Colonel said.

'Russia? Probably China,' said Ernie, releasing my hand. 'We have a few people from Tubabao here.'

Colonel Brighton didn't notice the correction. He flipped through some files on Ernie's desk, picked one up and indicated a door at the end of the room. 'Come this way, Anya,' he said.

I followed the Colonel into his office. The sun through the windows was brilliant and the room was hot. The Colonel opened the slats on the windows and turned on a fan. I sat in the chair opposite his desk and found that I was facing not only Colonel Brighton but the long, sour face of the British King, whose portrait hung on a wall behind him. The Colonel's office was orderly, with files and books packed neatly along the sides of the walls and a framed map of Australia in the far corner. But his desk was in chaos. It was overloaded with files and looked in danger of collapse. The Colonel placed the file he was carrying on top of the others and opened it.

'Anya, I have a letter here from Captain Connor of the IRO saying that you worked for him. That you speak good English, which is obvious, and can type.'

'Yes,' I said.

Colonel Brighton sighed and leaned back into his chair. He considered me for a long time. I shifted in my seat, wishing he would say something. Finally, he did.

'Can I persuade you to work for me for a month or two?' he asked. 'Until they send me more staff from Sydney. We are in rather a mess. This camp is not at all what it should be, especially not for women. And there will be another thousand people arriving here over the next fortnight.'

The Colonel's admission that the camp conditions weren't acceptable was a relief. I thought we might have been expected to live with them.

'What do you want me to do?' I asked.

'I need someone who can help me, Dorothy and Ernie. We urgently need to do something about the cleanliness

264

of the camp, so I want you to take over the filing and other general duties. I can pay you above the allowance and will give the employment officer a special recommendation for you when you finish.'

The Colonel's offer took me by surprise. I hadn't known what to expect from him, but I certainly hadn't been expecting that he would offer me a job on my first day at the camp. I had only one American dollar left from Tubabao and I couldn't sell the jewels I had brought from Shanghai until I got to Sydney. Some extra money was just what I needed.

The Colonel's honesty gave me confidence to tell him that I thought the toilets and food were serious problems, and that we were in danger of an epidemic.

He nodded. 'Until yesterday's intake we were just managing. This morning I organised for the Sanipan company to come three times a day, and Dorothy is assembling new teams for the kitchens right now. There's no time for mucking about. As soon as I see a problem, I do my best to fix it. The only difficulty is that I have far too many problems to fix quickly.' He pointed to the files on his desk.

I wondered if I should accept the job and go, as he had a lot to do, but he seemed to enjoy talking to me so I asked him why the Australian government was bringing so many people into the country if it couldn't provide adequate places for them to live.

Colonel Brighton's eyes lit up and I realised he had been waiting for me to ask that question. He strode over to the map and picked up the pointer. I had to pinch my lips together to stop myself from laughing.

'The government has decided on a policy of populate or perish,' he said, indicating the Australian coast with the pointer. 'We were nearly invaded by the Japanese because there weren't enough people to guard our shores. The government is bringing thousands of people into the country to build the nation up. But until we build the

economy, no one is going to have a decent place to live.'
He walked over to the window and leaned against the
frame. If he had been someone else, the way he stood
with his feet apart and his chin thrust into the air would
have seemed overdramatic, but it fitted so well with his
character that I stopped wanting to laugh and found myself
listening to him attentively.

'All I can say to apologise is that there are plenty of
native-born Australians living in packing crates.'

The Colonel returned to his desk; his whole face was
red with excitement and he spread his hands over the files
in front of him. 'You. Me. Everyone here, we are part of a
grand social experiment,' he said. 'We are going to become
a new nation and we are either going to sink or swim. I'd
like to do my best to see us swim. I think you would like
to see us do the same.'

Colonel Brighton's words were like a drug; I could feel
the blood begin to rush through my veins and had to
remind myself to stay calm or else I'd get swept up in what
he was saying. The Colonel made living in a shabby,
depressing camp sound almost exciting. He may not have
been a good listener but he was obviously a passionate and
enthusiastic man. I was sure I wanted to work with him,
if only for the fun of seeing him every day.

'When would you like me to start?' I asked.

He rushed towards me and shook my hand. 'This afternoon,' he said, glancing back at the files on his desk.
'Straight after lunch.'

TWELVE

Wildflowers

After my meeting with Colonel Brighton I hurried back to the hut with a pitcher of water and a glass from the kitchen. I was surprised to find Irina sitting up in bed, talking with Aimka Berczi.

'Here's your friend,' said Aimka, standing up to greet me. She was wearing a bottle-green dress and holding an orange in one of her delicate hands. I assumed she had brought it for Irina. Neither the deep tone of her dress nor the colour of the orange brought any life to her face. In the daylight her skin seemed as unearthly as it had the night before.

'I'm glad,' said Irina, her voice croaking. 'I'm dying of thirst.'

I balanced the pitcher on the upturned box near her bed and poured her a glass of water. I put my palm to her forehead. Her temperature was gone but she was still pale.

'How are you feeling?'

'Yesterday I thought I was dying. Now I just feel sick.'

'I thought Irina might still be ill this morning,' said Aimka, 'so I brought her the employment and English class registration forms.'

'The questions are all in English,' Irina said, taking a sip of water and grimacing. I wondered if the tea had tasted bad this morning because of the water.

'Never mind, once you've finished the English course you'll be able to complete them,' I said.

We all laughed and the mirth brought a spot of colour to Aimka's face.

'Aimka speaks six languages fluently,' said Irina. 'Now she's teaching herself Serbian.'

'Goodness,' I said, 'what a talent for languages you have!'

Aimka brought one of her lovely hands to her throat and lowered her eyes. 'I came from a family of diplomats,' she said. 'And there are plenty of Yugoslavians here to practise with.'

'I imagine you would have to be a good diplomat to be a block supervisor,' I said. 'Do you know about Elsa?'

Aimka dropped her hands to her lap. I found it hard to keep my eyes off them, they were like two lilies against the green of her dress. 'It seems we have all the tensions of Europe in this camp,' she said. 'People argue over border towns as fiercely as if they were still living in them.'

'Do you think there is something we can do for Elsa?' Irina asked.

Aimka shook her head. 'I've always had trouble with her,' she said. 'Elsa's never happy wherever I put her and she doesn't make an effort to be friendly with the others. In another hut I have a German and Jewish girl together who can't do enough to help each other. But then they are young, and Elsa is old and set in her ways.'

'Russians say that as long as you have good food no one will argue,' I told her. 'If the peasants had been well fed there wouldn't have been a revolution. Perhaps people wouldn't be so tense if the food was better. Whatever we had for breakfast this morning was barely edible.'

'Yes, I hear endless complaints about the food,' Aimka replied. 'It seems that the Australians are fond of over-cooking their vegetables. And of course there is too much mutton. But during the siege of Budapest I was boiling my shoes to eat, so I don't find much to complain about here.'

I blushed. I should have known better than to be so flippant.

'What have you been doing this morning, Anya?' Irina asked, coming to my rescue.

I told them about my job with Colonel Brighton and about his passion for 'populate or perish'.

Irina rolled her eyes and Aimka laughed. 'Yes, he's a character, Colonel Brighton,' Aimka said. 'Sometimes I think he's quite mad, but he has a good heart. You'll do well to work for him. I will see if I can get Irina a job at the crèche, anything to save her from the stupid employment officer.'

'He was trying to give Aimka work as a domestic,' Irina explained.

'Really?'

Aimka rubbed her hands together. 'I told him that I spoke six languages and he told me that was a useless skill in Australia, except for the English. He said that there were no jobs for interpreters and I was too old to get any other kind of work.'

'That's crazy,' I said. 'Look at all the people in this camp. And Colonel Brighton told me this morning that there are more camps just like it all over Australia.'

Aimka snorted. 'That's the problem. *New Australians*, indeed. They want us all to be British. I went to Colonel Brighton and told him that I spoke six languages. He almost jumped out of his chair to kiss me. He put me to work straightaway as an English teacher and a block supervisor. Every time I see him now he says, "Aimka, I need twenty more of you." So, for all his faults, he has my admiration.'

Irina shuddered and coughed. She pulled a handkerchief from under her pillow and blew her nose. 'Excuse me,' she said. 'I think this means I'm getting over it.'

'We'd better go to the Red Cross tent,' I said.

Irina shook her head. 'I just want to sleep. But you should go and ask them about your mother.'

269

Aimka glanced at us curiously and I told her briefly about my mother.

'The Red Cross here won't be able to help you, Anya,' she said. 'It's just a medical unit. You'll need to see someone at the headquarters in Sydney.'

'Oh,' I said, disappointed.

Aimka patted Irina's leg and put the orange on the box next to the pitcher. 'I'd better get going,' she said.

After Aimka left, Irina turned to me and whispered, 'She was a concert pianist in Budapest. Her parents were shot by the Nazis for hiding Jews.'

'God,' I said, 'there are three thousand tragic stories in this tiny place.'

After Irina had fallen asleep again, I gathered our clothes and rushed to the laundry, which consisted of four cement tubs and a boiler. I scrubbed the dresses and blouses with my last bar of soap. After hanging them out to dry, I went to the supply office where the clerk, a Polish man, kept glancing from my throat to my breasts.

'All I can offer you is ex-army shoes, ex-army coats or an ex-army hat. If you would like any of those.' He pointed to an elderly couple trying on odd pairs of boots. The old man's legs trembled and he leaned on his wife's shoulder for support. The sight of them broke my heart. I thought old people should be enjoying the fruits of their labour, not starting over again.

'No soap?' I asked. 'No towels?'

The store clerk shrugged. 'This isn't the Paris Ritz.'

I bit my lip. Shampoo and scented soap would have to wait until payday. At least our clothes were clean. Perhaps Aimka would lend us something and we could pay her back.

Lunch was announced over a loudspeaker hooked to the wall of the supply hut, first in English and then in German. I saw the old woman flinch at the sound of '*Achtung!*'

270

'Why do they announce things in German?' I asked the store clerk.

'Sensitive, isn't it?' he said, smiling from the corner of his mouth. 'They figure that thanks to the Nazis we all understand orders in German.'

I dragged my feet to the dining hut, dreading another unpalatable meal. Most people were already seated when I arrived but the atmosphere in the room had transformed since the morning. The diners were smiling. The brown paper was gone and each table had been decorated with jars of blue flowers. A man walked by with a bowl of soup and a piece of brown bread. Whatever was in the bowl smelled mouth-watering, and familiar. I glanced at the crimson soup and thought I must be dreaming. Borscht. I picked up a bowl from a pile on a table and stood in line in front of the servery window. I almost jumped for joy when I found myself face to face with Mariya and Natasha from Tubabao.

'Ah!' we all cried out together.

'Come,' said Natasha, opening the bench door. 'Almost everyone has been fed now. Eat with us in the kitchen.'

I followed her into the back room, which not only smelled of beetroot and cabbage but bleach and bicarbonate of soda as well. Two men were busy washing down the walls and Natasha introduced them as her father, Lev, and her husband, Piotr. Mariya filled my bowl to the brim with the fresh borscht while Natasha found me a chair and poured us all cups of tea.

'How is Raisa?' I asked them.

'She's not bad,' said Lev. 'We were worried that she wouldn't make the trip but she's tougher than we thought. She's in a hut with Natasha and the children and seems happy there.'

I told them about Ruselina and they shook their heads in sympathy. 'Give Irina our love,' said Mariya.

On the shelf next to me was a bunch of the blue flowers

271

I had seen earlier. I fingered the tubular petals and the elegant stems.

'What are these?' I asked Natasha. 'They're lovely.'

'I'm not sure,' she said, wiping her hands on her apron. 'I think they're Australian. We found them on a little track down past the tent section. They are pretty, aren't they?'

'I like the trees here,' I said. 'They are mysterious, as if they are hiding secrets in their trunks.'

'Well, you'd like this walk then,' said Lev. He put down his scrubbing brush, sat at the table and began drawing a map for me on a piece of brown paper. 'The track is easy to find. You won't get lost.'

I swallowed a spoonful of borscht. After what I had been eating the past few days, it was liquid heaven. 'This is delicious,' I said.

Mariya pointed with her chin to the dining hall. 'I'm sure we will have a lot of complaints about Russian food. But it's better than what the Australian chef was serving. It's good nourishing work food.'

Some more people came to the window and held up their plates, asking for seconds. Lev and I exchanged smiles. I watched Natasha and Mariya attend to them. When I had seen the family's tent on Tubabao, for some reason I had thought they must be rich. But now I realised there was nothing in that tent which they hadn't created themselves from the materials available to them. If they had funds they wouldn't be in a migrant camp. I realised that they must simply be industrious and hardworking, determined to make the best of whatever life handed them. I watched Mariya point and make faces with the diners, trying to communicate with them. I was full of admiration.

I returned to Colonel Brighton's office just before two o'clock. I was surprised to hear voices arguing and hesitated before pushing open the door. Dorothy was at her desk and smiled when I slipped inside but cut the expression short when she recognised me. I was confounded by what I had done to inspire such dislike in her so quickly.

The Colonel and Ernie were standing in the doorway of the Colonel's office. A woman was with them, her gloves and hat poised in her hands. She was in her fifties and had a pretty face and lively eyes. The group turned to look at me when I said, 'Good afternoon.'

'Ah, there you are, Anya!' said the Colonel. 'Just in time. We have toilets that are a threat to our health, food going bad in the heat, and people who can't speak any of the languages in which we have been trying to communicate with them. Nonetheless, my wife has decided that what we need most urgently is a tree-planting committee.'

The woman, who I took to be his wife, rolled her eyes. 'People take one look at this camp and feel depressed, Robert. Plants, trees and flowers will take away the starkness and make people feel better. We should try to make the camp more of a home. That's what a lot of these people have been missing for years. A home. Anya will tell you.'

She nodded her head at me. I sensed I was about to be used as a tie breaker and was careful not to speak too soon.

'It's not a home,' said the Colonel, 'it's a holding centre. The army didn't mind the way it looked.'

'That's because if it was beautiful they would never have gone off to war!'

Rose folded her arms across her chest, bouncing her hat in her hand. She was short and feminine but her arms were muscular. She had made a good point, I thought, and I wondered what the Colonel would say in reply.

'I'm not saying your idea is a bad one, Rose. I'm just saying that I have to get these people fed first and get them speaking some sort of English. I have hundreds of doctors, lawyers and architects who must be taught some manual skills if they and their families are going to survive in this country. The professional jobs will go to the British immigrants, whether they are better qualified for them or not.'

273

Rose sniffed at this and pulled a notebook from her handbag. She flipped it open and began reading from a list. 'Look,' she said, 'this is what the Dutch ladies suggested we could plant: tulips, daffodils, carnations . . .'

Colonel Brighton glanced at Ernie, throwing his hands up in exasperation.

Rose looked up at them. 'Well, if you don't like flowers, other people have suggested cedars and pines for shade.'

'Good gracious, Rose,' said Ernie. 'We'd have to wait twenty years for those trees to grow.'

'I think Australian trees are beautiful. Wouldn't they grow quickly in their own climate?' I asked.

They all turned to me. Dorothy stopped typing and looked over a letter, pretending to proofread it.

'Apparently there's a forest walk near here,' I continued. 'Maybe we can find some seedlings and plant those.'

Colonel Brighton was staring at me and I thought that I had made an enemy of him by siding with his wife. But his face broke into a smile and he clasped his hands together. 'Didn't I tell you I had found a smart one? That's a brilliant idea, Anya!'

Ernie coughed into his fist. 'Colonel, if you don't mind me saying . . . I think it was Dorothy and I who found Anya's file.'

Dorothy threw down the letter she was reading and resumed typing. She must have regretted finding my file, I thought.

Rose slipped her arm around my waist. 'Robert thinks it's a brilliant idea because it will save him money,' she said. 'But I think it's a good idea because while the roses and carnations will remind people of Europe, the native plants will help them remember that they now have a new home.'

'And they will attract more native birds and wildlife to the camp,' said Ernie. 'And hopefully fewer rabbits.'

'Well, you win then,' said the Colonel, shooing us out of

274

his doorway. 'I'll lend you Anya to help with your tree-planting committee. Now go away all of you. I have serious work to do.'

He made a sulky face and slammed his door. Rose winked at me.

Irina was unwell for the rest of the week but the following Monday, when she was feeling better, we set out on our seedling-finding mission along the bush track near the camp. Rose had lent me a field guide to Australian wildflowers, and although I found the book difficult to follow, I took it with me anyway. Irina was in a good mood because she had started working at the crèche and enjoyed it, but also because she had received a telegram to say that Ruselina had arrived safely in France and, despite the taxing journey, was already showing signs of improvement.

'Arrived safe. Feeling better. Tests good. French men charming,' the telegram read. Ruselina had learned English and French at school, Irina told me, but those words were the first her granddaughter would learn to say in English. She brought the telegram with her and read the message over and over again.

The track started past the tent sites and wound its way into a valley. I was thrilled to see the eucalypts up close and breathe in their oily scent. I'd learned from Rose's book that many Australian wildflowers bloomed year round but it took me a while to spot them in the underbrush. I was used to picking roses and camellias but after a while I began to see that some of the hardy plants had fruits like roller-brushes or flowers twisted into what looked like Art Deco flourishes. Then I began to find lilies with exquisite petals, and bell-shaped flowers in every colour imaginable. When I had told some of the other migrants that I was going to plant native flowers around the camp, they had screwed up their noses. 'What? Those ugly withered things? They're not flowers,' they said. But the deeper Irina and I moved

275

along the track, the more I saw that they were wrong. Some of the plants had feather flowers, berries and nuts all on the one stem, while others looked as graceful as seaweed floating in the ocean. I thought about what a modern artist once said about his art: 'You have to train your eye to see things in a fresh way. To see the beauty of the new.' That artist was Picasso.

I turned to see what Irina was doing and found her tiptoeing behind me and whacking a stick into the leaf matter.

'What are you doing?' I asked her.

'I'm scaring the snakes away,' she said. 'They said in the camp that the ones in Australia are deadly. And fast. Apparently they chase you.'

I laughed at the idea but secretly resolved to watch where I trod.

'You should speak in English to me,' Irina said. 'I must learn it quickly so that we can get to Sydney as soon as possible.'

'All right,' I said in English. 'How do you do? I'm very pleased to meet you. My name is Anya Kozlova.'

'I'm very pleased to meet you too,' said Irina. 'I am Irina Levitskya. I am almost twenty-one years old. I am Russian. I like singing and children.'

'Very good,' I said, reverting back to Russian. 'Not bad at all for only one lesson. How were things at the crèche today?'

'I loved it,' she said. 'The children are cute. And well behaved. But some have such sad faces. I want to have a dozen children when I get married.'

I spotted some of the flowers I had seen in the dining hall and squatted down to dig them out with my spade. 'A dozen?' I said. 'That's taking "populate or perish" very seriously.'

Irina laughed and held out the sack for me to drop the plant inside. 'Only if it's possible. My mother couldn't have any more children after me and Grandmother had a stillborn baby before she gave birth to my father.'

'She must have been very happy when he was born,' I said.

'Yes,' said Irina, shaking down the plant to the bottom of the sack. 'And even sadder when he grew to thirty-seven and was killed by the Japanese.'

I looked about me for some other plants. I thought about Mariya and Natasha and how I had been wrong about them being rich. I might be wrong about them being blessed too. Where were Natasha's brothers and sisters, uncles and aunts? Not all Russians had one-child families. They must have lost loved ones in the revolutions and wars too. It seemed no one could escape pain and tragedy.

I pointed to a patch of purple and white violets. They would make a good ground cover. Irina followed me and I began to dig the plants out with my spade. I felt sorry to be taking them away from their home, but I whispered to them that they would be well cared for and that we were going to use them to help people feel happier.

'By the way, Anya, I never asked you how you learned to speak such good English. Was it while you were working as a governess?' Irina asked.

I looked up at her. Her eyes were wide and interested, waiting for my answer. I knew then that Ivan had never told her the truth about me.

I turned back to my digging, too ashamed to face her. 'My father liked reading books in English and taught me. But he approached it more as an exotic language than a practical one, like Hindi or something. At school we had classes so I learned how to speak. But I became much more fluent in Shanghai because I had to use it almost every day.' I glanced up at Irina before continuing, 'But not as a governess. That was a lie.'

Irina's face twitched with surprise. She crouched down

next to me and looked straight into my eyes. 'What's the truth then?'

I took a deep breath then found myself telling her all about Sergei, Amelia. Dmitri and the Moscow-Shanghai. The more I talked the wider her eyes became, but there was no judgement in them. I felt guilty that I had been deceitful but relieved to be finally telling her the truth. I even told her about Ivan's proposal.

When I'd finished, Irina stared into the forest. 'My goodness,' she said after a while. 'You've surprised me. I'm not quite sure what to say.' She stood up, wiped the dirt from her hands and kissed the top of my head. 'But I'm glad you've told me about your past. I can understand why you didn't want to talk about it. You didn't know me. But from now on you must tell me everything because we are like sisters.'

I leaped up and threw my arms around her. 'You are my sister,' I said. Something wriggled in the scrub and we both jumped back. But it was only a lizard catching the last rays of afternoon sun. 'My God!' laughed Irina. 'How am I ever going to survive this country?'

Irina and I stopped in our tracks when we reached our hut and heard shouting in several languages coming from it. We pushed open the door and saw Aimka standing between Elsa and a Hungarian girl with short black hair.

'What's happened?' asked Irina.

Aimka pursed her lips. 'She says Elsa stole her necklace.'

The Hungarian girl, who was built like a man, shook her fist and shouted at Elsa. The old woman, far from looking afraid as I would have expected, tossed her head arrogantly.

Aimka turned to us. 'Romola says that Elsa was always watching her whenever she took the necklace off and put it in the pocket of her suitcase. I tell them all the time not to leave precious things in the huts.'

I glanced at my matroshka doll sitting on the shelf I'd made with a piece of wood I'd found on a rubbish pile and thought about the jewels hidden in the hems of the dresses in my suitcase. I hadn't expected people would be stealing from each other.

'Why does she assume I've taken it?' Elsa said in English, presumably for my benefit. 'I've been here for weeks and nothing's gone missing. Why doesn't she ask the Russian girls about it?'

The blood rushed to my face. I'd been making an effort to be friendly to Elsa since we arrived and I couldn't believe she was saying such things. I translated what she had said to Irina. Aimka didn't translate what Elsa said for the other girls but the Hungarian girl who could speak English did. Everyone turned to us.

Aimka shrugged. 'Anya and Irina, let's satisfy everyone by searching your things.'

The skin on the back of my neck prickled with anger. It wasn't difficult to understand how people might come to hate Elsa. I strode over to my bed and ripped the blankets off and flung aside the pillow. Everyone except Romola, Elsa and Aimka turned away, embarrassed at what I was being made to do. I opened the lid of my suitcase and gestured that they were welcome to rummage through it, but I promised myself that once they had, I was going to keep my dresses in the administration office. Inspired by my indignation, Irina flung open the lid of her suitcase then grabbed the sheets off her bed. She picked up her pillow and pulled the slip off it. Something tinkled. Irina and I stared down at the floor to see what it was. Neither of us was able to believe it when we saw a silver chain with a ruby cross lying at our feet. Romola climbed over our sheets and snatched up the necklace, staring at it with joy. Then she glared at us, her eyes burning into Irina.

Elsa's face was flushed. Her hands under her chin were like claws.

'You put that necklace there,' I said to her. 'You liar!'

Her eyes widened and she laughed. The nasty laugh of someone who believes they have won. 'I don't think I'm the liar here. Aren't you Russians famous for it?'

Romola said something to Aimka, who was looking as frazzled as we were. But I was worried to see the frown forming on her forehead. 'Irina,' she said, taking the necklace from Romola, 'what's the meaning of this?'

Irina looked from Aimka to me, speechless.

'She didn't take that necklace,' I said. 'Elsa did.'

Aimka glanced at me and then straightened her back. There was a change in her face. Her expression was a mix of disappointment and disgust. She pointed at Irina with one of her pianist's fingers.

'This doesn't look good, does it?' she said. 'I expected better from you. We are very strict about these things. Pack your bags and bring them with you.'

Irina wobbled on her feet. She had the dazed look that honest people get when they are accused of something they couldn't even imagine doing.

'Where are you taking her?' I asked Aimka.

'To the Colonel.'

The mention of the Colonel's name was a relief. He was a reasonable man who would get to the truth of the matter. I kneeled down to help Irina with her bag. It didn't take us long to collect everything because she hadn't had time to fully unpack.

After we'd fastened the clasps on her suitcase, I folded my blankets and started to pack my own bag.

'What are you doing?' asked Aimka.

'I'm coming too,' I said.

'No!' she said, holding up her palm. 'Not if you want to keep your job with the Colonel. Not if you ever want to get a job in Sydney.'

'Stay,' Irina whispered to me. 'Don't make it bad for yourself too.'

I watched Aimka march Irina out the door. Elsa flashed

her eyes at me before tucking in her blankets and turning down her bed. I felt such rage that I imagined myself pummelling her back with my fists. I grabbed the matroshka doll off the shelf and finished packing my suitcase. Romola and her English-speaking friend didn't take their eyes off me the whole time.

'Go to hell!' I screamed at them. I picked up my suitcase and slammed the door behind me before rushing out into the darkness.

The night air didn't make me feel any better. What was going to happen to Irina? Surely they wouldn't send her to gaol? I imagined her pitiful uncomprehending face in a courtroom. 'No, stop it,' I told myself. They were not going to put her in gaol over that. But she might be punished in some other way and that was not fair. They might put it on her record and make it hard for her to get a job. I heard laughter from one of the huts. A woman was telling a story in Russian and other women's voices were egging her on. God, I thought, why weren't Irina and I put in there?

I heard the door to our hut slam, and turned to see the two Hungarian girls running towards me. I thought they might be coming to beat me up and I picked up my suitcase to defend myself. But the girl who could speak English said, 'We know your friend didn't take the necklace. Elsa did. You'd better go to the Colonel and try to help your friend. We will write a note but anonymous, okay? Don't trust Aimka.'

I thanked them and ran to the administration office. Why had I let Aimka stop me? Did I care more about my job than Irina?

When I reached the Colonel's office I saw that the light was still on inside. Irina and Aimka were just coming out the door. Irina was weeping. I ran to her and threw my arms around her shoulders. 'What happened?' I asked.

'She'll have to move her things to a tent,' Aimka said. 'And she won't work at the crèche any more. She's been warned once and if it happens again she will be more severely punished.'

Irina tried to say something but couldn't. I was confused by Aimka's sudden coldness. I was starting to get the impression she was enjoying seeing Irina punished.

'What's happened to you?' I said to Aimka. 'You know she didn't take it. You said yourself Elsa was a troublemaker. I thought you were our friend.'

Aimka snorted. 'Did you? Why did you think that? I've only known you a few days. Your people stole plenty of things when they came to liberate us.'

I was lost for words. Aimka's mask was slipping away but I couldn't yet see what was underneath. Who was this woman, this pianist who at first had seemed so intelligent and kind? Only a few days before she had criticised those who brought their national conflicts with them to Australia. Now it seemed that her real problem with us was that we were Russians.

'She said if we want to be together, you can come to the tent too,' Irina sniffed.

I looked into Irina's bloodshot eyes. 'Of course I'll come with you,' I told her. 'Then neither of us will have this bitch as our block supervisor.' I had never used such a word before and I shocked myself, but somehow I was proud of myself too.

'I knew you were common,' said Aimka.

The door to the Colonel's office swung open and he stuck his head out. 'What's all this commotion?' he asked, scratching his ear. 'It's late and I'm trying to work.' The Colonel did a double take when he saw me. 'Anya, is everything all right?' he asked. 'What's going on?'

'No, Colonel Brighton,' I said, 'everything is not all right. My friend has been wrongly accused of theft.'

The Colonel sighed. 'Anya, come inside for a moment, will you? Ask your friend to wait. Aimka, that's all for the evening.'

Aimka glowered at the Colonel's tone of regard for me. She squared her shoulders before heading down the path back to the huts. I told Irina to wait and followed the Colonel into his office.

The Colonel sat down at his desk. He had circles under his eyes and he seemed annoyed, but I didn't let that worry me. My job planting trees and filing letters wasn't as important to me as Irina.

He sucked on the end of his pen, then pointed it at me and said, 'If you speak to Rose she will tell you that I always make snap decisions about people and that once I've made my decision I never change my mind. The one thing she will neglect to tell you is that I have never been wrong. Now, I made a decision about you the moment I met you. You were honest and prepared to work hard.'

The Colonel walked around his desk and loomed dangerously close to the map of Australia. I wondered if there was going to be another lecture on 'populate or perish'.

'Anya, if you say your friend didn't take that necklace, I believe you. I had my own doubts anyway and checked her file. There's a letter in there from Captain Connor, just like there was for you. He wrote about her bravery in caring for mental patients during a typhoon. Now if Captain Connor was like me, a busy man, which I imagine he was, he wouldn't have had time to set down reports on just anybody. He'd have to have had a good reason for praising them.'

I wished Irina could be in the room to hear what the Colonel was saying, although she wouldn't have been able to understand it anyway.

'Thank you, Colonel,' I said. 'I appreciate what you're saying.'

'I didn't assign her to a tent to punish her,' he said, 'but to get her away from Aimka. But I'll say no more on that because I'm desperate for people who can speak languages.

I'll get Irina something better when I can, but for the moment she'll have to make do with a tent.'

I wanted to hug him but that wouldn't have been appropriate. I thanked him again and headed towards the door. The Colonel opened a notebook and began writing.

'And Anya,' he said, as I was about to close the door, 'don't tell anybody about this conversation. I cannot be seen to be playing favourites.'

The weeks following the necklace incident were miserable. Although Colonel Brighton hadn't put a black mark against Irina's name, and even Romola and her friend, who was called Tessa, tried to piece enough Russian together to tell her they knew she wasn't to blame, Irina lost her enthusiasm for Australia. The situation wasn't helped by our new accommodation. Our tent was pitched at the edge of the camp, away from the other tents which were occupied by Sicilian men waiting for transport north to the cane fields, and a long way from the women's facilities. If I tried to stand up straight the roof of the tent scraped the top of my head, and our floor was nothing more than dirt, which made everything we owned stink like dust. At least I didn't have to spend a lot of time there, but Irina, with no job, spent her days lying in bed or milling around the post office waiting for more news from Ruselina.

'France is far away,' I tried to reassure her. 'It will take weeks for a letter to get here and Ruselina can't send telegrams all the time.'

The only thing Irina showed any enthusiasm for was her English classes. At first that made me feel better. I'd return to the tent and find her practising her vowels or reading the *Australian Women's Weekly* with a dictionary. I thought as long as she kept up that interest, things would get better. That was until I realised the English practice was part of her preparation to go to the United States.

'I want to go to America,' she told me one morning when

284

I returned from my shower and was dressing for work. 'I must take the chance that they will let Grandmother in when she's better.'

'Everything will settle down,' I told her. 'We'll save some money and get jobs in Sydney soon.'

'I'll perish here. Do you understand, Anya?' she said. Her eyes were bloodshot. 'I don't want to stay in this ugly country with its ugly people. I need beauty. I need music.'

I sat down on her bed and took her hands in mine. Irina was voicing my worst fears. If she had given up hope for a good life in Australia, how was I supposed to maintain it?

'We are not migrants,' I told her. 'We are refugees. How can we leave? We must at least try and make money first.'

'What about your friend?' she said, clutching my sleeve. 'The American?'

I didn't dare tell her that I had thought about writing to Dan Richards many times myself. But we had signed a contract with the Australian government and I doubted there was much Dan could do to help us now. At least not until our two years were up. I'd heard the punishment for breaking the contract was deportation. Where were they going to deport us to? Russia? We would be executed there.

'I promise that I'll think about it if you promise to spend the day with Mariya and Natasha,' I told her. 'They said they need help in the kitchen and that the job pays well. Irina, we will work hard, save up some money and go to Sydney.'

At first she wouldn't agree, but then she thought about it and decided that if she worked in the kitchen she could start saving up for America. I didn't argue with her. As long as she didn't spend all day alone I would be happy. I waited for Irina to dress and fix her hair and we walked to the dining hall together.

Irina's state of mind must have worried Mariya and Natasha too, because when I returned to the tent in the early evening, Lev was busy clearing the long grass that surrounded it and Piotr was building us a wooden floor.

'Irina's terrified of snakes,' Piotr said. 'This ought to put her mind at ease.'

'Where is she?' I asked.

'Mariya and Natasha took her to the cinema hall. There's a piano there and Natasha wants to start playing again. They are trying to convince Irina to sing.'

There was a pick in the sack of tools they had brought. I asked if I could use it to dig a garden patch at the front of the tent.

'The one you made around the entrance and the flag-pole is beautiful,' said Lev, straightening up and tossing aside his sickle. 'You have a talent for gardening. Where did you learn?'

'My father had a spring flower garden in Harbin. I must have learned from watching. He said it was good for your soul to put your hands in the earth every once in a while.'

Piotr, Lev and I spent the rest of the daylight hours making improvements to the tent. When we had finished, it was hardly recognisable. The interior smelled of pinewood and lemon. Outside I'd planted a ring of bluebells and daisies and some grevillea. The trimmed lawn was a great improvement.

'Everyone in the camp is going to be jealous now,' laughed Lev.

Working with Mariya and Natasha improved Irina's depression a little, but not much. She didn't want to go on living in a camp forever, and we still had no idea when we could go to Sydney. I tried to cheer her up by taking her into the town which could be reached in twenty minutes on the local bus. Several other people from the camp were travelling into the town that day, but none of them spoke Russian or English so we couldn't ask them anything about it. When the bus reached the outskirts of the town, we saw that the streets were as wide as two Shanghai blocks. They were flanked on either side by sandstone bungalows and cottages with white picket fences. Elms, willows and tall liquidambars shaded the roads with their sprawling limbs.

The bus terminated in the main street, which was lined with houses with cast-iron railings and shops with corrugated-iron awnings. A Georgian-style church was situated on the corner. Dust-covered cars were parked front end to the kerb, side by side with horses tied to water troughs. Across the road we saw a pub that was three storeys high and had a Toohey's Beer poster of a man playing golf painted on its side.

Irina and I strolled past the draperies, hardware and general stores to an ice-cream parlour that was playing Dizzy Gillespie on a transistor radio. Afro-Cuban jazz seemed so out of place in the dry, dusty environment that even Irina smiled. A woman in a button-down dress served us chocolate ice-cream on cones, which we had to eat quickly because the ice-cream started to melt the moment we stepped out of the store.

I noticed a man with a pockmarked nose staring at us from a bus stop. His face was red and his eyes white with drink. I told Irina that we should cross the road.

'Go home, reffos,' the man growled at us. 'We don't want you lot here.'

'What did he say?' Irina asked me.

'He's just a drunk,' I said, trying to hurry her along. I didn't want Irina to collect any evidence about ugly Australians.

'Go home you bloody reffo sluts!' the man screamed at us. My heart thumped in my chest. I wanted to look over my shoulder to see if he was following us, but I didn't. I knew it wasn't wise to show fear.

'Bloody reffo sluts!' the man screamed again. Someone from the pub opened a window and shouted back, 'Shut up, Harry!'

To my surprise, Irina laughed. 'I understood that,' she said.

Behind the main street was a park bordered by pine trees, with ornate fountains and flowerbeds bursting with marigolds. A family was sitting on a blanket near a bandstand draped in bougainvillea. The father wished us good morning when we passed. Irina wished him good morning back in English, but we felt self-conscious after the incident with the drunk and didn't stop to talk.

'This park is pretty,' I said to Irina.

'Yes, it's an improvement on the camp.'

We sat down on the steps of the bandstand. Irina picked clover flowers from the grass and started to make a chain. 'I didn't think there was anything civilised around us,' she said. 'I thought we were in the middle of nowhere.'

'We should have come here sooner,' I replied, encouraged that Irina was talking about something positive for a change.

She finished her chain and hung it around her neck. 'I would hate me if I were you, Anya,' she said. 'Just think, if it wasn't for me and Grandmother, you'd be in New York now.'

'I'd be on my own in New York,' I said. 'And I'd rather be with you.'

Irina lifted her eyes to mine. They were filled with tears. I knew that I couldn't have said anything more true. No matter how hard life in Australia seemed, there was nothing to guarantee that life in America would have been any better. It was people who were important, not the country in which you lived.

'The only thing that matters,' I said, 'is that Ruselina gets better and we bring her here.'

Irina took the flower chain from around her neck and put it around mine. 'I love you,' she said.

Apart from Irina's unhappiness, what had unnerved me most about the necklace incident was the way Aimka had turned on us. I couldn't understand why she had been so warm towards us in the beginning if, deep down inside, she resented Russians. The mystery was solved several weeks later when I met Tessa in the laundry.

'Hello,' I said, my hands deep in soapy water.

'Hello,' Tessa replied. 'How is your friend?'

'Getting better.'

Tessa reached into her pocket and took out a matchbox. She struck a match and lit the boiler, then used the same match to light her cigarette. 'I heard your tent is pretty nice, yeah?' she said, blowing out a stream of smoke from the corner of her mouth.

I squeezed out a blouse and dropped it in the rinsing tub. 'Yes,' I said. 'It's a palace now.'

'Things are pretty unhappy where we are,' she said. 'Aimka sets Elsa up against us. We are young, we want some of the men around sometimes, you know? Aimka should put Elsa in with some older women or some other uptight Germans who want to follow the rules. But Aimka won't do it. She's always baiting everybody.'

'I don't understand her,' I said, shaking my head. 'She came from a family in Budapest that used to hide Jews during the war. They must have been kind people.'

Tessa's eyes nearly sprang from her head. 'Who told you that?' She stubbed out her cigarette and took a step towards me, glancing over her shoulder before whispering, 'She's Hungarian but she lived in Poland. She was a collaborator. She helped send Jewish women and children to their deaths.'

I returned from work that day feeling that there were whole layers of existence I knew nothing about. Something had happened in Europe that would probably never be fully understood. I had thought Shanghai was full of deceit and corruption, but suddenly Shanghai life as we had lived it seemed fairly simple: if you had money, you enjoyed life; if you didn't have money, you couldn't.

*   *   *

289

One morning, at the beginning of February, I was in the administration office, sorting correspondence and eavesdropping on the Colonel and Ernie talking about problems with the camp.

'The town and the camp are two separate communities and we need to do something to integrate them,' the Colonel said. 'How are we ever going to get these people out into society and get Australians to accept them if we can't do it in a country town where people are friendly?'

'I agree,' said Ernie, pacing as much as he could in the small area behind his desk. 'There have been protests against non-British migrants in Sydney, and even in the town there have been incidents.'

'What sort of incidents?'

'Some of the stores have had their windows broken. They reckon it's because they served people from the camp.'

The Colonel shook his head and stared at his feet.

Dorothy stopped typing. 'It's a nice town,' she said. 'The people are good. It's just a few of the riffraff who behave like that. But they are just stupid boys. No one should be afraid.'

'That's the thing,' said the Colonel. 'I'm sure the people of the town would like the folks here if they could just get to know them.'

'Some of the other camps have held concerts in their local towns,' said Ernie. 'There are lots of talented people here. Perhaps we can try something like that?'

The Colonel pinched his chin and considered the suggestion. 'You know what,' he said, 'we could try that. Just something small to start with. I'll ask Rose to organise it with the CWA. Do you have some musicians in mind?'

Ernie shrugged. 'It depends what kind of music they want – opera, cabaret, jazz . . . There's plenty of people who could do it. I'll find someone. You just tell me what and when.'

I jumped up from my pile of paper and startled them. 'Excuse me,' I said, 'I have a suggestion.'

The Colonel smiled at me. 'Well,' he said, 'if it's as good as your one about the native trees, I'm all ears.'

'I can't believe you got me into this!' Irina cried. Her voice echoed around the ladies' room of the church hall, the venue for the Country Women's Association's social nights. The tiled area had three cubicles and its walls were the shade of stale bubblegum. It reeked of slimy water.

She held up her hair so that it wouldn't get caught when I zipped her into my green cheongsam. I could see a red rash forming on the back of her neck.

'I didn't know you got so nervous,' I said, my own voice beginning to tighten. 'I thought you liked performing.'

Natasha, who was squeezing herself into a wasp-waisted dress, snorted. She lifted her fingers one by one and cracked her knuckles. 'I've never had so much riding on one performance,' she said. 'Colonel Brighton's acting as if the success of "populate or perish" is dependent on us tonight.' Natasha's hand shook when she applied her lipstick. She had to blot her mouth with a handkerchief and start again.

I straightened the cheongsam over Irina's hips. We'd had to take it out for her fuller figure and restitch the side splits so that they started from the knee and not the thigh. Irina tied a Spanish shawl over her shoulders and knotted it at her bust. We'd decided that the red flamenco dress was too sexy for her Australian debut, and had gone for an exotic but modest look instead.

Irina and Natasha twisted their hair into Judy Garland rolls. I helped with the pins. Whatever they were feeling inside, no one could deny they both looked beautiful.

I left Irina to do her makeup and primped my hair in the mirror. Rose had collected an assortment of powders, lipsticks and hair sprays for us. It was amazing how a few cosmetics boosted our self-esteem after we had gone without the most basic things for months.

291

'Go take a peek, Anya,' said Irina, balancing herself against a sink to pull on her stockings. 'Tell us what it's like out there.'

The performers' toilets were down a flight of stairs that started from the wing of the stage. I lifted my skirt and hurried back up the steps. There was a gap in the side of the curtain and I peered through it. The hall was filling up quickly.

The Colonel and Rose were introducing the president of the local CWA to some of the migrants who had been hand-picked to represent the camp. There was a pharmacist from Germany, an opera singer from Vienna, a Hungarian linguistics professor, a professor of history from Yugoslavia and a Czechoslovakian family who had been chosen for their impeccable manners. Ernie was talking with Dorothy, who was wearing a yellow dress with a flower in her hair. Ernie was making some sort of joke, waving his hands like a butterfly, and Dorothy was batting her eyelids.

'Ah ha, I see,' I whispered. 'Why didn't I notice that before?'

Irina and Natasha were looking over the music when I returned to the ladies' room. 'The hall is full,' I said.

I saw both of them swallow and decided it was better not to say anything more. They had been expecting to perform for about twenty people, but there were already almost a hundred out there.

There was a knock at the door and the Colonel and Rose popped their heads inside.

'Good luck, girls,' Rose said. 'You look gorgeous.'

'Don't forget,' said the Colonel, 'we are depending on you—' Rose dragged him away before he could finish.

I glanced at my watch. 'We'd better go up there,' I said.

With a strained 'Good luck' I left Irina and Natasha on the stage and took a seat at the far end of the front row. The hall had filled up to capacity. The minister was rushing around looking for extra chairs. I hoped they would turn the lights off before the curtains opened. I wasn't sure it would be good for Irina and Natasha to see how many people had turned up.

The CWA president walked up the stairs to the front of the curtain. She was a buxom woman with wiry hair kept in place by a net. She welcomed everyone and then handed the microphone to the Colonel to introduce the performers. The Colonel pulled out some notes and started telling the audience about the day-to-day running of the camp and the importance of new migrants to Australia's future. I noticed Rose signalling to him to keep it short.

'Thank God he didn't bring his cardboard signs,' I heard Ernie whisper to Dorothy.

When the Colonel mentioned 'populate or perish' I almost groaned. Rose crawled along the front row and behind the curtain. The curtain suddenly opened on a surprised Irina and Natasha. Natasha rolled her fingers down the keyboard and the audience started clapping. The Colonel thanked everyone for coming and took his seat. He glanced over and smiled at me. Rose slipped back next to him, unnoticed.

Irina started with a song called 'The Man I Love', which she sang in English. Her voice sounded tight. Rose and I had helped translate the words of the songs she and Natasha knew. Rose had also bought the music to some new pieces. But as soon as I heard Irina singing I knew we had made a mistake. English wasn't a language she could relax with. I could see how constricted her throat was, her eyes looked dull. She wasn't Irina at all.

I glanced around the audience. Most of them were listening politely, but here and there I saw a frown. Irina stumbled over some of the words and blushed. A couple towards the back whispered to each other. A few minutes later they stood up and made their way along the row to the door. I wanted to get up and run away too. I couldn't watch the humiliating disaster that was unfolding before my eyes.

The shawl slipped from Irina's shoulder and under the stage lights the combination of red and green didn't work, she looked like a lampshade. My eyes flitted over the audience again. The dresses there were white, pink or baby blue.

Irina moved on to a French song. She sang some of the verses in English and some of them in French, which had been my idea, so that the number would keep some of its original flavour. Irina could sing the French with gusto, but faltered on the English. Far from sounding exotic, the song sounded broken down and strange.

I pulled a handkerchief from my bag and wiped down my palms. What was I going to say to the Colonel? I glared at Dorothy whose face was expressionless. She'd probably have a field day with this. I imagined myself trying to comfort Irina after the concert. 'We tried our best,' I would say. It had taken weeks to cheer Irina up after the necklace incident. What would happen after this?

Another couple got up to leave. The French song ended and Natasha hit the first note of the next one, but Irina put up her hand to stop her. Her cheeks were flushed and I thought she was going to cry. Instead she started to speak.

'My English not good,' she said, breathing heavily into the microphone. 'But music say more than words. This next song I sing in Russian. I sing it for my best friend, Anya, who taught me to love this beautiful country of yours.'

Irina nodded to Natasha. I recognised the sad melody.

'They told me you would never return, but I didn't believe them.
Train after train returned without you, but in the end I was right.
As long as I can see you in my heart, you are with me always.'

We had cut the song from the programme, thinking it would be too sad for the occasion. But Irina's body was alive with the song, emanating power through her vibrant voice and the language of her heart. The woman next to me opened her handbag and pulled out a handkerchief. I looked over my shoulder at the audience. A change had come over them. There was no fidgeting or movement, instead jaws hung slack, eyes were moistened and tears glistened on cheeks. They were as mesmerised by Irina as the people on Tubabao had been.

Irina closed her eyes but I wanted her to open them and see what was happening, what her voice was doing to people. They had probably never heard a word of Russian in their lives before and yet they all seemed to know what she was singing about. They may have not known revolution and exile, but they knew grief and they knew war. They knew what it was like to have stillborn babies and sons who never came home. I thought again about Natasha and Mariya's tent on Tubabao. No one misses out on the hardness of life, I told myself. Everyone just tries to find what happiness and beauty they can.

The music stopped and Irina opened her eyes. The hall was silent for a moment then the audience broke out into loud applause. One man stood up and shouted, 'Bravo!' More people stood up to join him. I turned to look at the Colonel; his face was as delighted as a boy about to blow out the candles on his birthday cake.

It wasn't until a few minutes later that the applause died down enough for Irina to speak again. 'Now,' she said, 'we have happy song. And this big hall. Plenty of room. Dance if you like.'

Natasha's hands flew across the keyboard and Irina started to sing a jazz number that I had first heard at the Moscow-Shanghai.

'Whenever I look at you
It's like the sun is out and the sky is blue.'

People glanced at each other. The Colonel scratched his head and shifted in his seat. But the audience couldn't resist the catchiness of the tune: they tapped their feet and thrummed their fingers on their laps, but no one got up to dance. Irina and Natasha weren't discouraged this time, they rolled their shoulders and gave the song all they had.

'So don't be shy
Time will just go by
And if time goes by and you're still shy
Well, before we know it we'll be saying goodbye.'

Rose elbowed the Colonel so hard he jumped out of his seat. He straightened his uniform then offered her his hand. They moved out to the front of the stage and danced a quick step. The audience applauded. Ernie grabbed Dorothy's arm and they started dancing too. A farmer, who had come in his overalls, stood up and walked over to the Viennese opera singer. He bowed and gave a flourish of his hand. The linguistics professor and the history professor started stacking chairs against the walls to make more room. Soon everyone in the room was dancing, even the minister. At first the women were too self-conscious to dance with him, but he managed on his own, shuffling his feet and clicking his fingers until one of the daughters from the Czechoslovakian family stepped forward to join him.

'So when I ask you to dance
Give me this one chance
Tonight is the night for romance.'

The following day, the local paper reported that the Country Women's Association's social night had lasted until two o'clock in the morning and had only come to an end when the police arrived to ask the participants to lower the noise. The article went on to say that the CWA's president, Ruth Kirkpatrick, had declared the evening 'an astounding success'.

THIRTEEN

Betty's Café

Sydney seemed different the second time I saw it. The skies had opened and torrential rain was beating down around the colonnade where Irina and I were waiting for a tram. Pools of water ran around our feet and splattered mud onto our new stockings, which had been Rose Brighton's parting gift. I stared at the stone walls and massive arches of Central Station and mused at how our trip back to Sydney had seemed much faster than the one we had taken inland.

I tucked my handbag under my arm and thought about the envelope inside it. In my imagination I could see the address written in bold print. *Mrs Elizabeth Nelson, Potts Point, Sydney.* I was tempted to pull the envelope out and study it again, but I had already memorised not only the address but the directions Colonel Brighton had written down for me. The moisture in the air would only smudge the ink, so I left the envelope alone.

A few days after Irina's concert, Colonel Brighton had called me into his office. I looked from the King's portrait to the Colonel to the envelope he pushed across the desk to me. He stood up from his chair and paced towards the map, then back to his desk again. 'Rose and I know a lady in Sydney,' he said. 'She owns a coffee lounge in the city. She's looking for some help. I spoke to her about you and Irina. She has some Russian chappie doing the cooking for her and she seems very happy with him.'

The Colonel sank back into his chair, twirling a pen between his fingers and considering me with grave eyes. 'Waitressing is not what you're used to, I know,' he said. 'I've been trying to get you some secretarial work but it seems there's not enough to go round for *New* Australians. Betty will give you time off if you want to do night classes, and she won't make trouble for you with the employment office if you find something better once you get there. She has space in her flat and can give you cheap board to help you out.'

'Colonel Brighton, I have no idea how to thank you,' I stammered, half out of my chair with excitement.

He waved his hand. 'Don't thank me, Anya. I hate to lose you. It's Rose who has been at me every day to do something for you.'

I clutched the envelope in my hand and took a deep breath. The prospect of leaving was both exciting and frightening. As much as we hated it, camp life was a safe haven. I wondered what we would have to face once we were fending for ourselves.

The Colonel coughed into his fist and frowned. 'Work hard, Anya. Make something of yourself. Don't just marry the first man who asks you. The wrong man can make you miserable.'

I almost choked. It was too late. I had already married the first man who had asked me. And he had made me miserable.

'You're preoccupied,' said Irina, dabbing at her neck with her handkerchief. 'What are you thinking about with such a serious face?'

The walls of Central Station snapped back into focus and I remembered that I was in Sydney.

'I was wondering what the people will be like here,' I said.

'If Mrs Nelson is anything like the Brightons, then we can be sure that she's crazy.'

'That's true,' I laughed.

299

A bell rang and we looked up to see the tram approaching.

'Sad too, though, I imagine,' said Irina, picking up her suitcase. 'Rose said Mrs Nelson's husband died a year ago and that she lost both her sons in the war.'

The conductor reeked of perspiration and I was glad to hurry past him to take a seat at the back of the tram. The floor was slippery from muddy shoes and dripping umbrellas. There was an advertisement for the Immigration Department in between one for Raleigh's tomato sauce and another for Nock & Kirby's Hardware Store. In the immigration advertisement a man in a hat was shaking the hand of a short man in an old-fashioned suit. 'Welcome to your New Home' the slogan read. Someone had scrawled over it in red crayon: 'No More Bloody Reffos!' I saw that Irina had noticed. She'd heard the word 'reffo' enough times by now to know it wasn't a friendly message. But she didn't make any comment. I glanced around at the other passengers. Men and women, they all looked alike in their grey raincoats and sombre hats and gloves. As long as Irina and I didn't speak, we could be one of them.

Irina rubbed at the fogged-up window with her glove. 'I can't see a thing,' she said.

By the time Irina and I reached Potts Point the rain had lifted. The shop awnings were dripping and steam was wafting up from the street. The powder and lipstick we had applied before leaving the train at Central had evaporated. My hands felt plump and Irina's skin was shiny. The mugginess made me think of a magazine article I had read about New Orleans. It said that human relationships were at their most raw and sensual in a hot, humid atmosphere. That was true in Shanghai. Would it be true in Sydney too?

We walked along a street that sloped towards the harbour. I was amazed at the mix of trees that grew out of sections of the footpath: giant maples, jacarandas and even a palm tree. Some of the terrace houses looked genteel with wrought-iron balconies, black and white tiled verandahs and pots of aspidistras in their entranceways. The other houses were badly in need of a coat of paint. They must have been grand once too, but their shutters were half rotted and some of the windowpanes were broken. We passed a house that had its front door open. I couldn't resist peering into the dingy corridor. It reeked of something close to opium mixed with wet carpet. Irina tugged my arm and my eyes followed the drainpipe up to the open third-floor window. A man with a beard streaked with paint was leaning out and pointing at us with an artist's brush.

'Good afternoon,' I said.

His wild eyes rolled back. He saluted and shouted: '*Vive la Revolution!*'

Irina and I quickened our pace, almost running down the street. But it wasn't easy to move speedily with a suitcase each.

Towards the end of the street, near a flight of descending sandstone stairs, was a house with a ball gown displayed in its ground-floor window. The dress was daffodil yellow with a white fox-fur trim. The backdrop of the window was pink satin with silver stars embroidered onto it. I hadn't seen anything as glamorous since Shanghai. My eye fell to the gold plate by the door: 'Judith James, Designer'.

Irina called out to me from across the road. 'This is it!'

The house she was standing in front of was neither elegant nor shabby. Like most of the other houses in the street, it was a terrace with wrought-iron trimmings. The window frames and verandahs sloped to the left and the path to the door was cracked in places, but the windows gleamed and there wasn't a weed in the small garden. Pink geraniums blossomed near the mailbox and a maple stretched towards the third-floor windows. But it was the gardenia plant blooming from the strip of grass in front of the verandah that caught my eye. It reminded me that I was finally in the city that would help me find my mother.

I took the envelope from my bag and looked at the number again. I knew it but I was frightened that such serendipity was a dream. A gardenia still blooming in late summer had to be a good omen.

One of the doors on the second-floor verandah opened and a woman stepped out. She balanced a cigarette holder on the rim of her lip and rested one hand on her waist. Her sharp-eyed expression didn't change when Irina and I said hello and put our suitcases down near the gate.

'I heard you're a singer,' she said, pointing her chin at Irina and folding her arms over the ruffled neckline of her blouse. With her capri pants, spike-heeled shoes and bleached-grey hair she looked like a taller, tougher, tartier version of Ruselina.

'Yes, I do the cabaret,' said Irina.

'And what use are you?' the woman asked, looking me up and down. 'Besides beautiful. Can you do anything?'

I gaped at her rudeness and struggled for something to say. Surely this woman couldn't be Mrs Nelson?

'Anya, she is smart,' Irina answered for me.

'Well, you'd better come on in then,' the woman said. 'We're all geniuses here. I'm Betty, by the way.'

She lifted her hand to her beehive hairdo and squinted. Later I would learn that this gesture was Betty Nelson's version of a smile.

Betty opened the front door for us and we followed her through the entrance and up the stairs. Someone was playing 'Romance in the Dark' on a piano in the front room. The house seemed to have been subdivided into an apartment on each floor. Betty's was on the second. It was almost railroad-style with windows at the front and rear. At the back of the house, at the end of the corridor, there were two identical doors. 'This is your bedroom,' Betty said, opening one of the doors and leading us into a room with peach-coloured walls and a linoleum floor. The two chenille-covered beds were pushed against opposite walls, with a bedside table and

302

lamp between them. Irina and I put our suitcases near the armoire. My eyes fell to the towels and the sprigs of daisies that had been left on our pillows.

'You girls hungry?' Betty asked. It was more a statement than a question and we scurried after her into the kitchen. A collection of battered pans hung over the oven, and the furniture had been propped under the legs with pieces of folded cardboard because the floor sagged in the middle. The tiles above the sink were old but the grout was clean. The tea towels had lace trimmings and the air smelled like butter cookies, bleach and cooking gas.

'Through there is the living room,' Betty said, pointing to double-glass doors beyond which was a room with polished floorboards and a wine-red rug. 'Take a look if you like.'

The room was the airiest in the house, its high ceiling decorated with wedding-cake swirls. There were two tall bookshelves and a lounge with matching armchairs. A wireless stood in the corner next to a stand with a maidenhair fern on it. Two French doors led out onto the verandah.

'Can we look outside?' I called out.

'Yes,' Betty replied from the kitchen. 'I'm just putting the kettle on.'

From the verandah, crammed between two houses, there was a slip of a view of the harbour and the lawns of the Botanic Gardens. Irina and I sat for a moment in the wicker chairs, surrounded by pots of spider plants and fishbone ferns.

'Did you notice the photograph?' Irina asked me. She was whispering although she was speaking in Russian.

I leaned back and peered into the living room. On one of the bookshelves was a wedding photograph. From the blondeness of the bride and the ritzy gown with fitted bust and straight skirt, I guessed it was Betty and her late husband. Next to that photograph was one of the man in a double-breasted suit and hat. The groom, several years later.

'What?' I asked Irina.

'There are no pictures of the sons.'

While Irina helped Betty make the tea, I found the bath-room, a closet-sized space off the kitchen. The room was as well scrubbed as the rest of the flat. The rose-patterned mat on the floor matched the shower curtain and the skirt around the basin. The bathtub was old with a stain around the plughole, but the water heater was new. I caught sight of my reflection in the mirror above the sink. My com-plexion was clear and lightly tanned. I leaned closer and stretched the skin of my cheek between my fingers where the tropical worm had eaten my flesh. The skin was smooth and soft, only a light brown patch remained where I had been so hideously marked. At what point had it healed so well?

I returned to the kitchen and found Betty lighting a cigarette from the stove flame. Irina was sitting at a card table covered with a sunflower cloth. There was a vanilla cupcake perched on a plate in front of her and at the setting opposite there was another cupcake. 'These are our "Welcome to Sydney" cakes,' Irina said.

I sat down opposite her and watched Betty pour the boiling water into a pot and cover it with a cosy. The piano from downstairs started up again. *I've got the Sunday evening blues,*' Betty sang along with it. 'That's Johnny,' she said, pointing with her chin towards the door. 'He lives with his mother, Doris. He plays at some of the clubs up at Kings Cross. We can go to one of the more respectable ones sometime if you like.'

'How many people live in this building?' I asked.

'Two downstairs and one upstairs. I'll introduce you to everybody once you've settled in.'

'And how about the café?' asked Irina. 'How many people work there?'

'Just one Russian cook at the moment,' Betty said, bring-ing the pot to the table and sitting down with us. 'Vitaly.

He's a good boy. A hard worker. You'll like him. Just don't either one of you fall in love with him and run off, okay? Not like my last kitchen hand and waitress.'

'What happened?' asked Irina, peeling the paper mould off her cupcake.

'They left me flat out on my own for a month. So if one of you girls even thinks about falling in love with Vitaly, I'll cut your little fingers off!'

Irina and I froze, our cupcakes poised halfway between our mouths and the plates. Betty glared at us, her hand to her beehive and a squint in her eyes.

I woke in the night with a start. It took me a few seconds to remember that I wasn't in the camp. A streak of light from the window of the third-floor apartment reflected off the house behind ours and shone across my bed. I breathed in the freshly laundered scent of the sheets. There was a time when I'd slept in a four-poster bed with a cashmere cover and gold paper on the walls around me. But I'd lived with canvas and dust so long that even a single bed with a soft mattress and crisp sheets seemed luxurious to me. I listened for the sounds of the night that had become familiar in the camp – the breeze through the trees, scurrying animals, the cry of a night bird – but it all was quiet except for the faint whistle of Irina's breathing and an insomniac upstairs listening to the radio. I tried to swallow but my mouth was dry. I slipped out of bed and felt my way to the door.

The apartment was silent except for the tick of the clock in the corridor. I ran my hand down the frame of the kitchen door for the light switch and flicked it on. There were three glasses turned upside down on a tea towel on the draining board. I picked one up and turned on the tap. Someone moaned. I peered into the living room and saw that Betty was asleep on the lounge. She had a coverlet pulled up around her neck and her head was resting on a pillow. From the pair of slippers by the side of the lounge and the hairnet she was wearing, it was clear she had intended to go to sleep there. I wondered why she didn't sleep in the other bedroom, then decided that there was probably more air in the living room. I made my way back to my bed and pulled the sheet around me. Betty had said that we would have one and a half days off a week. It was Sunday and my half-day would be Friday morning. I'd already looked up the address of the Red Cross. As soon as I could, I would be heading to Jamison Street.

Early the following morning, Betty sent Irina and myself out into the backyard to pick passionfruit off a vine that sprawled over the fence.

'What do you think of her?' Irina whispered to me, holding open a string bag so I could toss in the purple fruit.

'At first I thought she was strange,' I said, 'but the more she talks, the more I like her. I think she's nice.'

'Me too,' said Irina.

We presented Betty with the two bags of fruit. 'I use it for the Tropical Ice-cream Boat,' she told us.

Afterwards we caught the tram with Betty to her coffee lounge in the city. The decor was somewhere between an American diner and a French café. It was split into two levels. On the first level there were round tables with straw chairs. On the second level, which was reached via four stairs, there were eight musk-pink booths and a counter with stools. Each booth had a picture of an American movie star hanging on the wall above it: Humphrey Bogart, Fred Astaire, Ginger Rogers, Clark Gable, Rita Hayworth, Gregory Peck and Bette Davis. I eyed the one of Joan Crawford when we passed it. Her severe eyes and tight mouth reminded me of Amelia.

We followed Betty through two swing doors with round windows in them and down a short corridor into the kitchen. A young man with spindly legs and a cleft in his chin was mixing flour and milk over a bench. 'This is Vitaly,' said Betty. The man looked up and smiled. 'Ah, here you are,' he said. 'Just in time to help me with the pancake mix.'

'No work for you just yet,' said Betty, taking the string bags from us and putting them on the table in the centre of the room. 'Sit down and talk for a bit before the customers start arriving. You need to get to know each other.'

The café's kitchen was as clean as Betty's one at home, though the floor was straight. There were four cupboards, a gas stove with six rings, a large oven and two sinks. Betty pulled an apron from one of the cupboards and tied it around her waist. I noticed the two pink uniforms hanging on a peg, one of which I guessed would be mine. I was to help Betty as a waitress. Irina was going to be Vitaly's assistant in the kitchen.

Vitaly brought in chairs from the back room and we sat around the table.

'How about eggs for you all?' Betty asked. 'You girls only had toast this morning and I don't want my staff half starved and on their feet all day.'

'I know you two from Tubabao,' Vitaly said to us.

'Ah yes, I remember,' laughed Irina. 'You asked me for my autograph after the concert.'

I stared at Vitaly's ruddy cheeks, sandy hair and protruding eyes, but I couldn't recall him at all. We told him about our camp and he said that he'd been sent to a place called Bonegilla.

'How old are you?' Irina asked him.

'Twenty-five. And how old are you?'

Betty cracked some eggs into a bowl and glanced over her shoulder. 'Don't try to speak in English just because I'm here,' she said. 'You can speak Russian to each other.' She patted her hair and squinted. 'That's as long as you're not sharing juicy gossip. Or, for that matter, if one of the customers comes in. I don't want my staff carted off as Communist spies.'

We clapped and laughed. 'Thank you,' Irina told her. 'That is much easier for me.'

'And you, Anya,' Vitaly said, turning to me. 'You seemed familiar to me from somewhere before Tubabao. I wanted to introduce myself to you, but then I heard you were from Shanghai and I assumed we couldn't have known each other after all.'

'I'm not from Shanghai,' I told him. 'I am from Harbin.'

'Harbin!' he said, his eyes flashing. 'I am from Harbin too. What's your last name?'

'Kozlova.'

Vitaly thought deeply for a moment, rubbing his hands together as if he were trying to entice a genie from a lamp.

'Kozlova! Daughter of Colonel Victor Grigorovich Kozlov?'

My father's name took my breath away. It had been a long time since I had heard it. 'Yes,' I said.

'Then I do know you,' Vitaly said. 'Although you might have been too young to remember me. My father was friends with your father. They left Russia together. But we moved to Tsingtao in 1938. I remember you though. A little girl with red hair and blue eyes.'

'Is your father with you?' Irina asked him.

'No,' said Vitaly. 'He's in America with my mother and eight brothers. I am here with my sister and her husband. My father doesn't trust my brother-in-law, so he sent me to look after Sofia. Are your parents with you, Anya?'

His question caught me off guard. I looked down at the table.

'My father died in a car accident before the end of the war,' I said. 'My mother was deported from Harbin. By the Soviets. I don't know where they took her.'

Irina reached over and squeezed my wrist. 'We are hoping that the Red Cross in Sydney might be able to trace Anya's mother in Russia,' she told Vitaly.

He rubbed the cleft in his chin then rested his fingers on his cheek. 'You know,' he said, 'my family is looking for my uncle. He stayed in Harbin and also went to the Soviet Union after the war. But he wasn't forced. He and my father had very different ideas. My uncle believed in the principles of Communism and never served in the army with my father. He wasn't exactly an extremist. But he was a supporter.'

'Have you heard from him?' Irina asked. 'Perhaps he would know where Anya's mother was sent.'

Vitaly snapped his fingers. 'He might, you know. It's possible they were on the same train from Harbin to Russia. But my father has only heard twice from my uncle since his return, and even that was only through people we knew. I do recall that the train stopped in a place called Omsk. My uncle went on from there to Moscow, but the rest of the passengers were taken to a labour camp.'

'Omsk!' I cried. I had heard the name of that town before. My mind turned over, trying to remember where.

'I can ask my father to try to make contact again,' said Vitaly. 'My uncle is afraid of my father and what he might say to him. We always have to rely on other people to convey the messages, so it will take time. And of course everything is checked and censored nowadays.'

I was too overwhelmed to speak. In Shanghai, Russia had seemed like an entity too big for me to tackle. Suddenly, in a coffee lounge on the other side of the world, I had more information about my mother's whereabouts than ever before.

'Anya!' Irina cried. 'If you can tell the Red Cross that you think your mother is in Omsk, they might be able to trace her for you!'

'Hey, hang on a minute!' said Betty, setting three plates of scrambled eggs and toast before us. 'You're not being fair. I said you could speak in Russian if it wasn't anything exciting. What's going on?'

All three of us started to speak at once, but we couldn't make any sense to Betty that way. Irina and Vitaly stopped talking and let me explain. Betty glanced at her watch. 'What are you waiting for?' she said to me. 'I've lasted without you for a month, I'll last without you for another morning. The Red Cross will open at nine o'clock. If you leave now, you should be the first person there.'

I dodged in between the secretaries and office workers, hardly taking in anything of George Street as I raced towards downtown. I glanced at the map Betty had drawn for me on a serviette. I turned into Jamison Street and found myself standing outside Red Cross House ten minutes before it opened. A directory was posted on the glass door. My eyes scanned over the blood transfusion service, the convalescent homes, the hospital and repatriation departments, to the tracing department. I checked my watch again and paced back and forth on the pavement. My God, I thought, I'm finally here. A woman walked past me and smiled. She must have thought I was desperate to donate blood.

Near the door was a window displaying Red Cross handicrafts. I glanced over the satin-covered coathangers and crocheted blankets and told myself that I would buy something for Betty on the way out. She had been kind to give me time off work before I had even started.

When a clerk opened the doors I headed straight for the fire stairs, not wanting to wait for the elevator. I burst into the tracing department and startled the receptionist, who was settling into her desk with a cup of tea. She pinned on her volunteer's badge and asked me how she could help. I told her I was trying to find my mother and she handed me some registration forms and a pen. 'It's hard to update the tracing files,' she told me, 'so make sure you include as much information as you can this morning.'

I took a seat by a water cooler and flipped through the forms. I didn't have a photograph of my mother and I hadn't noted the number of the train that took her from Harbin. But I filled in as much information as I could, including my mother's maiden name, her year and place of birth, the date I last saw her and a physical description. I paused for a moment. The image of my mother's despairing face with her fist to her mouth came back to me and my hand started to tremble. I swallowed and forced myself to concentrate. There was a note at the bottom of the last form explaining that, due to the number of inquiries and the difficult process of gathering information, it could take six months to several years to receive a reply from the Red Cross. But I didn't let that discourage me. 'Thank you! Thank you!' I wrote next to the disclaimer. I gave the forms back to the receptionist. She slipped them into a file and told me to wait until a tracing officer called me.

A woman with a child in her arms walked into the waiting area and asked the receptionist for forms. I looked around the room, noticing for the first time that it was a museum of grief. The walls were covered in pictures with notes under them that read: 'Lieba. Last seen in Poland 1940'; 'My beloved husband, Semion, disappeared 1941'. The photograph of a little brother and sister holding hands almost broke my heart. 'Janek and Mania. Germany 1937.'

'Omsk,' I said to myself, rolling the name over my tongue as if that might help me unlock the memory. Then I remembered where I had heard that name before. It was the town where Dostoyevsky had been imprisoned as a political exile. I tried to recall his novel *Notes from the Underground* but all I could remember was the darkness and misery of the main character.

'Miss Kozlova? My name is Daisy Kent.'

I glanced up and saw a bespectacled woman in a blue jacket and dress staring down at me. I followed her through a paper-flooded administration area, where volunteers were checking and filing forms, to an office with a frosted-glass door. Daisy asked me to sit down and closed the door behind us. The sun was burning through a window and she closed the blinds. The fan rotating on one of the filing cabinets did little to relieve the stuffiness of the room. I was finding it hard to breathe.

Daisy pushed her glasses higher up on her nose and studied my registration form. I looked over her shoulder at the poster of a nurse with a red cross on her cap comforting a wounded soldier.

'Your mother was taken to a labour camp in the Soviet Union, is that correct?' Daisy asked.

'Yes,' I said, leaning forward.

Her nostrils quivered and she folded her hands in front of her. 'Then I'm afraid the Red Cross can't help you.'

My fingers and toes turned to ice. My mouth fell open.

'The Russian government doesn't admit to having labour camps,' Daisy continued. 'Therefore it is impossible for us to determine where they are and how many there are.'

'But I think I know the town. Omsk.' I heard the tremble in my voice.

'Unfortunately, unless it's a war zone, we can't help you.'

'Why?' I stuttered. 'The IRO said that you could.'

Daisy sighed and clenched her hands. I stared at her neat trimmed nails, not able to believe what I was hearing. 'The Red Cross does all it can to help people, but we can only assist in countries involved in international or national wars,' she said. 'This is not the case in Russia. They are not considered to be breaking any humanitarian rules.'

'You know that's not true,' I interrupted. 'Labour camps are the same in Russia as they are in Germany.'

'Miss Kozlova,' she said, taking off her glasses and pointing them at me, 'we are supported by the Geneva Convention and we have to abide by their strict guidelines or we wouldn't exist at all.' Her voice was clinical rather than kind. I got the impression that she had faced these types of questions before, and had decided it was better to crush all hope at the outset rather than be drawn into an argument.

'But surely you have some connections?' I went on nervously. 'Some organisation that can at least give you information?'

She slipped my papers back into the folder as if to demonstrate the futility of my case. I didn't move. Did she expect me to just leave?

'Can't you do anything to help me?' I asked.

'I've already explained to you that there is nothing I can do.' Daisy picked up another folder from the pile next to her and started writing notes on it.

I saw that she wasn't going to help me. I couldn't reach that soft part which I had believed existed in everyone, except perhaps people bent on revenge, like Tang and Amelia. I stood up. 'You weren't there,' I said, a tear leaking out of my eye and running down to my chin. 'You weren't there when they took her away from me.'

Daisy dropped the folder back onto its pile and lifted her chin. 'I know this is distressing but . . .'

I didn't catch the last part of her sentence. I rushed out of her office and crashed into a table in the administration area, sending files sliding across the floor. The receptionist glanced up at me when I ran by but said nothing. Only the photographs on the wall in the waiting area, with their sad, lost eyes, showed me any sympathy.

I arrived back at the coffee lounge just as the mid-morning rush was beginning. My head was pounding and I was nauseous with the tears I was holding inside. I had no idea how I would get through my first day of work. I changed into my uniform and pulled my hair into a ponytail, but as soon as I walked into the kitchen my legs gave way beneath me and I had to sit down.

'Don't be put off by the Red Cross,' Betty said, fetching a glass of water and putting it on the table in front of me. 'There's more than one way to skin a rabbit. Maybe you

313

can join the Russian–Australian Society. You might find something out through them.'

'You might find yourself being investigated by the Australian government as a possible spy as well,' said Vitaly, slicing a loaf of bread. 'Anya, I promise I will write to my father tonight.'

Irina took the slices from Vitaly and began buttering them for sandwiches. 'The Red Cross is inundated and has to rely on volunteers,' she said. 'Vitaly's father can probably do more to help you anyway.'

'That's right,' said Vitaly. 'He'd like a project. Believe me, he will see it through to the end. If he can't find my uncle, he will get another contact for you, somehow.'

On Friday I spent my morning off in the State Library. Bathed in the ethereal light from the library's vaulted glass ceiling, I pored over Dostoyevsky's *Notes from the Underground*. It was difficult to read such a complex work in translation. I used a Russian–English dictionary to help me and persevered with it until it became clear that it was a fruitless endeavour. It was a dark novel about the nature of humanity, but it gave me no clues to my mother other than to confirm what I had already found out from an atlas: Omsk was in Siberia. Finally I had to admit that I was clutching at straws.

I returned to Potts Point, tired and defeated. The sun was hot but a sea breeze was starting to whip up from the harbour. I picked one of the geraniums near the gate and studied it while I walked up the path. A man burst through the front door, pushing a hat down onto his head. We almost collided. He stepped back, startled at first, then a smile spread over his face.

'Hello,' he said. 'You're one of Betty's girls, aren't you?'

The man was in his early thirties and his jet-black hair and green eyes reminded me of Gregory Peck's portrait in the coffee lounge. I noticed his glance drop from my face to my ankles and back again.

'Yes, I live with Betty,' I said. I wasn't going to give him my name until he told me his.

'I'm Adam. Adam Bradley,' he said, reaching out his hand to shake mine. 'I live upstairs.'

'Anya Kozlova,' I said.

'Watch out for him! He's trouble!' a woman's voice called out.

I turned around to see a pretty girl with blonde hair waving to me from across the street. She was wearing a pencil skirt with a fitted blouse and carrying a bunch of dresses over her arm. She opened the door to a Fiat and draped the clothes on the back seat.

'Ah, Judith!' Adam shouted back. 'You've called me out before I've even had a chance to start afresh with this beautiful young woman.'

'You'll never start afresh,' the woman laughed. 'Who was that à la mode waif I saw you sneaking home the other night?' The woman turned to me. 'By the way, I'm Judith.'

'I'm Anya. I saw your dress in the window. It's beautiful.'

'Thank you,' she said, smiling with big white teeth. 'I'm off to a show this weekend but drop in and see me any time. You're tall, slim and gorgeous. I could use you as a model.'

Judith slipped into the driver's seat of her car, did a U-turn and came to a roaring stop in front of us.

'Do you want a lift to the newspaper, Adam?' she asked, leaning over to the passenger window. 'Or is it true reporters don't work afternoons?'

'Hmm,' said Adam, tipping his hat to me and opening the car door. 'It was nice to meet you, Anya. If Judith can't get you a job, maybe I can.'

'Thanks, but I already have a job,' I said.

Judith tooted the horn and slammed her foot on the accelerator. I watched the car zoom up the street, narrowly missing two dogs and a man on a bicycle.

I walked up the stairs to the flat. I still had two hours

until I had to return to the coffee lounge to help with the Friday afternoon crowds. I went into the kitchen and decided to make myself a sandwich. The air in the flat smelled stale and I opened the French doors to let in the breeze.

A door banged at the back of the flat. I guessed it was either the bedroom door or that I hadn't closed the entrance door properly. I walked back inside to fix it. The front door was shut and so was the tilting window above it. I glanced around the corner and noticed that the door to my room was shut too. I heard another bang and saw that it was the door to the room next to ours that was opening and shutting in the breeze. I grasped the knob, intending to pull the door shut tightly, but curiosity got the better of me. I pushed the door open and peered inside.

The room was slightly larger than the one I shared with Irina, but like ours it had two single beds pushed against opposite walls. The covers were maroon with black tassels and there was a chest of drawers under the window. The air was old but the room had been dusted and the rug was clean. Hanging on the wall above one of the beds was a framed poster for a cricket match held in 1937, and some athletics ribbons were pinned above the other wall. My gaze moved from the fishing tackle on top of the wardrobe, to the tennis racket behind the door, to the photograph on top of a small dresser. In the picture two young men in uniform were standing either side of a smiling Betty. There was a ship in the background. Next to the photograph was a leather album. I opened the cover and found myself looking at a sepia photograph of two blond toddlers sitting in a boat. They were both holding up birthday cards with the number two on it. Twins. My hand flew to my mouth and I collapsed onto my knees.

'Betty,' I wept. 'Poor, poor Betty.'

Sadness washed over me in waves. My mother's crying face flashed before me. I understood what the room represented. It was a place for memory and private grief. Betty kept all the pain she felt inside in this room so that she could go on with her life. I understood why she kept it because I had a place like that too. It wasn't a room, it was the matroshka doll. That was something I retreated to when I needed to still believe that the mother I had lost had at some time been a part of my life. It was a way of reminding myself that she wasn't a dream.

I stayed in the room, crying until my ribs hurt and my eyes were so dry that I couldn't cry any more. After a while I got up and stepped out into the hall, closing the door tightly behind me. I never mentioned the room to Betty, although from that afternoon on I felt a special bond with her.

'I'm just stepping out to the bank,' Betty said one slow after-noon. She slipped on a light coat over her uniform and checked her lipstick in the shine of the coffee percolator. 'You'll be right with any customers, Anya, won't you?' she asked, squeezing my arm. 'Vitaly's in the kitchen if you get stuck.'

'Sure,' I told her.

I watched her step out onto the street. It was one of those overcast days that was neither hot nor chilly, but if you didn't wear a jacket you felt cold and when you put one on you felt too warm.

I wiped down the counter and the tables although they were already clean. About half an hour later I heard the front door open and looked up to see a group of girls saunter into the lounge and take the Joan Crawford booth. They were wearing office suits with straight skirts and pumps, and hats and gloves. They seemed to be in their late teens, but they were trying to look sophisticated by lighting up Du Mauriers and shooting puffs of smoke towards the ceiling.

They gave me the once-over when I approached their

table. One of them, a girl with large shoulders and pimples on her cheeks, whispered something and the other girls laughed. I could feel trouble coming.

'Good afternoon,' I said, ignoring their rudeness and hoping they only wanted small orders. 'What can I get you to drink?'

One of the girls, a plump brunette with her hair pulled back too tightly from her face, said, 'Vell, let me see . . . I would like you to brrring me some vater and perrrhaps some coffee to drrrink.'

Her imitation of my accent brought squeals of laughter from the other girls. The pimply girl slapped her hand on the table and said, 'And I would like some coffee and a rhubarb crumble. Make sure you bring me rhubarb crumble now, and not rrrhubard crrrumble. I believe there's a difference.'

My hand moved to my throat. I clutched my notepad, trying to keep my dignity, but my face blushed. It shouldn't have mattered. Part of me knew that they were only ignorant girls. But it was hard to stand there in my waitress's uniform and not feel like a second-rate person. I was a migrant. A 'reffo'. Someone the Australians didn't want.

'Speak E-n-g-l-i-s-h or go back to where you came from,' one of the girls muttered under her breath.

The hate in her voice took me by surprise. My heart started to pound. I looked over my shoulder but I couldn't hear Vitaly or Irina in the kitchen. Maybe they were in the lane, putting out the garbage.

'Yeah, go back,' the plump brunette said. 'We don't want you.'

'If you have a problem with her perfectly good English, you are welcome to get your coffee on King Street.'

We all looked up to see Betty standing in the doorway. I wondered how long she had been watching. Judging by the tautness of her mouth it had been long enough to catch the gist of what was going on. 'You'll pay another shilling or two for your drinks there,' she told them, 'so that's two shillings less for your diet pills and pimple cream.'

A couple of the girls hung their heads in shame. The plump girl fingered her gloves and smiled. 'Oh, we were just joking,' she said, trying to dismiss Betty with a wave of her hand. But Betty was on top of her in a minute, her face right up to the girl's, her eyes narrowed. 'You don't seem to understand, young lady,' she said, hovering over the girl in a manner that would have made anyone frightened of her. 'I'm not making you an offer. I'm the proprietor of this place and I'm telling you to get out now.'

The girl's face turned red. Her lip quivered and I could see she was about to cry. It made her look uglier and, despite myself, I felt sorry for her. She stood up, knocking over the napkin dispenser in her hurry to get away. Her friends sheepishly got up and scuttled out after her. None of them looked sophisticated any more.

Betty watched them leave and turned to me. 'Don't you ever let anyone speak to you like that, Anya. You hear?' she said. 'Never! I have some idea of what you've been through, and I'm telling you, you are worth twenty of them!'

That night, after Irina had fallen asleep, I lay awake thinking about how Betty had come to my defence, like a lioness rushing in to save her cub. Only my mother would have been so fierce. I heard the tap in the kitchen and wondered if Betty was having trouble sleeping too.

I found her sitting on the balcony, staring at the sky, with an inch of ash on the cigarette that glowed like a fire-fly in her fingers. The floorboards creaked under my feet. Betty's shoulder twitched but she didn't turn around to see who was behind her.

'Looks like rain tomorrow,' she muttered.

'Betty?' I slipped into the chair next to her. I'd interrupted her thoughts and it was too late to stop myself now.

She glanced at me but said nothing. In the glimmer of the light from the kitchen her skin was pale and her eyes were small without makeup. The fan of wrinkles on her forehead and the grooves around her mouth glistened with cold cream. Her features were softer, less dramatic, without the mask of cosmetics.

'Thank you for what you did today.'

'Hush!' she said, flicking her ash over the side of the balcony.

'I don't know what I would have done if you hadn't come.'

She squinted. 'You would have told them to "piss off" yourself sooner or later,' she said, fingering her hairnet. 'There's only so much a person can take before they start to fight back.'

I smiled, although I doubted what she said was true. When those girls had called me a worthless refugee, I'd believed them.

I leaned back into the chair. The air from the ocean was fresh but not cold. I breathed it in and filled my lungs with it. When I'd first met Betty her harsh manner had made me afraid of her. Suddenly, sitting next to her and seeing her in her nightdress with the ribbon laced around the neckline, I found the thought of that ludicrous. She reminded me of Ruselina. She emanated the same strength and fragility. But perhaps I only knew that she was fragile because I had seen her secret room.

Betty blew a spiral of smoke into the air. 'Words can kill you,' she said. 'I know. I was number six in a family of eight. The only girl. My father made no bones about telling me how worthless he thought I was, and that I wasn't worth the food he put in my mouth.'

I recoiled. I couldn't imagine what kind of father would say such a thing to his daughter. 'Betty!' I cried.

She shook her head. 'When I was thirteen I knew that I had to get away or let him murder what was left inside of me.'

'You were brave,' I told her. 'To make the choice to leave.'

She stubbed out her cigarette and we both fell silent, listening to the sound of a car starting down the road and the thrum of late-night music from the strip.

After a while Betty said, 'I made my own family because the one I'd been given at birth was no good. Tom and I didn't have much in the beginning, but God did we laugh. And then when the boys came . . . Well, we were happy.'

Her voice faltered and she took another cigarette from the pack on the armrest. I thought about the room. How the things that had belonged to her sons had been so lovingly kept.

'Rose told us that you lost your sons in the war,' I said. I was surprised at myself. On Tubabao I would never have asked anybody about their past. But then I had been in so much pain, I couldn't have borne anybody else's. Suddenly I had an urge to let Betty know that I understood her anguish because I felt it too.

Betty clenched her fist in her lap. 'Charlie in Singapore and Jack a month later. It broke Tom's heart, he didn't laugh so much after that. And then he was gone too.'

The same feeling of grief that had overcome me in the sons' room gripped me again. I reached out and touched Betty's shoulder. To my surprise she took my hand and held it in her own. Her grasp was bony but warm. Her eyes were dry but her mouth quivered.

'You're young, Anya, but you know what I'm talking about,' she said. 'Those girls in the lounge today, they're young but they don't know a bloody thing. I sacrificed my sons to save this country.'

I slipped out of my chair and kneeled beside her. I did understand her sorrow. I imagined that, like me, she was afraid to close her eyes at night because of the dreams, and that even among friends she was in a world of her own. But I couldn't imagine the magnitude of the loss of one

321

child, let alone two. Betty was strong, I felt the foundations of her verve pulsing through her, but at the same time I knew that if she was pushed too far she would shatter.

'I'm proud,' she said. 'Proud that because of young men like my sons, this country is still free and kids like you can come and make new lives here. I want to do all I can to help you. I won't have people calling you names.'

Tears stung my eyes. 'Betty.'

'You, Vitaly, Irina,' she said, 'you're my children now.'

FOURTEEN

Society

One evening in July, Betty was teaching me the secret of her beef and pineapple casserole when Irina rushed into the kitchen waving a letter. 'Grandmother's coming!' she cried.

I wiped my hands on my apron, took the letter from her and read the first few lines. The French doctors had declared Ruselina recovered and the consulate was preparing the papers for her to travel to Australia. So much had happened since I had last seen Ruselina, I couldn't believe it when I read that she was expecting to be in Sydney at the end of the month. The time seemed to have flown by.

I translated the news for Betty. 'Wait till she hears how well you're speaking English now,' she said to Irina. 'She won't recognise you.'

'She won't recognise me because you've been feeding me so well,' replied Irina, smiling. 'I've put on weight.'

'Not me!' protested Betty, slicing some bacon and batting her eyelids. 'I think it's Vitaly who's been over-feeding you. Whenever the two of you are in the kitchen all I hear is giggling!'

I thought Betty's joke was funny but Irina blushed.

'Vitaly should have his Austin fixed up by the time Ruselina arrives,' I said. 'We can take her for a trip to the Blue Mountains.'

Betty rolled her eyes. 'Vitaly's been working on that

Austin of his since I first employed him and it still hasn't been out of his garage! I think we'd better count on the train.'

'Do you think we can find a flat for Grandmother close by?' Irina asked Betty. 'We don't have much time.'

Betty slipped the casserole dish into the oven and clicked on the timer. 'I have another idea,' she said. 'There's a room downstairs that belongs to me, I've been using it for storage. But it's large and pleasant. I'll clear it out if you like it.'

She reached to a jar on top of the kitchen cupboard, pulled out a key and handed it to Irina. 'You and Anya have a look and see what you think. Dinner won't be ready for a while.'

Irina and I raced down the stairs to the first floor.

The room Betty had told us about was at the end of the hall, behind the stairs.

We opened the door and stepped inside, finding ourselves in a cramped space filled with cupboards, suit-cases and a four-poster bed. The air smelled of dust and mothballs.

'That bed must have been in our room once,' I said. 'It was probably Tom and Betty's.'

Irina pushed open a sliding door under the stairs and switched on the light. 'There's a basin and toilet in here,' she said. 'I guess Grandmother could take her baths upstairs.'

I opened the doors of a carved armoire. It was packed with Bushell's tea.

'What do you think?' Irina asked me.

'I think you should take it,' I said. 'Betty needs to sell this stuff sooner or later, and if we clean up the room it will be nice.'

Ruselina's ship sailed into the harbour on a sublime Sydney morning. The humidity of summer had been familiar to me because Shanghai's climate was similar, but I had never

324

known winter days with bright sunshine glistening in the trees and the air so crisp it seemed you could bite it like a fresh apple. Unlike Harbin, there was none of the drawn-out descent into winter, followed by months of snow, ice and darkness. Sydney's kind version of winter put a bounce in my step and roses in my cheeks. Irina and I decided to walk to the wharf to meet Ruselina. We practically skipped and couldn't help secretly laughing at the Australians wrapped up in their jackets and coats and complaining of the 'bitter cold' and 'chilblains'.

'It must be fifty-five degrees above or more,' I said to Irina.

'Grandmother will think it's summer,' she laughed. 'That kind of temperature was a heatwave when she lived in Russia.'

We were relieved to see that the ship that brought Ruselina to Australia was not as crowded as the one we had seen on our first day in Sydney, although the wharf was full of people waiting for the passengers to disembark. There was a Salvation Army band playing 'Waltzing Matilda' and some journalists and photographers taking pictures. A line of people were descending the gangway in an orderly fashion. A group of boy scouts rushed forward to hand out apples to the passengers as they came ashore.

'Where did this ship come from?' I asked Irina.

'It started from England and picked up a few other passengers on the way.'

I didn't say anything but I did feel hurt that the Australians seemed more keen about British migrants than us.

Irina and I searched the faces for Ruselina's.

'There she is!' Irina cried, pointing towards the middle of the line.

I blinked. The woman coming down the ship's gangway wasn't the Ruselina I had known on Tubabao. A healthy tan had replaced her ashen complexion and she was walking without the aid of a stick. Gone were the dark patches beneath her skin that had been familiar to me. She spotted us and called out. 'Irina! Anya!'

We both rushed forward to meet her. When I hugged her it was like squeezing a cushion instead of a twig.

'Let me see you!' she cried, taking a step back. 'You both look so well. Mrs Nelson must be taking good care of you!'

'She is,' said Irina, wiping away a tear. 'But what about you, Grandmother? How are you feeling?'

'Better than I ever imagined,' she replied. Seeing the sparkle in her eye and her glowing skin up close, I could believe it.

We asked her about her sea voyage and about France and for some reason she answered us only in English although we were speaking to her in Russian.

We followed the other passengers to the southern end of the wharf, where the luggage was being unloaded. Irina and I asked Ruselina about the passengers on the ship and she lowered her voice and said, 'Irina and Anya, we must speak only English now that we are in Australia.'

'Not when we are speaking to each other!' laughed Irina.

'Especially when we are speaking to each other,' said Ruselina, pulling out a brochure from her handbag. It was the IRO introduction to Australia booklet. 'Read that,' she said, opening it to an earmarked page and passing it to me.

I read from the paragraph marked with an asterisk.

Perhaps the most important thing is to learn to speak the language of the Australians. Australians are not used to hearing foreign languages. They are inclined to stare at people whose speech is different. Speaking in your own language in public will make you conspicuous and make Australians regard you as a stranger . . . Also, try to avoid using your hands when speaking because if you do, this will make you conspicuous.

'It seems very important to them that we are in no way "conspicuous",' said Irina.

'That would explain the strange looks we've been getting,' I said.

Ruselina took the booklet back from me. 'There's more. When I applied for my entry into Australia they sent an official to the hospital to inquire whether I had any Communist sympathies.'

'Was that a joke?' asked Irina. 'We of all people. After all we've lost. As if we would be Reds!'

'That's what I told him,' said Ruselina. '"Young man, do you seriously believe I could support the regime that put my parents before the firing squad?"'

'It's the tensions in Korea,' I said. 'They think every Russian is a spy for the enemy.'

'It's worse if you are Asian,' said Irina. 'Vitaly says they don't even let people with dark skin into the country.'

A crane roared and we looked up to see a bundle of luggage in a net being unloaded onto the wharf.

'There's my suitcase,' said Ruselina, pointing to a blue bag with a white trim. When the official told us we could go and pick it up, we lined up with the other passengers.

'Anya, that black case over there is also mine,' said Ruselina. 'Can you manage it? It's heavy. Irina can take the suitcase.'

'What is it?' I asked, although I knew as soon as I felt the weight and smelled the machine oil.

'It's a sewing machine I bought in France,' said Ruselina. 'I'm going to take in some dressmaking so that I can help you two.'

Irina and I glanced at each other. 'It's not necessary, Grandmother,' said Irina. 'We have a room for you. The rent is low and we can pay it until our contracts are up.'

'You can't possibly afford to do that,' said Ruselina.

'Yes, we can,' I told her. But I didn't tell her that I had sold the jewels I had brought with me from Shanghai and

327

opened a bank account. I didn't get as much money as I had hoped for the stones because, as the jeweller explained, there was something of a glut of migrants selling jewels in Australia. But I did have enough to pay for Ruselina's room until our contracts were up.

'Nonsense,' said Ruselina. 'You must save as much money as you can.'

'Grandmother,' said Irina, rubbing her hand down her side. 'You've been so sick. Anya and I want you to take it easy.'

'Bah! I've had it with easy,' said Ruselina. 'Now I want to help you.'

Back at Potts Point we found Betty and Vitaly arguing in the kitchen. The apartment smelled of roast beef and baked potatoes and, although it was winter, all the windows and doors were open to let out the heat.

'He wants to cook some strange foreign dish,' said Betty, shrugging her shoulders. She wiped her fingers on her apron and reached out to shake Ruselina's hand. 'But I want nothing but the best for our guest.'

'I'm pleased to meet you, Mrs Nelson,' said Ruselina, shaking Betty's hand. 'I want to thank you for taking care of Irina and Anya.'

'Call me Betty,' the other woman said, stroking her beehive. 'And it's been a pleasure. I feel like they are my daughters.'

'What foreign dish do you want to make?' Irina asked Vitaly, playfully punching his arm.

He rolled his eyes to the ceiling. 'Spaghetti bolognaise.'

Midday in winter was still warm enough to eat outside and we carried the card table to the verandah and brought out more chairs. Vitaly was given the job of carving the meat and Irina dished out the vegetables. Ruselina sat down next to Betty and I couldn't help staring at them. They were a strange juxtaposition. Apart you could tell they were different women, but side by side they looked uncannily alike. On the surface they had nothing in common: one was an old-world aristocrat reduced in circumstances through wars and revolutions; the other was a woman from a working-class family, who through scrimping and saving had come to own a coffee lounge and a house in Potts Point. But from the first words they spoke to each other Ruselina and Betty had an easy rapport, like women who have been friends for years.

'You were very sick, love,' said Betty, lifting Ruselina's plate so Vitaly could put some meat on it.

'I thought I was going to die,' said Ruselina. 'But now I can honestly say that I've never felt better in my life.'

'It's them French doctors,' said Betty, squinting. 'I reckon they would fix you up all right.'

Ruselina laughed at Betty's innuendo. I was surprised that she understood. 'They certainly would have, if only I was twenty again.'

Dessert was parfait served in tall glasses. Looking at the layers of ice-cream and jelly topped with fruit and nuts, I had no idea how I was going to fit it in after our heavy meal. I sat back, resting my hands on my stomach. Betty was telling Ruselina about Bondi Beach and how she wanted to move there when she retired. Irina was listening, with more enthusiasm than I would have expected, to Vitaly's stroke-by-stroke account of the laps he had done in the tidal pool that morning. 'You're not affected by the cold, that's for sure,' Irina said to him. I looked at everyone's smiling faces and felt a tingle of joy inside. Despite my longing for my mother, I realised I was happier than I had been in months. I'd been worried about so many things but everything was turning out well. Ruselina had arrived in good health and spirits. Irina seemed to be enjoying working at the coffee lounge and going to her English classes at the technical college. As for me, I loved Betty's little flat. I felt more comfortable there than I had in the mansion in Shanghai. I had loved Sergei but the house had been a den of angst and deception. Here in Potts Point everything was as calm and as welcoming as it had been in Harbin, even though the two cities, and my father's and Betty's taste, couldn't have been more different.

'Anya, you're crying,' said Ruselina.

Everybody became quiet and turned to look at me. Irina passed me her handkerchief and grasped my fingers. 'What's wrong?' she asked.

'Did something upset you, love?' asked Betty.

'No,' I said, shaking my head and smiling through my tears. 'I'm happy, that's all.'

Ruselina's dressmaking endeavours got off to a slow start. Many women migrants who had never worked before were taking up dressmaking to supplement their husband's wages, and although Ruselina's needlework was close to perfection, the younger women could work faster. The only kind of dressmaking Ruselina was offered was outwork with factories. Without telling us, she agreed to take ten cocktail dresses a week from a factory in Surry Hills. But the detail in the dresses was so labour-intensive that she had to work from six in the morning until late at night to meet the deadline, and in less than a fortnight she was pale and feeble again. Irina forbade her to take on any more work from the factory, but Ruselina could be stubborn when she wanted to be.

'I don't want you to support me when I can do it myself,' she argued. 'I want you to save money so you can get back to your singing career.'

It was Betty who took control of the situation.

'You've only been in the country a few weeks, love,' she told Ruselina. 'It takes a while to meet people. Dressmaking work will come to you by and by. Anya and I will need new uniforms soon, so why don't I commission you to do that? And then I think this flat could do with some nice curtains.'

Later, while I was reading the newspaper in the kitchen, I overheard Betty tell Ruselina, 'You mustn't get so worried about them. They are young. They will find their own way. The coffee lounge is doing better than ever and you all have a roof over your heads. I'm happy to have you here.'

The following week Betty gave me an afternoon off instead of a morning and I spent it on the verandah, reading a novel. Four hours passed and I didn't even notice. Then for some reason I glanced up and the window of Judith's studio caught my eye. She had a new dress on display. A sage-coloured gown made of silk and covered in a layer of tulle.

'Why didn't I think of that before?' I asked myself, putting down the book and standing up.

Judith's face broke into a smile when she opened the door and saw me on the step.

'Hello, Anya,' she said, 'I was wondering when you would show up.'

'I'm sorry I didn't come earlier,' I said, 'but a friend arrived to live with us and we have been trying to get her settled in.'

I followed Judith through a tiled entrance into the front room where two gold chaises longues sat on either side of a gilded mirror.

'Yes, Adam told me. A refined elderly lady, he said.'

'I came to see if you might have some work for her. She comes from a time when sewing was an elevated form of art.'

'Ah, that sounds good,' said Judith. 'I have enough cutters and sewers at the moment, but it would be good to know that I had someone who could help out during our busy periods. Tell her to come and see me whenever she has a chance.'

I thanked Judith and looked at the crystal vases filled with roses on the mantelpiece. There was a statue of Venus on a bronze stand over by the window. 'This room is beautiful,' I said.

'My fitting room is through here.' Judith opened a set of saloon doors and showed me a room with white carpet and teardrop chandeliers hanging from the ceiling.

Two Louis XV chairs were covered in rose chintz. She pulled aside a pair of gold lamé curtains and we entered a part of the studio with a different atmosphere. There were no curtains on the windows and the afternoon light fell sharply onto the workbenches covered with pincushions and scissors. A group of dressmaker's dummies were propped at the back of the room, looking as though they were having a committee meeting. It was after five o'clock and Judith's staff had gone home for the day. The room had the ambiance of an empty church.

'How about some tea?' Judith asked, moving towards a kitchenette in the corner. 'No, let's have some champagne.'

I watched her set down two glasses on a workbench and twist the cork on the champagne bottle. 'I can relax better here than I can in the other room,' she laughed. 'The front room is all about show. This room is closer to my soul.'

She handed me a glass and the first sip went straight to my head. I hadn't drunk champagne since the Moscow-Shanghai. In Judith's studio, those days seemed a lifetime away.

'Are they your latest designs?' I asked her, pointing to a rack of dresses in organdie covers.

'Yes.' She put down her glass, crossed the room and wheeled the rack towards me. She unzipped one of the covers to show me a lace dress with cap sleeves and a v-neckline that opened wide at the shoulders. The dress was lined with bronze silk which looked as expensive as the outside of the dress.

'People are wearing stiff petticoats,' she said, 'but I like the material to fall close to the body, so that it drapes over

332

the figure like a waterfall. That's why I need models with good legs.'

'The detailing is gorgeous.' I ran my fingertip over the silver beads on the bodice. My eye caught the price tag. Some Australians would have considered the amount a deposit for a block of land. I remembered I had bought such dresses in Shanghai and not even considered the price. But after all I had been through, my priorities had changed. Still, I couldn't help but be charmed by the extraordinary dress.

'I have an Italian woman who does the beading for me and another who does the embroidery.' Judith put the dress back in its cover and took out another to show me. It was an evening gown with a cowl neck and bust in lavender, an underbust in turquoise and a black skirt with rosettes around the hem. She turned the dress over and showed me the soft bustle at the back. 'This one's for a play that will be showing at the Theatre Royal,' she said, holding the dress against her body. 'I get a lot of work from the theatre companies and quite a bit from the racing crowd. Both are all about glamour.'

'Sounds like exciting clientele,' I said.

Judith nodded. 'But I'd really like to get society women wearing my clothes because they're photographed for the papers all the time. And also because they're snobby about Australian designers. They still think it's more prestigious to buy their clothes in London or Paris. But what looks good in Europe doesn't necessarily translate well here. The old social circle is a tight one though. It's hard to break in.'

She held out the dress towards me. 'Do you want to try it on?'

'I look better in simpler designs,' I said, putting down my glass.

'Then I have the dress for you.' She unzipped another bag and pulled out a dress with a black scooped bodice and a straight white skirt with black piping on the hem.

'Try this on,' she said, guiding me to the fitting room. 'It has matching gloves and a beret. It's part of my spring collection.'

Judith helped me to unhook my skirt and slipped my sweater onto a padded coathanger. It was the practice of many couturiers to help their customers change their clothes and I was glad I was wearing the new underwear I had bought from Mark Foys a few days earlier. It would have been embarrassing to be seen in the threadbare undergarments I had been wearing since Tubabao.

Judith zipped me into the dress and placed the beret at an angle on my head, then walked around me in circles. 'You'd make a good model for the collection,' she said. 'You've got the right aristocratic look.'

The last person who had said I was aristocratic was Dmitri. But Judith made it sound more like a personal quality than a mere asset. 'An accent in Australia is a disadvantage,' I said.

'That all depends on the circle in which you move and how you present yourself.' Judith gave me a wink. 'The owners of the top restaurants in this city are all foreigners. One of my competitors is a Russian woman in Bondi who claims to be a niece of the Tsar. It's a lie of course, she's far too young. But everyone laps it up. She tells her clientele what to wear or not to wear with such authority that even some of the society matrons cower in her presence.'

Judith picked up the hem of the dress and smoothed it between her fingers, her mind ticking over. 'If I can get you seen at the right places wearing my clothes, it might be the boost I need. Will you help me?'

I looked into Judith's blue eyes. What she was asking me wouldn't be too difficult. After all I had once been the hostess of Shanghai's greatest nightclub. And after wearing faded clothes and seconds for so long, it was nice to wear a beautiful dress.

'Sure,' I said. 'It sounds like fun.'

*   *   *

The sight of my reflection in Judith's mirror took my breath away. After five fittings, two of which were probably unnecessary, the dress she had created for my 'debut' into Australian society was ready. I fingered the cyclamen chiffon gown and smiled at her. The dress had a gathered bodice, boned for support, and spaghetti straps. The flowing skirt stopped just above my ankles. Judith draped the matching wrap over my shoulders and blinked her eyes. She could have been a mother dressing her daughter for a wedding.

'It's an amazing dress,' I said, glancing from Judith back to the mirror. It was true. Of all the dresses I had worn in Shanghai, none had been as feminine or as finely cut as this one Judith had designed for me.

'It's been quite a production,' she laughed, pouring out two glasses of champagne. 'Here's to the success of the dress.' She emptied her glass in three gulps and, when she saw the surprise on my face, added, 'Better drink up for Dutch courage. Girls of our station in life mustn't be seen drinking in public.'

'I thought you wanted me to be a displaced Russian aristocrat,' I teased Judith. 'Didn't you say the one in Bondi drinks like a fish?'

'You're right. Forget I said that.' She checked her own crepe de Chine gown in the mirror. 'Just be yourself. You're charming just as you are.'

Chequers nightclub was in Goulburn Street, but unlike the Moscow-Shanghai with its stairs leading upwards, it was at basement level. The minute I put my foot on the staircase, Judith turned around and smiled at me and I knew I was on show. Although several women turned to admire my dress, none of the press photographers took a picture of it. I did, however, overhear one of the reporters say, 'Hey, that's not that American starlet, is it?'

'Don't worry about the photographers,' said Judith, linking arms with me. 'If they don't know you, they won't take your picture. Did you see all those women admiring your dress? You're the belle of the ball.'

The club was filled to capacity. Everywhere I looked I saw silk brocade, chiffon, taffeta, mink and fox fur. I hadn't seen anything like it since the days of the Moscow-Shanghai. But there was something different about the crowd at Chequers. With their bright chatter and golden good looks, they lacked the darker, hidden layer that one sensed in Shanghailanders. They didn't seem to be people who were living on the razor's edge of fortune or ruin. Or so I thought.

We were shown to a table one row back from the dance floor and not far from the stage.

'We might see Adam,' Judith said, scanning the crowd. 'I think he's got his eye on a trainer's daughter.'

I watched the couples turning on the dance floor; there were a few very good dancers. I noticed a man whose feet glided so smoothly that his upper body didn't jerk at all and a woman so light in her step that she made me think of a feather skimming the breeze. The romantic music carried with it a memory of the Moscow-Shanghai. I thought of how Dmitri and I had danced in the last days after I had forgiven him for his affair with Amelia. How close we had seemed then. Much closer than when we were younger or when we first married. I wondered if my life as a refugee would have been easier if he had come with me. I flinched. Wasn't that the reason people got married? To support each other. I was beginning to think that every part of our relationship had been an illusion. How else could he have given me up so easily?

'Hello,' I heard a familiar voice call out. I looked up to see Adam Bradley smiling at us.

'What's happened to your racing girl?' Judith asked.

'Well,' said Adam, glancing over my dress, 'I was hoping Anya would dance with me so I could make her jealous.'

'If her father finds out, you're going to get a broken

nose, Adam,' said Judith. 'And I'll only let Anya dance with you because it's a good chance to show off the dress.'

Adam led me out onto the crowded floor. I shook off my sad thoughts about Dmitri. There was no point spoiling the evening with regret about something I couldn't change, and a sour look didn't go with my dress, which was attracting admiring glances from some of the other dancers. The colour was bold against the other black, white and pastel dresses and the chiffon glimmered like a pearl under the lights.

'Actually,' said Adam, glancing around, 'it could do my career a lot of good to be seen with you. Everyone is looking at us.'

'I hope it's not because the zip has come undone,' I joked.

'Hang on, I'll just check,' he said, slipping his hand low on my back.

'Adam!' I reached around and put his hand in a more respectable position. 'That wasn't an invitation.'

'I know,' he grinned. 'I don't want both Judith and Betty on my case.'

The band started up a slower number and Adam was about to lead me when I heard a voice beside us say, 'May I have the next dance?'

I looked up to see an older man with short eyebrows and a square jaw looking back at me. His protruding lower lip made him resemble a benevolent bulldog. Adam's eyes nearly popped out of his head.

'Ah yes, sure,' he said. But I could tell by the way he gripped me that he wasn't pleased to have been cut out.

'My name is Harry Gray,' the man said, leading me away gracefully. 'My wife sent me over here with strict instructions to save you from Adam Bradley and to find out who made your dress.'

He indicated somewhere behind us with his chin. I glanced over my shoulder to see a woman sitting at a table near the dance floor. She was wearing a champagne-coloured dress with a beaded bodice, her grey hair swept into a low chignon.

'Thank you,' I said. 'I would like to meet your wife.'

When the dance finished. Harry led me to the table where the woman was waiting. She introduced herself as Diana Gray, women's editor for the *Sydney Herald*. Something flashed in the corner of my eye and I glanced up to see Judith peering at me over the top of a menu and giving me a thumbs-up sign.

'How do you do, Mrs Gray?' I said. 'My name is Anya Kozlova. Thank you for sending your husband to me.'

'Anything to save a becoming girl like you from Adam Bradley. Won't you sit down, Anya?'

It was hard to take my eyes off Diana. She was a beautiful woman. She wore no makeup except for a slash of dark red lipstick and spoke with a clear accent, which I took to be British. I was impressed that she could pronounce my name properly.

'Now tell me about your dress, Anya.'

'It's by the designer Judith James,' I replied. 'She's Australian.'

'Really?' said Diana, standing up and waving to someone over the other side of the dance floor. 'I haven't heard of her, but I think we should get a picture of it for the paper.'

A girl with short dark hair and an expensive-looking dress made her way to the table, with a photographer in tow. My heart skipped a beat. A picture of the dress in the paper was more than even Judith had expected.

'We're waiting to get a photograph of Sir and Lady Morley before they leave for the evening,' the girl told Diana. 'If we miss out we will be the only paper here without them.'

'Okay, Caroline,' Diana said, 'but take a photo of Anya in this beautiful dress first.'

'Anya who?' the girl asked, not even looking at me.

338

'Kozlova,' Diana answered. 'Now hurry up, Caroline.'

Caroline pinched her face like a wilful child. 'We only have two plates left. We can't afford to waste any. The colour won't come up in the paper and that's the best thing about the dress.'

'The best thing about the dress is the girl who's wearing it,' said Diana, pushing me out onto the dance floor and sticking me into a pose with Harry. 'There, that way you can get the whole dress,' she told the photographer.

I did my best not to waste a plate when the photographer took the picture. I looked over to where Judith was sitting. Judith was half out of her chair with her hands in the air.

Afterwards, back in her studio, Judith downed a brandy nightcap while I changed from my gown back into a cotton dress.

'Cinderella after the ball,' I said.

'You were marvellous, Anya. Thank you. And that dress will be yours as a present. I just want to hold on to it for a week, in case anyone wants to see it.'

'I can't believe that we got it into the paper,' I said.

Judith shifted in her chair and put her glass down. 'I don't expect it will make it that far. Not with her royal highness, Caroline Bitch, social editor, in charge.'

I sat down next to Judith and slipped on my shoes. 'What do you mean?'

'Caroline Kitson doesn't include anyone in the social page who can't help her achieve her own ambitions. What I'm happy about is that Diana Gray took a liking to you. She'll talk about you and the dress, and that's good for both of us.'

I kissed Judith goodnight and headed across the street. My legs ached from the dancing and I could hardly keep my eyes open. But when I slipped into the bedroom in the dark, Irina sat up and turned on the light.

'I was trying not to wake you,' I said apologetically.

'You didn't,' she smiled. 'I couldn't sleep so I decided to wait up for you. How was it?'

I sat down on my bed. I was exhausted and wanted to go to sleep, but I had been spending a lot of time with Judith and hardly any with Irina for the past few weeks, and I felt guilty. Besides, I had missed her companionship. I told her about Diana Gray.

'The nightclub seemed like a good venue,' I said. 'You should try out for the cabaret.'

'Do you think so?' Irina asked. 'Betty has asked me to sing at the coffee lounge on Saturday afternoons. The lounge on King Street has got a jukebox now and Betty wants to compete with something more upmarket. She's even going to buy a piano so Grandmother can play.'

The idea sounded cute, but given Irina's initial passion for New York I wondered why she didn't react more keenly to what I had told her about Chequers. I could understand that she would want to help Betty out, but not why she wouldn't want to try for a professional cabaret as well.

'Anya,' she said, 'I have something to tell you.'

The way she hesitated made me nervous. For some reason I thought she might start talking about going to America again, although she seemed happy in Australia.

'And I don't want Betty to find out, okay? Not yet anyway.'

'Okay,' I agreed, feeling my throat tighten.

'Vitaly and I are in love.'

Her confession took me by surprise. All I could do was look at her. I knew that she and Vitaly got along well, but I hadn't seen anything further than friendship coming out of that.

'I know. You aren't impressed,' she said. 'He's goofy and he's not handsome. But he's sweet and I love him.'

From the starry look in her eyes I had no doubt it was true. I grabbed her hand. 'Don't say that,' I said, 'I like Vitaly

340

a lot. You took me by surprise, that's all. You never told me you liked him that way.'

'I've told you now,' she grinned.

When Irina had fallen asleep, I shut my eyes and tried to sleep too but I couldn't stop my mind from racing. If Irina was in love with Vitaly I could only wish her happiness. It was natural that she should fall in love and want to get married some day. But where did that leave me? I had been so occupied with trying to get by day to day, and longing for my past, that I had forgotten there was a future to consider. Dmitri's face flashed before me. Why had I thought about him so much during this evening? Was it possible I still loved him? He had betrayed me for an easy life in America, but when I tried to imagine myself falling in love with another man the thought alone was enough to make me grit my teeth with pain. What would I do when Irina was gone? I would be all alone.

Judith was right about the social editor and the photograph. I flipped through the morning and afternoon editions of the *Sydney Herald* the next day but my picture wasn't in either of them. I wondered why Diana hadn't been more insistent with someone who was junior to her. After work I stopped by the bookstore in the Cross to look for something new to read. I'd decided I was going to be doing a lot of reading now that Irina would be occupied with Vitaly, I chose a book of Australian poems and bought a dictionary, then dawdled along the strip, looking at all the couples talking together in cafés and bars, before going home.

When I stepped into the flat I was surprised to see Adam sitting in the living room, talking with Betty.

'Well, look who's here,' said Betty, standing up and putting her arm around me. 'It seems you made a big impression on someone last night.'

I glanced at Adam, wondering if he was upset over our interrupted dance, but he was smiling. 'Anya,' he said,

341

'Diana Gray asked me to find out if you would be interested in working for her. They have an opening for a beauty editor in the women's section.'

I'd had so many surprises in the past twenty-four hours that I could hardly react, but the first thing I thought of was Betty and the coffee lounge. Working in an office would be better than being a waitress. And working for a newspaper sounded interesting. But Betty had been good to me and I couldn't just leave her. I turned to Betty and told her this.

'Don't be silly,' she said. 'It's a wonderful opportunity. How could I hold you back? Colonel Brighton warned me that someone would recognise how bright you are and snap you up.'

'You won't be paid as much at first as you have been with Betty,' said Adam, 'but it's a good starting position.'

'What will you do at the lounge?' I asked Betty.

'Irina's English is good enough now,' she said. 'I think it's time she came out of the kitchen.'

'You see, Anya,' said Adam. 'You're doing Irina a favour.'

'Oh,' I said, trying to look innocent. I was sure that was the last kind of favour Irina would want.

FIFTEEN

The Key

I accepted Diana Gray's offer and began work at the paper the next day. Besides Diana and Caroline, there was Ann White, the fashion editor, a pale girl who wore her hair pulled back into a tight ponytail, and Joyce, Diana's secretary. There were also three reporters, Suzanne, Peggy and Rebecca who covered events such as society weddings, balls, ocean liner arrivals and departures and polo matches. Joyce helped with the daily tasks of running copy to the subeditors and sending out the patterns that were featured in the section. Ann spent most of her time staring at pictures while Caroline spent hers on the telephone, gossiping, which was the greater part of her job.

Although I was given the title of 'Beauty Editor' I wasn't really much more than a D-ranking journalist. My job was to write about new products that came on the market and to give beauty tips which I collected from the girls at the cosmetic counters. Every week I told women how to make themselves attractive. I instructed them to dip their elbows into lemon halves to keep them white or to rub petroleum jelly into their cuticles to make their nails strong. I did none of those things myself, except to clean my face thoroughly before I went to bed.

Betty sniffed out Vitaly and Irina's secret long before they were ready to admit it and saw it as a chance to take a holiday with Ruselina down the coast. 'Tom and I always promised ourselves a break but we never got the chance to take one. I'm going to train you two up to be managers so I can retire. You can buy me out of the business as time goes by.'

At Christmas Irina and Vitaly announced their engagement with the marriage set for November the following year. Apart from still missing my mother, my life in Australia was happy and I was sure that I was going to have my best year yet. But I was wrong. Something would happen to turn my life upside down, all over again.

I returned to the flat in Potts Point one evening and found it deserted. I knew that Irina and Vitaly were at the pictures. There was a note on the coffee table from Betty saying that she had gone for a dip in the Domain baths. She'd drawn a map in case I wanted to join her. It was hot that day, a real Sydney heat wave. It was half past seven but the sun was still burning. I kicked off my shoes and opened the doors and windows. I found Ruselina lying on the banana chair on the balcony, wearing a Chinaman's straw hat and sunglasses and catching the beginnings of the evening sea breeze. Down on the street I could hear the happy shouts of children playing under a hose.

'It's what the Australians call "stinking hot", isn't it?' Ruselina said.

I asked her if she wanted some lemonade.

'Thank you. A telegram came for you today, Anya,' she said. 'I put it on the kitchen table.'

I rushed to the kitchen, wondering who would have sent me a telegram. My heart leaped with excitement when I opened the envelope and saw that it was from Dan Richards, my American friend. The telegram said that he was coming to Sydney the following week and asked me to meet him at the consulate on Tuesday at eleven o'clock.

'Hey,' I called, running out to Ruselina, 'it's from Dan, my old friend. The one who tried to help us get to America. He's coming to Sydney next week and wants to see me.'

I couldn't imagine any surprise more wonderful than seeing Dan again. We had kept up correspondence over the years, mainly Christmas cards but occasionally a letter. He was the father of two children by now.

'An overseas visitor! How wonderful for you!' said Ruselina, tilting her hat so she could get a better look at me. 'Is he bringing his wife and children?'

'I don't know,' I said. 'I assume he will be, though the youngest is barely five months old. He must be coming on either a holiday or business.'

I read the message again. I was puzzled about why Dan had sent me a telegram rather than writing a letter and giving me more notice. I hoped that he was bringing Polly and the children. I had never met his wife but had always been intrigued by her. Dan described her as a lively and strong-minded woman. I knew that she would have to be someone special to have inspired such loyalty in a man.

I was wide awake at five o'clock on the morning I was supposed to meet Dan. I'd slept well but I couldn't lie in because of the anticipation of seeing him again. I'd already prepared my best summer dress. It was ironed and hanging on the wardrobe door, a cherry-red shift with a matching hat, one of Judith's creations. The hat was decorated with a trim of gardenias. The dress was simple and flattering, it was the hat that gave it balance and personality. My meeting with Dan would be the first occasion I'd have to wear it. I slipped out of bed without disturbing Irina and went to the kitchen. I made tea and marmalade toast and tiptoed out onto the balcony, careful not to wake Betty when I passed her on the lounge. But there was little chance of that. Betty was a sound sleeper. As soon as she put on her pyjamas and her hair net she was usually out cold until her alarm went off in the morning.

The street was summery green and the harbour was dazzling in the early sunlight. I could hardly believe that in a few hours I would cross paths with Dan Richards again. I closed my eyes and saw him as he had been during those language and culture afternoons in Shanghai. So gallant and dashing, trying to pronounce the Russian words I wrote down for him. I laughed when I thought of his red hair and freckled skin. His charming, boyish smile. There had been a time when I thought I could fall in love with him. That made me smile too and I was glad that I never had. He was a good man, a kind man, but we would not have been suited to each other. Besides the fact that he was happily married, I was too complicated for him. But I was glad that we had remained good friends. He had been loyal to me and generous. I was lucky to have had his help when I needed it.

A pain pinched my stomach. Another memory came floating up like a piece of wreckage from the depths. It was at odds with the summer breeze and the joy I had been feeling just a second before. Another day, another city, another consulate . . . *I'm looking for my husband.* Gunfire in the distance. The terror in the eyes of the people crowding the halls. *Please don't worry. Everything has been chaotic here.* Chinese antiques and books half packed into boxes. A photograph of a man I loved. Dan's grim mouth. *Anya, is this your husband. Dmitri Lubensky?* A ship waiting in the dock. Its funnel billowing steam. *Good God, Anya!* Dan struggling with my luggage, his arm tucked under my elbow to stop me from stumbling. Papers clutched in my hands. My legs weak with shock. *Trust me, there will be a day when you'll be glad that man's name doesn't belong to you.*

'Anya.'

The murky river transformed into the blue harbour again.

'Anya.'

It was Irina standing in the doorway holding out a plate of bacon and eggs.

'What time is it?' I glanced over my shoulder at her. Her smile disappeared.

'Anya,' Irina asked, her eyes darkening. 'Why are you crying?'

To my relief the American consulate in Sydney bore no resemblance to the one in Shanghai, save for the American flags in its reception area. Its decor was functional leather and wood. It was businesslike rather than chic and its uniformed guards looked purposeful and serious. It had none of the opulent atmosphere of its counterpart in Shanghai. Dan Richards was waiting for me. He was sitting in a wing-backed armchair with his leg crossed over his knee, reading the *Daily Telegraph*. The paper was folded out full in front of his face but I could tell it was him from the spray of red hair poking out over the edge of it, and his long, thin legs.

I crept up to him and grabbed the top of the paper. 'You should be reading my paper,' I said, 'not the competition's.'

Dan dropped the newspaper and stared up at me, his face breaking into a smile. 'Anya!' he cried, leaping out of his seat. He grabbed me around the shoulders and kissed me on the cheek. He hadn't changed at all. He was still the same boyish Dan, despite being a father twice over. 'Anya!' he shouted again. 'You're beautiful!'

The guards and the receptionist squinted at him, not impressed by the commotion he was causing. But Dan was oblivious to them and didn't change his tone. 'Come on!' he said, taking my arm and wrapping it around his. 'There's a place a few blocks from here where we can have coffee and a bite to eat.'

The restaurant Dan took me to was called the Hounds. It was exactly the kind of place one would expect diplomats to dine at. It was elegant but comfortable with a scrolled ceiling, solid chairs and dark wood tables. An old smell like leather and books pervaded it. There was an open

347

fireplace in the dining area that of course was not in use at this time of year. The windows had been thrown open and Dan and I were seated at one overlooking a courtyard of clay pots of dwarfed lemon trees and planters full of overgrown herbs.

The waiter pulled out my chair for me. He handed me the menu with a stiff smile.

Dan watched him walk away and grinned at me. 'Anya, you've stunned him. You are absolutely gorgeous. It makes me look good to be seen with you, and I'm an old married man.'

I was about to ask him where Polly and the children were but the waiter returned too quickly with the coffee pot and I lost my chance.

'Gosh, looking at this is making me hungry,' said Dan, glancing at me over the top of his menu. 'Would you like an early lunch? I heard the roast chicken is very good.'

It was the first time I'd looked directly at him. He was the same jolly Dan but there was something in his expression, a flash in his eyes, that made him seem ill at ease.

The waiter came with his notepad and left with Dan's order for chicken and mine for mushroom soup. I saw it there again. The troubled expression on Dan's face. The nervous constriction of his throat. For the first time that day I had a sense of foreboding. I became frightened that something had happened, some disaster had befallen Polly and his children. But surely he would have written to me of that before coming. Perhaps it was just tiredness. The trip from New York to Sydney was a long one.

He took one of the rolls from the basket and began buttering it, glancing up at me now and again and smiling. 'I can't get over how well you look, Anya. I can see why the beauty business suits you. Tell me, what do you do on a typical day at the paper?'

Yes, there was something there. He was Dan but not

carefree Dan. Whatever it was that was troubling him would have to wait, I decided, until after the food arrived. There was something important he had to tell me but I did not want the waiter to interrupt us. So I let myself be lulled into friendly chatter and talked with him of day-to-day things. About Sydney and Australians, Diana, Betty's café, the apartment in Potts Point, and my love for Australian fashion.

It seemed ages before the food arrived. When it did, Dan tucked straight into his meal and appeared no closer to telling me what was on his mind.

'So how is the soup?' he asked. 'Here we are in this hot country eating hot food, it doesn't seem right, does it? Would you like some chicken?'

'Dan.'

He glanced up at me, still smiling.

'Where is Polly?'

'She's in America. With the children. They're all well,' he said, carving a slice of chicken and putting it on my side plate. 'Elizabeth is three, can you believe it?'

'Are you here on business then?' I asked. My voice broke.

Dan stared at me. It was an honest, compassionate look. The expression of a man who does not wish to deceive his friend. He put down his fork. His eyes clouded over. The change in mood between us was so sudden that I was shocked. I could feel my face blanch. The blood hummed in my ears. Whatever it was he had to tell me, it was lying there covered between us, like a body in a mortuary waiting for identification. Dan drew a breath. I braced myself.

'Anya,' he began, 'I didn't come here for business. I came because I have something important to tell you.'

There was no stopping what was coming now. I had unleashed it. Perhaps it needn't have ever come out if I hadn't asked. It was bad news. I could tell by the strange tone of Dan's voice. It was a tone I had never heard him use before. We were going to talk of something distressing, something forbidden. But what on earth could it be?

'Anya, I haven't slept this past week,' he said. 'I have been tormented by what is the right thing to do by you. I know from every piece of correspondence you have sent me, and from seeing you now, that you are happy in your new life and your adopted country. I tried to write at least ten letters and ended up destroying them all. What I have to convey to you doesn't belong in a letter. So I have come myself, believing in your fortitude and comforted by the fact that you are surrounded by true friends.'

His speech was so wordy it almost made me laugh with nerves. 'What is it?' My voice was calm, but inside I was screaming with panic.

Dan reached across the table and grabbed my wrist. 'I have news of your husband. Dmitri Lubensky.'

White spots danced before my eyes. I shrank back into my chair. A hot breeze from the courtyard washed over me. I smelled the sage and the mint. Dmitri. My husband. Dmitri Lubensky. I repeated his name to myself. He was connected to my past; I could not associate him with anything in the present. His name was the smell of brandy and the sound of trombones and drums from a brass band at the Moscow-Shanghai. He was tuxedos and velvets and oriental carpets. He was not part of the Sydney restaurant where I sat opposite Dan. He was not in the heat or the blueness of the Australian sky. Pictures flashed across my mind in fractured pieces: a bowl of shark's fin soup, the rumba on a crowded dance floor, a room full of wedding roses. I took a sip of water, barely able to hold the glass steady in my trembling hand. 'Dmitri?' was all I could manage to get out.

Dan pulled a handkerchief from his pocket and dabbed at his brow. 'I have no idea how to tell you this . . .'

Dan was speaking to me through a fog. I could barely hear him. Dmitri's name had been like a blow. I had not

350

been prepared for it. *We were going to have coffee and cake. Dan had come on business. We were going to spend the morning laughing and talking about our lives.* Everything seemed to be spinning around. Dan and I were not the same people we had been ten minutes ago. There was a taste like metal in the back of my throat.

'Anya, a little over a week ago I was sitting at the breakfast table when Polly brought in my letters and my newspaper. It was going to be a normal day like any other day, except that I was running late and would have to read the paper at my office. After I dressed I picked the newspaper up from the table to put it in my briefcase. I stopped when I saw the picture on the front cover. I knew the man's face in an instant. The article said the police were trying to identify him. He'd been shot in some sort of robbery that went wrong and was unconscious in hospital.'

My hands were wet. They were soaking the tablecloth, making patterns like butterflies. Dmitri. Robbery. Hurt. Shot. I tried to picture it but could not.

'When I saw the photograph my first thought was of you,' Dan continued. 'Should I tell you? Everything in my soul told me that I should not. That you had a new and happy life and the way the man had treated you had been nothing short of abominable. Deserting his young wife! How could he have been sure that you would have gotten that next boat? If you had waited just a few hours more you would have been left behind and executed by the Communists.'

Dan sat back in his chair, his brow knotted. He picked up his napkin, refolded it and dropped it into his lap again. It occurred to me that this was the first time I had seen him look angry.

'But I knew I had a moral duty to the police and the government to come forward and at least identify Dmitri,' he said. 'So I called the police sergeant listed in the article. He took down my statement and told me that the priest

351

at the hospital was also keen to speak to anyone who knew the man. I didn't know what that was about, but I felt obliged to call anyway. I telephoned the hospital and the priest told me that Dmitri was in bad shape, conscious at last but mostly delirious. He'd been shot trying to defend a seventeen-year-old girl. When I heard that it stopped me in my tracks. "And who is Anya?" the priest asked me. "He keeps calling out for Anya." I told him I would be there on the next flight.'

It was so hot in the room. The heat seemed to be coming in great waves. Why don't they set up a fan, I thought. Do something about the air circulation. I fumbled with my hat. I took it off and laid it on the chair next to me. It seemed such a silly, frivolous thing now. How stupid I was to have been so delighted with it. Everything was shifting. I felt my chair lift. The ceiling seemed to come closer. It was as if I was riding the crest of a wave and at any moment I would be tugged underwater.

'Anya, this is a terrible shock to you,' said Dan. 'Can I get you a brandy?'

Dan seemed better. What he had been dreading was already underway. Suddenly he could be himself again, my strong friend helping me through another crisis. 'No,' I said, the room swaying before my eyes. 'Just more water.'

He signalled to the waiter to refill my glass. The waiter kept his eyes averted, trying to be discreet. But there was something morbid about him. His pale hands pouring the water seemed hardly human. His clothes smelled like an old church. He had the air of a funeral director rather than a waiter.

'Please continue,' I said to Dan. 'What happened when you saw Dmitri? Is he all right?'

Dan shifted in his seat. He didn't answer my question. The sensation came over me that everything was about to change. That everything I had felt since Shanghai was about to be turned over. I had not understood Dmitri. The man

I was hearing about was not the man I had imagined for so long. Where was his easy life? His nightclub? Where was Amelia?

'I arrived in Los Angeles the day after I saw the newspaper article,' Dan said. 'I went straight to the hospital. The priest was waiting for me there. Since I'd given the police Dmitri's name they had done a background check. It seems he had been working for a gangster called Ciatti, helping him run an illegal gambling den downtown.

'On the night he was shot he was at some big gun's house in the hills. The guy didn't trust banks and it was rumoured that he had stashes of money and jewels all over the place. Ciatti somehow knew about that and figured he could pull a walk-in, walk-out job. Easy money when his gambling business was going down. He used a couple of his thugs to enter the place. Dmitri was just the driver. He was left with the car. But it went wrong when the big gun's seventeen-year-old granddaughter turned up at the door. Her appearance hadn't been figured into the plan. Dmitri watched her run up the steps to the house, knowing she was heading straight for a death trap. In fact, Ciatti was already pistol-whipping the girl when Dmitri burst inside. There was an argument. Dmitri struggled with Ciatti, copping a bullet in the lung and one through the top of his head. The screams and gunshots got the attention of the neighbours and Ciatti and his men fled the house.'

'He saved someone?' I asked. 'Dmitri saved a girl he didn't know?'

Dan nodded. 'Anya, when I saw him in the hospital he was incoherent most of the time. When I asked him about what happened that night he seemed convinced that the girl he had saved was you.'

I felt a rip down my centre, as if something that had been buried for years was reawakening. I rubbed my hands over my face but couldn't feel my fingers or my cheeks.

Dan watched me. I had no idea what his taut expression

meant. I had no idea what anything meant any more. 'But Dmitri also had moments of lucidity,' he said. 'And in those moments he told me of a girl he once loved. A young woman who had danced the bolero with him. It was almost as if he understood who I was, and that I had come to represent you. "You'll tell her, won't you?" he begged me. "You'll tell her that I always thought of her. I ran away because I was a coward, not because I didn't love her."

'"How will she know?" I asked him. "How will I convince Anya of that when you left her to die?" Dmitri didn't answer me for a long time. He fell back on his pillow, his eyes rolled back in his head. I thought he was lapsing into a coma again, but he suddenly looked at me and said: "As soon as I got to America, I knew I had been a fool. That woman? Do you think that she loved me? She left me overnight. When I asked her why, she said it was to defeat Anya. I can never explain to you the hold she had over me. How she could sing the worst in me to life. Not like sweet Anya, who could bring out the best. But between the two there must have been more blackness in me or how else could Amelia have won?"

'The nurse came in to check on him then,' Dan said, running his fingers through his hair. 'She checked his pulse and his drip and said that I had asked enough questions and I should leave and let him be. I turned once again before I left the room and looked at Dmitri, but he was already asleep.

'The priest was waiting for me outside. "Dmitri went to the IRO office the day he arrived in Los Angeles," he told me. "There wasn't any record of an Anya Lubenskya. So he asked them to check under Anya Kozlova. When he found out she had changed back to her maiden name, he said he knew that she would be all right. That she knew how to survive." I asked the priest when Dmitri had told him this, and he said it had been that morning. During his confession.

'I went to see Dmitri the following day. His condition

354

had deteriorated again. He was very weak. I hadn't slept all the previous night, so heavily was he weighing on my mind. "But you didn't go back to her, did you?" I said to him. "You didn't try to help her any further after that?" Dmitri looked at me with sadness on his face. "I loved her enough not to ever want to hurt her again," he said.'

Tears stung my eyes. All the time Dan had been talking my mind had been racing ahead. I would go to Dmitri. I would help him. By his very deed he had shown me that he was not a monster. He had saved a seventeen-year-old girl. And he had saved her because she had reminded him of me.

'How soon can we get back to America?' I asked Dan. 'How long before I can see him?'

Tears welled up in Dan's eyes. He suddenly seemed old. It was a moment of agony. We stared at each other without saying anything. He reached into his jacket and pulled out a brown packet and handed it to me. My trembling fingers fumbled with the wrapping. Something fell out and tinkled onto the table. I picked it up. A wrought-iron key with a Parisian bow. Although I had not seen it for years, I recognised it immediately. The key to our apartment in Shanghai.

For eternity.

'He's gone, isn't he?' I asked, tears streaming down my cheeks. I was barely able to speak.

Dan reached over the table and grabbed my hands, holding them tightly as if he were afraid that I would fall.

The restaurant was filling up with people, the lunchtime crowd. All around us were happy faces. The patrons were chatting over their menus, pouring wine, clinking glasses, kissing each other's cheeks. The waiter seemed lively all of a sudden, running backwards and forwards with the orders. Dan and I clung to each other. Dmitri was dead. I felt the knowledge of it spread across my chest and enter my heart. The irony of it seemed too much. Dmitri had fled to find

355

riches and instead found pain and death. I had become a refugee and had never once gone hungry. All the past years I had been trying to hate Dmitri, he had never stopped thinking of me.

I clutched the key in my palm.

For eternity.

Later, much later, when I moved into my apartment in Bondi and found the strength to take the key from the box where I had hidden it the day Dan gave it to me, I had a lock made to match it. It was the only way I could think of to share my life and good fortune with Dmitri.

For eternity.

PART THREE

SIXTEEN

Bondi

A few days after New Year's Eve 1956, I was sitting in my flat on Campbell Parade, looking out to the beach and watching the crowd that spilled over it like mismatched clothes from a basket at a jumble sale. On the first day of January the seas had been high with waves over fifteen feet. The lifesavers were frantic, dragging people from the surf and rescuing two boys who had been washed onto the rocks. But today the sea was flat and flocks of seagulls bobbed lazily on its surface. It was hot and I had all the windows open. I could hear the sound of children playing on the sand and the whistle of the lifesavers urging people to swim between the flags. The ocean might have looked calm, but underneath it was riddled with dangerous rips.

I was working on an article for the women's section, where I had been appointed fashion editor the year before. Ann White, after exhausting herself on coronation gowns and the Queen's wardrobe for her royal visit to Australia, had married into the Denison family. Her flair for fashion was considered a bigger asset to the department store dynasty than her dowry and she was appointed head fashion buyer for their Sydney store. We saw each other at social occasions and had been out for lunch two or three times. It was ironic that after our shaky start we should have ended up needing each other's patronage.

For the article I was writing I had asked three Australian

designers to submit their ideas on how they would dress Grace Kelly for her wedding to Prince Rainier of Monaco. Judith put forward the most beautiful gown, an ivory organza sheath dress with a taffeta bust and swan-down collar, but the dresses submitted by the other designers were also worthy of the title haute couture. One was a mermaid-line dress with curved seams and fishtail hem, and the other was sable-trimmed brocade and iridescent silk. That dress had been submitted by a Russian who had come to Sydney via Paris. Her name was Alina, and when I wrote her name on the back of the photographs to go with the article, I started thinking about my mother.

Stalin had died in 1953, but that hadn't stopped the West and the Soviet Union entwining themselves in a Cold War that made any sort of transfer of information impossible. Vitaly's father had never heard back from his brother, and I had written to every organisation I could: the Russian–Australian Society, the United Nations, the IRO and many other smaller humanitarian organisations. But none had been able to help me. It seemed that Russia was impenetrable.

Australia was far removed from anything my mother and I had known together. I couldn't see her in the trees or associate her with the sea. I still harboured my terror that I would forget the details of her: the shape of her hands, the exact colour of her eyes, her scent. And yet I could not forget her. Even all those years later she was still the first person I thought of when I woke up in the morning and the last person I imagined before I turned out the light. We had been separated for almost eleven years and yet, somewhere in my heart, I still believed that my mother and I would see each other again.

I slipped the article and photographs into an envelope and laid out my clothes for the office. A few weeks before I had put together a fashion spread titled 'Too Hot for the Beach' featuring the new bikini styles that were making

360

their way to Australia from Europe and America. Because swimsuits were intimate wear, I had asked the model if she would like to keep the bikinis she had posed in, but she told me that she already had drawers full of swimming costumes from other shoots. So I'd brought the swimsuits home to wash, intending to give them to the junior reporters. I opened my wardrobe and rummaged through the straw bag where I thought I had put the bikinis after they had dried on the line. But they weren't there. I stared at the empty interior of the bag, puzzled. I wondered if I'd been so busy with deadlines that maybe I had already taken the swimsuits to the office and simply forgotten. At that moment Mrs Gilchrist, the building supervisor, knocked on the door.

'Anya! Telephone!' she shouted.

I slipped on my sandals and rushed to the shared telephone in the hall.

'Hello,' Betty whispered when I picked up the receiver. 'Could you come and get us, love?'

'Where are you?'

'At the police station. The police won't let us go unless someone comes to pick us up.'

'What's happened?'

'Nothing.'

I heard Ruselina talking to someone in the background then the sound of a man's laughter.

'Betty, if nothing's happened, what are you two doing at the police station?'

There was a moment's pause before she said, 'We've been arrested.'

I was too surprised to say anything. Ruselina called something out but I couldn't catch it.

'Oh,' said Betty, 'Ruselina asked if you would mind bringing us some clothes.'

I hurried to the police station, my mind overflowing with possible scenarios of what Betty and Ruselina might have done to get themselves arrested. Betty had retired, and after selling the house in Potts Point had bought a three-bedroom apartment for herself and Ruselina and the bedsitter above it for me. Vitaly and Irina were living in a house in Tamarama, one suburb away. Since moving, Betty and Ruselina had begun to exhibit odd behaviour. Once they leaped off the rocks near the headland with knives between their teeth, claiming they were 'going to fight the sharks in honour of Bea Miles', who had been Bondi's crazy lady for a number of years. The tide was out and the sea was calm and clear so they hadn't been in much danger of drowning, but the sight of our dear old ladies floating around in an unpatrolled area was enough to terrify Irina and myself. We made Vitaly jump in after them to coax them back to shore.

'Don't worry so much about them,' Vitaly told us after-wards. 'They've both had tragedies in their lives but have had to be strong and carry on regardless. This is the time in their life when they want to let go and be irrespon-sible. They're lucky to have found each other the same way you two have.'

I hadn't telephoned Vitaly and Irina before I left for the police station. Irina was four months pregnant and I didn't want to upset her. But all the way to the station I couldn't help worrying. Why couldn't Betty and Ruselina take up painting or bingo like other old ladies? The Bondi tram rattled past and I glanced up. Out of the corner of my eye I saw a solitary old woman sitting on a bench in the park. She was throwing bits of bread to the seagulls. The image of her lonely figure seemed to burn itself into my mind, and I began to wonder if I would be that old lady in another fifty years' time.

When I turned up at the police station Betty and Ruselina were sitting in the waiting area in their terry-towelling robes. Betty was blowing rings of smoke into the air. Ruselina grinned when she saw me. There was an elderly man sitting next to her wearing a white singlet and shorts. His skin was as brown as leather hide and he was leaning with his elbows on his knees, deep in thought. In the opposite corner of the room a solid-looking man in a bib-style swimsuit and shorts was holding an icepack to his jaw. I read the word 'Inspector' printed on the ribbon around his straw hat.

The sergeant in charge stood up from his desk. 'Miss Kozlova?'

I glanced at Betty and Ruselina but they weren't giving anything away.

'What's happened?' I asked the sergeant, lowering myself into the chair opposite his desk.

'Don't worry,' he whispered, 'nothing serious. It's just that the beach inspector is strict about "decency".'

'Decency?' I cried. Ruselina and Betty giggled.

The sergeant opened his desk drawer and pulled out a diagram of a man and a woman standing on a beach. He pushed it towards me. There were lines and measurements drawn over the figures. My head was swimming. Decency? What on earth had Betty and Ruselina done?

The sergeant pointed to various parts of the picture with his pen. 'The legs of the swimming trunks, according to the inspector, must be at least three inches long, and women's swimsuits must have straps or other support.'

I shook my head, not understanding. Ruselina and Betty had elegant one-piece suits. I had bought them for them from David Jones last Christmas.

'Your grandmothers' costumes,' whispered the sergeant, 'are a little too brief.'

There was another giggle from Betty and Ruselina. Suddenly what had happened dawned on me. 'Oh God! No!'

I strode over to Betty and Ruselina. 'Come on,' I said. 'Open up!'

Ruselina and Betty opened their robes and strutted around the reception area, mimicking catwalk models.

Betty was wearing high-cut sarong pants with a strapless bikini top. Ruselina's costume was patterned like a tuxedo with a v-shaped neckline. They were the bikinis from the fashion shoot. Although both women were in good shape for their age, they certainly weren't the young women the costumes had been designed for. Betty's bony hips were far too skinny for her pants and Ruselina's bust wasn't quite up to a low-cut front, but they both walked with an elegant poise.

I watched them dumbstruck for a few seconds then burst out laughing.

'I don't object to you wearing those costumes,' I told Betty and Ruselina later, when we were sitting in the local milkbar and drinking strawberry shakes. 'But why do it on the beach that has the strictest inspector?'

'Getting chased by that old fart was half the fun!' cackled Betty. Ruselina started to laugh too. The owner of the milkbar glanced over at us.

'Who was the other guy at the station?' I asked. 'The one in the shorts.'

'Oh, him,' said Ruselina, a twinkle in her eye. 'Bob. He was a real gentleman. When the inspector started marching us off the beach, Bob stepped in and told him not to "manhandle ladies".'

'Then he bopped the inspector one on the chin,' said Betty, slurping her shake.

I glanced down at the airy pink bubbles of my own drink and thought about how the two old ladies who had looked after me for so long were turning into my children.

'What are you doing this afternoon, Anya?' asked Betty. 'It's Saturday. You want to come to the pictures with us? *East of Eden* is showing.'

'I can't,' I shrugged. 'I've got to finish an article on wedding dresses for tomorrow's paper.'

'What about your own wedding, Anya?' said Ruselina, sucking up the last lick of icy milk through her straw.

'You'll never find a husband if you're always working so hard.'

Betty patted my knee under the table. 'Ruselina, you sound like a Russian babushka,' she said. 'She's still young. There's no hurry. Look at her marvellous career. When she's ready she'll pick someone out at one of those glamorous parties she's always going to.'

'Twenty-three's not that young to be married,' said Ruselina. 'It's only young compared to us. I was married at nineteen, and that was considered quite late in my day.'

After I said goodbye to Betty and Ruselina I walked upstairs to my own flat and lay down on the bed. My bedsitter was small, most of it was taken up by my bed, and one of the walls was nearly all windows. But I had a view of the sea and a corner with plants and an over-stuffed armchair and a desk where I could write or think. It was my retreat and I felt comfortable there. Away from people.

You'll never find a husband if you work so hard, Ruselina had said.

I turned and looked at the matroshka dolls lined up on my dresser. There were five altogether, two after me. A daughter and a granddaughter. That had been my mother's vision for our lives. She probably once believed that we would all live out our days peacefully in the house in Harbin, adding a new extension each time another member of the family came along.

I lay back down on the pillows and squeezed the tears from my eyes. To have a family I would need a husband. But I had grown so used to living without a man's love, I didn't even know where to begin. It was four years since I had found out about Dmitri's death, seven years since he had left me. How many years would it take to stop mourning?

Diana was already at her desk when I arrived at the paper. I dropped into her office to say hello.

'What are you doing this Friday night, Anya?' she asked, fingering the collar of her Givenchy-style dress.

'Nothing special,' I told her.

'Well, I have someone I want you to meet. Why don't you come over for dinner around seven? I'll have Harry pick you up.'

'Okay, but who is it you want me to meet?'

Diana's face broke into a smile that showed all her pearly teeth. 'Is that a yes or a no?'

'It's a yes but I'd still like to know who it is I'm meeting.'

'Don't you trust me?' she asked. 'A dashing young man, if you must insist. He's been dying to meet you ever since he spotted you at the Melbourne Cup ball. He said he followed you around all night but you paid him no attention. Which, I might add, sounds just like you, Anya. He's the best-looking man on this paper, has a great sense of humour and couldn't even get you to say "boo".'

I blushed. My embarrassment seemed to make Diana even more amused. I wondered if she'd had some way of reading my mood that afternoon and had worked quickly to find a solution.

'Wear that gorgeous crepe evening dress you bought at the sales. It looks so lovely on you.'

'I will,' I said, unnerved by the uncanny coincidence. It was as if Diana were my fairy godmother and she was granting me a wish.

'And Anya,' she called after me when I turned to go.

'Yes?'

'Try not to look so terrified, darling. He doesn't bite, I'm sure.'

I didn't say a word to Ruselina or Betty about Diana's dinner party. I was proud of myself for at least agreeing to meet a young man, although the thought still terrified me. Telling them about the dinner meant I wouldn't be able to back out of it if I decided not to go.

When Friday night came around, I felt queasy and had second thoughts about turning up. But I couldn't offend Diana. I wore the dress she had suggested. It had a fitted bodice, wide shoulder straps and a panelled skirt. I slipped my feet into silk shoes with pointed toes and swept my hair to one side with a diamanté clip.

Just after half past six Harry came to pick me up in his navy Chevrolet. He opened the car door for me and squinted at the late sun glistening on the beach. 'It looks so calm after those terrible storms,' he said.

'I read in the paper that the lifesavers pulled one hundred and fifty people from the water on New Year's Day,' I told him.

Harry slipped into the driver's seat and started up the motor. 'Yes, your beach was one of the worst hit. They say the storm churned up so much seaweed that one of the lifesavers got his line caught in it. It dragged him under and he started to drown. The rescue boat couldn't break through the waves to reach him.'

'Goodness,' I said. 'I hadn't heard about that.'

'One of his mates got him out though,' said Harry, turning the car into Bondi Road. 'A big guy who's just come up from Victoria. They say he tunnelled through the water like a torpedo. He's Russian too. You might know him.'

I shook my head. 'Probably not. I only seem to get to the beach these days after everyone else has left.'

Harry laughed. 'Diana says you work hard,' he said.

Diana and Harry lived in a Tudor-style house overlooking the water at Rose Bay. When we pulled into the driveway Diana, gorgeous in a red silk dress, ran out to greet us. 'Come along, Anya,' she said, gliding me like a tango dancer into her house. 'Come and meet Keith.'

The interior of the house was spacious with modern white flooring and walls. Recessed shelves lined the hallway, displaying photographs of Diana with celebrities, and the knick-knacks she had collected from all over the world.

I stopped to look at the porcelain piggy collection she had brought back from London and laughed. As glamorous as she was, Diana did not take herself too seriously.

Diana tugged me into the living room and nearly sent me flying into the lap of the young man who was sitting on her modular lounge. As soon as he saw us he rose, a smile breaking out on his clean-cut face. 'Hello,' he said, reaching out his hand to shake mine. 'I'm Keith.'

'Hello,' I said, taking his hand. 'I'm Anya.'

'Good,' said Diana, patting my back. 'I'm going to see to dinner, you two have a chat.'

With that Diana rushed out of the room. Harry was just at that moment stepping inside the room, a bottle of wine in his hand. Diana grabbed him and yanked him down the hall as if he were a bad actor being whipped off stage.

Keith turned to me. He was handsome with cobalt blue eyes, blond hair, a neat nose and plum-like lips. 'Diana has told me wonderful things about you,' he said. 'And apparently you have a rice story I have to hear over dinner.'

I blushed. Diana hadn't told me anything about Keith. But then I hadn't exactly asked either.

'Keith works on the sports pages,' said Harry, walking into the room with a platter of cheese and saving me from making a fool of myself. I realised then that he must have been standing outside the door, listening.

'Really? How wonderful,' I said, sounding like Diana and not at all like myself.

Harry winked at me behind Keith's back. Diana glided in with a tray of olive halves on crackers. She must have been waiting outside the door too. 'Yes,' she said. 'He won an award for his coverage of the Melbourne Cup.'

'That's wonderful,' I said, turning to Keith. 'I didn't. They obviously didn't think my piece on Cup hats was impressive enough.'

Keith's eyes widened for a moment, until Harry and Diana laughed and he felt safe enough to join in too.

'A girl with a sense of humour,' he said. 'I like that.'

Harry set up a dining table in the greenhouse terrace. Diana laid it with a cream tablecloth and a royal blue place setting. She twisted sprigs of fuchsia around the base of the candlestick. It had been a long time since I had experienced such relaxed elegance. It was an effect my father had been good at creating. I rubbed the edge of the linen cloth between my fingers and relished the weight of the silverware. In the centre of the table Diana placed a bowl of cabbage roses. I breathed in their sweet-scented fragrance. The candle flickered and I saw Sergei standing in the shadows, his arms laden with wedding flowers. Dmitri floated out of the darkness towards me and took my hands in his own. 'Let me go, Dmitri. Please,' I said inside my head. But moments later I saw that I was in a bath full of petals. Dmitri was scooping up water by the handful. But the more water he drank the lighter he got. And he began to fade away.

'Anya, are you okay? You're terribly pale,' said Diana, tapping my arm. I squinted at her, disorientated.

'It's the heat,' said Harry, getting up from the table and opening the windows wider.

Keith picked up my glass. 'I'll pour you some water.'

I rubbed my forehead. 'I'm sorry. Everything is so beautiful, I forgot where I was.'

Keith set down my glass in front of me. A drop of water slid down the side and splashed onto the tablecloth. It looked like a tear.

Dinner was poached scallops mornay with creamed mushrooms. The conversation was light and Diana kept it moving along with a deft hand. 'Keith, you must tell Anya about your parents' farm. I heard from Ted that it's lovely' and 'Anya. I saw the most gorgeous antique samovar in Lady Bryant's home but neither of us had any idea how it worked. Could you explain it to us, darling?' I was aware of Keith's eyes on me and I was mindful to pay attention to him when he spoke, and not to discourage him, as Diana had accused me of doing in other similar situations. I wasn't crashing into love as I had with Dmitri. I felt like a flower waiting for a bee.

After the plates had been cleared, we moved to the lounge room for apricot chiffon pie and vanilla ice-cream.

'Now,' said Diana, waving her spoon in the air, 'you simply must tell Keith your rice story.'

'Yes,' laughed Keith, moving closer to me. 'I must hear it.'

'I haven't heard this one myself,' said Harry. 'Every time Diana tries to tell it to me she begins laughing so much . . . well, I never get to hear the end of it.'

The food and wine had relaxed me and I felt less shy. I was happy that Keith was sitting close to me. I had warmed to him. I was glad he wasn't afraid to show that he liked me too. My re-entry into the world of romance wasn't turning out as badly as I had feared.

'Well,' I began, 'one day I went to visit my best friend and her husband and we started talking about all the food we missed from China. Of course, rice in this country must be the hardest ingredient to find and nearly all the dishes of our childhood contain rice. So we decided to go to Chinatown one day and bring home enough rice to last us for three months.

'That was in 1954, when Vladimir Petrov and his wife were given asylum in Australia in return for rooting out Russian spies, and rooting out spies became foremost in a lot of people's minds, including the old lady next door to my friends' house. She saw us lugging sacks of rice up the drive and speaking in Russian, and called the police.'

Keith laughed and rubbed his chin. Harry chuckled. 'Go on,' he said.

'So two young constables came and asked us if we were Communist spies. But Vitaly somehow persuaded them to stay for dinner. We cooked risotto Volgii, made with bulgur, broccoli and silverbeet sautéed in onion and garlic and served with a side dish of eggplant and yoghurt. Now, refusing to drink with Russians can be extremely difficult, and refusing to drink with a Russian man is downright insulting. So Vitaly managed to convince the police that the only way to boost true "international friendship" and repay him for the "best meal" they had tasted in their lives was to down a few glasses of vodka. When the policemen were so drunk their faces were turning strange shades, we piled them into a taxi and sent them back to the station, where you can imagine their sergeant wasn't very happy with them. And although Mrs Dolen at number twelve still reports us regularly, we haven't heard from the police since.'

'Goodness,' bellowed Harry, winking at Keith. 'She's a rascal. You watch out for her!'

'I will,' said Keith, grinning at me as if there were no one else in the room. 'Believe me I will.'

Afterwards, when Harry was taking the car out of the garage to drive me home, Keith walked with me to the door. Diana rushed past us out into the garden, pretending to search for her nonexistent cat.

'Anya,' Keith said to me. 'Next week it's my friend Ted's birthday. I would like to take you to the party. Will you come?'

'Yes, I'd love to.' The words rushed out of my mouth before I had time to think about them. But I felt comfortable with Keith. There didn't seem to be anything hidden about him. Unlike me. I was full of secrets.

After Harry had dropped me home, I opened the windows and lay down on my bed, listening to the sea. I shut my eyes and tried to remember Keith's smile. But I had already started to forget what he looked like. I wondered if I sincerely liked him, or whether I was only making myself like him because I thought that I should. After a while all I could think about was Dmitri. It was as if just as I was preparing to let go his hold on me for good, my memories

371

of him returned stronger than before. I tossed and turned in my bed, our wedding night playing over and over again in my head. The only true happy moment of our marriage. Before Sergei's death. Before Amelia. My soft wet body covered in petals pressed against the hardness of Dmitri's burning skin.

Ted was Keith's photographer on the sports pages and he lived on Steinway Street in Coogee. When we arrived at his birthday party, people were already spilling out of the doors and windows of the fibrocement house. 'Only You' was spinning on the record player and a group of guys and girls in neck scarves and shirts with the collars turned up were crooning along to it. A blond man with sideburns and his cigarette packet tucked in his shirtsleeve hurried over to us. He slapped hands with Keith and then turned to me.

'Hello, lovely. Are you the girl Keith has been telling me about? The Russian fashion queen?'

'Give her a break, Ted,' laughed Keith, then turning to me added, 'It takes a while to get used to his humour. Don't worry.'

'So it's your birthday, Ted,' I said, holding up the present Keith and I had brought: a Chuck Berry record wrapped in spotted paper and sealed with a bow.

'You guys didn't have to . . . but put it on the table,' Ted smiled. 'Lucy is making me open them up all together later.'

'She's turning you into a girl,' said Keith.

The lounge room was a hothouse, steamy with the heat of bodies pressed together and the summer night. People were sprawled over the carpet and lounge, smoking and drinking soda or beer straight from the bottle. Some of the girls turned to look at me. I had worn a sleeveless torso dress with a high shoulder to shoulder neckline. The other girls were wearing Capri pants and body-hugging shirts. Their hair was short, in the style many Australian women preferred then, and brushed forward, like pixies. Mine was still long and I wore it loose with curls at the ends. Their glances made me uncomfortable. They didn't seem very friendly.

A group of men and women were sitting on the floor in a circle, a bottle poised in the middle. I knew the game: spin the bottle. But not this version of it. Each participant had a beer by his or her side and when the bottle was spun and the tip had settled on a member of the opposite sex, the spinner had a choice of either kissing that person or taking a swig of beer. If they chose to drink, the person being rejected for a kiss had to take two swigs of beer.

'Just another Australian excuse to drink,' said Keith.

'Russians are the same. Well, the men at least.'

'Really? I bet Russian men would rather kiss girls than drink beer though, given the choice.'

Keith was looking at me in that direct way of his again, but I couldn't hold his stare. I glanced down at my feet.

Keith drove me home in his Holden. Whenever he wasn't looking, I sneaked glances at him. Studying the texture of his skin, noticing for the first time the freckle on the corner of his nose, the light spray of hair around his wrist. He was good-looking, but he wasn't Dmitri.

When we reached my apartment building he pulled the car to the kerb and turned the engine off. I twisted my hands and prayed he wouldn't try to kiss me. I wasn't ready for anything like that. He must have sensed my uneasiness because he didn't kiss me. Instead he talked about the tennis matches he was covering and what nice guys Ken Rosewall and Lew Hoad were to interview. After a while he squeezed my hand and said he would walk me to my door.

'Next time I will take you somewhere more classy,' he said. He was smiling, but I sensed disappointment in his words. I stammered, not sure what to say. He had mistaken me for a snob. I wanted to assure him how much I liked him but when I said, 'Goodnight, Keith,' it came out tight and wrong.

Instead of going to bed happy, I couldn't sleep. I lay awake, terrified that I had ruined a relationship even before I was sure whether or not I wanted it.

The next day Irina and Vitaly came to meet me for our planned picnic on the beach. Irina was wearing a smock dress although she was barely starting to show. I suspected that she was too excited to wait until she got fatter. A few weeks earlier she had come over with patterns for baby clothes and sketches of how she was going to decorate the nursery. I couldn't help sharing her sense of joy. I knew she was going to be a wonderful mother. I was surprised to see that Vitaly had put on weight since Irina had found out she was pregnant, but I refrained from any 'eating for two' jokes. The extra weight suited him. His skinny gauntness was gone and his face was more handsome when it was round.

'Who was the guy you were with last night?' he asked me before he had even put his foot in the door. Irina jabbed him in the ribs.

'We promised Betty and Ruselina we would find out.' Vitaly grimaced, rubbing his side.

'Betty and Ruselina? How did they know I was with someone?'

Irina swung the picnic basket onto the table and packed in the date loaf and plates I'd prepared for the day. 'They were spying on you as usual,' she said. 'They turned off the lights in their flat and pressed their faces to the window when he dropped you off.'

Vitaly picked a corner off the loaf and took a bite. 'They tried to listen to what you two were saying but Betty's stomach kept rumbling and they didn't hear a thing.'

I took the loaded basket from Irina. It wasn't too heavy but I didn't want her to carry anything. 'They make life difficult when they do that,' I said. 'I'm self-conscious enough as it is.'

Irina patted my arm. 'The secret is to get married and move a suburb away. That's not too far but not too close either.'

'If they keep it up I won't get married,' I said. 'They'll scare men away.'

'Tsch!' snorted Vitaly. 'Who is this suitor, Anya? Why didn't you ask him along today?'

'I met him through Diana. And I didn't invite him today because I haven't seen you two for ages and I wanted to spend the day with you.'

'Too early to introduce him to the family, I see,' said Vitaly, wagging his finger at me. 'But I have to warn you that your wedding dress is already being discussed downstairs.'

Irina rolled her eyes. 'I can't believe it,' she said, pushing me and Vitaly out the door.

On any Sunday in summer Bondi Beach was packed with people. Irina, Vitaly and I had to walk to the Ben Buckler headland before we could find somewhere to sit. The glare was dazzling. It reflected off the sand and the wall of beach umbrellas much the same way snow glistens from the rooftops and trees in the northern hemisphere. Vitaly spread out the towels and set about planting the beach umbrella while Irina and I donned our sunglasses and hats. The lifesavers were training in the surf, their brown-skinned muscles shimmering with the residue of the sea and sweat.

'I saw some of them training in the pool the other weekend,' said Vitaly. 'They were swimming with water-filled kerosene cans tied to their belts.'

'I guess they have to be strong to fight the sea,' I said.

A sweets vendor passed by, the zinc cream on his face melting like ice-cream in the sun. I called out to him and bought three vanilla cups, handing one each to Irina and Vitaly and opening my own.

'The lifesavers are good-looking, heh?' Irina giggled. 'Perhaps Anya and I should join the club.'

'You'll be swimming with more than a weighted kerosene can around your waist in a few months, Irina,' said Vitaly.

I watched the lifesavers go through their drills with the belt. One of them stood out from the others. He was taller than the other men and solidly built with a square face and thick jaw. His fellow lifesaver, performing the part of the near-drowned victim, was securely held and in no danger of being dropped. Every task that lifesaver performed was executed with vigour and single-mindedness. He whipped the belt around his waist and sprang into the ocean without hesitation, dragging his victim from the surf without strain and mock-resuscitating him on the beach as if life on earth depended on it.

'That one is very impressive,' said Vitaly.

I nodded. Again and again with effortless energy the lifesaver bounded into the waves, in search of the next person in need. He ran like a stag in the forest, fast and carefree. 'He must be the one Harry was talking about the other night . . .' I stopped mid-sentence. A tingle ran over my skin.

I jumped up, shielding my eyes from the sun with my hand. 'Oh my God!' I cried.

'What is it? Who is it?' Irina asked, standing up next to me.

I answered her by waving my arms at the lifesaver and calling out, 'Ivan! Ivan!'

SEVENTEEN

Ivan

Betty and Ruselina were listening to the radio and playing cards at the table by the window when we burst into the flat, one after the other, with Ivan in tow. Betty glanced up from her cards and squinted. Ruselina turned around. Her hand flew to her mouth and her eyes welled with tears. 'Ivan!' she cried out, getting up. She rushed across the rug towards him. He met her halfway, hugging her so furiously that her feet swung off the ground.

When Ivan put Ruselina down, she clutched his face between her hands. 'I thought we would never see you again,' she said.

'You're not half as surprised as me,' Ivan said. 'I thought you were all in America.'

'Because of Grandmother's illness we had to come here,' said Irina. She glanced at me and I felt guilty, although that hadn't been her intention. But I *was* the one who was supposed to have written.

Ivan spotted Betty wavering by the couch. He greeted her in Russian. 'This is my friend Betty Nelson,' Ruselina explained. 'She's Australian.'

'Oh, Australian,' said Ivan, moving towards Betty to shake her hand. 'Then we'd better speak in English. I am Ivan Nakhimovsky. An old friend of Ruselina and the girls.'

'I am pleased to meet you, Mr Nak . . . Mr Nak . . .' Betty tried, but she couldn't get out his last name.

'Ivan, please,' he grinned.

'I was just about to start on dinner,' Betty told him. 'I can't offer you the traditional roast because we've all been playing around this weekend and no one's done the shopping. But I hope sausages and vegetables will be okay for you?'

'Let me go home first and change into something more presentable,' Ivan said, looking down at his water-splattered T-shirt and shorts. There were grains of sand caught in the hairs on his legs.

'No,' laughed Vitaly. 'You are presentable as you are. Anya's the only person who still gets dressed up for "bangers and mash". Being casual is the only aspect of Australian life she hasn't adopted.'

Ivan spun around and smiled at me. I shrugged. He had hardly changed since Tubabao. His face had remained young with the same mischievous grin. The scar had faded a little- with his tan. He still moved with his bear-like gait. When I recognised him on the beach, I ran towards him on impulse. It was only when he looked up and realised who I was that I remembered the tension of our last days together and became fearful. But there was a warm twinkle in his eye and I understood that somewhere between Tubabao and Sydney I had been forgiven.

'Sit down, Ivan,' I said, leading him towards the lounge. 'We want to hear all your news. I thought you were in Melbourne. What are you doing in Sydney?'

Ivan sat down, with Ruselina and me on either side of him. Vitaly and Irina took the armchairs. We spoke in English because, in between cutting and boiling the vegetables, Betty would come in to catch parts of the conversation.

'I've been here for a couple of months,' he said. 'I've been setting up a new factory.'

'A new factory?' repeated Ruselina. 'What is it that you do?'

'Well,' said Ivan, resting his hands on his knees, 'I'm

still a baker of sorts. Only now I work in frozen foods. My company packages pies and cakes for supermarkets.'

'*Your* company!' Irina cried, her eyes wide. 'It sounds like you are a success!'

Ivan shook his head. 'We are a small company, but we grow substantially each year and this year looks as though it will be our biggest one yet.'

We urged him to tell us how he'd got his business started. I suspected he was being modest about his company being small. Many migrants had set up their own family businesses after their contract requirements had been met, but I'd never heard of anyone owning factories in two major cities.

'When I came to Australia I was put to work in a bakery,' he continued. 'There was another New Australian working there, a Yugoslavian by the name of Nikola Milosavljevic. We got along well and agreed that when we finished our contracts we would go into business together. So that's what we did.'

'Was it just the two of you?' asked Vitaly. 'That sounds like hard work.'

'It was,' said Ivan. 'That was a crazy year, but Nikola and I were so sure of our success that we worked every day of the week on no more than four hours' sleep. It's amazing how you can keep going when you are passionate about something.'

Betty placed a plate of buttered peas on the dining table and wiped her hands on her apron. 'You sound like Anya. She's the only person who works as hard as that.'

'Not as hard as that,' I laughed.

'What do you do?' Ivan asked me.

'She's the fashion editor with the *Sydney Herald*,' Irina told him.

'Really?' said Ivan. 'I'm impressed, Anya. I remember the article you wrote for the *Tubabao Gazette* about the clothes in *On the Town*.'

I blushed. I'd forgotten about the article and sketches I did for the *Gazette* and all my gushing enthusiasm for New York. 'Ivan, no one wants to hear about me. Tell us more about you,' I said.

'Well, my job doesn't sound half as interesting as yours but I will continue,' he said. 'After we had been working hard at expanding our business for a year, a new supermarket opened up in a nearby suburb, so we approached the manager about selling our pies to him. He told us all about what was happening in America with supermarkets and frozen foods.

'Nikola and I thought the concept sounded feasible. So we began to experiment with freezing our pies. It took us a while, but when we got the balance of ingredients and technique right, we were able to get backers and open our first factory. And, if things work out in Sydney, Nikola will look after the Melbourne operation and I will stay here.'

'We'll make sure we buy lots of your pies then,' said Ruselina, clasping his hand. 'It would mean so much to have you here.'

Betty called us to the table and insisted that Ivan, as our guest of honour, sit at the head of it. She placed me at the other end, opposite him.

'It's an appropriate setting,' laughed Vitaly. 'The King and Queen of Australia. They are both foreigners but Ivan spends his free time pulling Australians from the water and she supports their fashion designers and sells cards at Christmas time to save the bushland.'

Ivan's eyes flashed at me. 'Perhaps we both feel we owe this country a lot, Anya?'

Ruselina patted Ivan's arm. 'You do work a bit too hard,' she said. 'All those hours at your factory and all those hours on the beach. Even in your free time you push yourself.'

'Not to mention the danger of being drowned or eaten by a shark,' said Irina, snapping a sausage in half with her teeth.

I shivered although she was joking. I glanced up at Ivan and a foreboding came over me that something too dreadful to imagine would happen to him. I couldn't bear the thought that a passionate, kind man could just be snuffed out while he was at his peak. I calmed myself by drinking my water slowly and breathing into my napkin, hoping no one would notice my panic. They didn't. Everyone was busy chatting about the storms that had churned up the beaches on New Year's Day and asking Ivan about life-saving techniques. My breathing slowed and my head became clear again. What a stupid thought, I told myself. Something too dreadful to imagine has already happened to him. What damage can the sea do to you that a human being can't?

At eleven o'clock Ivan excused himself, saying that he had to be at his factory early in the morning.

'Where do you live?' Vitaly asked him.

'I'm renting a house on the hill,' he said.

'We'll drive you home then,' said Vitaly, slapping Ivan's back. I was pleased to see that the two men were getting along. They must both have been happy to have met another culinary male.

Ruselina, Betty and I stood on the pavement, waving, while the others piled into Vitaly's car. Ivan wound down his window. 'Would you like a tour of the factory?' he asked us. 'I can show you around next weekend.'

'Yes!' we all cried out together.

'Where there are cakes, we will follow,' said Betty, patting her hair.

I didn't hear from Keith at work on Monday. Each time the copy boy arrived or my telephone rang, I jumped, expecting some word from him. But none came. I repeated the same pattern on Tuesday. On Wednesday I saw Ted stepping into the elevator in the lobby. 'Hi, Anya. Great party. Glad you made it,' was all he could say before the doors clanged shut.

381

I went home with the gloom of disappointment hanging over me. I had blown it with Keith.

It wasn't until Thursday that I saw him again. The Lord Mayor was preparing for the games.

Keith was there with Ted who had jumped into the line of photographers waiting to get a picture of the stars.

'Listen,' said Keith, turning to me, 'if you're still willing to go out with me after Ted's birthday, can I take you to the pictures this Saturday night? *The Seven Year Itch* is showing and I heard it's pretty funny.'

I smiled. 'That sounds good.'

A door opened and the mayor entered the room followed by the guest athletes. 'Better go,' said Keith, signalling to Ted. 'I'll give you a call.'

'Apparently one of his Victorian employees drowned,' said Irina. 'She was an elderly lady from Italy and didn't realise how unpredictable the sea down south could be. That's how he got interested in surf clubs.'

'Is Ivan married?' Betty asked.

We were all silent, wondering who should answer that question. The car tyres rattled over the seams in the concrete road in a steady rhythm.

'He was,' said Ruselina eventually. 'She died in the war.'

Ivan was waiting for us outside the factory gate. He was wearing a navy suit that had obviously been tailored for him. It was the first time I had seen him dressed up. The factory's newness compared to those on either side of it was given away by the unblemished bricks and mortar. A stone chimney towered above the roof with the words 'Southern Cross Pies' on it. There were a dozen trucks in the delivery yard with the same lettering on their sides.

'You look good,' I told him when we piled out of the car.

He laughed. 'Being told that by a fashion editor will go straight to my head.'

'It's true,' Ruselina said, taking his arm. 'But I hope you're not wearing it just for us. It must be close to ninety degrees today.'

'I never feel the heat or the cold,' Ivan answered. 'Being a baker working with frozen foods means I no longer feel the extremes.'

The main area of the factory resembled a giant aircraft hangar with galvanised-iron walls and windows running the length of the room. The machinery was stainless steel and hummed and whirred rather than clanked and creaked as machinery did in the factories of my imagination. Everywhere I looked there were louvre vents, butterfly vents and ventilating machines. It was as if the motto of the factory was 'Keep breathing'.

Ivan started the tour in the delivery area where we watched men stacking sacks of flour and sugar, while others carried trays of eggs or fruit to the enormous refrigerators. 'It's like a kitchen, only a million times bigger,' said Betty.

I could understand why Ivan had become immune to heat when we walked into the cooking area. I was awestruck by the size of the rotating ovens and, although dozens of fans spun in their metal cages, the room was hot and the air was thick with spices.

Ivan led us past the conveyor belts where women were packing the pies into waxed boxes and then on to the demonstration kitchen, where the chef had prepared a table of pies for us to try.

'You'll be pied out by the end of the day,' said Ivan, gesturing for us to be seated. 'For mains we have potato and meat, chicken and mushroom, shepherd's or vegetable pies. And for dessert there is lemon meringue pie, custard and strawberry tart or cheesecake.'

Vitaly took a bite of his shepherd's pie. 'This is as good as the fresh, Ivan.'

'I'm sold,' said Betty. 'I'd give up cooking and have these any day.'

After lunch we could barely walk back to the car. 'That will teach us for being greedy,' laughed Ruselina.

Ivan had given us an armful each of whatever had been our favourite pies to take home with us. Vitaly opened the boot and we lined up to put our goodies inside.

'The pies were delicious,' I told Ivan.

'I'm glad you could come,' he said. 'I hope you don't really work every weekend.'

'I try not to,' I lied.

'Why don't you show Ivan where you work?' suggested Betty.

'I would like that,' he said, taking the pies from me and stacking them into the boot with the others.

'Ivan, where I work is boring to look at,' I said. 'It's just a desk and a typewriter with pictures of dresses and models spread around. But I will take you to visit my friend Judith if you like. She's a designer and a true artist.'

'Very good,' he smiled.

We all took turns kissing Ivan goodbye and then waited for Vitaly to open the car doors and let the hot air out.

'Why don't you come over for dinner tonight?' Betty asked Ivan. 'We can listen to records and I'll buy a bottle of vodka if you like. For you and Vitaly. He'll finish at the lounge about eight o'clock.'

'I don't drink, Betty. But I'm sure Anya could knock back my share,' Ivan said, turning to smirk at me.

'Oh, forget her,' said Vitaly. 'She won't be joining us. She has a date with her boyfriend.'

A shadow passed over Ivan's face but he continued to smile. 'Her boyfriend? I see,' he said.

I could feel my own face blanch. He's thinking about how he asked me to marry him and I refused, I thought. It was natural that the mention of Keith should make us uncomfortable, but I hoped it was something that would pass. I didn't want there to be bad feelings between us.

I saw Betty out of the corner of my eye. She was looking from Ivan to me with a perplexed expression on her face.

My second date with Keith was more relaxed than the first. He took me to the Bates Milkbar in Bondi where we had a booth to ourselves and drank chocolate shakes. He didn't ask me about my family but talked about his own childhood in rural Victoria. I wondered if Diana had filled him in on the brief facts I had given her about my past, or whether it was the Australian custom not to ask about someone's personal life unless they brought it up. It was sweet and light to be with Keith, like Ivan's lemon meringue pie. But at what point would we need to talk seriously? I couldn't imagine blighting our fun outings with stories of my bleak past. His father and uncles hadn't gone to war, he wouldn't know what it was like. He seemed to have an endless supply of aunts and uncles and cousins. Would he be able to understand me? And how would he react when I told him that I had been married?

Later, after the picture, when Keith and I came out of the Six Ways theatre we found that the evening had turned from sticky hot to balmy with a Pacific breeze blowing in from the ocean. We marvelled at the size of the moon.

'What a perfect evening for a walk,' Keith said. 'But your flat isn't very far away.'

'We could walk there and back a few times,' I teased.

'But there would be another problem,' he said.

'What?'

He reached into his pocket for his handkerchief and wiped his brow. 'There aren't any air vents on the way to blow your skirt up.'

I thought of the scene in *The Seven Year Itch*, where Marilyn Monroe stood over a subway vent and her skirt blew right up to her hips in front of a drooling Tom Ewell, and laughed.

'That was a man's scene,' I said.

385

Keith put his arm around me and led me towards the street. 'I hope it wasn't too rude for you,' he said.

I wondered what kind of girls Keith had dated before to worry about a thing like that. The picture was tame compared to the Moscow-Shanghai. 'No. Marilyn Monroe is very pretty,' I said.

'Not as pretty as you, Anya.'

'I don't think so,' I laughed.

'Don't you now? Well, you're wrong,' he said.

After Keith dropped me home, I sat by the window watching the foam dance on the blackness of the night ocean. The waves seemed to roll in and out in time with my breathing. I had enjoyed myself with Keith. He'd kissed me on the cheek when we reached the doorstep, but his touch was light and warm and had no expectations behind it, although he had asked me out for the following Saturday night.

'Better book you up before another fellow gets in,' he said.

Keith was loveable, but when I climbed into bed and closed my eyes, it was Ivan I was thinking about.

Thursday was a short day at work because I had finished my fashion section two weeks in advance. I was looking forward to leaving the office on time and doing some late-night shopping before going home. I had one of Ivan's pies left in my refrigerator, and I imagined myself warming it up and then climbing into bed with a book. I took the stairs to the lobby and stopped in my tracks when I saw Ivan waiting there. He was wearing his smart suit, but his hair was wild and his face was pale.

'Ivan,' I cried, leading him towards one of the lounges. 'What's happened?'

He didn't say anything and I started to worry. I wondered if that foreboding feeling I'd had was coming true. Finally he turned to me and threw his hands up in the air.

'I had to see you. I wanted to wait until you arrived home, but I couldn't.'

'Ivan, don't do this to me,' I pleaded. 'Tell me, what's happened?'

He pressed his hands onto his knees and looked into my eyes. 'This man you are seeing . . . is it serious?'

My mind went blank. I didn't know how to answer him, so I said the only thing I could think of. 'Maybe.'

My answer seemed to calm him. 'So you're not sure?' he asked.

I felt that anything I said would carry more weight than it should so I remained silent, deciding that it was better to hear Ivan out first.

'Anya,' he said, running his hands through his hair, 'is it impossible for you to love me?'

He sounded angry and my spine prickled. 'I met Keith before I saw you again. I'm just getting to know him.'

'I knew how I felt about you the moment I met you on Tubabao and then again when I saw you on the beach. I thought that now we have met again, your feelings might be clear to you.'

My mind blurred. I had no idea how I felt about Ivan. I did love him at some level, I knew that, otherwise I wouldn't have worried about his feelings. But perhaps I didn't love him the way he wanted me to. He was too intense and it frightened me. It was easier to be with Keith. 'I don't know what I feel—'

'You're not clear on very much, Anya,' Ivan interrupted. 'You seem to live your life in emotional confusion.'

It was my turn to be angry but the lobby was filling with *Sydney Herald* workers leaving for the evening and I kept my voice low. 'Perhaps if you didn't suddenly jump on me with your feelings, then I would have time to understand mine. You have no patience, Ivan. Your timing is dreadful.'

He didn't answer me and we both remained silent for

387

a few minutes. Then he asked, 'What can this man give you? Is he Australian?'

I thought about his question, then answered. 'Sometimes it is easier to be with someone who makes you forget.'

Ivan stood up and glared at me as if I had slapped him. I glanced over my shoulder, hoping no one from the women's section – or worse, Keith – would see us.

'There's something more important than forgetting, Anya,' he said. 'And that's understanding.'

He turned and rushed out of the lobby, mingling with the crowd pouring out onto the street. I watched the flow of suits and dresses, trying to sort out what had just happened.

I didn't make it home for the relaxing evening I had planned. I sat on the beach in my work dress, stockings and shoes, my handbag by my side. I sought solace in the ocean. Maybe I was destined to be alone, or maybe I was incapable of loving anyone. I clutched my face in my hands, trying to sort out my jumbled feelings. Keith wasn't making me decide anything, and even Ivan's outburst wasn't what was causing me to feel pressure. It was something else inside me. Since I had learned of Dmitri's death, I had become tired and weary. A part of me didn't see a future no matter what I decided.

I watched the sun go down and waited until the air turned too cold to sit outside any longer. I dawdled along the promenade and stood outside my apartment building for a long time, gazing upwards. Every window had a light in it except for mine. I pushed my key into the entrance door and jumped when it opened before I turned it. Vitaly was standing in the hallway.

'Anya! We've been waiting for you all evening!' he said, his face uncharacteristically tense. 'Quick, come inside!'

I followed him into Betty and Ruselina's apartment. The old women were sitting on the lounge. Irina was there too, perched on the edge of an armchair. She leaped up when she saw me and clutched me in her arms.

'Vitaly's father has received a letter from his brother after all these years!' she cried. 'It includes news about your mother!'

'My mother?' I mumbled, shaking my head.

Vitaly stepped forward. 'Enclosed with the letter to my father was a special one for you. He has forwarded it from the States by registered mail.'

I stared at Vitaly in disbelief. The moment didn't seem real. I had waited so long for it that I didn't know how to react when it happened.

'How long will it take?' I asked. My voice didn't sound like my own. It sounded like Anya Kozlova, thirteen years of age. Small, frightened, lost.

'It will take seven to ten days to arrive,' replied Vitaly.

I hardly heard him. I didn't know what to do. I wasn't really capable of doing anything. I paced around the room in circles, clutching at the furniture to calm myself. On top of everything else that had happened today, it seemed that the world had lost all substance. The ground lurched under my feet the way the ship that had taken me from Shanghai had rolled on the waves. I would have to wait seven to ten days for news that had taken almost half my lifetime to reach me.

EIGHTEEN

The Letter

It was impossible to behave normally while waiting for the letter from America. If ever I felt calm, it was only moments before I began to unravel again. At the paper I would read copy over three times and not take in anything. At the store I would pile tins and packets into my basket and arrive home with nothing I could use. I was covered in bruises from walking into chairs and tables. I stepped off footpaths and onto busy streets without looking, until honking horns and angry drivers set me straight again. I wore my stockings inside out to a fashion parade, and called Ruselina 'Betty' and Betty 'Ruselina', and Vitaly 'Ivan' when I wasn't thinking. My stomach churned as if I had drunk too much coffee. I woke in the night with fevers. I felt totally alone. No one could help me. No one could reassure me. Surely the letter contained bad news or why would it have been sealed and addressed to me? Perhaps Vitaly's parents had read the contents and, rather than be bearers of bad news, had simply forwarded it on to me.

Yet despite my rationalisations and preparations for the worst, I hoped against hope that my mother was alive and that the letter was from her. Though I could not imagine what such a letter would contain.

After the seventh day, time was marked out by daily visits with Irina to the post office where we waited in line to face the hostile glare of the postal clerks.

'No, your letter hasn't arrived. We will send you a card when it does.'

'But it's a very important letter,' Irina would say, trying to elicit some sort of sympathy. 'Please understand our anxiety.'

But the clerks only looked down their noses at us, dismissing our private drama with a wave of their hands as if they were kings and queens instead of government employees. And even when the letter hadn't arrived after ten days, and I felt the bones of my ribs collapse inward, crushing my lungs and cutting off my breath, they couldn't find enough kindness in their hearts to call the other post offices in the area to check if the letter had gone astray. They behaved as if they were rushed off their feet, even when Irina and I were the only customers.

Vitaly telegrammed his parents but they only verified the address.

To help take my mind off the letter I went with Keith one afternoon to the races. I watched from the balcony while he interviewed the trainers. After Keith had called in his story and the results to the paper, he met me in the bar for a drink. He bought me a shandy, which I politely tried to drink while he explained to me the life of the racing world: the outsiders and favourites, the weights and barrier draws, jockeys' tactics and bookmakers' odds. I noticed for the first time that afternoon that he called me Anne and not Anya. I wondered if he was purposely anglicising my name or if he really couldn't hear the difference. When I told him about the letter and my mother, he threw his arm around me and said, 'It's better not to think about sad things.'

Despite that, I longed for his company. I ached for him to hold my hand, to yank me from the whirlpool that was swallowing me. I wanted to say, 'Keith, see me. See that I am drowning. Help me.' But he couldn't see it. He walked me to the tram stop, gave me a peck on the cheek and sent me back to my mindless loneliness while he continued to drink at the bar and hunt down stories.

I opened the door to my flat. The silence inside was both comforting and oppressive. I switched on the light and saw that Ruselina and Betty had cleaned it. My shoes were polished and lined up in pairs by the door. My nightdress was folded at the foot of the bed with a pair of cloth slippers tucked underneath it. On my pillow they had placed a cake of lavender soap and a washcloth. The washcloth was hand-embroidered with flowers and bluebirds. I unfolded it and saw the words: 'For our precious girl'. My eyes filled with tears. Perhaps something would change for the better. Even though something inside me said that the arrival of the letter would make things worse. I still tried to hope otherwise.

Betty had baked a batch of her ginger biscuits and left them in a jar on my desk. I took one out and nearly broke my teeth trying to bite it. I put the kettle on and made some tea, softening the biscuits in it before eating them. I lay down on the bed with the intention to rest for a moment, but I fell into a deep sleep.

I woke up an hour later to a knock at the door. I struggled to sit up, my limbs heavy with sleep and sadness. I saw Ivan through the peephole. I opened the door and he strode into the flat, his arms laden with frozen pies. He headed straight to the kitchenette and opened the door to my mini-fridge. The only thing in it was a jar of mustard on the top shelf. 'My poor Anya,' he said, stacking the packages. 'Irina told me about your terrible wait. I am going to stand outside the postmaster's office tomorrow until he tracks down that letter.' Ivan closed the refrigerator door and threw his arms around my shoulders, squeezing me like a Russian bear. When he broke away, his eyes fell to my waist. 'You're so thin,' he said.

I sat down on the bed and he took a seat at my desk, rubbing his chin and staring out to the dark ocean.

'You're very kind to me,' I said.

'I've been awful to you,' he replied, not looking at me. 'I've tried to force you into feelings you don't have.'

We lapsed into silence. Because he wouldn't look at me, I stared at him. At his big hands, fingers linked on the table; his broad and familiar shoulders; his wavy hair. I wished that I could love him the way he wanted me to because he was a good man and he knew me well. I realised then that the lack I had felt for Ivan had been the lack in myself, nothing to do with him.

'Ivan, I'll always care about you.'

He stood up, as if I had given him the signal to leave, whereas in truth I wanted him to stay. I wanted him to lie on the bed next to me so I could snuggle up to him and fall asleep on his shoulder.

'I'm moving back to Melbourne in a fortnight,' he said. 'I've hired a manager for the Sydney factory.'

'Oh,' I said. It was as though he had stabbed me.

After Ivan left I lay on the bed again, feeling the gap inside me widening and spreading, as if I were bleeding to death.

The day after Ivan's visit I was at my desk at the paper working on an article on iron-free cotton. Our office faced west. The summer sun was streaming through the glass windows, turning the women's section into a hothouse. The wall fans whirred pathetically against the oppressive heat. Caroline was working on an article about what the Royal family liked to eat at Balmoral. Every time I glanced at her, I noticed that she was slowly slumping forward a bit more, drooping like a thirsty flower. Even Diana looked faded, little strands of hair adhering to her shiny forehead. But I could not get warm. My bones were like ice, freezing me from within. Diana told the junior reporters that they could roll their sleeves up if they needed to, while I put on a sweater.

My telephone rang and my heart fell to my feet when

I heard Irina's voice. 'Anya, come home,' she said. 'The letter is here.'

On the tram home I could barely breathe. The terror was becoming more real. Once or twice I thought I would faint. I hoped Irina had called Keith as I had asked. I wanted him and Irina to be there when I read the letter. The hum of the traffic made me think of the hum of my father's car when he took my mother and me for Sunday drives. Suddenly her image loomed up in front of me much clearer than it had for years. I was taken aback by the vividness of her dark hair, her amber eyes, the pearl studs in her ears.

Irina was waiting for me outside the apartment. I stared at the envelope in her hand and stumbled. It was grubby and thin.

'Do you want to be alone with this?' she asked.

I took the letter from her. It was light between my fingers. Perhaps it said nothing at all. Perhaps it was just a pamphlet from Vitaly's uncle on the righteousness of the Communist party. I wanted to wake from the nightmare and be somewhere else.

'Keith?' I asked.

'He said he has to finish an urgent article, but he will be over as soon as he can.'

'Thank you for calling him.'

'I'm sure it's good news,' said Irina, biting her lip.

Across the road, next to the beach, was a patch of grass under a pine tree. I nodded towards it.

'I need you,' I told her. 'More than ever.'

Irina and I sat down in the shade. My hands were jelly and my mouth was dry. I ripped open the envelope and stared at the Russian handwriting, not able to read a sentence at a time, but rather looking at all the words at once and not taking in anything. 'Anna Victorovna' was all I could read before my vision blurred and my head began to swim.

'I can't,' I said, passing the letter to Irina. 'Please read it to me.'

Irina took the paper from me. Her face was grave and her mouth quivered. She began to read.

'Anna Victorovna,

My brother has informed me that you have been seeking news of your mother, Alina Pavlovna Kozlova, after she was taken from Harbin for transportation to the Soviet Union. When your mother was deported that day in August. I was on the same train. However, unlike your mother, I was returning to Russia of my own free will and so was in the rear passenger carriage along with the Russian officials who were overseeing the transportation.

About midnight the train was travelling towards the border when it came to a sudden halt. I remember the look of surprise on the face of the officer next to me, so I knew that the stop had not been expected. In the gloom outside I could just make out the military car parked near the front of the train and the outline of the four Chinese men who stood in its headlights. It was an eerie sight. Those four men and the car in the middle of nowhere. There was some discussion with the train driver, and before long the door to our carriage was prised open and the men entered. I could tell from their uniforms that they were Communists. The officials in the carriage stood up to greet them. Three of the men were unremarkable Chinese but the fourth will stay in my mind forever. He had a serious, dignified and intelligent face but his hands . . . they were stumps in padded gloves and I swear I could smell the flesh rotting. I knew immediately who he was, although I had never met him. A man named Tang, the most notorious of the leaders of the Communist resistance in Harbin. He had been interned in a Japanese camp, sent there by a spy who had posed as a fellow Communist.

He had no time for our greetings and immediately began asking after your mother and which carriage she was on. He seemed nervous about something and kept glancing out the windows. He said he had orders to take her off the train. I knew about your mother too. I had heard of the Russian woman who had housed a Japanese general. I knew that she had lost her husband, although I didn't know about you then.

One of the officials objected. He said all the prisoners had been spoken for and must be delivered to the Soviet Union. But Tang was adamant. His eyes were red with fury and I became concerned that there would be some violence. Finally the official acquiesced, assuming, I guess, that arguing with the Chinese would only delay the train. He put on his coat and with a nod of his head led Tang and the other Chinese through the train.

A short time later I saw the men leave the train. The woman I believe was your mother was with them. The Soviet official returned to the carriage and ordered us to close the shutters. We did so but the bottom slat of mine was broken and I could see some of what was going on outside. The men marched the woman to the car. There was some sort of argument and then the lights of the train went out and a round of shots rang through the night air. The noise was horrendous but the silence afterwards was even more chilling. Some of the prisoners began to cry out, demanding to know what was going on. But a few moments later, the train started to move. I bent down and peered through the broken slat. All I could make out was the body of someone I believe to be your mother lying on the ground.

Anna Victorovna, let me assure you that your mother's death was quick and without torture. If there is any comfort then take it from the fact that the fate awaiting her in the Soviet Union would have been far worse . . .'

The sun dropped like a ball and the sky turned dark. Irina stopped reading; although her lips continued to move she made no sound. Betty and Ruselina were watching us from the step but when I looked at them they read my expression and crumbled. Betty grasped the railing and stared at her feet. Ruselina sank down onto the steps, clutching her head in her hands. What had we expected? What had I expected? My mother was dead and had been for years. Why had I lived in hope? Had I really believed that I would see her alive again?

For a few moments I didn't feel anything. I was expecting someone to arrive and say the letter was a mistake or that it was another woman who was taken from the train. They would take the letter back and wipe out everything it had said and I could go on living again. Then, suddenly, like a house struck by an explosion, I crumbled from inside. The pain gripped me so hard I was sure I would split open with it. I fell back against the pine tree. Irina stepped towards me. I grabbed the letter and tore it to shreds, throwing the pieces towards the sky. I watched them drift like snowflakes into the summer air.

'Curse you!' I screamed, shaking my fist at the handless man who was probably long dead but had still found a way to hurt me. 'Curse you!'

My legs gave way. My shoulder slammed into the ground but I didn't feel anything. I saw the sky above me and the beginning of stars. I had fallen like that twice before. Once in snow when I was following the General on the day I met Tang. The other time when Dmitri told me that he loved Amelia.

Betty and Ruselina crouched over me. 'Call a doctor!' Ruselina screamed to Irina. 'She's bleeding from the mouth!'

I had an image of my mother on the isolated plains of China, lying face down in the dirt. She was full of puncture wounds from the bullets, like a beautiful fur coat ruined with moth holes, and bleeding from the mouth.

Some people say that knowing is better than not knowing. But it wasn't so for me. After the letter I had nothing to hope for. No pleasant memories to draw on, no happy daydreams about the future. Everything behind or ahead came to a stop with the sound of bullets ringing out in the night.

The days rolled on with a relentless summer heat and no respite. 'Anya, you must get out of bed,' Irina scolded me daily. But I didn't want to move. I shut my blinds and curled up in my bed. The smell of musty cotton and the darkness were my comforts. Ruselina and Betty brought me food, but I couldn't eat. Apart from having no appetite, I had bitten my tongue when I had fallen down and it was painfully swollen. Even the melon they cut up for me stung it. Keith didn't come to see me the night I got the letter. He came a day later and stood in the doorway, half turned to me and half to the hall, a bunch of wilted flowers in his hand. 'Hold me,' I said, and he did for a few minutes, although both of us understood then that there was nothing of substance between us.

Never mind, never mind, I told myself after he left and I knew it was over between us. He would be better off with a happy Australian girl.

I tried to understand the sequence of things, how it had all come to this final blow. Just a few weeks earlier I had been at the Town Hall talking to sports stars; Keith and I seemed to be falling in love; and, although my searching had come to a dead end, somewhere I still had the possibility that I might find my mother. I tortured myself by remembering all the times I thought I had somehow been getting closer to her. I recalled the gypsy in Shanghai who stole my necklace, then Tubabao where I had been certain I could feel my mother's presence. I shook my head with the irony of how angry I had been with the Red Cross when Daisy Kent had said that they wouldn't be able to help me. As it turned out my mother had never even left China, she'd been executed only a few hours after I last saw her. Then I remembered Sergei's sad face and Dmitri's warning against expectations. I wondered then if they had known my mother was dead, but had chosen not to tell me.

I had believed for so long that one day the great void

my mother's absence had left in me would close, and suddenly I had to admit that it would not.

A week later Irina stood in my doorway with a towel and sunhat in her hand. 'Anya, you can't lie there forever. Your mother wouldn't have wanted that. Let's go to the beach. Ivan's competing in the carnival. It's his last before he goes back to Melbourne.'

I sat up, even now I don't know why. Irina herself looked surprised when I moved. Perhaps after a week in bed I realised that the only thing that might stop the pain would be getting up. My mind was foggy and my legs were weak, like those of someone who has suffered a long illness. Irina took my getting up as permission to open the blinds. The sunlight and sounds of the ocean were a shock to my vampire-like state and I lifted my hand to shield my face. Although we were going swimming, she insisted that I shower and wash my hair.

'You're too pretty to go anywhere looking like that,' she said, fingering my straggly mane and pushing me towards the bathroom.

'You should have been a nurse,' I mumbled, then remembered what terrible nurses we had been on Tubabao the night of the storm. As soon as I stepped into the shower and turned on the taps I felt spent again. I lowered myself onto the edge of the bath, buried my face in my hands and began to cry.

It's my fault, I thought. Tang went after her because I got away.

Irina brushed my hair away from my face but paid no attention to the tears. She pushed me towards the stream of water and began lathering up my hair with strong fingers. The shampoo smelled like caramel and was the colour of eggs.

The carnival was a sudden return to the world of the living. The beach was crowded with oil-slathered sunbathers, women in straw hats, children with rubber rings, men with zinc cream on their noses, old people sitting on blankets, and lifesavers from every club in Sydney. Something had happened to my hearing in the past week. My tubes were blocked. Sounds would seem unbearably loud one second and then fade away into silence the next. The discomfort caused by a baby's crying made me cover my ears, but when I dropped my hands away I could hear nothing at all.

Irina grabbed my hand so that we wouldn't lose each other trying to squeeze our way to the front of the crowd. The sun sparkling off the water that morning was deceptive, because the ocean was full of rips and the waves were high and dangerous. Three people had been pulled from the sea already, even though they had been swimming between the flags. There was talk of closing the beach and cancelling the carnival, but the boat race was judged safe enough.

The lifesavers marched behind their club flags as proudly as military men. Manly, Mona Vale, Bronte, Queenscliff. The lifesavers from North Bondi Surf Life Saving Club wore bib and brace-style costumes in the club colours of chocolate, red and white. Ivan marched as the belt man. With his head held high, his scar seemed invisible in the bright sunlight. I felt for the first time that I was seeing his face as it really was, the jaw set in the determined expression of a classic hero. Scattered throughout the crowd, clusters of women were shouting encouragement to the men. Ivan cringed from their attention at first, assuming it wasn't for him, but egged on by the other guards he accepted a hug from a blonde woman and the kisses her friends blew to him. Seeing his shy pleasure brought me the only happiness I had known the whole week.

If I had been wiser, healthier in the heart, I might have married Ivan when he asked me, I thought. Perhaps we would have given each other some happiness and comfort.

400

But it was too late for that. It was too late for anything except regrets.

Ivan and his team pulled their boat to the water's edge. The home crowd cheered for them, whistling and shouting, 'Bondi! Bondi!' Irina called out and Ivan turned to us, his eyes meeting mine. He smiled at me and I felt the warmth of it run straight to my heart. But the minute he turned away I became cold again.

The whistle blew and the teams crashed into the water. They thrashed against the high waves which broke over the bows. One boat was twisted sideways in the surf and over-turned. Most of the lifesavers jumped out in time but one was caught underneath and had to be rescued. The race official ran out to the shore, but it was too late to call the others back, they were beyond the breakers. The crowd became silent then, because everyone understood that the excitement was over, that the race could be fatal in these conditions. For ten minutes the four remaining boats were out of sight beyond the waves. My chest twisted into a knot. What if I lost Ivan too? Then I saw the oars of the returning boats, high above the waves. Ivan's boat was in the lead, but no one cared any more about the race. I struggled with my sense of dread. I heard the wood groan and saw it start to split apart, like pieces of straw from an old hat. The lifesavers' faces were frozen with fear but Ivan's expression was calm. He shouted orders to his team and by some miracle they held the boat together with their bare hands while Ivan held the rudder steady and got them back onto the sand. The supporters for North Bondi went wild. But Ivan and his team were not concerned with their victory. They leaped out of their boat and jumped back into the waves, helping the other teams pull their boats onto the beach. When everyone was safely back on the sand, the crowd let out a roar. 'Show us the man!' they chanted. 'Show us the man!' The guards around Ivan lifted him into the air as if he were as light as a ballerina. They carried him towards the crowd and threw him into a mob of girls, who jumped on him, giggling and squirming.

Irina turned to me, laughing. But I couldn't hear her. I had lost all sense of sound. Her tanned skin glinted in the sunlight; the salty air had given her pretty mermaid curls. She rushed towards Ivan and began a playful tug of war with him over his cap. The crowd moved forward and I was jostled further and further towards the back of it until I found myself standing alone.

Like a fist into my stomach the pain returned, even harder and sharper than before. I clutched my gut and sank to my knees. I retched but could bring nothing up. It was my fault my mother was dead. Tang shot her because of me. I had got away and he couldn't hurt me so he went after her. Olga too. I killed them all. Even Dmitri. He would have come looking for me if I hadn't changed my name.

'Anya!'

I stood up and ran to the water's edge, feeling the relief of the cooler sand on my burned feet.

'Anya!'

She was calling out my name.

'Mama?' I cried, padding over the wet sand. When I reached the rockpool, I sat down. The midday sun was high. It had turned the water as clear as glass and I could see schools of fish in the waves, and the dark shadow of the rocks and the seaweed that clung to them. I glanced back along the beach. The carnival crowd had dispersed and most of the lifesavers were relaxing, drinking sodas and talking to girls. All except Ivan, who had taken off his cap and was jogging along the sand. I couldn't see Irina.

I heard her call again and turned back to the ocean. My mother was standing on the rocks, looking at me. Her eyes were as transparent as the water. Her hair was loose about her shoulders and flapped in the breeze like a black veil. I stood up and breathed deeply, finally understanding what

I had to do. Once I allowed the first thought, all the other thoughts came quickly. I was elated, realising how easy it would be, what the answer had always been. The pain would stop and I would defeat Tang. My mother and I would be together again.

The wet sand felt light and soft under my feet, like snow. The icy cold rush of water over my skin was invigorating. At first I had to struggle against the ocean and it tired me. But then I thought of the boats, fighting against the waves, and used all my strength to wade into the deep water. A wave rose like a shadow above me, then crashed down, sending me swirling to the sandy bottom. My back struck the ocean floor. The blow winded me and I could feel the water seeping from my throat into my lungs. It hurt at first, but then I looked up and saw my mother standing on the rocks above me and I sensed myself moving into a new world. I closed my eyes, listening to the sea ripple and bubble about me. I was in my mother's womb again. For a moment I was sad, thinking how Irina would miss me. I thought of them all, Betty, Ruselina, Ivan, Diana. They would say I had so much to live for, that I was young and pretty and clever. I was guilty that all those things never meant as much to me as they should have. They never stopped the loneliness. And now I would never be lonely again.

Suddenly I was pulled up and thrown to the surface, lifted high on the crest of a wave like a child tossed up in her mother's arms. For a moment my sense of sound returned and I could hear the cries and laughter of the people on the beach, the waves crashing on the shore. But a second later I was plunged down again. This time the water rushed into my nostrils and throat more quickly, as if I were a leaky boat. 'Mama, I'm coming,' I cried. 'Help me! Help me!'

The water was heavy in my lungs, bubbles rose from my mouth and nostrils and then stopped. I could feel it, the cold creeping through my veins, the exhaustion. I closed my eyes against the pain and let the current rock me back and forth.

There was movement next to me. A flash of sunlight on flesh. I wondered what it was: a shark or a dolphin coming to witness my last moments? But then human arms slipped under my shoulders and dragged me to the surface.

The sunshine burned my salty eyes.

In the distance a woman was screaming. 'No! Oh my God! No!'

Irina.

A wave washed over me. The ocean ran over my face and hair. But the arms lifted me higher and I was thrown over someone's shoulder. I knew my rescuer. Another wave crashed over us, but still he held onto me, his fingers digging into my thighs. I coughed and spluttered. 'Let me die,' I tried to say, with nothing coming out but water.

But Ivan didn't hear me. He lay me on the sand and put his head against my chest. His wet hair brushed against my skin but he must have heard nothing. He turned me on my chest and pressed his hands on the back of my ribs, then rubbed my limbs vigorously. The sand on his palms scratched my skin and I felt the grit on my lips. His fingers were shaking and the leg he had pressed against mine trembled. 'Please don't,' he shouted at me, tears choking his voice. 'Please don't, Anya!'

Although my cheek was pressed against the sand, I could see Irina standing at the water's edge, sobbing. A woman had thrown a towel over her shoulders and was trying to comfort her. My heart ached. I did not want to hurt my friends. But my mother was waiting for me on the rocks. I wasn't the strong person everyone thought I was, and only she knew that.

'Let it go, mate. Let it go,' I heard another lifesaver say

when he kneeled down to examine me. 'Look at the colour of her face. The froth on her lips. She's gone.'

The other one touched my arm, but Ivan shoved him away. Ivan wouldn't let me go. I struggled against him when he pressed down on me, fighting everything he did to save me. But his will was stronger than mine. He beat his fists against me until something like a ferocious wind blew into my lungs. I felt a sharp spasm and the ocean gave way to the rush of air. Someone picked me up. I saw a crowd and an ambulance. Irina and Ivan were standing above me, holding onto each other and weeping. I turned my head to the rocks. My mother was gone.

Every evening for the next week Ivan came to visit me in St Vincent's Hospital, his hair smelling of Palmolive soap and a gardenia in his hand. His face was sunburned and he walked slowly and stiffly, exhausted from the traumatic weekend. Whenever he arrived, Betty and Ruselina, who spent their days reading to me or listening to the radio while I slept, got up to leave. They always acted as though there were important things to be said between Ivan and myself, and drew the green curtain around us for privacy before scuttling off to the cafeteria. But Ivan and I said very little to each other. We had a communication that went beyond words. Love, I saw, was more than feelings. It was the actions you took too. Ivan had saved me and breathed life into me with as much determination as a woman giving birth. He had pounded life into me with his fists and would not let me die.

On my last night at the hospital, when the doctors declared my lungs clear and strong again, Ivan reached out and touched my hand. He looked at me as if I were a priceless treasure he had plucked from the sea, and not a suicidal young woman. I remembered what he had said about understanding being more important than forgetting.

'Thank you,' I said, intertwining my fingers with his. I

knew then that whatever had stopped me from loving him was gone. When he touched me I wanted to live again. He had a will strong enough for both of us.

NINETEEN

Miracles

We Russians are pessimists. Our souls are dark. We believe that life is suffering, relieved only by momentary sketches of happiness that pass as quickly as clouds on a windy day, and death. Australians, however, are pessimists of the oddest sort. They, too, believe life is harsh and that things go wrong much more than they go right. However, even when the ground they depend on for food turns as dry as a rock and all their sheep and cattle die, they will still lift their eyes to the sky and wait for a miracle. To me that suggests that deep in their hearts they are optimists. And perhaps this is the way my new country has changed me. For the year I turned thirty-six, when hope began eluding me, I experienced two miracles one after the other.

The year before, Ivan and I had moved into our new home in Narrabeen, on the Northern Beaches. The house had been a two-year project that had started with the inspection of a corner block of land on a hill. It was covered in eucalypts, angophoras and tree ferns and looked over the lagoon. Ivan and I fell in love with it at first sight. He walked the boundary, pushing aside the green fronds of the fishbone ferns and stumbling over rocks, while I fingered the grevillea and native fuchsia and began envisioning a garden alive with the exotic, verdant plants of my second homeland. Two years later a split-level home stood on it with feature walls of apple or orange and wall-to-wall carpet.

The two bathrooms were mosaic-tiled and wood-panelled. The Scandinavian kitchen overlooked a swimming pool, and the triple windows of the lounge room opened onto a balcony facing the water.

There were four bedrooms: ours, the main bedroom with an ensuite; one on the ground level, which I used as an office; a guest room with two single beds; and a sunny room next to ours with no furniture at all. That room was our sadness, the only grief we knew in an otherwise happy marriage. Despite all our efforts, Ivan and I had not been able to conceive a child and it began to seem unlikely that we ever would. He was already forty-four, and in those days, at thirty-six, I was considered well past a woman's prime. Yet, with no words spoken, we had left a room for her, as though we were hoping that by providing a beautiful place for our baby, she would finally appear. That is what I meant by looking to the sky and hoping for a miracle.

I had often seen her, that child who would not become a reality. She was the one I had thought of in Shanghai when I cried out for a child to love. She had not come, I thought, because Dmitri was not the right man to be her father. But Ivan was a good man, a man capable of great love and sacrifice. He listened to me and remembered what I told him. When we made love he would cup my face in his palms and gaze tenderly into my eyes. But still the child had not come. I called her my little running girl for whenever I saw her that is what she was doing. Sometimes in the supermarket I would see her peeking through the canned goods, her tousled black hair limp over her amber-coloured eyes. She would smile at me with her shiny rose-coloured lips, her grin bejewelled with miniature teeth. Then as quickly as she appeared she would run away from me. She came to the garden of our new house, where I worked like mad to make up for the loss I felt by not being able to bring her into being. I would hear her cheerful laughter among the crimson bottlebrushes, and when I turned I would catch just a glimpse of her chubby baby legs running away from me. Running and running so fast that I could never catch her. My little running girl.

Irina and Vitaly, however, had been more than fertile. They had produced two girls, Oksana and Sofia, and two boys, Fyodor and Yuri, and were talking about the possibility of one more. Irina approached forty like a duck to water. She was proud of her wide hips, her thickening olive skin, the few grey hairs on her crown. I, on the other hand, still looked something like an adolescent in a grown woman's body, thin and nervous. My only concession to my age was to wear my long hair in a chignon as my mother had done.

Irina and Vitaly had bought the coffee lounge from Betty and opened another one in North Sydney. They'd moved into a house in Bondi with a neat front garden and a carport. They would scare the local population by jumping into the ocean midwinter with half a dozen of their other Russian Club friends. I once asked Irina whether she regretted not pursuing her singing career. She laughed and pointed to her happy children eating at the kitchen table. 'No! This is a much better life.'

I had quit my job at the *Sydney Herald* when I married Ivan, but after years of childless boredom I accepted Diana's offer to write a column for the lifestyle section. Australia in the sixties was a different country to the one I had known in the fifties. Young women were leaping off the pages in the women's section and into all areas of journalism. 'Populate or perish' had changed the face of the nation from a British clone to a cosmopolitan country, with new foods, new ideas and new passions blending in with the legacy of the old country. The column kept me in touch with the world a couple of days a week and stopped me from thinking too much about what I didn't have in my life.

We also experienced a sad loss. One day when I went

to visit Ruselina and Betty in their flat, I was shocked to find that vibrant, energetic Betty had suddenly become old. Her shoulders stooped and her skin hung over her like a loose dress.

'She's been listless like that for a couple of weeks now,' whispered Ruselina.

I insisted that Betty go to her doctor for a checkup. He sent her to a specialist and we returned the following week to get the results. While Betty spoke with the doctor I sat outside in the waiting room, flipping through magazines, sure that the door to the consulting room would open any minute and the doctor would tell me that Betty needed vitamins or a change of diet. I wasn't prepared for the grave expression on his face when he called my name. I followed him into his room. Betty was sitting in a chair, clutching her handbag. I turned to the doctor and my heart lurched when he told me the verdict. Inoperable cancer.

We nursed Betty at the flat in Bondi for as long as we could. Irina and I were concerned about how Ruselina would take her friend's illness, but she was stronger than the rest of us. While Irina and I took turns to cry, Ruselina played cards with Betty and cooked her favourite foods. They took evening walks on the beach, and when Betty could no longer stand without the aid of a stick, they sat outside the front door and talked for hours. One evening when I was in the kitchen I overheard Betty say to Ruselina, 'I'll try and come back as one of Irina's children, if she decides to have any more. You'll know it's me. I'll be the naughty one.'

When Betty became too sick to stay at home, her decline was more rapid. I looked at her in the hospital bed and thought how small she had become. I decided to test my theory by measuring the distance from her feet to the end of the bed with my hand, and I found that from the time she had been admitted to hospital, she had shrunk three inches. As I pulled my hand away, Betty turned to me and said, 'When I see your mother, I'll tell her what a beautiful girl you turned out to be.'

Then one evening in September, while Ruselina was on watch, we were all called to the hospital. Betty's condition had worsened. She was barely conscious. Her cheeks were sunken and her face was so pale that it looked moonlit. Towards the morning, Ruselina began to turn ashen herself. The nurse came in to check on us. 'She'll probably still be here until the afternoon, but not long after that,' she said, patting Ruselina's shoulder. 'You should get something to eat and have a lie-down.'

Irina stood up, understanding that if Ruselina didn't take a break, she wouldn't have the strength for what was to come. Vitaly and Ivan went with the women while I stayed behind to keep watch.

Betty's mouth was open, and her uneven breathing and the hum of the airconditioning were the only two sounds in the room. Her eyes flickered now and then, as if she was dreaming. I reached out and touched her cheek and remembered the first day I saw her, standing on the balcony in Potts Point with her beehive hairdo and cigarette holder. It was hard to believe that she was the same wasted woman who lay before me. It occurred to me that if my mother had not been taken away from me prematurely, then we would have faced a similar separation one day. I realised then that whatever time we have with someone is precious, something to be treasured and never wasted.

I leaned closer and whispered, 'I love you, Betty. Thank you for taking care of me.'

Her fingers twitched and she blinked. I like to think that if she'd had the strength, she would have touched her hair and squinted one more time.

The day after Betty died, Irina and I went to collect Ruselina's clothes from the flat. She was too distressed to return there herself and stayed at Irina and Vitaly's house. Irina and I stood together in the third bedroom, where Betty had recreated her sons' room in Potts Point. Everything was clean and in its place, and I suspected Ruselina must have been dusting it while Betty was ill.

'What should we do about this room?' I asked Irina.

Irina sat down on one of the beds, her face deep in thought. After a while she said, 'We should keep their photographs because they are family. But the rest we can give to charity. Betty and her boys don't need these things now.'

At the funeral, against all Russian or Australian tradition, Ruselina wore a white dress with a corsage of red hibiscuses pinned to the lapel. And after the wake she took a bunch of candy-coloured balloons and released them into the sky. 'For you, Betty,' she shouted. 'For all the havoc you are causing up there.'

I don't know whether I believe in reincarnation or not, but I have always thought it fitting that Betty had the possibility to be born anew in the middle of the flower power generation.

One year after we'd moved into our new home the first miracle happened. I fell pregnant. The news renewed Ivan and shaved twenty years off his demeanour. He walked with a bounce, smiled at everything and nothing, and stroked my belly before falling asleep at night. 'This child will heal us both,' he said.

Lilliana Ekaterina was born on August twenty-first that year. In between contractions, the nurses and I listened to the radio broadcast of the Soviet invasion of Czechoslovakia, and I thought about my mother more than I had allowed myself to since the news of her death. I thought of the mothers and daughters in Prague. What would become of them? The nurses held my hands when the birth pangs were intense and joked with me when they subsided. And when

Lily slid from me after sixteen hours of labour, I saw my mother there before me in her shock of dark hair and her unusual eyes.

Lily was a miracle because she did indeed heal me. I believe our bond to our mother is the most significant we have. The death of the one who brought us into the world is one of the biggest turning points in our lives. But most people have at least some time to prepare. Having my mother taken away from me when I was thirteen left me feeling lost in the world, like a leaf blown about by the wind. But becoming mother to Lily retied the cord. Holding her warm body in my arms, her face nuzzling my breast, grounded me to everything that was good and worth living for. And she healed Ivan too. He had lost what was most precious to him early in his life, and now in middle age, in a country full of sun and far from bad memories, he could rebuild his dream again.

Ivan built a pinewood letterbox, twice the size of any other letterbox in the street, to honour Lily's homecoming. On the front of it he glued a woodcut of a man, his wife and their baby. When I was strong enough to garden again, I planted a mat of violet dampiera around it. A baby huntsman set up home in the box and would scurry away whenever I opened the lid to pick up the afternoon mail. One day a few weeks later the spider decided to take up residence elsewhere, and that was the day I got the letter. The letter that was to bring about the second miracle and change everything.

It was jumbled up with the other letters and bills, but the moment I touched it my fingers tingled. The stamp was Australian but the envelope was so marked with fingerprints it looked as if it had passed through a hundred hands before reaching me. I sat down on the bench by the pool, surrounded by pots of gardenias, the only non-native plants in the garden, and opened it. The message struck me like a bolt of lightning.

If you are Anna Victorovna Kozlova, the daughter of Alina and Victor Kozlov from Harbin, please meet me on Monday at noon at the Hotel Belvedere dining room. I am able to arrange for you to see your mother.

The letter fell from my fingertips and fluttered in the breeze onto the grass. I watched it float for a moment like a paper boat. I tried to think who the letter's author could be, who after all these years would contact me with news of my mother.

Ivan came home and I showed him the letter. He sat down on the couch and was quiet for a long time.

'I don't trust the author of this letter,' he said. 'Why doesn't he give his name? Or ask you to telephone him first?'

'Why would someone lie about my mother?' I asked.

Ivan shrugged. 'A Russian spy. Someone who wants to take you back to the Soviet Union. You may be an Australian citizen now, but who knows what they would do to you if you ended up there. Tang?'

It could have been Tang trying to trap me, but in my heart I didn't believe that. Surely he would be dead by now or too old to pursue me. There was something else. I stared at the handwriting again, trying to unlock its secret.

'I don't want you to go,' Ivan said, looking at me with tears in his eyes.

'I have to,' I said.

'Do you believe your mother is alive?'

I thought about it but couldn't separate what I longed to believe from what seemed most likely.

Ivan rubbed his face, covering his eyes with the heels of his palms. 'I will go with you.'

Ivan and I hid our anxiety over the weekend by digging in the garden. We pulled out weeds, moved plants and built a rock garden along the driveway. Lily lay in her pram on the

414

balcony, sleeping in the spring air. But despite our physical exertion, Ivan and I couldn't sleep on Sunday night. We tossed and turned and mumbled together. Finally we had to sip a glass of hot milk each and resign ourselves to only a few hours' rest. On Monday we drove to Irina and Vitaly's house and left Lily with Irina. When we got back into our car, I turned around to take one last look at my daughter bundled up in Irina's arms. I began to breathe sharply then, terrified that I may never see her again. I turned to Ivan and saw by the set of his jaw that he was thinking the same thing.

The Hotel Belvedere was long past its 1940s heyday. Ivan and I stepped out of the car and contemplated the neon sign over the doorway, the built-up grime on the walls, the scattered pot plants in the entrance. We looked in the dusty windows but could only see our own worried reflections staring back at us. Ivan clasped my hand and we stepped into the dark interior.

To our relief the hotel lobby was more welcoming than its exterior. The air was stuffy with mustiness and the lingering aroma of tobacco, but the worn chairs were clean, the tables polished and the tattered carpet vacuumed.

In the dining room a waitress stepped out from behind the counter and thrust a menu at us. I told her that we had come to meet someone. She shrugged as if meeting someone in a place like the Hotel Belvedere could only be a cover-up for something else, and her attitude made me agitated again. A young woman sitting by the window blinked at us then turned back to her book, more interested in the latest murder mystery than in a Russian couple clinging to each other in the middle of the room. Two tables from her an obese man was listening to a transistor radio, an earplug strung from his ear and a newspaper in his lap. His hair was shaved close to his skull so that his head looked small on his body. I turned to him but he stared back without recognition. The dining booths were down an aisle and out the back. I walked in front of Ivan, checking out the faded velour seats. I stopped as if I had struck an invisible wall. I felt him even before I saw him. I lifted my eyes to the last booth in the corner. He was aged, shrunken, staring back at me. I felt coldness on my cheek and remembered the first day he had come to our house and how I had hidden under a chair in the entranceway. The protruding, wide-spaced eyes, so unusual for a Japanese, were unmistakable.

The General stood up when he saw me, his lips trembling. He was shorter than me now, and no longer dressed in uniform but in a checked flannel shirt and a baseball jacket. However, he still stood erect and with dignity, his eyes flashing. 'Come,' he said, beckoning to me. 'Come.'

Ivan slid into the seat next to me, silent and respectful, understanding that the man must be someone I knew. The General sat down too, his hands placed in front of him on the table. For a long while none of us could speak.

The General took a deep breath. 'You are a grown woman,' he said. 'Beautiful but much changed. I can only tell it is you by your hair and your eyes.'

'How did you find me?' I asked, my voice barely audible.

'Your mother and I have been searching for you for a long time. But war and the Communists have prevented us from reaching you until now.'

'My mother?'

Ivan put his arm around me, protectively. The General glanced at him, as if seeing him for the first time.

'Your mother could not leave Russia to come here as easily as I. So I came to see you.'

My whole body began to shake. I couldn't feel my toes or my fingers. 'My mother is dead,' I cried, half standing. 'Tang took her from the train and shot her. She has been dead for years.'

'You must tell us this story clearly,' Ivan said. 'My wife has endured so much. We were told that her mother was

416

dead. That she was taken from the transportation train from Harbin and executed.'

The General's eyes widened at Ivan's speech and, just as it had on that first day in Harbin, his face reminded me of a toad.

'Anya, your mother was indeed taken from the train before she reached the Soviet Union. But not by Tang. By me.'

I sat down again and began to cry.

The General took my hands in his, a gesture more Russian than Japanese. 'You forget,' he said, 'I was an actor. I pretended to be Tang. I took your mother from the train and faked the execution.'

I looked at him through blurry eyes, this man of my childhood who was speaking to me. I listened in a daze when he told me that his name was Seiichi Mizutani and that he had been born in Nagasaki. His father had owned a theatre and when he was ten the family moved to Shanghai where he learned to speak fluent Mandarin. The General's family moved between cities frequently, entertaining the Japanese who were migrating to China in ever increasing numbers, and had even made a trip to Mongolia and Russia. But when the Japanese officially invaded China in 1937 the General's wife and daughter were sent back to Nagasaki and the General was forced to become a spy. The year before my mother was taken away he brought in his biggest catch, the most notorious leader of the Chinese resistance. Tang.

'I befriended him,' the General said, his eyes fixed on our clasped hands. 'He trusted me. He told me his dreams for China. He was passionate, he was bright, he was self-less. He used to always come to see me with whatever food he could find. "For you, my friend," he would say. "I stole this from the Japanese for you." Or when he couldn't bring food, he would bring a fan or a piece of poetry or a book. It was two years before I turned him in. Until then I used him to root out others.'

The General took a sip of water. His eyes were heavy and I saw the pain in them. 'I am responsible for turning him into the monster he became,' he said. 'My betrayal deformed him.'

I closed my eyes. I could never forgive Tang for what he had done, but at least I could finally understand why his hate had been so relentless.

After a while the General continued his story. 'The day I left your home we had been told nothing except that Japan had surrendered and that Nagasaki and Hiroshima had been destroyed. It was years before I had any idea of the extent of what had been done to my city: a third of it destroyed; hundreds of thousands of people killed and injured, and thousands who became sick later and died slow painful deaths. As I was departing from Harbin I met my aide. He told me that your mother had been questioned and that she was being transported back to the Soviet Union. I was sorry but decided that I could only save myself and that I must get back to Japan to discover the fate of my wife and daughter. However, on the road I had a terrible vision. I saw my wife, Yasuko, standing on a hill on the horizon, waiting for me. I moved closer to her and realised that she was cracked and dry like a broken clay pot. There was a little shadow standing in the crook of her arm, and the shadow was crying. It was Hanako, my daughter. The shadow came running to me but disappeared as soon as she touched me, burning into my side. I lifted my shirt and saw the flesh was peeling like a banana skin from my ribs. It was then that I understood they were dead and it was because I had been negligent with you and your mother that they had been killed. Perhaps the spirit of your father had taken revenge on me.

'I had to move quickly then. I knew the train would approach the border by evening. I was afraid and unsure of what to do. Each idea that came to me seemed doomed for failure. Then I remembered that Tang had worked with

418

the Soviets. I stole some rags from a farmhouse and used them to bind my hands. I stuffed them with dead mice to imitate the smell of decaying flesh that had hung around Tang ever since he had escaped from the camp. By impersonating him I was able to secure a plane to the border, where I convinced three of the Communist guards to come with me to intercept the train and execute your mother.'

The General stopped for a moment, pursing his lips. He was no longer the awesome figure of my childhood. He was a frail, trembling old man, weighed down by the heaviness of his memories. He glanced up at me as if he had heard my thoughts. 'It was probably the most outrageous plan I had ever made,' he said. 'And I was not sure if it would work or if it would only get your mother and myself killed. When I stormed into the prison carriage your mother's eyes opened wide and I knew that she recognised me. I had one of the guards drag her by the hair to the door, and she struggled and screamed like an actress. Up until the last moment, the guards thought we were going to shoot your mother. Instead I pushed her to the ground, wrestled the gun off the guards, shot out the lights of the car and then shot them.'

'Where did you go afterwards?' Ivan asked. I dug my fingers into his arm, grounding myself. He was the only thing that was solid. The walls of the dining room seemed to be shifting, closing in on me. My head was light. Everything was unreal. My mother. My mother. My mother. She was coming back to life before my eyes so many years after I had accepted her death.

'Your mother and I hurried back to Harbin as best we could,' the General said. 'The journey was treacherous and took us three days. Your mother's appearance was more conspicuous than mine and that put us in danger. By the time we reached the city the Pomerantsevs were gone and so were you. Your mother collapsed when we found the burned-out shell of your home. But a neighbour told us

419

that you had been rescued by the Pomerantsevs and sent to Shanghai.

'Your mother and I decided that we would go to Shanghai to find you. We couldn't go through Dairen because the Soviets were stopping the Russians who were trying to escape by sea. Instead we travelled south by rivers and canals or by land. At Peking we stopped in a house not far from the railway station, intending to travel to Shanghai by train the following morning. But it was there that I realised we were being followed. At first I thought I was imagining things, until I saw the shadow lingering behind your mother when she went to buy the tickets. The shadow of a man without hands. "If we go to Shanghai, we will lead him straight to her," I told your mother, for I knew Tang was no longer interested in only me.'

I squeezed Ivan's arm tighter when I realised how close my mother had come to reaching me. Peking was only a day away from Shanghai by train.

'The Japanese had always been interested in Mongolia,' the General said, his voice sounding more urgent, as if he were remembering the terror he had lived through. 'Part of my spy training had been to memorise the routes the European archaeologists had used to make their way through the Gobi Desert. And of course I knew about the Silk Road.

'I told your mother that we must head north to the border where we would lose Tang in the rugged terrain. For where we were going, a man without hands would perish, even a man as determined as him. My goal was to get your mother to Kazakhstan and then make the journey to Shanghai myself. At first your mother resisted but I told her: "Your daughter is safe in Shanghai. What use will you be to her dead?"

'It may seem that taking your mother to Kazakhstan was putting her into the hands of the Soviets. But the

420

art of the spy is to blend in, and Kazakhstan was in chaos after the war. Thousands of Russians had fled there to escape the Germans, and there were many people without identification papers.

'Experienced riders could have made the trip in three months, but the journey to Kazakhstan took us almost two years. We bought horses from a tribe of herders but we had to be careful not to push them beyond their endurance and we could only travel over the seven-month summers. As well as the Soviet presence on the border and Communist guerillas, we faced dust storms and miles of stony desert, and one of our guides died from a viper bite. If not for the few words of Mongolian I knew, and the hospitality of local tribes, your mother and I would have perished. I don't know what happened to Tang. I have never seen him since and he obviously never found you. I like to think that he died pursuing us in the mountains. It would have been the only fitting release for his tortured soul. Killing us would not have given him that.

'Your mother and I reached Kazakhstan wasted by the journey. We found rooms in the home of an old Kazak woman. When my strength returned, I told your mother that I would go back to China and search for you. "You were separated from your daughter because of me," I told her. "I did things during the war in order to protect my family, but in the end I could do nothing to save them. I must make amends or they will not rest in peace."

'"It's not because of you that I lost my daughter," your mother answered. "The Soviets would have transported us both to a camp after the war. At least I know that she is safe. Perhaps I too have a chance because of you."

'Your mother's words touched me deeply and I dropped to my knees and bowed to her. I realised then that there was a bond between us. Perhaps we had formed it during our journey when we depended on each other for survival. Perhaps it is something from a former life. I had such a bond with my wife, that is how I knew that she had died in Nagasaki.

'Although I could move more easily through China alone, I was delayed by the battles waged by Communist and Nationalist armies. There were bands still loyal to the warlords wandering the country, and every step was a dangerous one. Trains were easy targets, so I travelled by water or foot. All the time I pondered the question of how I would return that distance with a White Russian girl. But as it turned out I could not find you in that monster of a city known as Shanghai. I searched for Anya Kozlova in the Russian cabarets, the stores and restaurants. I had no picture of you. Only a description of a girl with ginger hair. It was as if you had vanished. Or perhaps your people were suspicious of me and wanted to protect one of their own. Finally, someone told me that he believed there was a Russian girl with red hair at a nightclub called the Moscow-Shanghai. I sped there, full of expectation. But the owner, an American woman, told me that I was mistaken. The redheaded girl was a cousin who had long since returned to the United States.'

Nausea rose up in my belly. My mind turned over the dates. The General must have reached Shanghai late in 1948, when I was sick with influenza and Dmitri was betraying me with Amelia. The General's story had made Tang seem more human; he was a man distorted by the cruelty that had been done to him. But Amelia was an abomination. If the General had found me in the days when Sergei was alive, she would have been glad to have seen the back of me. But her only motive for her actions after his death was her spite.

'The Communists were closing in on the city,' the General said. 'If I didn't leave soon I would be trapped there. I was torn between looking for you and getting back to your mother. For I had experienced another vision: your mother stretched out on a burning bed. She was in danger.

'Indeed, when I did make it back to Kazakhstan the old woman told me that your mother had become seriously ill with diphtheria, but she had improved with the boiled horse meat and milk tonics the woman had been administering. I dared not show my face to your mother until she had recovered. When I did finally go into the room where your mother was resting, she sat up and looked beyond me. When she saw that I had failed her, that I had not brought you back, she fell into a depression so deep I thought she might try to kill herself.

'"Don't despair," I told her. "I believe that Anya is alive and safe. When you are better we will head west to the Caspian Sea." The Soviet presence in Kazakhstan had increased and the border with China was more closely guarded. I thought that if your mother and I could escape to the West, we might be able to get out of Kazakhstan by boat. Your mother closed her eyes and said, "I don't know why, but I trust you. I believe you will help me find my daughter."'

The General stared into my eyes and said, 'I realised then that I loved her, and that I couldn't expect or deserve her love until I found you.'

I was momentarily struck dumb by this revelation. And yet there was another feeling tingling under my skin. Twice after my father's death I had heard his voice promise me that he would send someone. I had been blessed with many people who had helped me in my life, but I suddenly understood who my father had meant.

'How did you find me?' I asked.

'When we reached the sea, we found that the Soviets were patrolling the coastline as well. There seemed to be no escape, but the situation worked in our favour. We were given jobs in a hotel where the party-privileged took their summer vacations. It was while we were working there that we befriended a man named Yuri Vishnevsky. Through him we found out that the Russians from Shanghai had been evacuated to America. After a while your mother approached Vishnevsky to help us move to Moscow. She told him that Moscow had been the city of her family and that she had always wanted to see it. But I knew her real reason. In Kazakhstan we were cut off from the rest of the world, but in Moscow we would not be. There were tourists and business people, government officials and foreign teachers. People with permission to cross borders. People who could be bribed or pleaded with.

'Three years ago we moved to Moscow where, in between our jobs in a factory and a store, we devoted our lives to finding you. We spent our time around the Kremlin Palace, Red Square and the Pushkin Museum, pretending that we wanted to practise our English while we were really accosting tourists and foreign diplomats with details of you. Some of them agreed to help us but many turned away. We didn't hear from anyone for a long time, until one American woman contacted the Russian Society in San Francisco for us. They contacted the IRO and found out that an Anya Kozlova had been sent to Australia.'

The General stopped. Tears flowed out of his eyes and dripped down his cheeks. He made no attempt to wipe them away and blinked through them at me. 'Can you imagine the joy when we received such news? The American woman was very kind and contacted the Red Cross in Australia to see if they could help any further. One of their retired volunteers remembered a young woman who had come to see her in 1950. The girl was beautiful and her story had made an impression on her. The volunteer had been heartbroken that she could not help the girl search for her mother, and had kept her details on file, although it was against the rules.'

'Daisy Kent,' I said to Ivan. 'I always thought she wasn't willing to help me at all!' Perhaps her empathy had only appeared to me as reticence.

'We were so close to finding you,' the General said. 'Your

424

mother changed in the years she was without you. She lacked stamina and was chronically ill. But the moment she heard you were in Australia it was if she became a young, courageous woman again. She was determined that whatever it took we would find you.

'We contacted Vishnevsky, who by that time had become a good enough friend to be trusted. He agreed to get papers for me, but said that your mother must stay behind as a guarantee of my return. I arrived in Australia two weeks ago and the Red Cross booked me a room in a hotel. I managed to trace you to a migrant camp and then to Sydney, but nothing after that. The Registrar of Births, Deaths and Marriages would not tell me if you had married or not. That was confidential information, even in a situation such as mine. But I was determined not to fail as I had in Shanghai. One day I was sitting in the hotel room, full of despair, when a newspaper was delivered under the door. Without thinking I picked it up and flipped through it. I came across a column signed off by "Anya". I called the newspaper but the telephonist said the columnist's name was not Anya Kozlova but Anya Nakhimovsky. "Is she married?" I asked. The woman said that she believed the writer was married. I looked up your address in the telephone book. Something told me that I had found the Anya I was looking for, but I couldn't give away who I was or what I was doing to every Russian in Sydney. So I wrote you an anonymous note.'

There the General sighed, exhausted, and said, 'Anya, your mother and I have searched all these years for you. You have lived in our hearts every day. And now we have found you.'

TWENTY

Mother

The Red Army Chorus bellowed out the 'Volga Boat Song' in a rumble that sounded like thunder. From the cabin speakers, the beat was monotonous but the melody flooded my head. The chant blended with the hum of the plane and became a hymn. The exertion and valour in the singers' voices reminded me of the men who had dug my father's grave in Harbin. Such spirit seemed to belong much more to them than the Red Army. 'Mother,' I whispered to the clouds that skimmed underneath the plane like a carpet of sun-lit snow. 'Mother.' The tears stung my eyes. I grasped my fingers in my lap until they were purple. The clouds were celestial witnesses to the most significant event of my life. Twenty-three years earlier my mother and I had been parted and, in less than a day, we would see each other again.

I turned to Ivan, who was cradling Lily in the crook of his arm while trying to keep the tea in the plastic cup from spilling onto his lap. It wasn't an easy feat for a large man in a small space. He had barely touched the tray of garlic sausage, *pirogi* and dried fish. If we were in Australia, I would have teased him, asking him what kind of Russian he thought he was if he couldn't stomach such typical Slavic fare. But jokes like that were for a country like Australia and could not be repeated in the Soviet Union. I studied the faces of our fellow passengers, surly-looking men in badly cut suits and a handful of mask-faced women. We didn't know who they were but we knew to be careful.

'Shall I take Lily?' I asked Ivan. He nodded, lifting her through the gap between the tray and his leg, not letting go until he was sure I had her firmly in my grasp. Lily looked at me with her jewel-like eyes and pouted, as if she were blowing me a kiss. I stroked her cheek. It was something I did when I needed to replenish my faith in miracles.

I thought of the washing basket on the lounge in the family room, spilling over with Lily's summer clothes, bibs, towels and pillowcases. It was the only mess we had left behind and I found it comforting that we hadn't left the house perfectly tidy. It made it seem that it was still our home, that there were things left undone that would need to be attended to when we returned. For I had understood the look that passed between Ivan and myself when we locked the front door before leaving for the airport: there was a risk that we wouldn't be coming back.

When the General told me that my mother was alive, the news had filled me with a joy equalled only by the rapture I had experienced when Lily was born. But four months had passed since we last saw the General and there had been no word since. He had warned us that this would be the case. 'Don't try to contact me. Just make sure you are in Moscow on February the second.' There was no chance of speaking to my mother before leaving – there wasn't a telephone in her building, and there was the problem of surveillance. We hadn't been sure what to expect from the Soviet embassy, so the long application process and the eight-week wait for our visas had been agony, like pushing ourselves through a sieve. Even when the visas were issued without questions and I found myself at Heathrow Airport, boarding the plane bound for Moscow, I still wasn't sure if my nerves had made it through to the other side all in one piece.

The stewardess wiped her hands on her crumpled uniform and poured me another cup of lukewarm tea. Most of the attendants were older women, but this one made no attempt to straighten the strands of grey hair that were bulging from under her ill-fitting cap. She didn't smile when I thanked her. She simply turned her back.

They couldn't afford to be friendly to foreigners, I reminded myself. Conversing too much with me could get her time in prison. I turned back to the clouds and thought about the General. In the three days he had spent with us, I had hoped that he would have started to seem more like a normal man and less of an enigma. After all, he ate, drank and slept like a mortal. He answered my questions about my mother – her health, her living conditions, her daily life – with frankness. I was horrified to hear that they didn't have hot water in the apartment, even in winter, and that my mother was suffering pains in her legs. But I was overjoyed when the General told me that my mother had some good female friends in Moscow who would take her to the *banya* for a steam bath when she needed some relief from the pain. It reminded me that I'd had Irina, Ruselina and Betty to stand by me through the worst times of my life. But I was too afraid to ask the General about his relationship with my mother and he never answered the question I asked him at Sydney Airport: 'When we take my mother out of Russia, are you coming too?' He kissed Ivan and me, and shook our hands, leaving us with the words: 'You will see me one more time.' I watched him disappear through the departure doors, an old man withered by time but with a proud march-like step, and realised that he had remained as much of a mystery to me as ever.

Lily gurgled. Her brow was furrowed, as if she was reading my thoughts. I rocked her to reassure her. My worst moments in the months leading up to the trip were putting her to bed and kissing her soft cheek, knowing that I would soon be taking her from the safety of Australia and placing her in danger. I would give my life for Lily's any time without hesitation, and yet I couldn't bring myself to make the trip without her. 'I want Lily to come with us,' I told Ivan one night when we were getting into bed. I prayed for him to become angry with me and tell me that I was crazy. I hoped he would insist that Lily stay with Irina and Vitaly. Instead he leaned over and turned the light back on, studying my face in its glare. He nodded solemnly and said, 'This family must never be separated.'

There was a 'clack' and the Red Army Chorus was cut off mid-verse. The pilot's voice echoed around the cabin. *Tavarishshi.* Comrades, we are about to make our descent into Moscow. Please prepare yourselves by fastening your seat belts and returning your seats to the upright position.'

I held my breath and watched the plane sink into the mass of clouds. The light changed from copper to grey and the sky disappeared, as if we had plunged into the ocean. The cabin rocked from side to side and flecks of snow lashed against the windows. I couldn't see anything. There was a dipping sensation in my stomach and for a few weightless minutes it seemed as if the engines had stopped and the plane was falling. Lily, who had been good the whole way from London, started to cry from the change in pressure.

The woman in the seat opposite leaned over and said to her in a cheery voice, 'Why you cry, you pretty baby? All is well.' Lily fell quiet and smiled. The woman intrigued me. Her French perfume was stronger than the fumes left by the Bulgarian cigarettes the men had been smoking, and her Slavic skin was beautifully madeup. But she couldn't have been a typical Soviet woman as they weren't able to leave the country. Was she a government official? A KGB agent? Or the mistress of someone important? I hated the feeling that we couldn't trust anyone, that because of the Cold War no one's kindness could be taken at face value.

Gaps appeared in the clouds and through them I saw snow-covered fields and birch trees. The slipping sensation gave way to another, stronger feeling, that of being drawn into a magnet. My toes stretched downwards, as if I were being dragged to the ground by a force too big to imagine. I knew what that force was: Russia. Gogol's words, read so long ago in the garden in Shanghai, came back to me: 'What is there in it, in that song? What is it that calls and weeps, and grips our heart? . . . Russia! What do you want from me? What is that unattainable and mysterious bond between us?'

Moscow was a fortress city, and I understood how apt that image was. It was the last wall standing between myself and my mother. I hoped that, armed with my husband and child and the determination born of years of pain, I had the courage to face it.

The clouds disappeared like a curtain being whisked away and I could see the plains of snow and the murky sky. The airport was beneath us but I couldn't see the terminal, only rows of snowploughs, and men in thick jackets and fur earmuffs standing by them. The runway was as black as slate. Despite Aeroflot's reputation and the icy conditions, the pilot brought the plane to the ground with the gracefulness of a swan landing on a lake.

When the plane came to a stop, the stewardess told us to head for the exit. There was a crush of people, and Ivan took Lily from me so he could hold her above the mass of travellers pushing against each other to get to the plane door. A gust of scouring wind burst through the cabin. When I approached the exit and saw the terminal building with its sooty windows and the barbed wire on its outer walls, I knew that the sun and warmth of my adopted country were far away. The air was so cold it was blue. It stung my face and made my nose run. Ivan pushed Lily further inside his coat to protect her from the bitter wind. I tucked my head down and kept my eyes on the stairs. My boots were fur-lined but as soon as I stepped onto the tarmac and headed towards the terminal bus, my feet began to freeze. I experienced another deeper sensation too. When I touched the ground in Russia, I knew that I was completing a journey begun long ago. I had returned to the land of my father.

Inside Sheremetievo Airport's dingy, fluorescent-lit arrivals area, the reality of what Ivan and I were about to do started to dawn on me with a lead-like sense of dread. I heard the General whisper in my ear: 'You mustn't make a slip. Everyone who comes into contact with you will be questioned about your behaviour. The maid at your hotel, the taxi drivers, the woman you pay roubles to for your cheap postcards. Take it as a matter of course that your room will be bugged.'

In my naivety I had protested, 'We are not spies. We are just a family trying to reunite.'

'If you are from the West, you are a spy, or at least a bad influence, as far as the KGB is concerned. And what you are planning to do will be looked upon as the highest treason,' the General warned me.

I'd been practising for months to keep my face still, to answer questions without hesitation and in a succinct manner, but as soon as I saw the soldiers near the exit gate wearing their guns slung on their backs and the customs officer parading his German shepherd, my legs turned to jelly and my heart pounded so loudly in my chest that I was terrified I would give us away. When we left Sydney on Australia Day, the sun-bronzed customs officer had given us a miniature flag each and wished us a 'happy holiday'.

Ivan passed Lily to me and we took a place in line behind the handful of foreigners from the flight. He reached into his coat pocket for our passports and opened them to the pages with our new surname, Nickham. 'Don't deny your Russian heritage, if asked,' the General had advised us, 'but don't draw attention to it either.'

431

'Yeah, Nickham's a lot easier to say than Nakhim-ov-sky,' the moon-faced clerk at the Australian Registry of Births, Deaths and Marriages had laughed when we gave him the form for a request for a name change. 'A lot of you New Australians are doing it. Makes it easier all round. Lilliana Nickham. She'll be some sort of actress, I'm sure.'

We didn't tell the clerk that we were anglicising our name so we could get our visas passed through the Russian embassy without problems. 'Anya, the days of Stalin's purges of the descendants of nobility are over and you and Ivan are Australian citizens,' the General had explained. 'But drawing attention to yourselves could put your mother in danger. Even under Brezhnev, if we admit to having relatives abroad we can end up in a mental asylum, to cleanse us of any capitalist ideas we may have absorbed.'

'*Nyet! Nyet!*' The German man in front of us was having some sort of dispute with the customs officer in her glass booth. She pointed to his letter of invitation, but each time she gave it back to him he would push it through the slot of her window again. After a few minutes of this stalemate exchange, she waved her hand impatiently and let him through. Then it was our turn.

The customs officer read our papers and examined every page of our passports. She frowned at our pictures and stared at the scar on Ivan's face. I clutched Lily close to me, drawing comfort from her warmth. I tried not to lower my eyes – the General had said it would be taken as a sign of deception – and I pretended that I was studying the row of party flags which took up an entire wall. I prayed that he was right and we shouldn't try to pass ourselves off as Soviets – even with Vishnevsky's inside help the General told us he couldn't get us the residency papers, and even if he could, if questioned it would be clear that we weren't native Muscovites.

The customs officer held up Ivan's passport and stared from it to him as if she were trying to unnerve him. We could hardly deny our Slavic eyes or our Russian cheek-bones, but some of the British and American foreign correspondents in Moscow were children of Russian immigrants. What was so unusual about us? The officer frowned and called over her colleague, a young man with clean-cut features, who was sorting through some papers behind her. White spots began to dance before my eyes. Was it possible we weren't even going to make it past the first point? The male officer asked Ivan if Nickham was his real name and what was his address in Moscow. But he asked the question in Russian. It was a trick and Ivan didn't miss a beat.

'Of course,' he answered in Russian, and gave the address of our hotel. I saw that the General had been right. Compared to the sandpaper voice barking flight details over the loudspeaker, Ivan's Russian was an elegant, pre-Soviet language that hadn't been heard in Russia for fifty years. He sounded like an English person reading Shakespeare or a foreigner who had learned his Russian from second-hand textbooks.

The male customs officer growled and grabbed the ink pad from his comrade. With a quick succession of loud bangs he stamped our papers and handed them back to Ivan, who calmly gathered them into his travel wallet and thanked the officers. But the woman officer had one final thing to say to me when I passed: 'If you're from a warm climate, why do you bring such a young baby to this country in winter? Do you want her to die of cold?'

The window seal in the taxi had a leak in it and I pressed my arm over the hole to prevent the whistling draught from blowing on Lily. I hadn't seen a car in worse condition since Vitaly bought his first Austin. The seats were as hard as wooden planks and the dashboard was a tangle of wires and jangling screws held together by cellulose tape. When he needed to indicate, the driver opened the window and thrust his hand into the freezing air. Most of the time he didn't bother.

At the airport exit, the traffic was jammed. Ivan pulled Lily's shawl around her nose and mouth to block out the built-up exhaust fumes. The driver patted his pocket, and then sprang out of the car. I saw that he was attaching the windscreen wipers. He jumped back in the car and slammed the door. 'I'd forgotten I'd taken them off,' he said. I looked at Ivan, who shrugged. I could only assume the driver had taken the wipers off because he was afraid they'd be stolen.

A soldier tapped on the window and ordered the driver to move to the side of the road. I noticed the other taxis and cars were doing the same. A black limousine with its curtains drawn glided past like a sinister hearse. The rest of the cars started up their engines again and followed in its wake. A word hung in the air of the taxi but none of us voiced it. *Nomenklatura*. The party-privileged.

Through the water-spotted window I could see that the highway was flanked by birch trees. I stared at their thin white trunks and the snow balanced on their bare limbs. The trees were like creatures from a fairytale, mythical beings in a story my father might have told me before bedtime when I was a girl. Although it was early afternoon, the sun was slipping away and darkness was falling. After a few miles, the trees started to give way to blocks of apartments. The buildings were drab with small windows and no embellishments. Some of them were half finished, with cranes perched on their roofs. Every so often we would pass a snow-covered playground or courtyard, but more often than not the buildings were crammed side by side, the snow around them stained and icy. For miles they stretched on, exhibiting a uniform grimness, and all the while I was aware that somewhere in this city of concrete my mother was waiting for me.

Moscow was a city of layers, its pattern of growth like the rings of a tree. Each mile took us deeper into the past. In an open plaza, watched over by a towering statue of Lenin, people were standing in a line outside a store where the clerks were adding up the totals on abacuses. A grocer sat by his stock, which he kept under a plastic sheet lest his potatoes freeze in the bitter cold. A man or woman, I couldn't tell, bundled up in a padded coat and felt boots, was selling ice-cream. An old babushka held up the traffic, limping across the road with an armload of bread and cabbage. Further on, a mother and her child, wrapped like a precious parcel in a woollen hat and mittens, waited to cross the street. A trolley bus rumbled by, its sides caked in mud. I studied the occupants, who were barely visible through their layers of scarves and fur.

These are my people, I thought, and tried to take in the truth of it. I loved Australia and it had loved me, but somehow I felt drawn to the people around me, as if we had all been cut from the same stone.

Ivan tapped me on the arm and pointed out the front window. Moscow was transforming before our eyes into charming cobblestoned avenues and majestic buildings with pastel walls, gothic apartment buildings and Art Deco street lamps. Draped in whiteness, they were pure romance. Whatever the Soviets had to say about the Tsars, the buildings erected by the monarchy remained things of beauty, despite the climate and neglect, while the Soviet buildings that loomed over them were already suffering from peeling paint and chipped masonry.

I tried to keep the distaste off my face when I realised that the block of glass and cement that the taxi driver had pulled up in front of was our hotel. The monstrous building dwarfed everything around it and was incongruous against the backdrop of the golden domes of the cathedrals within the Kremlin. It was as if they had deliberately tried to make something awful. I would have preferred to have stayed in the Hotel Metropol, magnificent in all its imperialist glory. The travel agent had tried to persuade us out of the hotel the General had told us to book by showing us pictures of

435

the Metropol's lavish fittings and the famous stained-glass ceiling. But it was also the KGB's favourite haunt to watch rich foreigners and we were not in Moscow for a holiday.

The foyer of our hotel was artificial marble and red carpet. It stank of cheap cigarettes and dust. We had followed the General's instructions to the letter and, although we were a day early, I searched every face in the lobby for him. I told myself not to be disappointed when I couldn't find him among the sombre men reading newspapers or loitering around the magazine stand. A dour-faced woman looked up from her cramped space behind the reception desk. She had startling pencilled-in eyebrows and a mole on her forehead as big as a coin.

'Mr and Mrs Nickham. And our daughter, Lily,' Ivan said to her.

The woman flashed a gold-toothed grimace that wasn't a smile and asked us for our passports. While Ivan filled in the registration form, I asked the woman as casually as I could manage if there were any messages for us. She checked our room box and returned with an envelope. I started to open it and noticed that the woman was watching me. But I couldn't take the envelope away half-opened, that would have looked unnatural. So I hoisted Lily higher onto my chest, as if she were becoming heavy, and made my way over to a chair. My heart thumped with anticipation, but when I opened the piece of paper in the envelope I found that it was a sightseeing itinerary from Intourist. I felt like a child who wanted a bicycle for Christmas and got a school case instead. I had no idea what the itinerary meant. From the corner of my eye, I could see that the receptionist was still staring at me, so I slipped the envelope into my bag and lifted Lily into the air. 'How's my pretty girl?' I cooed at her. 'How's my pretty girl with the wiggly nose?'

When Ivan had completed the form, the receptionist handed him our key and called over the bellboy, an elderly man with bowed legs. He pushed the trolley with our suitcases on it in such an erratic manner that I began to suspect he was drunk, until I noticed that the trolley had a wheel missing. He pressed the elevator button and then leaned against the wall, exhausted. There was another man, about the same age, with bags under his eyes and holes in the elbows of his cardigan, sitting behind a table of dusty trinkets and matroshka dolls. There was a smell about him, like garlic mixed with some sort of antiseptic. He examined every inch of us, including our luggage, as if he were trying to lock our image into his memory. In any other country I would have assumed he was an old man trying to supplement his pension, but after the General's stories about the KGB, the man's stern-faced curiosity sent a shiver through me.

Our room was small by Western standards and unbearably hot. The tasselled lampshade dangling from the ceiling threw an orange glow over the worn carpet. I inspected the steam heater under the window and discovered it was the kind that couldn't be adjusted. A man's tinny voice was praising the Soviet constitution. Ivan stepped around the bed to turn the radio off and found that there was no on-off switch. The best he could do was turn the volume down to static level.

'Look at this,' I said, pulling aside the lace curtains. Our room faced the Kremlin. The pink-brick walls and the Byzantine churches glistened in the fading light. The Kremlin was where the Tsars used to be wed and crowned. I thought of the black limousine we'd seen at the airport earlier and remembered that new Tsars resided there now.

While Ivan sorted out our bags, I laid Lily on the bed, undoing her heavy clothes and changing her into a cotton jumpsuit. I took our scarves and hats out of her basket and secured it between the pillows of the bed before laying her in it. She blinked her eyes sleepily. I stroked her tummy until she fell asleep, then sat back and watched her. The pattern on the bedcover caught my eye: intertwined

437

branches, like vines, with pairs of doves perched on them. I remembered Marina's grave in Shanghai, with the two engraved doves on her headstone, one fallen in an attitude of death, the other standing loyally by. Then I thought about the itinerary. My stomach heaved. My mother had been a day away from me in Peking before she had been thwarted by Tang. The General had come right to the door of the Moscow-Shanghai before Amelia had sent him away. What if, just as I was about to see my mother, the KGB had caught wind of our plans and had taken her away to a labour camp? This time for real.

I looked up at Ivan. 'Something's gone wrong. They're not coming,' I mouthed to him. He shook his head and stepped towards the bed, turning the volume on the radio up a notch. I took the itinerary from my handbag and handed it to him. He read it once, then again with a puzzled look on his face, as if he were trying to find clues in it. He gestured for me to follow him to the bathroom, and after he had turned on the tap, he asked who had given it to me. We had not booked an Intourist guide, although guides were compulsory for foreigners. I told him I was afraid that the itinerary had something to do with the KGB.

Ivan rubbed my shoulder. 'Anya,' he said, 'you're tired and you're thinking with an overheated brain. The General said the second. That's not until tomorrow.'

There were circles under his eyes and I reminded myself that the situation was a strain for him too. He had spent days and nights putting his business affairs in order to make things easier for his partner while he was away, and in case he didn't come back. Ivan was willing to sacrifice everything for my happiness.

I felt the months of waiting bear down on me. With only a few hours left till our scheduled meeting date, it wasn't the time to lose faith. And yet, the nearer the time came, the more doubtful I felt. 'I don't deserve you,' I said to Ivan, a tremble in my voice. 'Or Lily. I'm not a deserving mother. Lily might get the flu and die.'

Ivan studied my face. His mouth broke into a smile. 'You Russian women always think like that. You're a beautiful mother and Lily's a tubby, healthy baby. Remember after she was born, you and Ruselina rushed off to the doctor because she "didn't cry much and slept right through the night" and he examined her and said, "Half your luck."'

I smiled and leaned my head against his shoulder. Be strong, I told myself, and went over the General's plan again in my mind. He had said that he was going to get us out through East Germany. When he first told me that I had visions of guards in watchtowers, bloodhounds, tunnels and being shot at as we made a run for the Wall, but the General shook his head. 'Vishnevsky will get you a permit to cross the border, but you will still have to be wary of the KGB. Even the *Nomenklatura* are watched.' I wondered who this Vishnevsky was, and what my mother and the General had done to make friends with such a highly placed official. Or was it possible that there was some compassion behind the Iron Curtain?

'Thank God I married you,' I said to Ivan.

He put the itinerary on the basin shelf and clicked his fingers, his smile growing wider. 'It's a plan,' he whispered. 'Weren't you the one who told me that we are in the care of a master spy? Have faith, Anya. Have faith. It's a plan. And a good one too, knowing the General.'

The next morning, while we sat in the hotel restaurant for breakfast, I wavered between hopefulness and anguish about what the day would bring. Ivan, on the other hand, seemed calm, tracing the grain of the table with his finger. The waitress automatically brought us scrambled eggs and two pieces of toast, although the Russian breakfast of black bread, dried fish and cheese looked more appetising. Lily chewed the collar of her playsuit while we waited for the

439

waitress to warm her bottle in a saucepan. When she returned, I dripped a bit onto my wrist. It was the perfect temperature and I thanked the waitress. The girl wasn't afraid to smile, and said to me, 'Russians, we love babies.'

By nine o'clock we were in the foyer, coats, gloves and hats bundled on the seat beside us. Lily was sleepy after her meal and Ivan tucked her up in his coat. Our reasons for going along with the Intourist guide were precarious, but it seemed our best chance for the moment. Ivan believed that the General had arranged the tour to throw the KGB off our scent, to make us look like normal tourists, and that we would meet my mother somewhere along the way. I, on the other hand, couldn't help worrying that the tour was a trick by the KGB to get information out of us.

'Mr and Mrs Nickham?'

We turned around to see a woman in a grey dress, with a fur coat slung over her arm, smiling at us. 'I am Vera Otova. Your Intourist guide,' she said. The woman had the upright bearing of someone who had been trained in the army. She was the right age to have fought in the last war, perhaps forty-seven or forty-eight. Ivan and I stood up to shake her hand. I felt fraudulent. The woman smelled of apple blossom perfume and her hands were manicured. She seemed nice enough, but I couldn't be sure whether she was friend or foe. The General had told us, if questioned, to deny everything about our plan. 'Anyone I send to you will know who you are. There will be no need for you to say anything. Beware. They could be a KGB agent.'

It was going to be up to Vera Otova to let us know whose side she was on.

Ivan cleared his throat. 'I'm sorry that we overlooked booking a guide when we left Sydney,' he said, taking Vera's coat and helping her into it. 'Our travel agent must have done it for us.'

A dark look washed over Vera's face, but was quickly

dispelled again by her gap-toothed smile. 'Yes, you must have a guide for Moscow,' she said, perching her woollen beret on her head. 'It makes life much easier.'

I knew that was a lie. It was necessary for foreigners to have guides so they wouldn't go to places they weren't supposed to and see what the government didn't want them to see. The General had told us about it. The tours were set for museums, cultural events and war memorials. We would never get to see the real victims of Russia's corrupt Communism: chronic alcoholics dying in the snow, old women begging outside train stations, homeless families, children who should be in school digging up roads. But the lie didn't make me dismiss Vera as a fake immediately. What else could she have said in a crowded hotel foyer?

Ivan helped me into my coat and then bent towards the seat, lifting Lily up out of the folds of his coat.

'A baby?' Vera turned to me, her smile fixed on her face. 'No one told me that you were bringing a baby.'

'She's a good baby,' said Ivan, bouncing Lily in his arms. Lily, suddenly wide awake, giggled and pulled his hat towards her mouth so that she could chew on it.

Vera's eyes had a squint to them. I couldn't tell what she was thinking when she touched Lily's cheek. 'A gorgeous baby. Such beautiful eyes. The colour of my pin,' she said, pointing to the amber brooch in the shape of a butterfly that she wore on her collar. 'But we might have to make some . . . modifications to our program.'

'We don't want to go anywhere we can't take Lily,' I said, slipping on my gloves. My remark seemed to unnerve Vera; her eyes grew wide and her face flushed. But she quickly recovered. 'Of course,' she said. 'I quite understand. It was the ballet I was thinking about. They don't allow children under five inside the auditorium.'

'Perhaps I can stay behind with Lily,' suggested Ivan. 'You can take Anya. She would love to see a ballet.'

Vera bit her lip. I could see she was trying to work something out in her mind. 'No, that would never do,' she said. 'You can't come to Moscow and not see the Bolshoi.' She fiddled with the wedding ring on her finger. 'If you don't mind, while we are at the Kremlin I'll put you with a group tour and I'll go see if I can arrange something.'

'You let me know whatever you need to *arrange* things,' Ivan said as we followed Vera towards the hotel doors.

Vera's heels tapped on the floor tiles in a staccato rhythm. 'Your travel agent said that you both speak excellent Russian but I don't mind to speak in English,' she said, her chin disappearing as she wrapped her long scarf several times around her neck. 'You tell me which language you prefer. You can practise your Russian if you like.'

Ivan touched Vera's arm. 'I say that when in Russia do as the Russians do.'

Vera smiled. But I couldn't tell if it was because she was charmed by Ivan or because she had won some sort of victory.

'You wait in here,' she said. 'I'll get a taxi to come to the door.'

We watched Vera rush outside and say something to the doorman. A few moments later a taxi pulled up. The driver got out and opened the passenger doors. Vera signalled to us to come out and get inside the car.

'What was that all about?' I asked Ivan when we stepped into the revolving door. 'All that stuff about "You let me know whatever you need to arrange things."'

Ivan linked his arm with mine and whispered, 'Roubles. I think what Madame Otova was talking about was a bribe.'

The entrance of the Tretyakov Gallery was as calm as a monastery. Vera passed a voucher to the woman in the booth and held up our tickets to us. 'Let's put our things away in the cloakroom,' she said, waving for us to follow her down a flight of stairs.

442

The cloakroom attendants wore shabby blue coats over their dresses and scarves on their heads. They were bustling between the rows of hangers with armloads of bulky overcoats and hats. I was shocked at how old they were; I wasn't used to seeing women in their eighties still working. They turned and looked at us, and nodded when they saw Vera. We handed our coats and hats over to them. One of the women saw Lily's face poking through the shawl and jokingly handed me a number for her. 'Leave her,' she said. 'I'll take care of her.' I looked into the woman's face. Although her mouth was turned down, like those of the other attendants, merriness shone in her eyes. 'I can't. She's a "valuable",' I smiled. The woman reached out and tickled Lily's chin, nodding.

Vera took her eyeglasses from her handbag and studied the special exhibitions programme. She indicated the entrance to the gallery, and Ivan and I were about to head in that direction when one of the attendants called out. '*Tapochki! Tapochki!*' She was shaking her head and pointing to our boots. I looked down and saw that the snow on our boots had melted into puddles around our feet. The woman handed us each a pair of *tapochki*, felt overshoes. I slipped mine on over my boots, feeling like a naughty child. I looked down at Vera's shoes. Her dry leather pumps looked as good as new.

In the main foyer a group of schoolchildren were lining up in front of a plaque, reading it while their teacher looked on with the kind of reverence a priest displays when he puts on his robes. A Russian family waited behind the children, curious about the plaque too, and were followed by a young couple. Vera asked us if we wanted to read the plaque. Ivan and I said yes. When it was our turn we stepped closer to the plaque and I saw that it was a dedication for the museum. As well as acknowledging the museum's founder, Pavel Tretyakov, the plaque announced: 'After the dark days of the Tsars and after the Great

Revolution, the museum was greatly able to expand its collection and make many masterpieces available "to the people".'

I felt the hairs on the back of my neck bristle. What it meant was that after the Bolsheviks cut the throats of the noble and middle-class families or sent them to die in labour camps, they stole their paintings. The hypocrisy made my blood boil. Those families had paid the artists for their paintings. Could the Soviets say the same? There was no mention on the plaque that Tretyakov had been a wealthy merchant whose lifelong dream was *to make art available to the people*. I wondered if sometime in the future, the authorities would try to rewrite Tretyakov's background and make him out to have been a working-class revolutionary. My father's parents and sisters had been slaughtered by the Bolsheviks, and Tang's partner in separating me from my mother had been a Soviet officer. Such things were not easy to forget.

I glanced at the Russian family and the faces of the young couple. They were expressionless. I wondered if they were thinking the same things I was, but, like Ivan and I, had to keep quiet in order to protect themselves. I'd thought I had returned to my father's Russia, but I saw that wasn't the case. My father's Russia was only a remnant. A relic from a lost era.

Vera ushered us into a hall full of icons. '"The Virgin of Vladimir" is the oldest in the collection,' she said, leading us towards a depiction of the Virgin holding her child. 'It arrived in Kiev from Constantinople in the twelfth century.' I read on the plaque underneath that the icon had been painted over many times, but had kept its original despairing expression. Lily was quiet in my arms, fascinated by the colours around her, but I found it hard to feign interest in the artwork. I scanned the groups of elderly women in the museum's guide uniform who were sitting along the walls. My eyes were wide and watchful, looking for my

444

mother. She would be fifty-six years old. I wondered how much she would have changed since I last saw her.

Ivan asked Vera about the origins and themes of the icons, and slipped in questions about her personal life. Had she always lived in Moscow? Did she have any children?

'What is he up to?' I asked myself. I stopped in front of Rubliov's icon of winged angels to listen to her answers. 'I've only worked as a guide with Intourist since my sons went to university,' Vera told him. 'Until then I was a housewife.' I noticed Vera gave away little of herself when she answered his questions and she didn't ask Ivan anything about us or Australia in return. Was that because it wasn't wise to have such conversations with Westerners? Or was it because she already knew what was important to know?

I walked impatiently on, and noticed through an arch that the guide a few rooms down was looking in my direction. She had dark hair and long, narrow hands, the kind you find on tall women. Her eyes glinted like glass in the light. My throat constricted. I edged my way towards her but as I got closer I saw that the dark hair on her head was just a scarf and that one of her eyes was clouded with a cataract. The other was pale blue. She couldn't be my mother. The guide frowned at my stare and I quickly looked up at the portrait of Alexandra Struiskaya, whose gentle expression seemed too lifelike for comfort. Flustered by my mistake, I stumbled on through the gallery, stopping to examine the portraits of Pushkin, Tolstoy and Dostoyevsky. All of them seemed to be regarding me with a kind of anxious foreboding. I turned to the paintings of the noble-men and women for reassurance. They were dignified, elegant, dreamy. The colours floated up around them like magical clouds.

'What happened to you after your portraits were completed? Did you know what the fate of your sons and daughters would be?' I secretly asked them.

I waited by Valentin Serov's 'Girl with Peaches' for Ivan and Vera to catch up with me. I'd seen the picture in a book but was amazed at the sincerity the painting projected when I stood before it in real life. 'Look, Lily,' I said, holding her so that she faced the painting. 'You'll be as beautiful as that girl when you grow up.' The image of the girl's radiant youth, her carefree eyes, the brightness of the room in which she sat, brought memories flooding back of the house in Harbin. I closed my eyes, frightened that I might begin to cry. Where was my mother?

'I can see Mrs Nickham has a love of old art,' I heard Vera say to Ivan. 'But I think she will find that the best art in this museum belongs to the Soviet era.'

I opened my eyes and looked at her. Was she smiling or squinting at me? She led the way to the Soviet paintings and I followed dutifully, looking back at the 'Girl with Peaches' one more time. After all the ugliness I'd seen on my first day in Moscow, I could have stood in front of that painting for hours.

I did my best not to grimace while Vera spoke rapturously about the flat, lifeless art in the Soviet section. I thought if she used the terms 'social message', 'poetic simplicity' or 'the people of the revolutionary movement' once more, I would walk out of the museum. But of course I couldn't. Too much was riding on my good behaviour. Still, I found that the more I looked around the rooms, the more I found paintings that made me put aside my prejudices and acknowledge what I thought was good. There was a picture called 'Students' by Konstantin Istomin which caught my eye. Two delicate young women, caught in the dusk of a short winter's day, gazing at the fading light from their apartment window.

Vera stepped up behind me. Was I mistaken or did she click her heels? 'You like works that show femininity. And you seem to like dark-haired women,' she said. 'Come this way, Mrs Nickham, I think there is something in the next room which will be very much to your taste.'

446

I followed her, keeping my eyes to the floor, wondering if I had given myself away. I hoped that I would be able to express myself appropriately when she showed me another piece of Soviet propaganda.

'Here we are,' Vera said, positioning me in front of a canvas. I looked up and gasped. I found myself face to face with the close-up portrait of a mother holding her child. The first things I thought of were warmth and gold. The woman's fine brow, the way she wore her hair in a low chignon, her chiselled features, were those of my mother. She looked gentle, but also strong and courageous. The child in her arms had gingery hair and pouting lips. The image of me as a baby.

I turned to Vera and stared into her eyes, my questions too obvious to voice. What is the meaning of all this? What is it you are trying to say to me?

If Vera was setting out some sort of puzzle for us, then the pieces weren't coming together fast enough. I lay on the hotel bed, my back curved into the sag, and stared at the clock on the wall. Five o'clock. February the second was almost over and there was still no sign of my mother or the General. I watched the light fade into blackness through the grimy window. If I don't see my mother at the ballet tonight, then it's all over, I thought. My last hope is gone.

My throat tingled. I reached for the jug on the bedside table and poured myself a glass of the metallic-tasting water. Lily was curled up beside me, her fists bunched by the side of her head as if she were holding onto something. When Vera dropped us off at the hotel after the gallery, she asked me if I had anything 'to keep Lily quiet' during tonight's performance. I told her that I would bring her dummy and give her a dose of baby Panadol to help her sleep, though I had no intention of doing either. I would feed her, and that was it. If Lily started crying, I would sit in the foyer

447

with her. The way Vera was insisting on the ballet made me uneasy.

Ivan was sitting by the window, scribbling in his notebook. I opened the bedside drawer and pulled out the guest folder. A faded brochure for a resort on the Caspian Sea fell into my lap, along with a crinkled envelope with the hotel logo on it. I took the stub of pencil that was attached to the folder by a piece of twine and wrote on the envelope: 'Vera's waited too long to give me news of my mother. She doesn't have a heart if she can't understand what I'm going through. I don't believe she's on our side.'

I pushed my hair from my face, stood up on wobbly legs and handed my note to Ivan. He took it from me and, while he was reading it, I glanced down at what he had been writing in his notebook. 'I thought I was Russian, but in this country I don't know what I am. If you asked me a day ago what were the typical characteristics of the Russian people, I would have said their passion and their warm-heartedness. But there is no backslapping gregariousness in this place. Only cowering, stooping people with eyes full of fear. Who are these ghosts around me . . . ?'

Ivan wrote under my words on the envelope: 'I've been trying to figure her out all day. I think the painting was her way of trying to tell you. She probably can't talk because we are under surveillance. I don't think she's with the KGB.'

'Why?' I mouthed to him.

He pointed to his heart.

'Yes, I know,' I said. 'You're a good judge of character.'

'I married you,' he smiled. Ivan tore the page he had been writing on from his notebook and, together with the envelope, ripped them into tiny pieces which he carried to the toilet and flushed away.

'This is an impossible way to live,' he said, half to me and half to the hissing cistern. 'No wonder they look so unhappy.'

*   *   *

448

Vera was waiting for us in the hotel foyer. She stood up when she saw us step out of the elevator. Her coat was beside her but she'd kept the rose-coloured scarf over her hair. The apple blossom scent had given way to something stronger, lily of the valley, and I noticed a slash of lipstick on her lips when she smiled. I tried to smile back but it came out as a wince. I couldn't keep up the show. This is ridiculous, I told myself. If I don't see my mother at the Bolshoi, I'm going to confront her.

Vera must have noticed my irritable mood because she glanced away from me and spoke to Ivan. 'I think you and Mrs Nickham will enjoy tonight's performance very much,' she said. 'This is Yuri Grigorovich's *Swan Lake*. Ekaterina Maximova is the principal dancer. People are desperate to see this performance, which is why I wanted to make certain you wouldn't miss out. It was wise of your agent to book you tickets three months in advance.'

An alarm went off inside my head. Ivan and I didn't look at each other, but I could tell he was thinking the same thing. *We didn't see the travel agent until we had received our visas. We only went to see her a month before we left, and only to book our air tickets. Everything else we had organised ourselves.* Was the agent Vera was referring to the General? Or had the whole tour been a ploy to keep us separated? I glanced around the foyer for the General, but he was nowhere to be seen among the people chatting near the reception desk or waiting in the chairs. When we walked through the doors towards the taxi Vera had waiting, there was one thought in my mind: tonight would either end in me seeing my mother or inside the walls of the Lubyanka, the KGB headquarters.

Our taxi stopped in the square in front of the Bolshoi Theatre, and when I stepped out of it I was surprised to find that the air was fresh rather than cold, a Russian winter's version of balmy. A sprinkle of snow, as fragile as petals, fluttered against my cheeks. I looked across to the

449

theatre and drew a breath, the sight of it making me forget all the evils of Moscow architecture I had seen yesterday. My gaze followed the giant columns to Apollo and his chariot draped in snow on the pediment. Men and women, wrapped in fur coats and hats, were scattered about the colonnade, talking or smoking. Some of the women had fur hand-muffs and pouches. It was as if we had gone back in time, and when Ivan took my hand and we walked towards the steps, I felt as though I were my young father, accompanied by his bejewelled sisters, rushing up the stairs to be in time for the ballet. What would he have seen then? *Giselle* or *Salammbô*? Or maybe even *Swan Lake* choreographed by the infamous Gorky. I knew that my father had watched the great Sophia Fedorova II dance before she went mad, and Anna Pavlova perform before she left Russia for good, and that he'd been so taken with the latter that he had named me after her. I had the sensation of being lifted into the air, and thought that perhaps for a moment I would catch a glimpse of old through his eyes, like a child peering into a richly decorated shop window.

Inside the theatre doors, usherettes in red uniforms were urging people to take their seats, for if there was one thing that started on time in Moscow, it was the Bolshoi Ballet. We followed Vera up the stairs to the cloakroom and found over a hundred people already packed in there, each trying to push their way to the counters to check in their coats. The noise was louder than a crowd at a football stadium, and my jaw dropped when I saw a man shove an elderly woman aside in order to get by her. Her response was to pummel her fists into his back.

'You hold Lily,' Ivan said to me, 'I'll take your coats. You ladies are not going in there.'

'If you go in there, you'll get a black eye,' I warned him. 'Let's take everything with us into the theatre.'

'What? And make ourselves look uncultured?' He

grinned, then pointed to Lily. 'We're already sneaking in more than we should, remember.'

Ivan disappeared into the swarming mass of elbows and arms. I slipped the ballet programme out of my handbag and read the introduction. 'After the October Revolution classical music and dance became accessible to millions of workers, and on this stage the best revolutionary characters based on heroes from our history were created.' More propaganda.

Ivan returned twenty minutes later, his hair dishevelled and his tie askew.

'You look like you did on Tubabao,' I told him, patting down his hair and straightening his jacket.

He pressed a pair of opera glasses into my palm.

'You won't need them,' Vera said. 'You have excellent seats. Right near the stage.'

'I wanted them for the novelty,' I said, lying. I had wanted them so I could get a better look at the audience, not the stage.

Vera put her arm around me, but she wasn't being affectionate, she was trying to hide Lily as she guided me towards our section. The usherette slouching by our box seemed to be expecting us. Vera slipped something into the woman's fist and she pushed open the door, releasing a blast of violins tuning up and the pre-concert chatter. 'Hurry! Quick! Move inside!' the usherette hissed. 'Don't let anybody see you!'

I rushed to a seat near the front of the box and laid Lily down in my lap. Ivan and Vera slipped into the seats on either side of me.

The usherette held up her finger and warned me, 'The moment she cries you must leave.'

I had thought the outside of the theatre was beautiful but the auditorium left me breathless. I leaned over the balcony, trying to take in the red and gold interior all at once. There were five tiers of balconies, each ornamented in gold, reaching up to a crystal chandelier that hung from a ceiling decorated with Byzantine paintings. The air was tinged with the scent of old wood and velvet. The giant curtain across the stage was a sparkling montage of sickles and hammers, music scrolls, stars and tassels.

'The acoustics are the best in the world,' Vera told us, smoothing down her dress and smiling with such pride we could have been forgiven for thinking she had been responsible for the design.

From where we were seated we had a good view of the audience in the front section of the auditorium but not in the boxes above us or towards the back of the hall. Still, I searched for my mother and the General among the people making their way into their seats, but I didn't see their likenesses anywhere. From the corner of my eye I noticed that Vera was staring across the hall. I tried to be subtle and slowly followed her gaze to the box opposite us. At that moment the lights started to dim, but before they went out completely I caught a glimpse of an old man sitting in the front row. It wasn't the General but for some reason he seemed familiar. There was a rush of coughing and rustling before the orchestra hit the first note.

Vera touched my arm. 'Do you know how this is going to end, Mrs Nickham?' she whispered. 'Or are you trying to guess?'

I caught my breath. Her eyes looked pink in the glow from the stage, like a fox caught in the light. 'What?'

'Happily or unhappily?'

My mind blurred then came into focus. She was talking about the ballet. *Swan Lake* could have two endings. One where the prince was able to break the spell the wicked magician had cast and save the swan princess, and the other where he couldn't and the two lovers could only find each other again in death. I squeezed my fist so tightly I snapped the opera glasses.

The curtains swung open to reveal six trumpeters in red

452

capes. Ballerinas in festive dresses with huntsmen for partners dashed across the stage, Prince Siegfried leaping after
them. I hadn't seen a live ballet since Harbin, and for a
brief moment I forgot what I was doing in the theatre and
became transfixed by the dancers and the graceful shapes
they were making with their bodies and feet. This is Russia,
I told myself. This is what I have been trying to see.

I glanced down at Lily. Her eyes were sparkling in the
glittering light. My ballet lessons had been cut short when
the Japanese came to Harbin. But Lily? She was a child of
a peaceful country and could do anything she wanted. She
would never be forced to flee her home. When you are
older, Lily, I told her with my eyes, you can do ballet, piano,
singing, anything that makes you happy. I wanted her to
have everything I had missed out on. More than any of
those things, I wanted to give Lily her grandmother.

I heard the first strain of the swan theme and turned
back to the stage. The scenery had changed to a craggy
mountain and a blue lake. Prince Siegfried was dancing,
and the wicked magician, disguised as an owl, was mirroring the dance behind him. The owl was a terrifying shadow,
always near, lurking with ill intent, pulling the prince back
when he thought he was moving forward. I glanced across
at the man in the box Vera had been looking at earlier. In
the blue light he seemed unearthly. The blood drained from
my face and I clenched my teeth, convinced for a moment
I was looking at Tang. But the light in the theatre bright-
ened and I realised that wasn't possible. The man was white.

Even when the second scene finished and the lights came
up for the interval, I couldn't recover my senses. I handed
Lily to Ivan. 'I have to go to the ladies' room,' I told him.

'I'll come with you,' said Vera, getting out of her seat.
I nodded, although it wasn't my intention to empty my
bladder. I wanted to search for my mother.

We made our way through the crowded corridor to the
washroom. It was as chaotic as the cloakroom had been.

There was no line to wait for the stalls. The women stood in a huddle and pushed against each other to get to the front when a stall became free. Vera pressed a tissue as stiff as cardboard into my hand. 'Thank you,' I said, remembering that there was no paper to be found in public toilets anywhere in Moscow. The toilets in the Tretyakov Gallery hadn't even had seats.

A woman came out of the stall in front of us and Vera pushed me forward. 'After you,' she said. 'I'll wait for you outside.' I hooked the door behind me. The cubicle stank of urine and bleach. I watched through the crack in the door for Vera to go into a stall and, as soon as she did, I pulled the chain in mine and raced out of the ladies' room and into the corridor.

I scurried past the clusters of people chatting on the stairs and ran down to the first floor. There was a smaller crowd there and I searched every woman's face for someone who resembled my mother. She'll be grey now, I told myself, and there will be wrinkles. But in the jumble of faces around me, I couldn't find the one I was longing for. I pushed open the heavy doors and ran out onto the colonnade, thinking that for some reason she might be waiting out there. The temperature had dropped and the air bit through my blouse. Two soldiers were standing on the stairs, breathing puffs of condensation into the blackness. There was a row of taxis outside but no one else was in sight in the square.

The soldiers turned around. One of them lifted his eyebrow at me. 'You will catch cold out here,' he said. His skin was the colour of milk, his eyes like blue opals. I stepped back inside the theatre, feeling the warmth from the central heating rise up around me. The soldier's image stayed in my vision like a sunspot and I recalled the station in Harbin the day my mother was taken away. He reminded me of the young Soviet soldier who had let me escape.

By the time I tried to squeeze my way back up the

454

crowded staircase, the auditorium had emptied and the foyer was crowded with people. I managed to inch my way almost to the top and I noticed Vera leaning on the balustrade. She was turned away from me, talking to someone. My view of the other person was blocked by a plant urn. It wasn't Ivan because I could see him at the far end of the foyer with Lily bundled in his arms, peering out the window to the square. I craned my neck to see around the urn and caught a glimpse of a white-haired man in a maroon jacket. The man's clothes were clean and pressed, but the back of his shirt collar was frayed and his trousers had a worn sheen to them. He was standing with his arms folded across his chest and every so often he gestured with his chin towards the window where Ivan was standing. I couldn't hear what he and Vera were discussing above the hubbub of the crowd. Then the man shifted his foot and turned a degree. I caught sight of the pouches under his eyes. I knew I had seen his face before. He was the souvenir seller at the hotel. I pressed myself against the balustrade and strained my ears to listen to what he was saying. For a moment there was a lull in the chatter and I heard the man say, 'They are not simple tourists, Comrade Otova. Their Russian is too perfect. The baby is a front. It may not even be theirs. That's why they should be taken in for questioning.'

My breath caught in my throat. I'd guessed that the old man was spying for the KGB, but I'd had no idea that he suspected us. I stepped back from the balustrade, my legs trembling. I'd only half believed Vera was with the KGB, but I had been right. She had been setting a trap.

I darted up the staircase, pawing at people to get out of my way so that I could reach Ivan. But the crowd seemed to be jammed together shoulder to shoulder. I was hemmed in by mountains of poorly made suits and twenty-year-old dresses. Everyone seemed to reek of camphor or honeysuckle, the year's standard issue perfume. '*Izvinite.*

455

Izvinite. Excuse me. Excuse me,' I said, trying to push my way past them.

Ivan had seated himself discreetly by the window and was bouncing Lily in his lap, playing with her fingers. I tried to will him to look at me but he and Lily were too captivated by their game. Get to the Australian Embassy, I told myself. Grab Ivan and Lily and go there.

I glanced over my shoulder. At that same moment Vera swivelled on her heel and her eyes met mine. She frowned and glanced towards the stairs. I could see her mind ticking over. She turned to the man and said something before pushing her way through the crowd towards me.

My head throbbed. Everything seemed to be in slow motion. I'd felt this way once before, when was it? I remembered again the day on the station in Harbin. Tang inching towards me through the crowd. I grabbed and clawed at the people around me. A bell chimed for the next act and suddenly the crush of people loosened and began to fall away, like apples dropping from a burst bag. Ivan turned around and saw me. His face blanched.

'Anya!' he cried. My blouse was soaked. I touched my face, my hands were slippery with sweat. 'We have to get out of here,' I wheezed. The gripping sensation in my chest was so ferocious I thought I might be having a heart attack.

'What?'

'We have to . . .' but I couldn't get the words out fast enough. My throat was swollen with fear.

'My God, Anya,' Ivan said, clutching at me, 'what's happened?'

'Mrs Nickham.' Vera's fingers clamped on my elbow like a vice. 'We must get you back to your hotel immediately. It appears your flu has taken a bad turn. Look at your face. You have a fever.'

Her touch sickened me. I could barely keep myself upright. It was too surreal. I was about to be taken in for questioning by the KGB. I stared at the people hurrying through the doors back into the auditorium and resisted the urge to scream. I couldn't imagine anyone coming to our assistance. We were trapped. The best we could do was to cooperate, but deciding that didn't make me feel any calmer. I clenched my toes in my shoes, bracing myself for whatever would come next.

'Your flu?' Ivan cried. He touched the wetness of my blouse then turned to Vera. 'I'll get our coats. Can the hotel call a doctor?'

So this is how they do it, I thought. This is how they make their arrests in public and snatch you away in front of everyone.

'Give the child to me,' Vera said to Ivan. Her face was unreadable. I didn't know her well enough to imagine what she was capable of doing.

'No!' I screamed.

'You should think what is best in terms of the child,' Vera snapped at me; her voice was like nothing I had heard from her before. 'The flu is extremely contagious.'

Ivan passed Lily over to Vera. The moment I saw her arms wrap around Lily something inside me broke. It occurred to me as I watched them that in trying to find my mother I could lose my daughter. Whatever is to happen, I prayed, let it come. But let Lily be safe.

I glanced at the man with the white hair. He was looking at me with a fixed stare, holding his hands to his chest as if he were witnessing something distasteful.

'This is Comrade Gorin,' Vera said to me. 'You may know him from your hotel?'

'The flu can be very bad in Moscow in winter,' he said, shifting his feet. 'You must stay in bed and rest until you are better.'

He kept his limbs tucked in tight to his body, and the way he leaned with all his weight on his back foot would have been comical under other circumstances. It made him

457

seem afraid of me. I decided it must be his loathing of foreigners that produced such a posture in him.

Ivan returned with our coats and wrapped mine around me. Vera tied her scarf loosely around Lily's mouth, making it into a mask. Gorin watched her, his eyes growing larger. He took another step back from us and said, 'I must return to my seat or I'll miss the next act.'

Like a spider running back to his hole, I thought. He's leaving the dirty work to Vera.

'Take Lily,' I whispered to Ivan. 'Take Lily please.'

Ivan glanced sideways at me but did as I asked. When I saw Lily lifted out of Vera's arms and in her father's again, my head cleared. Vera pretended to help me down the stairs when she was really pressing me against the balustrade so I couldn't wriggle away. I willed myself forward, watching my feet on each step. They won't know what I don't tell them, I thought. Then I remembered all the stories I'd heard about the KGB putting babies into boiling water to make their mothers confess, and I became weak in the legs again.

The soldiers outside the theatre were gone. Only the line of taxis remained. Ivan walked ahead of us, his head tucked to his chest and his arms wrapped around Lily. One of the taxi drivers stamped out his cigarette when he saw us walking in his direction. He was about to get back into his cab when Vera shook her head at him and pushed me towards a black Lada waiting near the kerb. The driver was sitting low in his seat, his collar pulled up around his face. I gave out a cry and dug my boots into the snow.

'It's not a taxi,' I tried to tell Ivan, my words slurring out like a drunk woman's.

'It's a private taxi,' Vera muttered under her breath.

'We're Australian,' I told her, clutching at her shoulder. 'I can call the embassy, you know. You can't touch us.'

'You're as much an Australian as I'm a Pakistani,' Vera responded, opening the car door and shoving me into the back seat, behind the driver. Ivan climbed into the other side with Lily. I gave Vera a defiant glare and she ducked down so quickly that I flinched, expecting her to slap me. Instead she tucked my coat under my legs so that it wouldn't get caught in the door. The gesture was so motherly that I was struck dumb by the juxtaposition. She embraced me, letting out a laugh that sounded like a mixture of mirth and long-suffering patience.

'Anna Victorovna Kozlova, I will never forget you,' she said. 'You are your mother all over and I'll miss you both. It's a good thing I know that KGB informer has a mortal terror of germs or it would have been difficult to get you out of his clutches.' She laughed again and slammed the door. The Lada took off full throttle into the night. I spun around to look out of the rear window. Vera was heading back towards the theatre with her usual straight-spined gait. I clutched my fist to my head. What on earth was going on?

Ivan leaned forward and gave the driver the name and address of our hotel. The driver didn't respond and went in the opposite direction on Prospect Marksa, in the direction of the Lubyanka. Ivan must have realised that we were heading in the wrong direction too because he ran his fingers through his hair and repeated the name of the hotel to the driver.

'My wife is sick,' he pleaded. 'We must get her a doctor.'

'I'm fine, Ivan,' I told him. I was so frightened that my voice didn't sound like my own.

Ivan glared at me. 'Anya, what was all that back there with Vera? What's going on?'

My mind was swimming. My arms tingled from where Vera had hugged me but the gesture hadn't registered because I'd gone into shock. 'They are taking us for questioning but they can't do that until we've contacted the embassy.'

'I thought I was taking you to see your mother.'

The voice from the darkness sent pins and needles through

me. I didn't need to lean forward to know who the driver was.

'General!' Ivan cried out. 'We were wondering when you were going to show up!'

'Probably not for another day,' he said. 'But we had to change our plans.'

'Lily,' Ivan muttered. 'I'm sorry. We didn't think . . .'

'No,' the General replied, trying to keep the laughter out of his voice. 'It was Anya. Vera said she was being difficult and was drawing attention to herself.'

I cringed. I should have been ashamed of my stupid paranoia but all I could do was laugh and choke on my tears at the same time.

'Who is Vera?' Ivan asked, shaking his head at me.

'Vera is Anya's mother's best friend,' the General replied. 'She'd do anything to help her. She lost two brothers to Stalin's regime.'

I pressed my hands to my eyes. The world was spinning around me. I was changing, transforming from the person I had been all my life. A gap was opening up inside me. The void, so long buried by all the things I'd tried to fill it up with, rose to the surface. But instead of causing me pain, joy was rushing into the empty space.

'I had hoped that you would get to see the whole ballet,' the General said. 'But never mind.'

The tears ran in streams down my face. 'It was the version with the happy ending, wasn't it?' I said.

About fifteen minutes from the Bolshoi Theatre, the General brings the car to a stop outside an old apartment building, five floors high. A lump forms like a stone in my throat. What will I say to her? After twenty-three years what will our first words be?

'Come back down here in half an hour,' says the General. 'Vishnevsky has arranged an escort and you must leave tonight.' We close the car doors and watch the Lada

460

disappear down the street. I realise now how foolish it was of me to think that the General could be a normal man. He is a guardian angel.

Ivan and I walk through an archway, the ground under our feet sodden with snow, and find ourselves in a dimly lit courtyard. 'It was the top floor, wasn't it?' Ivan asks, pulling open a metal door which clangs shut behind us. Someone has nailed a blanket around the doorpost in an attempt at insulation. It is almost as cold in the hallway as it was outside, and dark too. Two shovels lean against the wall, melted ice pooled around their tips. We climb the five flights of stairs to the top floor because the elevator is broken. The steps are covered in dust and the stairwell smells of clay. Our heavy clothes make us pant and sweat. I remember that the General told me my mother has problems with her legs, and I cringe to think that she can't leave her apartment without help. I squint in the weak light and see that the walls are painted grey but the ornate ceiling mouldings and door frames depict faded birds and flowers. Their decorativeness suggests that the building was once a grand mansion. Each landing has a stained-glass window in the corner, but most of the panes have been replaced with cheap frosted glass or bits of wood.

We reach the landing on the top floor and a door creaks open. A woman in a black dress steps out. She balances herself on her walking stick and squints at us. I don't recognise her at first. Her hair is the colour of pewter and mostly hidden under a scarf. Her stout legs are twisted and veined beneath the skin-toned medical stockings. But then she straightens her back and our eyes meet. I see her as she was when she was in Harbin, in her smart chiffon dress, the breeze in her hair, standing by the gate, waiting for me to come home from school.

'Anya!' she cries out. Her voice breaks my heart. It is that of an old woman, not that of my mother. She lifts a trembling hand out to me and then clasps it to her bosom

461

as if she has seen a vision. There are liver spots on the backs of her hands and deep grooves around her mouth. She looks old for her age, a sign of the hardness of her life, while I look young. But her eyes are more beautiful than ever. They glisten like diamonds.

'Anya! Anya! My darling baby! My beautiful child!' she calls out, her eyes reddening with tears. I step towards her but falter. My courage runs out of me and I find myself weeping. Ivan puts his hand on my shoulder. His kind voice in my ear is the only link I have to reality. 'Show her Lily,' he whispers, nudging me forward. 'Show her grand-daughter to her.' He takes my arms and wraps Lily into them, tugging the blanket away from her face. Lily opens her eyes and stares at me in wonder. She has the same eyes as the woman who is reaching out to me now. Amber and beautiful. Wise and kind. She babbles and kicks her legs, then suddenly turns to the woman and leans with all her strength towards her, veering away from me.

I am in China again and I am twelve years old. I have fallen over and hurt myself and my mother wants to heal me. Each step towards her is awkward, but she opens her arms wide. When I reach her, she clasps me to her chest. The warmth of her rushes over me like steam from a hot spring. 'My darling daughter! My baby girl!' she murmurs, regarding me with such tenderness I think I will burst with it. We cradle Lily between us and gaze into each other's faces, remembering all that we have lived through. What was lost has been found. What was ended can be started again. Mother and I are going home.

Author's Note

Russians have a formal way of referring to each other based on their patronymic names. For instance, in *White Gardenia* Anya's full name is Anna Victorovna Kozlova. Victorovna is derived from her father's name, Victor, and Kozlova is the feminised version of his surname, Kozlov. When being addressed politely she would be referred to as Anna Victorovna, but among family and friends she would simply be called Anya. If you have read a Russian novel in translation you can understand how distracting this system can be for the Western reader. Why does a character who has been called Alexander Ivanovich for half the novel suddenly become Sasha?

To avoid this kind of confusion, I decided to use the characters' patronymic names only in very formal situations, such as in letters, Sergei's will, formal introductions and so on, in order to give a sense of the Russian custom. For most of the book I used the characters' informal names. I also had Anya continue to use her surname, Kozlova, when she arrived in Australia, although she may have chosen to drop the feminised ending of her name to simply Kozlov.

One of the most enjoyable aspects of writing *White Gardenia* was creating a story about the bond between a mother and daughter in a wider historical setting. I have made every attempt to be accurate and authentic in detail, however there were a couple of places where I had to play

God and condense history to keep the story flowing. The first instance was where Anya arrives in Shanghai soon after the announcement of the end of the Second World War. Chronologically speaking, while there would have been some Americans in Shanghai, Anya arrives there a couple of weeks before the main part of the American navy arrived to set up newsreels and get the city moving again. But because the main purpose of the scene was to show the jubilation at the end of the war, and how quickly Shanghai was able to recover, I felt comfortable pushing the events closer together. The other place I condensed history was on Tubabao. The refugees on the island endured more than one typhoon during their stay, but to describe every storm in detail would have shifted the focus away from Anya's emotional survival and her growing attachment to Ruselina and Irina.

George Burns once said, 'The most important thing about acting is honesty. And if you can fake that, you've got it made!' There are some places in *White Gardenia* where fictional settings were more suitable than real ones. The first example is the Moscow-Shanghai. While this nightclub is a creation of my imagination, based on the architecture of several of the Tsar's palaces, it is nonetheless true to Shanghai's spirit of decadence at that time. Similarly, the migrant camp Anya and Irina are sent to in Australia is not intended to represent a particular migrant camp in the central west of New South Wales, although most of my research revolved around the Bathurst and Cowra migrant camps. My reasoning here was that I wanted Anya to interact on a personal level with the camp director and didn't feel it would be fair to bring any of the real camp directors into the story in such a personal way. For this same reason, I created a fictional metropolitan newspaper for Anya to work on, the *Sydney Herald*, rather than use an actual paper of the time because I needed Anya to form a close relationship with her editor, Diana. The society families are also fictional and do not represent any real personalities of the time, although Prince's, Romano's and Chequers nightclub were the places to be seen in Sydney in the 1950s. I could describe my approach to these fictional creations in terms of the creed a fashionable friend once shared with me: 'If the hair and shoes are right, everything else in between will fall into place.' By this I mean that as long as my historical context was accurate and the day-to-day details of what people were eating, wearing and reading were true to the times, I was able to allow myself some freedom with the story in between.

Following on from this, I would also like to say that while the inspiration for the novel came from the journey my mother and godmother made from China to Australia, all the characters and situations in the novel are works of my imagination. The book is not a family history in fictional form and none of the main characters are meant to represent any actual person living or deceased.

It was a great pleasure researching and writing *White Gardenia*. I hope that reading it has brought you much pleasure too.

Acknowledgments

It has often been said that a writer's life is a solitary one, but it seems to me that the moment I put pen to paper (actually, fingers to keyboard) to write *White Gardenia* I was blessed with an incredible array of people willing to offer inspiration, information and support for the project.

To start out with, I would like to express gratitude to the two women who inspired me to write a novel about Russians in the first place: my mother, Deanna, and my godmother, Valentina. The tales of their lives in Harbin, Tsingtao, Shanghai and Tubabao captivated me as a child and enthralled me again as an adult. But it was more than the exotic locations that inspired the themes of the novel, it was their example of true friendship and love of life. Despite all the terrible things they have seen, the loved ones they have lost and the hardships they have endured, they have never lost their capacity to love, and to love fiercely. Their kindness and their sense of charity towards others is what makes them truly amazing. I would also like to convey my appreciation to my father, Stan, and brother, Paul, who believed that I could accomplish the task of researching and writing a novel with so much historical background, even before I had started!

I'm not sure if I can find the right words to say thank you to Selwa Anthony, who is such an enthusiastic, insightful and talented literary agent that some days I think I must have dreamed her up. Her faith in me is one of the most precious gifts I have ever received, and over the course of the novel's development, I am proud to say that Selwa has been not only a terrific agent but a wonderful mentor and friend.

Further to my list of blessings, I have to add my publisher, Linda Funnell, and my editor, Julia Stiles. What first-time novelist wouldn't be thrilled to find herself under the guidance of two of the most brilliant women in publishing? Their sensitivity, intelligence, care and sense of humour were tremendous gifts during the long and sometimes demanding process of rewriting and editing. I'd also like to thank Nicola O'Shea, senior editor at HarperCollins, whose organisational skills, diligence and passion for what she does made her a pleasure to work with. In fact, whenever I think about the collective talent, professionalism and enthusiasm of the HarperCollins team I can't help but be amazed. In particular I would like to mention Brian Murray, Shona Martyn, Sylvia Marson, Karen-Maree Griffiths and Vanessa Hobbs.

I would also like to thank Fiona and Adam Workman. If diamonds are a girl's best friend, then Fiona and Adam are best friends of the highest clarity and the ideal cut, depth and carat weight. Not only were they terrific sounding boards whenever I felt stuck, nurturing my creativity back to the surface with their gourmet cooking and sense of joie de vivre, but they sent me a treasure chest of primary sources, including the wonderful Kay Campbell and Theo Barker, who put together information for me on the Bathurst Migrant Camp and migrant camps in general while I was living in New York, and Joan Leyda and Peter Workman, who took time to share with me their lively and entertaining memories of Sydney in the 1950s. On the subject of Sydney in the 1950s, I would also like to thank legendary Australian fashion designer, Beril Jents; journalist and author, Kevin Perkins; Gary A Shiels and Aran Maree of North Bondi Surf Life Saving Club; and John

468

Ryan of the Australian Jockey Club for the invaluable information they all shared with me.

Thank you also to my other sources of information for their enthusiasm and time in answering my questions: Levon and Janna Olobikyan for first-hand accounts of Moscow in the 1960s; Andrea Lammel for dance terms and German phrases; Doctor Ludmila Stern of the University of NSW and Svetlana Aristidi for checking my Russian terms and patronymic names; Jan Wigsten of Nomadic Journeys and Graham Taylor of Karakorum Expeditions for explaining to me the practicalities involved in crossing the Gobi Desert; and Vicky Robinson for her insight into Polish.

There is also a multitude of people I would like to thank for making the rough parts of this writer's journey smooth and the joys even sweeter. Unfortunately, because of space I can't list them all, but I would particularly like to mention:

Jody Lee, Kim Swivel, Maggie Hamilton, Professor Stephen Muecke, Bruce Fields, Jennifer Strong, Alain Mentha, Andrea Au, Brian Dennis, Shilene Noé, Jeffrey Arsenault, Kevin Lindenmuth, Tom Nondorf, Craig Smith, Phyllis Curott, Arabella Edge, Christopher Mack, Martin Klohs, Kai Schweisfurth, Virginia Lonsdale, Olivia Rhee, and the members of Women in Publishing, New York. I would also like to thank my New York roommate, Heather Drucker, for not only generously giving me full use of her communications and word-processing equipment but for sharing the companionship of her two delightful cats. Sitting on my bed with my laptop, Sabine and Chaplin curled up and purring on either side of me, the snow piling up outside the window, created the perfect atmosphere for writing *White Gardenia*.

Thank you all!